ONE MORE *Chance*
A REDEMPTION NOVEL

RENO. R. MIST

POSH PANGOLIN PUBLISHERS

One More Chance, A Redemption Novel

Please note that the story, all names, characters, and incidents portrayed in this production are fictitious. No identification with actual persons (living or deceased), places, buildings, and products is intended or should be inferred.

Every effort has been made to trace or contact all copyright holders. The publishers will be pleased to make good any omissions or rectify any mistakes brought to their attention at the earliest opportunity.

Copyright © 2025 by Reno R. Mist

First Edition: June 2025

All rights reserved. No part of this publication may be reproduced, distributed, or transmitted in any form or by any means, including photocopying, recording, or other electronic or mechanical methods, without the prior written permission of the publisher, except as permitted by U.S. copyright law.

Book Cover by Get Covers: https://getcovers.com/
Book Art: Wenqing Yan, aka Yuumei Art, LLC

ISBN: 979-8-9989053-0-8 (ebook)
ISBN: 979-8-9989053-1-5 (Paperback)
Library of Congress Number: 2025909834

For permission requests, contact PoshPangolinPublishers@gmail.com
For author information, please contact Reno.R.Mist@gmail.com

Social Media
Website https://www.renormist.com
Tik Tok https://www.tiktok.com/@renormistauthor
Instagram https://www.instagram.com/reno.r.mist

CONTENT & TRIGGER WARNINGS

Your mental health matters

PLEASE NOTE THAT THIS STORY IS A WORK OF FICTION AND IS NOT INTENDED TO SERVE AS GUIDANCE OR ADVICE FOR NAVIGATING RELATIONSHIPS, MARRIAGE, SURVIVING BETRAYAL, OR ANY OF THE SENSITIVE TOPICS DEPICTED.

IF YOU FIND YOURSELF FEELING OVERWHELMED OR TRIGGERED WHILE READING, WE ENCOURAGE YOU TO PAUSE AND SEEK SUPPORT. PLEASE DON'T HESITATE TO REACH OUT TO A TRUSTED FRIEND, MENTAL HEALTH PROFESSIONAL, OR AN EMERGENCY RESOURCE IN YOUR AREA.

THIS BOOK CONTAINS MATURE AND POTENTIALLY DISTRESSING CONTENT, INCLUDING BUT NOT LIMITED TO:

- BETRAYAL (PHYSICAL, MENTAL AND EMOTIONAL)
- CHILD TRAFFICKING
- CONSTRUCTION MATERIALS USED IN POTENTIALLY DISTRESSING WAYS
- DETAILED SEX SCENES (WHICH INCLUDE BUT NOT LIMITED TO: ADULT TOYS, DEGRADATION, KINK EXPLORATION, PRAISE, RESTRAINTS, UNINTENTIONAL PUP PLAY, ROUGH SEX)
- DRUG USE
- INFIDELITY
- MENTAL ILLNESS (WHICH INCLUDE BUT NOT LIMITED TO: ANXIETY, DEPRESSION, GRIEF, LOW SELF ESTEEM, HYSTERICAL BONDING)
- MISCARRIAGE
- MURDER
- NAME CARVING ON SKIN
- PET INJURY (HE GETS BETTER FOR THOSE OF US WHO NEED TO KNOW AHEAD OF TIME)
- PREGNANCY
- STALKING
- SHARP THINGS (KNIVES, AXE, ETC)
- SUICIDE
- THEME PARKS (I SAID WHAT I SAID)
- VOMITING

PLEASE EMAIL ME AT RENORMIST@GMAIL.COM IF I MISSED ANY THAT NEED TO BE INCLUDED.

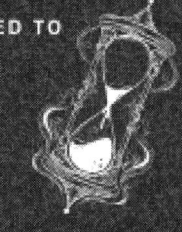

Contents

Dedication	IX
Acknowledgements	XI
Epigraph	XIII
1. Chapter 1	1
2. Chapter 2	7
3. Chapter 3	21
4. Chapter 4	30
5. Chapter 5	35
6. Chapter 6	43
7. Chapter 7	50
8. Chapter 8	62
9. Chapter 9	71
10. Chapter 10	78

11. Chapter 11 — 91
12. Chapter 12 — 101
13. Chapter 13 — 113
14. Chapter 14 — 121
15. Chapter 15 — 135
16. Chapter 16 — 152
17. Chapter 17 — 161
18. Chapter 18 — 169
19. Chapter 19 — 188
20. Chapter 20 — 195
21. Chapter 21 — 202
22. Chapter 22 — 207
23. Chapter 23 — 214
24. Chapter 24 — 231
25. Chapter 25 — 240
26. Chapter 26 — 252
27. Chapter 27 — 260
28. Chapter 28 — 265
29. Chapter 29 — 275
30. Chapter 30 — 284
31. Chapter 31 — 294
32. Chapter 32 — 299

33.	Chapter 33	302
34.	Chapter 34	312
35.	Chapter 35	319
36.	Chapter 36	333
37.	Chapter 37	346
38.	Chapter 38	357
39.	Chapter 39	372
40.	Chapter 40	375
Epilogue		388
To my Readers...		396
Fated Rebirth Preview		398

For every woman piecing herself back together

You're not broken. You're becoming.
Whether you stay, fight, leave, or rise
Your story still belongs to you.

Acknowledgements

For my husband,
Thank you for believing in me even when I doubted myself. Your strength and encouragement gave me the courage to tell this story.

For my daughter,
You are my light, my laughter, and my reminder that imagination has no limits. This book exists because of the wonder you inspire in me.

For my family and friends,
Thank you for your encouragement, and for reading draft after draft without (openly) threatening to block me. Your support means more than you'll ever know.

And lastly BookTok community and those surviving infidelity,
Thank you for being such an amazing community, sharing your stories, and letting your voices be heard.

Wherefore, O judges, be of good cheer about death, and know of a certainty, that no evil can happen to a good man, either in life or after death. He and his are not neglected by the gods; nor has my own approaching end happened by mere chance. - Socrates, as written by Plato.

Chapter I

I woke up mid-thrust, my body slick with sweat as the stench of stale perfume clogged my nose. For a moment, I didn't know where I was or even *who* I was. The room was dark except for a sickly orange light seeping through bedroom curtains.

Disoriented, I squeezed my eyes shut as nausea crashed over me in relentless waves. When I opened them again, the grim realization hit me. I was inside a body that wasn't supposed to exist anymore - my own.

A sharp gasp tore from my lips and I jerked back, blinking into the dim light of the bedroom as I stared at the familiar profile of someone I hadn't seen in years. Angie was on all fours, her blonde hair a tangled mess, mouth parted in a drunken moan calling out my name. Her hands clutched mine, her hips grinding against me, and the whole scene reeked of something worse than her perfume: regret.

I pulled out of her and fell back against the headboard, gasping, my heart in my throat as I fought hyperventilation. My skin crawled like writhing maggots.

Angie blinked up at me, her mascara smudged, her mouth curled into the pout that had once made me stupid. "Levi?"

"Angie?"

Her name curdled in my mouth, sour and metallic. It tasted of guilt, like copper on the back of my tongue. Years of rotten memories compressed into the pit of my stomach as I stared at her. She was not an ex, yet, but she was a gaping wound I'd left to fester, with her tinted smile I'd kissed too many times. She was a mistake already carved into the marrow of my bones.

The urge to vomit ripped through me, violent and consuming, as I stumbled off the bed and clawed blindly for my clothes. I glanced down at my cock, slick with her, and the sight hammered me with another tidal wave of nausea, stronger than any hangover I'd ever crawled through.

Behind me, she let out a confused, broken little cry as I searched the room naked and trembling. I heard the sharp intake of her breath, the rising panic in her voice as I grabbed fistfuls of clothes off the lush carpet.

"Levi, what the fuck?"

I caught my reflection in the mirror above the dresser. Smooth skin, no gray yet in my hair, no lines bracketing my mouth. I was maybe thirty-six again, at the peak of my selfishness. My younger, hotter, much dumber self: Old Me. Panic seized me as I stared at the narcissistic asshole in the mirror and collected my thoughts. I knew Angie wouldn't understand. Hell, *I* barely understood.

All I knew? I had died.

I had died years from this moment, in a distant future that seemed to no longer exist. And yet? There I was, trapped in my younger body.

I yanked my pants off the floor, shoving my legs into them with shaking hands, careful not to crush anything in the zipper. "Angie, I can't see you again," I said, the words scraping out of my throat raw.

I knew I needed to hurry out the door before I said something stupid. Nothing made sense right then.

Turning, I stared into her big blue eyes, disbelief and shock radiating from her as I pulled on my shirt.

Fuck, why come back to now? To this moment? Why not before I ever met her?

"I don't understand baby, what's going on?" Tears shimmered in her feathered eyes, blinking rapidly like a handheld duster. "You just moved in two days ago. You said you'd marry me." She sat up, covering herself with the wrinkled sheet.

Baby. Fuck, how I used to love being called that. But in that moment? Her voice was a knife in my ears. If only she knew how violently she repulsed me, how the thought of being inside her made me want to tear my own flesh off just to feel clean again. Yet there I was, dick limp and sticky in my jeans, soaked in her filth, with only one thought pulsing louder than the sickness in my gut.

How do I fix my marriage and earn back my family's trust?

The problem was, Angie had confirmed what I feared... I'd already moved out. The pain at home would still be raw; my absence a fresh wound on the family the Old Me had destroyed.

Despite Angie's pleas, my brain kept leaping from thought to thought. Somehow, I was back in time and nowhere near home. My last memory? My body, shattered, engulfed in a fireball of twisted steel and broken glass on the road home, twelve years into the future. In some cruel joke of time, I'd been dropped back into the exact moment my life began to unravel: a series of foolish choices by a foolish man-child. The ultimate betrayal. I looked down at my hands: unscarred, whole, and alive. Everything about me screamed before.

Fuck me. Home. I need to get out of here and get back home.

"Angie, we both knew this was never built to last, especially once the money dried up. I'll come get my stuff later." I hesitated. "Actually, fuck it. Burn it all if you want. I don't care."

Angie's shrill voice scraped against my skull as I grabbed my remaining clothes and stumbled for the door. I didn't look back. I couldn't.

Shame clung to me like a second skin, thick and suffocating, as I stormed down the three familiar steps of her house, a house I'd slithered in and out of for months, betraying my wife with every filthy, grinning lie.

Sloane. Hell, Sloane.

The Sloane I knew felt distant. One of my last memories of her struck me like a blade to the ribs: sharp, sudden, unforgettable. Despite every humiliation I dragged her through, despite the ocean of pain I'd nearly drowned her in, I still remember her calling me to wish me happy birthday - happy forty-eighth birthday. The two of us sipped coffee together at that cafe, a cafe that wouldn't even exist yet, on the corner of 7th and Spring Street. Her warm smile edged with lines. Her light touch on my arm when she laughed. The casual, yet tender, way she asked how I was holding up, even when I didn't deserve a single second of her consideration after all I'd done.

In my previous life, I had traded Sloane and my perfect life for sweat-stained sheets and empty orgasms: a hollowness that paled in comparison to what we'd built together. I had been left with a volatile mix of constant self-hatred and an endless, gnawing guilt that ate me alive, rotting every moment of my life like a cancer. While all of those heinous mistakes I'd made were a painful and distant memory for me, the revelation of my fuck-ups would be only a few days ago for this new life.

And we remember what happens next.

I had the grotesque privilege of knowing the horror on the horizon. The lonely condos, the hollow sex... Angie crying in the rain or shrieks of rage that reverberated in the halls. Then there was Slone's silence, Violet's disappearance, and finally Liam's series of incarcerations.

So what was I supposed to do? Relive the wreckage? Play it all again and hope for a different ending?

Fuck. I hadn't just ruined our family. I had obliterated Sloane, us, and everything we had built together. All I felt in that moment of clarity, coursing through my veins like ice water, was horror. I was a goddamn scumbag; a shell of a man in a skinsuit.

My death should have been my final punishment, my penance for the pain and suffering I had caused. Instead, I was somehow back again.

I stumbled out into the parking lot, the morning air sharp and cold against my skin. Somewhere in the distance, a siren wailed. The world felt too big, too real. Twelve years of knowledge burned behind my eyes as I slid into the driver's seat of my truck. The crisp, sterile smell of new leather and carpet smothered me, a reminder of how easily I'd buried guilt under the guise of waste and luxury.

As I breathed through the onslaught of nausea, tears pricked at my eyes. For the first time in years I let myself cry. I sat there for a long time, staring out the window of my truck, watching the bruised sky as the sun rose, feeling like some cruel god had dragged me out of the grave just to force me to witness the beginning of my own ruin. Not to change it, simply to watch it. Helpless. Aware.

Bile rose once again and I couldn't hold it back. I threw open the door, emptying out the remains of my stomach as the invasive thoughts kept coming.

I deserve this. This is Hell. This is my punishment for all I've done.

Hell or not, I knew something with bone-deep certainty: no matter how young my body, my soul was already rotting. And Sloane? Fuck, she would never look at me the same again.

Wiping the tears and vomit from my face, I crawled back in and started my truck. Anger coiled in my stomach as I came to the conclusion I needed.

Fuck whatever sadistic god brought me back and *fuck* whatever they had planned for me. I didn't care if it was intended as a curse, gift, or punishment. I had one more chance. I had to find Sloane and tell her how sorry I was before I lost her all over again.

Because I *refused* to lose her again.

Chapter 2

The first thing I did was check the date and time to confirm what I already suspected.

Twelve years. Twelve fucking years.

I sat there, trembling in the car, my hands unsteady as I tried to claw through the onslaught of my most recent memories from my previous life: from the death of Old Me. I had been driving. The light turned green. A horn, long, panicked, too late and then the impact. The sharp violent jerk as the front of a truck barreled into my truck at, what, seventy-five miles per hour? Maybe more? That bright burst of metal in my peripheral, a scatter of glass, and the sickening crunch as my body ceased to exist.

I could imagine all that must have remained of me: a mangled mess, my body nothing more than a stain to be scraped off the front of the truck's grill, a human carcass that couldn't even be recognized as one anymore.

Whatever god standing nearby in those solemn last moments must have taken pity after listening to me beg for ten years for another chance. That skeletal wave of his hand was all that was needed for a second opportunity, a time-travel resurrection, a get-out-of-death-free card.

Even now, as surreal as all of this felt, I knew that I could not fuck up my life again. The Old Me had blindly destroyed everything, and never took the time to appreciate how perfect my life had already been.

The feeling of desperation held taut as my chest heaved from the pressure. The thought of what I'd put Sloane through tore into my stomach, a knife of guilt stabbing into me. I *needed* to see Sloane.

Trying to ground myself, I checked my wallet and took an inventory of what cards and cash I had on me. Debit, credit, cash and a punch card to a coffee place Angie loved.

Well that is fucking trash now.

A small wave of relief passed through me when I remembered that my important documents, passport, birth certificate, social security card, were safe. Sloane had them. She'd been smart enough to suggest I leave them with her back when I was still in the midst of moving in with Angie.

Angie. My mistress.

Even the word felt filthy as it made my stomach twist.

Looking to the sky, I realized that I still had plenty of time left before Sloane woke up for the kids and her demanding job.

The constant chaos at the emergency vet clinic left her drained and I had been too stubborn to let her stay home with the kids until my business became a success. By that point, Sloane's love for the industry kept her working there as she held every paw and hand that came through those doors.

As for me, I was a builder by trade. Simple. Predictable. I built homes. Big, beautiful structures meant to last lifetimes and for a while,

I thought I was building a future, too. Business was booming. Money flowed in like water from a busted pipe, and I was arrogant enough to think it would never dry up since the housing market was on fire. I let myself believe I had outsmarted the system.

What I didn't know at the time, what none of us saw coming, was that the world was about to break. A slow, creeping apocalypse was already threading its way through airports, subways, and schools. A virus that didn't care how many zeroes I had in the bank and trust me when I say I had plenty. Like a bleak noir story, the end was already moving, silently and ruthlessly through the world, and by the time we realized it, we were all too late.

All the things I thought were permanent? Profit margins, business deals, my own sense of control? They meant nothing when our fluid-filled lungs collapsed from the onslaught of broken, damaged alveoli due to the danger in the air. So many deaths.

Regardless, I knew what to do. Fuck, things would be different. *I would be different.*

Fuck me, I need a drink.

Angie's foul taste and my own vomit still lingered on my tongue, sour and sticky, and I wanted to cleanse myself of her. I'd remove her memory from my very being if I could.

I stopped at the store and grabbed some clothes, a toothbrush, toothpaste, a bottle of water, and mints. Anything to feel clean again. As I was checking out, a rose bin sat next to me, its bright bouquets a contradiction to the rising storm inside of me.

Hesitantly I grabbed some; the sickly sweet flowers were a bitter contrast to what I'd done. Should I pick up a ring? No, that felt too ominous and negligent to the pain Sloane was enduring right now.

Standing in the parking lot, I brushed my teeth like a man possessed, gargling the taste of Angie away before popping several mints in my mouth. I rinsed my genitals in a brutal scrub, wishing I could peel the skin off and be done with it all. Had anyone tried to castrate themselves before? I was tempted to try.

After changing clothes, my finger scrolled relentlessly through old text chains, trying to piece together where I stood in this new life. My heart bled as I read the messages, each one a grim reminder of how far I'd fallen.

It seemed I'd taken a few days off to move, abandoning Sloane to juggle everything on her own. The kids. The chaos. The endless demands. I'd left her to carry the weight while I disappeared into my selfish spiral.

My last message to her was a cold, dismissive, *"Whatever,"* when she'd asked if I could spend some time with the kids and saying they missed me. I didn't even remember sending a response in my previous life much less this one... but there it was, my indifference staring back at me, like a branded scar.

Fuck, the Old Me is a complete asshole.

Hands trembling, I pulled up the photos from my phone. To my dismay, Angie's perky breasts were the most recent ones, bile threatening to take over again as I began to delete the mistake.

Then I saw it. My family. Little snapshots of the kids and of Sloane. My breath hitched as I stared at her youthful appearance, etching every line into my memory of her.

In my previous life, age had worn her down, leaving the mature woman I had grown to love and respect; fine lines added to a masterpiece on a perfect canvas.

In those photos, in this new life, she looked exquisite. It was as if Aphrodite herself had descended to sculpt every perfect curve and every beautiful flaw. There was still that quiet, unconditional kindness in her eyes, a quality I loved her for that transcended my two lifetimes.

Seeing her shattered me. I broke down, sobbing into the steering wheel, my whole body heaving as her photo lit up my phone screen. I kissed it, desperate, reverent, like a priest kissing a cross, as if it could bring me absolution as I whispered her name. She was my beginning, my middle, and whatever was left of this fucked up life I was trying to salvage.

Everything felt so alien and all so familiar. It was hard to grasp, comprehend, much less make coherent decisions but I was trying. I wanted to fix my mistake from twelve years ago, in a reality that was only a few hours old to me.

It took hours and the ghost of years' worth of therapy to steady my breathing. This time I would be devout. I would worship the very air she breathed and kiss her feet. These things I vowed to myself as I stared at her photo, time standing still before I truly felt like I could move on from her image.

The next step of my rebranding was my truck. I tore through it like I was trying to erase Angie from existence, scrubbing every trace of her from my life, as if I could will her away.

First, the trash went: empty condom wrappers, receipts for overpriced dinners I'd never even enjoyed, an empty beer bottle, fuck, all the crap that had piled up over time. Then, I dug deeper, pulling out anything that could remind me of her, the stupid little trinkets I'd bought to keep the lie alive, to keep her thinking she mattered more than she ever did. I threw it all away with a savage sense of urgency, each discarded piece a small victory in my fight to reclaim whatever was left of myself.

Somewhere in the back of my mind, the thought crept up, cold and detached: I needed to schedule a vasectomy. A permanent cut to make sure there was no chance I could ever fuck up again. No more mistakes. Fuck that future, and fuck the mess I'd made.

After I scrubbed the truck clean, I left the AC running, trying to fend off the suffocating humidity already creeping into the morning air. The truck hummed softly as I stared at the trash bag in the passenger seat. My hands still felt contaminated. No matter how much I scrubbed, the weight in my chest remained, suffocating. Nothing I did could wipe away the filth clinging to me. I exhaled a long, disgusted breath.

As I stood there listening to the soft, almost imperceptible hum of the radio, memories resurfaced with dizzying force, unwanted and invasive. The world outside blurred, like the edges of a nightmare creeping closer as my brain recalled what was to come. The chaos. The instability. The madness. Soon the world would collapse under its own weight and the fear of the impending pandemic crawled under my skin.

My hands clung to the truck door for balance, grounding myself even as cold sweat slicked my skin. I had to be smart. The world was going to crack wide open and before it did, I needed to be ready to profit off the collapse. I recalled the handful of companies that would bleed us dry during the impending pandemic, the ones that would explode from obscurity to become household names in the coming decade.

I climbed back into the truck with purpose. Plans swarmed my mind as I took the long way home, dragging out the drive. I pulled into a gas station, tossing the trash into a rusted bin while the pump clicked behind me.

I needed to steady my pulse before I walked through the door to my home. I couldn't barge in like some frothing madman, consumed by the knowledge of a horrific virus and the near societal collapse it would trigger.

Though, maybe I should? Hell, if nothing else it'll get me in the door.

Instead, I pulled into the driveway, practicing deep breathing exercises as my eyes caught the glint of Sloane's SUV parked in the garage. My heart sped up.

Well fuck, no amount of breathing exercises can help me right now.

I caught sight of other things I never noticed in my previous life. My daughter's little hand-drawn monsters littering the pavement, their crayon colored chalk faded but somehow still bright, standing out against the cold, gray concrete. Water guns lay discarded in the corner of the front yard, forgotten remnants of summer play, and a painful reminder of childhood innocence.

In that moment, something sharper hit me. I realized how much I had missed. I couldn't stop thinking about how much time I'd already wasted without my kids, and how little time I had left with to fix all I had broken.

The house loomed ahead, a modern two-story box of cold perfection, with its white brick and sharp black trim, the clean aesthetic a fucking mockery of everything that had crumbled in my wake. The place was a tribute to my once-pristine life, now marred by my own hand.

My only solace was that I'd been smart enough to buy the lots on one side, securing three and a half acres of land for whatever the hell I thought I could build. In my previous life, I had sold everything for pennies during the divorce; a transaction that even now made my stomach twist.

This time? I'd build something. Maybe I'd start a farm to fill the empty space with something that could grow? I was filled with purpose at the thought of watching my family experience joy in a safe space I would build for them; something I'd failed spectacularly at in my previous life.

Would that erase the trauma I inflicted on everyone and make things right? Maybe not... but it felt like the right thing, the only thing, to do.

The truck door slammed, louder than I intended, but enough to set off the little security camera above the garage door which blinked to life. Its cold, mechanical eye tracked my every step as I moved toward the house. Sweat slicked my palms, the roses trembling in my hands, and part of me mocked the pathetic gesture as I entered through the garage.

Inside, the house was still except for the soft pitter-patter of Rufus's paws on the hardwood, greeting me in his familiar way. His fluffy tail swayed low and slow, an old dog's awkward greeting, as he still recognized the man who had once called this place home.

"Hey buddy. I missed you."

Truth be told, I did miss him. Rufus had died in the middle of the divorce with Sloane while I had been locked down in Key West; partly for work, partly with Angie. It took years for the weight of his loss to fully settle in. I recalled the pain of not saying goodbye to such a good boy. The Old Me had been so selfishly balls deep in Angie, that he was oblivious to the struggles of his own family.

I placed the roses on the counter and reached back down for Rufus, hugging him tight as I caught a brief look of his confused face; comical yet everything I needed in that moment. My good boy looked so old.

I was petting him when I heard her voice break the silence from behind me. "Levi, what are you doing here?"

For a moment, I couldn't move. My hand stilled on Rufus, who used this opportunity to lean in and lick my face. I took a few deep breaths, telling myself I shouldn't cry but I felt tears prick the corner of my eyes.

"Levi?"

Fuck, her voice sounded so sweet yet broken. The approaching guilt washed over me for everything she had to go through. Years of regret and longing swelled, pressing against my ribs as I breathed out through my nose in steady, practiced exhales.

You can do this, big guy.

Trying to steady myself, heart pounding in my throat, I stood and looked at her. I'd spent hours memorizing her photo in the truck, but nothing could've prepared me for the jolt of seeing her in person. She looked so young, so heartbreakingly beautiful. Then and now, she still managed to steal the breath right out of me.

Sloane's red-rimmed hazel eyes stared back at me, her face pale from the little sleep I imagined she was getting as she tightened the robe around her curvaceous body, her tousled brown hair trickling down her face and frame.

Instantly I felt myself harden, balls tight and painful from the failed earlier tryst. Conflicting emotions of disgust and desire tore through me and I felt like a fucking animal. I wanted to punch myself.

"Hi, Sloane." I smiled at her, because I couldn't help it. I was so happy to see her and I'm sure I looked manic in that moment, drunk on the coursing adrenaline I had been battling earlier.

Sloane quirked a brow at me and took a step toward the island, completely ignoring the roses on the counter. "You aren't answering my question, Levi. Did you forget something while moving out?"

I shifted on my feet, feeling my cheeks heat at the low yet respectable blow she threw my way. "I actually came by to see you and the kids like you asked."

She was rummaging through the kitchen, looking for her coffee cup when I moved closer to the island to sit on one of the stools. Her icy voice cut me off before I could sit. "I never said you could stay Levi."

Sit. Stay. Speak. At this point, I would crawl to this woman if it meant I'd earn her forgiveness, but that wasn't what I needed to do right now.

Hand on the back of the chair, eyes downcast, I waited. Sweat pooled at the back of my neck as I felt her eyes on me, quietly sizing me up.

I know I look good.

Even with limited options, I'd managed to find a slim-fit black shirt that hugged my frame just right and a pair of dark navy jeans that fit like they were made for me. I'd chosen the clothes on purpose, the ones I knew she used to love seeing me in and would make her say, "Mmm, yeah... nothing like drywall dust and deltoids to get a girl going," whenever I flaunted my muscles like an idiot. Being a builder had its perks, after all.

Now is probably not the best time to do that though.

I met her eyes, already narrowed and assessing, and spoke before I lost my nerve, "Sloane. Can we talk?"

The broken laugh that escaped her shattered something inside me, a sound that felt like a crack in the earth beneath my feet.

Bad start. Abort. Abort.

She filled her cup with coffee, her hands steady but her eyes hollow. "Talk?" She scoffed, the word sour in her mouth. "What the hell is there left to talk about, Levi?"

Well fuck, here goes. "I want to get back together."

I knew the words were a death sentence as soon as I said them. I'd hardly finished the sentence before the coffee mug slipped from her hand and shattered on the floor, the sound of it exploding the silence like a gunshot. Hot coffee and ceramic shards flew everywhere.

"Fuck Sloane. Are you okay?" I rushed towards her.

She stepped back. Her breath caught as her face contorted with a flash of pain so raw I felt it tearing through me. She opened her mouth to speak, but no words came; only the silence of hurt and loss. Fuck. I had done this to her.

I took a tentative step away, as if backing up from a wounded animal, and collapsed onto the stool. My hands shook as I gripped the edge of the counter. My next words spilled out of me. "I'm sorry, Sloane. I'm so fucking sorry..." Hollow words falling out of a broken shell.

Her face twisted, the tears in her eyes shimmering but they didn't fall. Instead, fury replaced the hurt, blackening her eyes and even as the anger colored her face, I couldn't stop myself from admiring her like a lovesick fool.

Her voice broke me from my trance. "Don't you dare apologize to me now, Levi," she spat, each word sharp. "Not after everything you've done. Not after the lies, the fucking betrayal, the disrespect, everything you've dragged me through these last few days. You think a sorry can fix any of that?"

She was trembling now, her voice breaking between anger and agony, but she didn't stop. Her eyes never left me as she pulled from the deep abyss of her hurt. "You destroyed me, and now you want to come back like nothing ever happened? You don't get to walk back into my life like that. Not when you're the one who fucked it all up."

Tears streamed down her face and I felt my heart splinter. Instinctively, I reached for her, my hand only brushing air. "I want to-"

"It's always you, you, you, Levi!" Her voice rose, boiling over like a storm that had been waiting to break, "What about what I want?" She was unraveling in front of me, the woman I adored and cherished, spiraling into a whirlwind of anger and pain because of my choices... and nothing I said could help her hurt.

"Sloane, I'm begging you."

Her breathing was ragged, her chest heaving with the weight of it all as she seethed. "I don't give a *fuck* if you crawl on your hands and knees begging me to take you back, Levi."

Each word stabbed me in the gut, every syllable cutting deeper.

And yet, somewhere in the back of my twisted, traitorous brain, I imagined myself in a collar, on a leash. Because, apparently, pain only made me want her more.

"Do you have any idea what I've had to deal with? The tears? The anger from the kids? I've had to fucking protect them from this mess you created, while you..." Her voice faltered, but the rage was still there burning in her eyes. "While you fucked around like it was some game with that dipshit gym rat."

I couldn't speak. Couldn't find the words to defend myself, because what was left to say? She was right, and the weight of her fury crushed me.

Despite all this, seeing her in this little ball of rage and hearing her rip into me drove me wild with desire. I started to wonder if I'd had a kink for degradation that I'd never known about, or if it was just her presence stoking that heat within me.

Before I could respond, the sound of car doors slamming outside cut through the tension, jolting us both. Sloane froze, panic flickering across her tear-streaked face. Her eyes darted toward the door leading to the mudroom, and before she could say anything, I moved quickly from the stool, my limbs stiff with the need to *fix* something, anything.

I reached for her then, gently pulling her toward me, but she flinched away, her eyes burning with contempt.

"Levi... *why?*"

I grimaced, a bitter knot forming in my throat. "Sloane, we need to talk. I promise I'm hearing you." Years of therapy kicked in as I tried to salvage something. "I'll handle the kids. Go wash your face. Get dressed. You need a minute."

She shook her head, disbelief seeping into every inch of her. "I can't," she hissed. "You have no patience for them. You never have." My grip on her tightened as she tried to pull away. "And don't tell me what I need. You can't waltz in here looking good and expect me to fawn over your every word."

So she had checked me out. A small cheer went off as I changed tactics.

I grasped her hand gently, almost pleading with my eyes as desperation crept into my voice. "I'm not trying to tell you anything but do you want the kids to see us like this? Sloane, I need you to be logical, for a second."

I took a chance, my face a desperate plea of puppy dog eyes despite the rising fear that she might kick me in the balls or rip my face off. Both of which might make me come at this point from a sadistic game of edging I seemed to be playing with myself indiscriminately. Fuck who knows.

Her eyes bore into mine as my truth filled the space between us. I pushed a little more, ignoring the warmth of her body and the smell of her titillating my senses. "I'll have patience, Sloane. I promise. For them. For you. For all of it." I kissed her fingertips, my chest tightening with each soft touch.

She recoiled from me then, her body stiffening as she pulled out of reach. Violet and Liam's voices were closer.

I nodded towards our room. "Please Sloane. I am begging now. I'll even bark if you need me too."

Those words hung between us. She looked away towards where the kids were set to appear and I knew she was calculating in her head if this was a smart thing to do despite how desperately I needed her to trust me. *Please Sloane.*

Her decision was quick, a side-eyed glance to me as she nodded once. I watched the weight of everything settling onto her shoulders and without another word, she walked away.

The mud room door clicked and I turned to see my daughter...

The world froze, my lungs emptied, and tears blurred my vision. Violet... in my previous life, I hadn't seen her in nearly eleven years. Could I really do this? Was I ready to face one of my biggest failures from my previous life?

Oh, my baby girl, Violet.

Chapter 3

"Daddy!" Violet's excited scream shattered the empty silence of the house, and she rushed toward me, her face alight with the innocence only a nine-year-old could possess, wide and weightless. It took everything in me to not fall apart; burning her image into memory.

Seeing her now tore a hole in my heart. A brutal mix of relief and pain as I fought to stay grounded in the moment, ignoring the decade of torment I spent wondering what had happened to her. Like the world hadn't stolen her from me and buried her in every dream I clung to, just to stay sane and survive the grief of losing her.

Fuck all those years of not knowing.

Despite the years, I knew my baby girl. I dropped to my knees, knees that buckled under the weight of everything I was feeling, before she launched herself into my arms, her body as light as ever, brown braided hair wild and her unfiltered joy hit me like a punch to the ribs. Her cheeks were flushed from the heat mixed with the excitement.

"Daddy! Daddy!" she squealed. I forced a smile, the effort burning my insides.

"Violet!" I said, my voice too bright, too forced, as I kissed both of her hot cheeks. She still smelled like sun-warmed cotton and peanut butter.

I almost lost it then, tears threatening to spill, but somehow I kept myself together. I buried my face in her hair and tried to remember how to exist. Her tiny body clung to me and I was afraid she would vanish from my arms. I don't know if it was from relief, grief, or the overwhelming sense that nothing in this world made sense anymore but my heart pounded so hard against my chest, I thought I might be dying all over again with only her anchoring me to reality.

She giggled, pure and unfiltered. "Dawn took us to that pancake place this morning! For the start of school break! She let us get chocolate milkshakes with breakfast! Gluten free even!"

"That's so cool!"

She was vibrating with happiness, blissfully unaware of the tension her mother and I had shared or the turmoil in my chest. My lovely Violet, so innocent and wholesome.

Then I saw Liam.

He stepped in from the mudroom, quiet, watching me. His shoulders were hunched under his oversized black hoodie despite the stifling heat outside and I knew that hoodie might as well have been armor. His dark bangs covered most of his face, but I didn't miss the sharp edge in his amber eyes. He was a little carbon copy of me, filled with angst, whereas Violet, my artsy little devil, looked like her mother with the same temper.

My son stared at me and I could tell right away this wasn't moodiness. This was pain so similar to his mother's that my chest clenched.

Looking at my son, Liam had grown up more in the last few days than any kid should. He looked like a ghost wearing my son's clothes, a dark premonition of how I knew him from my previous life.

"Hey, Dad," he muttered. His gaze flicked to the floor, where the shattered remains of the ceramic mug glinted in the sunlight. "You and Mom fight again?"

Violet stiffened in my arms, her lips pursing in thought as she glanced back and forth between us.

"No," I said, softly. "No, bud. She dropped it. I was about to clean it up."

I smiled, even though it burned to lie to him and honestly, I didn't know if he believed me. I barely believed myself right now.

"You wanna help me clean it up?" I asked. "Was gonna say hi to Dawn, but..." I trailed off.

Violet's voice chimed in, hesitantly now. "She left when she saw your truck, Daddy. Dawn didn't even say bye. Called you a bad word though."

There was no bitterness in her voice and I knew truly that she didn't understand what exactly that meant. Sloane's parents and her sister Dawn were rightfully disgusted with me. I swallowed the humiliation and recalled that her parents only had another year to live before the virus ate away at them. Dawn, thankfully, would survive. My chest ached.

"It's fine," I lied.

Together, we cleaned up the broken mug and cold coffee. Violet talked nonstop, each word a tiny balm to the wreckage in my chest. Her science fair project, her volleyball game, her school reading list, all things I should've known about already. Things I'd missed while I was too busy wallowing in self-pity and fucking everything up.

I nodded and promised I'd be at the game. This time, I meant it and was looking forward to being a part of all their lives again.

Sloane came back out as we were finishing. Her eyes were still rimmed red and her damp hair clung to her neck, her expression unreadable. Even wrecked, she was beautiful and looked so damn untouchable as her walls were back up. I admired her in that fractured moment. My fierce, radiant wife, a pillar of grace holding the storm at bay for the children's sake and here I was, panting after her like a dog in heat, desperate and pathetic.

Disgust and shame weren't even the base of my vile personality anymore. I'd sunk far below that...mere shadows beneath the weight of my own darkness. Yet no matter how rotten I felt, no matter how much I deserved her contempt, I couldn't stop the ache in my chest on how badly I wanted to redeem myself to her, to claw my way back into her good graces, even if it meant swallowing my pride whole. I was willing to do anything for her and my family at this point.

"Hey," I said, awkwardly. "Shower help?"

She nodded once. Her arms crossed, fingers digging into her own skin like she had to physically hold herself together. "Yeah. Thanks. Are you... staying long?"

There was ice under the words, and I deserved every shard of it.

"No. Came by to see you all."

Liam let out a sharp, bitter laugh. He flopped onto the couch and turned the TV on, volume low. He didn't look at me again.

Violet stayed close, still buzzing with excitement, but her smile faltered as she sensed the tension between her parents. She was learning to read the room too well for her age and I hated that.

Despite how fucking awkward it felt to be standing in the kitchen, my heart was beating with joy being near them.

Don't be creepy, big guy. Smile. You got this.

The smile stayed plastered on my face. Sloane didn't say anything as she stared at me like she was trying to see through the mirage. Eventually she broke the silence, "Next time, text before you visit," she said.

I nodded. "Of course. I was too excited to see you all." I leaned over and ruffled Rufus' ears. "Especially Rufus."

"Uh huh." The disbelief in Sloane's voice sliced through whatever progress I thought we'd made earlier, dragging us right back to square one.

I glanced at my phone, briefly noting the time. "I'll leave in a few. Just need to make a few calls. I'm looking at places to stay nearby."

It was like an alarm went off in my head as Sloane froze. Her whole body went still, like she couldn't breathe.

Fuck, fuck, fuck.

"What?" she whispered, her posture ready to fight or flight at this point.

"I mean... I need to find a place. I'm not going far. I..." I stopped and tried to course correct. "It's not about abandoning anyone or forcing my way back in. I want to be close, for the kids and you if you'd let me."

From the couch, Liam cut in, his voice soaked in venom. "What about your girlfriend?" The word sliced through the air like a whip and I couldn't help but grimace.

Not helping, buddy. Fuck me, this is going poorly.

I tried to fix the failing conversation. "I made a mistake," I said quickly. "A stupid mistake. One I'm going to fix." The statement hung in the room, addressing anyone willing to listen. "That means getting my own place."

Sloane's hands trembled as she covered her mouth. Her eyes were filled with pain again and fresh tears. I was really hitting a record at this point. How much lower could I go?

"Levi... what are you saying?" she said.

Before I could answer, Violet lit up again from the dining room table she had been sitting at, her arts splayed in front of her. "You're coming home? For real?"

Fuck. My throat tightened.

"Violet," I said gently, "I... your mom and I need to work on things. Grown-up things. She has every right to set up boundaries and tell me what is best for you two. But I'm trying. I'm going to show her that."

Liam scoffed. "He's saying he doesn't want to be with us, Violet. Welcome to real life."

"Liam!" Sloane snapped. "That is enough."

Her voice cracked on the last word as all of us flinched at her tone. I had done this, made my wife a wounded animal lashing out.

"And *you*," she said, staring at me, "We'll talk. Later. Alone."

"Of course." I nodded before looking away, and forced myself to speak again, every effort in trying to sound casual. "I want to deposit a little more money in the joint account. For groceries. Or maybe something fun for the kids."

Puppy dog demeanor. I am a cute puppy dog.

Sloane raised a brow again, the tears now gone from the onset of anger she felt earlier as she busied herself in the kitchen. "You already gave us enough."

"I want to give more. For them. For you. Maybe... I don't know. A weekend trip? Disn-?"

Violet and Liam both gasped before I could finish the mention of the theme park, their voices screaming, "No way!" from behind me and

I knew I had won. It was a low blow, but I needed an excuse to wiggle my way back into their lives despite my brain telling me to take things slow. I was so afraid to lose her.

For a moment, a brief second, the tension dissolved as the kids rushed over; just two kids excited about rollercoasters and fireworks. It almost hurt worse that I had never offered this sooner and that I had to offer it now like a band aid.

Despite my own guilt, I knew it was effective. They swarmed her, Liam clinging to her arm, Violet tugging at her sleeve, voices overlapping in that breathless, frantic way only children can manage. I watched Sloane's resolve buckle under the weight of their excitement certifying that she couldn't tell them no to this. Her face cracked, a subtle unraveling followed by a single, reluctant nod.

The kids squealed, their joy vibrating through the kitchen like an aftershock and I stood there, hands jammed deep in my pockets. Watching. Memorizing. Her, them, this fractured fleeting slice of what I'd destroyed in my previous life.

Eventually, she calmed them enough to send them to their rooms to "pack." A temporary lie and a borrowed moment of silence for us.

Sloane stood in the kitchen, drained of her strength. Her shoulders slumped, arms hanging loose at her sides. She wasn't looking at me, but past me. Like if she met my eyes, she might shatter completely.

"Levi," she whispered, voice frayed at the edges. "Why are you doing this?"

The words echoed between us. Why?

Because you are my life, Sloane. You are my everything.

"Because I miss you all," I said instead, the words catching in my throat. "And because I want to fix what I broke. I know I can't ask you to forgive me. Not yet... but I'm here and I'm not going anywhere if you'd let me."

Her eyes finally found mine, and for a second, a flicker, I saw everything I'd ruined staring back at me. The trust I'd burned down. The love I'd taken for granted. The exhaustion I had helped carve into her face. She blinked hard, jaw tightening like she was holding back something too sharp to speak.

"I don't believe you," she said quietly. "You didn't just hurt me, Levi. You left me with everything. You left them."

A truth that would forever haunt me.

"I know," I said. "And I hate myself for it."

The silence between us was taut and raw.

"I'm not looking for pity," I added. "I... I don't want to waste this opportunity. However the hell I need to, I'll prove myself to you, to the kids. I need a second chance."

At that, her brow knit, ever so slightly, but enough to show her confusion.

"You think this is a second chance?" she asked, voice brittle. "You think you get to come back and decide that?"

"No," I said, realizing my mistake. I was so impatient and scared, it was causing me to rush my words into these fumbles. "I think I get to *try* if you allow me to have the opportunity. That's all I can do. Try and never stop trying."

"You've got a long road ahead of you, Levi," she said. I knew I had thrown her for a ringer. One day I said I was leaving her and now I'm begging to come back.

She motioned for me to sit. A silent command to an invitation with barbed edges. The irony wasn't lost on her nor was the power shift. I could see it in the way she held her chin, the flick of her eyes that told me she was still measuring whether I was worth the breath it took to speak to me.

"I'm going to get changed for work," she said, her fingers already undoing the top button of her blouse, not for seduction, but for control as she was reclaiming her body, her space, and finally her narrative to this story. "Wait here."

She paused at the threshold, turning back with one brow raised, the corner of her mouth twitching with something like disdain or amusement. "Oh... and what do you say?"

I hesitated. I could have said thank you or I'm sorry, but neither felt right.

Before I could stop myself, I said, "...Arf?"

Her eyes narrowed.

I cleared my throat. "Woof. I meant woof."

Her lips twitched. She didn't want to smile, but it betrayed her anyway.

"Good boy," she said, then walked away, leaving me equal parts humiliated, amused, and disturbingly aroused.

Sensing my banishment, Rufus padded over, tail low, eyes heavy with concern. He let out a soft whine and nudged my leg. I knelt beside him, fingers brushing over the soft fur of his ears.

"I know, buddy," I whispered. "I screwed everything up."

He licked my hand once, like a benediction. I scratched under his chin like I remembered he liked. "I promise you, Rufus, I'll do whatever it takes to earn my way back. Even if it takes me the rest of my life. I'm not quitting on them. Not again."

He added a small huff, as if he was confirming my vow.

Chapter 4

Leaving the house felt like peeling off a mask I barely held in place. Sloane had eventually said goodbye with that same exhausted caution in her voice, but I could sense a shift in her.

The kids waved through the window and I knew they were both already chattering about the trip. I waved back, even smiled, but inside I was rotting. My sense of self felt strained, the grim realization that I was struggling to fix things. Thank God they were still too young to realize it.

As I pulled away from the curb, the air inside the truck was thick with the scent of sweat and new leather. The sun glared down, too bright as I tried to plan my next step from here. A few blocks out, I passed the gym and my gut turned.

It was a sterile-looking place: sleek windows, steel trim, bold lettering. You'd never guess it was the site of my unraveling. I stared at it like a man watching the scene of a crime he'd committed. Fuck, I needed to cancel the membership.

That's where I met her. Angie.

She hadn't simply strolled into my life; she roared in like a wildfire looking for something to consume and I let her burn me. Hell, I kindled her flames.

But that fire didn't start with her. It was already smoldering in me, a dry brush left untended. Ego. Resentment. Years of unspoken bitterness I'd never admitted, not even to myself.

It had started on a Tuesday morning. I was skipping client calls, pretending to be productive while wasting time in a place where no one asked questions. The gym had become my temple of self-pity, a distraction wrapped in sweat and narcissism thanks to the sculptured six pack I had carefully created. I wasn't working out simply for health, I was trying to escape the monotony of life.

I ran on the treadmill, sweat pouring down my shirtless body, bored, angry, restless for reasons I couldn't name. It felt like I was breathing through gauze. Like the walls of my life were closing in and, instead of fixing it, I scratched at them.

That's when she walked in. Angie, the newest member of the gym and talk of the town thanks to her corporate daddy funding the next set of businesses looking to set up shop. Tight black leggings and flawless makeup even at 9 AM. She didn't belong in that place full of moms in oversized t-shirts and dudes sweating through their cheap tank tops.

She smiled at me while I was getting water. She wasn't coy, wasn't innocent. Fuck, she knew how attractive she was. I was helpless, caught up in the way she carried herself, completely unable to look away.

"You always scowl after cardio, or is that just for show?" Her rouge-painted lips curled into a smile that was all confidence and temptation.

I grunted some half-laugh and shrugged as I finished my water but already I was hooked. It had been months, maybe longer, since someone looked at me like I was interesting, not a walking to-do list or a constant disappointment.

The next day, she was there again... so was I.

It started off harmless: idle chatter, lifting tips, cardio jokes, dumb flirty jabs. She told me she was single, no kids, did some marketing consulting from home. She liked my sarcasm. Said I had "Alpha energy" which fed some starving, ugly thing within me that I hadn't known was there.

I should've turned away. I should've thought of Sloane's tired hands washing dinner plates after a ten-hour shift. Or the way Liam had started biting his nails until they bled from test anxiety. Or the way Violet still asked if I'd be home every night.

But I didn't. I looked away, ignoring the problems at home and focusing on this fantasy.

Each time we met up, Angie smiled like she already owned me. And a part of me, some bitter, broken part, smiled back.

Because I wanted someone to see me.

Because I wanted to feel *wanted*.

Because I was too damn selfish to appreciate the woman holding our family together with both hands while I whined inside my own head about how hard life was.

The mental gymnastics started early. It disgusts me to remember the things I said to Angie as I slipped deeper into the fantasy I was constructing.

"We can just be friends."

"Sloane and I haven't really talked in weeks."

That turned into flirtation, into inside jokes, into late-night texts that Sloane never saw. And Angie? She fed it.

"She sounds cold."

"You're not like other guys."

She knew exactly what strings to pull, and I was too arrogant to see I was another puppet.

I thought Angie was freedom. I thought she was validation. But she was a mirror, reflecting every ugly part of me I refused to face. Every choice I made with her came from a place of rot I hadn't treated and I justified it. Again and again.

I was bitter towards Sloane because she wanted to work. She loved the clinic and couldn't imagine a day without it. Ten or twelve-hour shifts, emergency surgeries, cases where some kid's dog came in mangled and she came home with its blood still under her nails. She was exhausted... always moving. The kids needed school lunches, rides, help with homework, doctors' appointments, orthodontist referrals.

I helped. Or, at least I thought I did. My self-centered ass couldn't see all the little things. I focused only on the obvious stuff: trash, dishes, the occasional school pickup when I "could spare the time." The mental load was always on her.

I had my phone, my secrets, my delusions of control. I made her the villain in my head just so I could feel righteous while betraying her. What I didn't see, the real weight, was how she carried it all. Emotionally. Logistically. Alone.

I only ever saw my own hunger.

Sloane had no idea. How could she? She was holding up the weight of our world, endlessly carrying the burden of our entire family *and* her career day in and day out like Sisyphus.

Hell, I'd come home to find her asleep at the table after grading Liam's science project or helping Violet practice reading. The house was clean because *she* cleaned it. Groceries were stocked because *she* planned every list. Doctor appointments? Calendars? Gift wrapping? Thank-you cards? Magic fairies didn't do that. *She* did.

I noticed all of it, but I didn't value any of it. Not the way I should have. Old Me had been incapable of appreciating her, because he was too busy feeling resentful that he wasn't being doted on. He was too blind to see she had nothing left to give.

So when Angie asked if I wanted to grab a drink one Friday night, I said yes. I said yes without thinking. Without guilt.

That night I met her, the bar was dim, music low, our booth tucked into a corner like a secret. I'd cleaned up after the gym, doing my best to look sharp and hoping to make an impression. But when I saw her, everything else vanished. I was star struck, blindsided by her presence. The rest of the world had slipped out of focus.

Angie wore red lipstick and a skin-tight dress that accentuated the tits her father had bought her. She touched my arm when she laughed. She asked, "Do you feel seen at home?"

I didn't answer right away.

She made me feel wanted, smart, and desirable. With Angie, I wasn't just a husband and father who mowed the lawn and cleaned out the gutters. She made me feel like *me* again. Except it wasn't *me*. Not really. It was a narcissistic sickness within me that needed to be the center of the universe.

"I see you," she said, dragging her fingers along the inside of my wrist. "I bet your wife doesn't even appreciate you anymore."

I could have stopped it right then. I should have stood up and walked away.

Instead, I kissed her.

Chapter 5

If that kiss was a match I'd lit, then what came next was a grenade: one that I'd pulled the pin on. It had been over a week since Sloane and I had spent any real time together. The tension between us was thick and stifling, as if it was competing with the humid June evening.

One thing to understand is that Sloane and I both had ravenous sex drives. This was a compatibility that had once been our superpower and, incidentally, the reason Liam arrived during our reckless, hormone-fueled early twenties after being high school sweethearts.

As we got older, we rarely went more than a day without touching, without grinding ourselves against each other. Sometimes it was a quickie in the shower, other times a stolen "lunch break" that had nothing to do with food. It wasn't glamorous, but it worked.

But that week, the rhythm had faltered. Life had gotten in the way with work schedules, kids' activities, bills, and noise. The distance grew slowly, and when we finally found ourselves alone, the pressure we hadn't spoken about all week detonated.

In hindsight, knowing what I now know, it's easy to see that most of our fights were foreplay masquerading as warfare; attraction hidden behind masks of anger.

This fight, however, was *not* that.

There was no artifice for our animosity, as our wounded prides escalated our heated words to cruelty. We were both too sharp, too stubborn. I recall how sick I was of Sloane always being right about everything. I remember how I desperately wanted help, but I didn't know how to ask for it without sounding weak.

On this particular evening, Sloane didn't even look up from her phone when I walked in. Dishes were piled in the sink, the kids were half-dressed watching TV, and she was slumped at the kitchen table with a mug of something gone cold. She didn't even say "hi." I was already wound too tight: long day, long week, long month.

Old Me, being the insensitive and self-centered prick that he was, snapped. "You could at least pretend to be happy to see me."

She looked up, slow and exhausted. I saw in her eyes that I was simply another demand she had to meet. "I'm tired, Levi. Can we not do this today?"

"Right," I muttered, yanking open the fridge. "Tired. Always tired."

She sighed. "Because I *am*. I just got home from work, Liam needed help with his homework, and Violet made herself a sandwich with *your* whole wheat bread. We really should consider being a gluten free home, Levi."

"But gluten free bread is gross," I said as I searched the fridge for a beer. "That's why I buy the good bread."

"I am too tired to have this argument right now."

I slammed the fridge shut. "You're always too tired. Too tired for dates. Too tired for sex. Hell Sloane, it feels like it's been weeks. It's like I'm invisible unless something breaks."

Her eyes flared, and I knew I'd crossed a line, but I didn't stop. I couldn't. The resentment was burning holes in my chest.

I asked, "When's the last time you even touched me like you wanted to? I get a pat on the back and a grocery list. That's it." I was grasping at straws, throwing out anything to get a reaction, anything to spark a fight, maybe even shout ourselves into some reckless, hot makeup sex.

She rose slowly. Her messy braids framed her face in wild loops and strands, a halo of chaos around a woman on the brink. Whatever angel she once was had long since handed the reins to something far more primal. I had summoned this version of her and now I was about to reap what I'd sown.

I saw the storm mounting in her eyes, fury rolling in with every breath. "You think I want this distance between us? You think I don't miss us too?"

"Then why won't you try? Why does it always feel like I'm begging for scraps of attention? Your sex toys get more action than I do most days."

"Because I'm drowning, Levi!" Her voice cracked. "I work, I parent, I clean, I schedule, I manage *everything*. Then you waltz in acting like sex is going to fix what's wrong with *us*, but you barely contribute to this household much less our marriage." She slammed her phone down, the sharp crack of the screen startling Rufus from his nap. "How is it that I'm failing *you* when I'm too exhausted to pretend I'm not broken anymore?" Her chest was heaving now, the tears in her eyes threatening to fall.

I opened my mouth to say something, anything, but nothing came.

She shook her head, her voice lower now, but no less cutting. "We're not young anymore. I get it. I'm not your fantasy, Levi. I can't climb into bed and pretend everything's fine. Not when I'm barely holding myself together and you're too wrapped up in your own bullshit to see that I need help, that I can't do this alone."

"Sloane, I *do* help," I said. My voice rose, getting defensive.

She blinked at me, then laughed, "Only when I beg, Levi." Her voice was brittle. "When I'm drowning in the mess and text you non stop, *then* you show up."

I opened my mouth, but she wasn't finished. Her eyes locked onto mine with sharp clarity. "You want to know why I don't want to have sex?" she asked. Her voice was cold and steady now. "It's because I already feel like I have a third child. And newsflash Levi, having a man-child isn't exactly a turn-on."

That one landed square in the chest. A clean, merciless blow as she turned and walked away, her shoulders heavy with the kind of surrender that only follows trying too hard for too long.

I stood there in the kitchen, hands clenched, jaw locked, wanting to scream but mostly feeling completely, irreparably alone. The first thought that flashed through me like lightning, fast and furious was, "How dare she treat me like this?"

She acted as if I was some burden she had to carry, nothing more than dead weight on her tired back. Was she blind to how hard I had worked my ass off to get us where we were? Why did I have to beg for affection from my own wife? Why was I not good enough for her anymore?

Fuck... Old Me was such a petulant narcissist.

My phone was already in my hand before I knew what I was doing.

> Wanna meet up?

The second I hit send, my stomach soured but not enough to stop me. I wanted to be seen. To feel wanted even if it was the wrong person. I was so consumed by my pain that I was blind to Sloane's.

Angie's text came back quickly.

> For you? Always.

That was all it took to hook me. Those three words gave me immediate and uncomplicated validation. Not like at home, where every word felt as if I was walking a tightrope. Not like Sloane, whose exhaustion had turned love into duty. Angie's words offered warmth where there had been cold, attention where there had been absence.

I knew it was wrong. I knew this wasn't connection. It was escape. A shortcut. A hit of something cheap that would burn out fast and leave me emptier than before.

But in that moment, I didn't care. I needed to feel something that wasn't rejection or inadequacy. I needed to feel *wanted*.

I'd told Sloane I needed to "get gas and clear my head." I didn't even bother with eye contact. She didn't argue. She was too tired. She didn't even kiss me goodbye. I got in the truck and drove.

The park I picked was nearly deserted, a few stray kids chasing the last of the fireflies and a couple joggers punishing their bodies in the heavy air. The late summer air was humid, oppressive, and stagnant.

Angie was already there, leaning against the restroom wall in cutoff shorts and a tank top damp with sweat. Her lipstick was a little too red for the hour, her grin a little too sharp.

"You're late," she said without looking at me.

"It's ninety degrees. You want me to rush through Hell?"

She smiled. "With what we are about to do, Hell is where you belong."

I almost laughed.

The sun was going down, bleeding orange across the sky. Shadows grew long between the trees. Crickets screamed from the tall grass. The tennis courts were deserted and the public bathroom stood isolated; a forgotten bunker in the heat-swollen stillness.

She took my hand without asking and I followed her inside.

The air reeked of piss and bleach. The cramped bathroom was dimly lit by a dying fluorescent bulb. The fan overhead hummed but did nothing to move the heat. There were scribbles on the stall walls, declarations of teenage heartbreak and crass symbols. A cracked mirror above the sink showed me a version of myself I hated.

She locked the door behind us and what followed wasn't affection. Hell, it wasn't even lust. It was something dangerous and sinister, fueled by self-loathing and delusion.

She touched me like she owned me and I let her because I didn't know who I was anymore without that attention, without someone pretending I was still worth something.

Our mouths crashed together in desperation. A sick transaction. Her hands were bruising on my back, mine on her waist as we ripped each other's clothes off. No trust, no intimacy.

Just raw need, sharpened to a knife's edge by guilt and narcissism.

"You think she'd cry," Angie hissed in my ear, nails raking down my spine, "if she knew what you let me do to you here?"

I flinched but I didn't stop. Cock and balls so heavy as I thrust into her so violently she had to cover her mouth to stop the screams.

I threw her on the sink as I rammed into her. I relished in the way her cunt squeezed around me before quickening to her release as I relentlessly pounded. It was everything my fantasy had fed me, and my orgasm hit me so hard, so overwhelming, I nearly collapsed.

Between the first lie and this moment, I had turned into a person I didn't recognize. Someone who breathed deception like it was oxygen. Someone who let himself be dragged into the dark and called it warmth.

When it was over, I sat on the toilet lid, elbows on knees, face in my hands. The stench of piss and bleach now mingled with sweat and sex. My chest heaved like I'd just escaped Hell. The truth was that my Hell had only begun.

Angie stood in front of the cracked mirror, painting her mouth red again like nothing had happened, like it hadn't meant anything.

Fuck, maybe to her it didn't. But to me? It was everything in me broken, rolled into a singular moment of regret disguised as validation.

The Old Me was abhorrent.

"This doesn't end when you say it does," she said, her voice low and deliberate. "Not when the chemistry between us is this fucking undeniable."

"I don't want this to end," I said. I was drunk on the attention, drunk on the idea that I was wanted. The way Angie looked at me? Like she couldn't get enough, like I was everything. I needed this lie. I needed something to cling to, so I could justify what I'd done.

She turned, brow cocked, a cruel little smirk tugging at her lips. "Who said it has to end? Move in with me."

I stared at the cracked tile behind her. If I looked at her, I would have have said yes in that moment.

She gave me a suggestive look and her smirk grew wider. She unlocked the door and walked out first, her laugh echoing down the corridor. I waited five more minutes before I left, knowing full well that the damage was done.

The devil had both my number and my soul, and I was too far gone to do anything about it.

Chapter 6

I drove home from the park with the windows down. The sweat drying on my neck was a reminder of the sin I'd committed. When I stepped into the kitchen, Sloane was sitting at the table with Violet asleep on her lap, one arm curled protectively around our daughter. A plate of cold dinner sat on the counter and the ice in her tea had melted.

It was at that moment, right there in the doorway, when I realized how small I'd become. How far I'd fallen. Not just as a husband, but as a man. Even as the heat of Angie's touch clung to my skin, I couldn't stop seeing Sloane's slumped shoulders, the weariness evident despite feeling the vindication I needed. Like a child throwing a tantrum, I couldn't see that I had it all and was destroying it piece by piece from the inside.

My narcissistic nature believed I could still control the narrative, bend the truth to serve me, twist guilt into justification. But all I was really doing was digging deeper, blind to the wreckage I was leaving behind. I kept telling myself I couldn't stop. That it wasn't about the sex. No, it was about the attention. It was the illusion of being valued that I drank like poisoned wine.

Angie and I continued to meet for weeks. We met in parking lots, cheap hotels, her home. I either didn't notice or didn't care that it was always her calling the shots, always whispering things that rewired my brain.

"You shouldn't have to beg to feel wanted."

Meanwhile, Sloane was forgetting to eat because Liam was sick and Violet's tooth was loose and there was a puppy on oxygen in the ICU and a dozen other battles Sloane was waging without me.

During all of this, I was lying to her face... but reality always comes calling.

The first crack was Liam's thirteenth birthday. I'd forgotten to RSVP to a skating party. One job. That's all I had to do. Sloane didn't yell. She just looked at me like she was so tired of being disappointed. Like she had stopped expecting anything better.

"Why can I never rely on you?" she asked.

Instead of answering her, I got defensive. Classic Old Me. Rather than sit with the truth of what she was sharing, I twisted it, turned the whole thing into an attack. I lashed out, accused her of not wanting me anymore, of making me feel like a burden in my own damn house. It was easier to turn the mirror on her than look into it myself.

That argument spiraled fast with sharp words flung like knives, both of us bleeding pride and somewhere in the middle of all that venom and fire, we crashed into each other like a storm meeting the sea. An angry, frantic, bruising kind of sex where clothes were ripped, lips bitten, nails dragged across skin like we were trying to mark territory.

It was the hottest and most toxic sex we'd ever had. Rage disguised as passion, our bodies saying what our words couldn't. We weren't making love that day. We were trying to outrun the distance between us, and prove we could still *feel* something even if it was through pain.

When it was over, we didn't collapse into each other like we used to with our post sex apologies and reconnection. Instead, it was a cold and suffocating silence. We got dressed in separate corners of the room, as if we were nothing more than strangers after a one-night stand, then walked away in opposite directions. We were somehow both angrier and emptier than before.

The truth was, I didn't like the mirror she held up. I didn't want to see what I was turning into. I hadn't fallen into an affair because Sloane failed me. I fell because I failed Sloane. I was the weakest man in the room. I confused validation for love. I confused sacrifice for neglect. I confused comfort for boredom.

My ego couldn't handle the passive-aggressive comments she made over the next day or two.

"You spend more time at the gym than at home."

"You are way too distracted, Levi."

My guilt, thinly disguised as feeling unappreciated, had been festering for weeks; ever since the affair with Angie started. That guilt twisted itself into something louder, something I could no longer ignore or excuse. I lied to myself that I was justified; that I deserved more. But the truth was simpler. I was a coward looking for a way out that didn't make me the villain.

I had already started packing. Bags stashed in the garage like ticking bombs.

A few nights after mine and Sloane's rage fueled fucking, on an evening we were meant to review the kids' schedules for the upcoming school year, I confessed to her. We were supposed to sit down at the kitchen table like we were still teammates, as if we still lived on the same side of the battlefield.

But I couldn't pretend anymore. I couldn't meet Sloane's eyes across that kitchen and act like I wasn't already halfway gone.

She looked too tired, too thin. She was a hollow eyed revenant of the woman I'd married, worn down from years of struggling alone; Old Me was too blind to see that he had done that to her. Fuck, Old Me was too immature to admit that he'd done anything wrong.

She was rinsing a glass in the sink when I said, "I need to tell you something."

Sloane didn't look at me. "Is this about the school forms? I signed them and left them in Liam's folder."

"No," I said. My throat burned, but I forced the words through anyway. "It's worse than that."

She stood there, averting her gaze, hands under the faucet, water running over her fingers like she hadn't heard me.

"I cheated."

No drama. No explanation. The truth, laid out cold on the kitchen floor.

She slowly looked up at me. Her face was eerily serene, but her eyes locked on mine, and in that moment, I knew I had detonated something we would never return from.

"With who?" she asked. Her voice was calm; far too calm. My mouth was dry and I'd realized then that I was genuinely afraid; she might have murdered me then and there.

I opened my mouth.

"Do not lie," she said, sharper now. "If you even *think* about sugarcoating it, Levi, I swear to God-"

"Her name's Angie. From the gym."

Sloane's lips parted, a dry sound escaping her throat. Not quite a gasp, more like a breath cut short. She laughed. Just once. One broken, humorless sound that made me want to crawl out of my own skin.

"From the *gym*," she echoed. "Jesus. Of course it was."

"I didn't mean for it to happe-," I began, but she held up her hand like a teacher reprimanding a toddler.

"Don't. Don't you *dare* give me that cliché garbage. Do you think I'm stupid? You didn't 'mean' to lie to me for who knows how long? You didn't 'mean' to betray me every time you came home and kissed me goodnight with her sweat still on your skin?"

Her voice cracked. The tears were there, welling fast, but she wasn't letting them fall.

I shook my head and stepped forward, heat rising in my chest. "I was lonely, okay? You were never around. Always working, always busy with the kids, the house, everything." I let out a bitter laugh. "It's not all on me. You were taking care of anything and everything else except *us*. At least *someone* made me feel wanted."

"Wanted?" she said, voice rising. "I gave you *everything*, Levi. I carried your goddamn ego on my back for years. I was up at 5 a.m. packing lunches while you slept in. I was cleaning vomit, paying bills, calling teachers, handling vet emergencies and you were what? Out screwing some gym rat?!"

I looked down, my hands clenched at my sides, heat pulsing in my temples. I was angry... at her, at myself, at life.

"You disgust me."

Those words hit harder than any slap ever could and just like that, something in me shut down. I told myself I couldn't stay. That it was easier to walk away, to start over with Angie, instead of face what I'd done. The truth? I was a coward and I hated her for making me feel like one.

"I'm moving out. I'm going to live with her," I said, steady and unapologetic. At that moment, the words didn't taste bitter. It felt like a release.

Somewhere along the long and twisted path that led me here, I had stopped seeing her as my wife and started seeing her as the *reason* I felt so small. To me, this felt like the next step. A natural result of weeks of what Old Me thought was being overlooked, unappreciated, and shut out.

Sloane didn't say anything at first. She stared at me like she didn't recognize who I was. The silence in the kitchen pressed down on me harder than any shouting ever could.

Then, she asked in broken, trembling whisper, "When?"

I gripped the edge of the counter, not because I was falling apart but because I needed to stay calm and in control. "Tonight."

I'd said it as a simple fact. As if it was the only logical conclusion. Why drag it out? Old Me thought he'd already given enough of himself; certainly more than anyone ever gave him.

A sharp sob broke out of her. "And the kids?"

I shook my head. My eyes stayed fixed on a crack in the tile because I had been too much of a coward to look at her. "We'll figure it out."

Leaving that night was the stupidest mistake I have ever made. But the worst part, the part I hate myself for the most, is that I didn't betray just my wife - I betrayed the mother of my children and the woman who gave up everything to build a life with me.

There were a thousand things Old Me could have done differently, could have done better. But Old Me picked the worst possible decision at every point and kept going... now I'm crawling through the wreckage and trying to rebuild something I'd set on fire.

If Sloane even lets me try, I know that every moment of healing, every tender glance from her, every night we spend rebuilding what I shattered, is a debt I know I'll never fully repay but... I am going to keep trying even if it takes the rest of this fucked up life.

Chapter 7

"I'd like to turn this in," I said. The cancellation letter shook as I handed it to Brandon, the manager of the gym I had used for an escape. I forced myself to smile. He looked down at it, then up at me too quickly.

Fuck, he knew.

There was a silence between us that grew heavy with everything unsaid. Brandon had seen the late nights, the lingering looks, and the way Angie used to drape herself over the front desk when she knew I was coming in. The man wasn't stupid.

He scratched the scruff of his beard as he read the letter, then folded it with deliberate care. "So... that's it, huh?" he asked, the question loaded with implication.

"Yeah. That's it."

This was the first real move. The first cut. This was part of the cleanse. Part of shedding the version of myself that had made these reckless and dumb decisions. This was just another step toward erasing the Old Me and tying off loose ends. One less place Angie might expect to find me. One less routine tethering the New Me to the Old Me.

"Shame to lose you, Levi. You and Angie were in here like clockwork," Brandon said, flipping the cancellation form over in his battered hands. The man looked better suited for fighting than running a place filled with mirrors and protein shakes. His words held a quiet condemnation wrapped in casual indifference.

I didn't flinch. He ran a gym, not a confessional.

I kept a polite curve to my lips. "Yeah... Just need to put my focus back where it should've been all along. My family."

Brandon snorted a laugh laced with bitterness and resignation as he slapped the counter. "Ain't that the truth? My wife's been on me for months about cutting back hours. Wants me home more. Says the kids barely know what I look like."

The irony wasn't lost on me as I glanced him over. He had the build of a man who used to compete and still clung to the title: broad shoulders, thick forearms, and a gut that spoke more of post-workout beers and skipped cardio than discipline. If I had any fucks left to give, I might've told him to go home and screw his wife like a man who still believed in vows. But honestly? I didn't care.

He shoved the cancellation form into a drawer with a thud, then looked up at me and asked, "You want me to give Angie the heads-up?"

I stiffened, my jaw clenching so tight it hurt, but I shook my head and forced the words out. "No. She doesn't need to know anything about me anymore."

There was a flicker of recognition in Brandon's eyes, a brief flash of understanding that didn't need to be spoken. He nodded slowly, not pushing it. "Alright, man. Take care of yourself."

I didn't respond, just turned and walked out, the door closing behind me with finality. The sun slapped me. Too bright. Too clean. It burned against the parts of me still rotting from the inside, but I kept walking.

The next step was mechanical, soulless in a way that made it easier. From the gym parking lot, the one I knew would get closed once the quarantines and shut downs happened, I opened my banking app. Numbers glared back like silent judges:

Joint Checking: $10,136.98
Individual Savings: $604,129.93
Individual Brokerage: $558,427.35
IRA: $742,008.94
Master Builders Inc. Checking: $5,457,814.55

All that money. All that success. Yet, Old Me had still managed to tear his life to pieces like it cost nothing. I knew that sometime this week I would need to add Sloane to all of the accounts I had setup in only my name; an effort for full transparency on how our money was being spent. I needed to ensure she knew that everything I owned - we owned. It was a huge step toward rectifying the financial insecurity I knew she had to feel while working her low paying job.

I moved $50,000 into our joint checking account with practiced fingers. I knew the money didn't fix anything, but I hoped it could help alleviate any worries she harbored over our finances. Who knows? Maybe she would make a frivolous purchase out of spite.

Hell, I wish my practical Sloane would do something like that for herself.

I sent her a quick text that I moved over some money and she should reserve a room at one of the deluxe hotels with the kids. I saw the brief check that showed she read it as I turned my attention back to the accounts. I made a mental note to call the accountant since I'd need to pause any major purchases given the market would soon freeze. My brief listening of the radio was enough that to feel the shift in the air after hearing the news about the West.

I flipped over to the talk radio station and let the angry voices spill through the speakers like static.

"Good morning. You're listening to GA 92.1 FM, a community radio. We know these are stressful times, and we'll be here with updates. Here are your headlines..."

The radio droned on, ranting about the election; another cycle of blame and bluster. Abortion had been the deciding wedge this time. Always something to divide us. Always someone to hate.

I turned the volume down, but let it hum in the background as the engine of the truck roared to life. Steading myself, I drove toward my business, toward my responsibility to support my family and those I had working for me.

The office building was a monument to Old Me. Tall. Stark. Polished. It had my company name on the sign: Master Builders Inc. That day, it felt as if I was driving up to someone else's empire. A man who'd built his business out of bravado and greed. A man who'd left his wife to carry the weight of the world while he played king.

Sloane had helped me name this place. We were sitting on the porch drinking cheap wine while she bounced ideas off her phone. She came up with Master Builders inspired by Liam's love of Legos. I laughed, kissed her, said it was perfect.

When I pulled in, Jose was already out front, puffing on a cigarette like always. He waved when he saw me, flicking the butt onto the gravel and crushing it under his boot.

"Hey, jefe," he said as he fell into step beside me. "Got good news. The Kew West deal's a go. Full green light. The investors want to break ground by next month. Our guys are already packing. Most of 'em can't wait to get away from the ol' ball n' chain." He laughed, but the sound felt hollow to my ears.

I didn't answer. I pushed open the office door and walked inside, tossing my phone onto the desk like it weighed a thousand pounds. I reached for my hard hat. Didn't even put it on. Just stared at it.

Might as well rip the bandage off.

"We're pulling out of that project," I said.

Behind me, I heard Jose stop in his tracks. "Come again?"

"I'm canceling Key West."

A pause then his voice rose, too sharp and too fast. "Boss, that deal's worth over two million dollars! We've already sent scouts down, already filed permits—"

I lifted my gaze to him as I put the hard hat back down and said, "I don't care." He stared at me as if I'd confessed I planned to burn the company down. "Listen, we're hemorrhaging money. Fuel, labor, materials. It's not sustainable. And Key West is a vanity project... and I'm done chasing vanity." My voice almost broke there.

Jose took a step forward and asked, "Is this about her?"

I didn't have to ask who he meant. My hands curled into fists on the desk. I took a breath, then another. "This is about me," I said. "I built this place chasing numbers. Chasing attention. I had a wife who loved me. Kids who needed me. But I was out there: traveling, expanding, grinding. I was starving for... something, but I had no clue what that something was. Through it all, I let myself become someone I wouldn't trust around my own daughter."

The room was quiet. Jose watched me, that calculating stillness of his settling in. He had been with me from the start. The most loyal second-in-command anybody could ever ask for. Through miles of misadventures together, I had helped pull him out of the chaos of border towns and broken promises. I helped him get his green card, helped him buy land, and together we'd poured the foundation for a house his sons could grow up in. He never forgot any of those things. That kind of loyalty doesn't come from a handshake; it's forged in debt, in gratitude, in survival. Jose would follow me through Hell if I asked, even if he didn't agree.

"I'm scaling back," I said. "Local builds only. No more chasing deals states away. I want to be home by dinner. I want to show up for my kids. I want, fuck, I *need*, to fix what I broke before there's nothing left to fix."

Jose rubbed the back of his neck, eyes dropping to the floor. "Damn, jefe... That's heavy."

I shrugged. "It's honest."

He nodded slowly before he looked back up. In an instant, his expression hardened, slipping into business mode without a second thought, "Alright. I'll start pulling the Florida crews back. What about the contracts?"

"Call the lawyer. Kill them. Pay what we need to pay. I don't care."

He hesitated for a second, then slapped my shoulder. His stone-cold facade slipped a bit as the weight of the moment broke through, "Good on you, man. Real talk, I was wondering when you were gonna come back to Earth."

Then you should've fucking said something, I wanted to say. But I held it back. I knew Jose would speak up if he thought I was about to run the business into the ground... but when it came to personal matters, we both tiptoed around the edges and only ventured into those conversations when necessary.

I handed him the clipboard for the contacts of the Key West jobs. "Thanks. Now get out there and let's fix this."

Jose walked out, leaving the door open.

I placed my hands over my face, feeling the weight of everything settle.

What none of them knew, what no one knew, was that I had twelve years' worth of hindsight now. And all that bravado, all that momentum... it was about to shatter.

A virus, microscopic and merciless, was already carving its path through the world. In weeks, borders would close. In months, economies would grind to dust. People would die, suffocate on their own breath while others hoarded toilet paper and hand sanitizer like it was gold. Society was about to crack and I was staring down the barrel of it, pretending I didn't already know the trigger had been pulled.

Fuck me, things are about to go bad.

I sank into my sleek, leather chair, its refined surface cold beneath me, and stared at the desk in front of me. Paperwork. Receipts. Financials scattered and there, underneath a pile of estimates and bills, I saw a photo of Sloane and the kids in a half-buried frame.

I pulled it free and wiped off the dust with my sleeve. Set it upright. Stared at it like I was praying to an alter, recognition hitting me as I recalled that trip to the Smokies. Violet's front teeth missing, Liam pretending he didn't want to smile. Sloane, flushed from the sun, eyes bright.

This company gave me money, prestige... hell, it gave me the illusion of power but it never gave me home. I already had that. Yet, somehow, I had buried it under ambition, late nights, and the lies I told myself about success. The next steps of redemption weren't about making more money or climbing higher. No, they meant getting things financially stable and securing the future so I could be home more. But even now, I wondered if I was too far gone to fix what I'd broken.

Can I rebuild the home I've demolished?

I threw myself into work: all of the shit that went into cancelling the Key West project, plotting the best investments to take advantage of the impending shutdowns, planning how to take care of my guys once the virus hit stateside and the housing market evaporated overnight.

The truth was, I had more reasons to cancel Key West than the impending pandemic. Yes, in my previous life that entire project had been stalled and then fucked sideways by the shutdowns and quarantines; it had proved to be one of the first major nails in the coffin of Master Builders Inc. But saving my company in this new life was not the only reason I was eager to cancel the trip to southern Florida. The thought of going down to that accursed place full of haunting memories was too much to bear… all because of who the Old Me had taken with him.

Angie.

It was our first trip together, her accompanying me to the Key West project in the midst of my divorce to Sloane. We had planned to treat it like a vacation while I was not on the job site, and the Old Me was stupid enough to believe it was a romantic lover's getaway.

Then the virus tore through the country, as it had throughout the rest of the world, and upended society as we knew it. It was as if the fucking thing was in a competition with itself to see which it could fill faster: graveyards or hospitals. Businesses weren't allowed to open, curfews enforced, travel restricted, and just… so, so many dead.

Angie and I were shut-in our hotel for months while my company, my life, and the rest of the world fell apart. Our relationship was new and I was a fucking idiot, so being quarantined together had seemed like a twisted blessing to the Old Me.

After that, Key West held a special place for us. It was where we later went to celebrate our one-year anniversary, where we went for her birthday, and ultimately it was the cause of our break-up as well.

I have to get to work. I am not wasting another second thinking about Angie.

I hammered through the next ten hours, the relentless grind of labor a welcome distraction from the mess I'd made of my life. The sun had started to bleed into the horizon by the time I walked through the parking lot toward my truck. I sat in it for a while, engine off, staring at the empty lot as exhaustion pressed on my shoulders.

My fingers twitched over the screen of my phone, hovering just above Sloane's name as if it might burn me. I was impatient to move back in but I knew she would still be wound tight. Despite that, I needed to call her to see how broken we truly were. I doubted she would be open to the idea and it was definitely a gamble, but I needed to try.

The longer I stared at her name, the more certain I became that she wouldn't answer... but I called anyway. One ring. Two. Three. Then her voice, clipped and wary.

"Levi?" Her tone was ice. Despite that, the sound of her voice sparked a warmth that spread from my chest down to my core; a burning reminder of how much she affected me.

"Hey," I said. My voice sounded small. "I didn't want to text this."

A pause then a quiet, "Okay."

I could hear the faint sound of the kids in the background: Violet laughing, Liam saying something sarcastic. My throat closed for a moment. I missed that noise. I missed them. I missed *her*.

"Thank you for the money. It seems excessive." Her voice was hesitant, as if she knew I was scheming something. I suppose, in a way, I was.

"Of course. Y'all should also check out that one deluxe hotel with the water park in it. I remember we had a great time at its neighbor."

Sloane's soft laugh filtered through and I couldn't help but close my eyes as my cock swelled, her voice a drug I could never quit. It was hard not to touch myself in the truck with her voice and laugh filling me.

"Levi, that was years ago." Her flat tone broke through the animalistic hunger I was holding back.

I took a deep breath as I adjusted myself. My voice came out hoarse when I said, "I've been thinking... I know I screwed everything up. I know I don't have the right to ask for anything. But I need to know... do you want me to look for a rental? Or..."

"Or *what*?"

Yep, definitely still mad. Rightfully so.

"... Or should I come home?"

The silence on the line stretched so long I thought the call dropped. I checked the screen. Still active.

Then, Sloane exhaled, and her breath shook. "You think this is something you get to just walk back into?"

"No," I said quickly. "No, Sloane. I don't think that. I'm not asking to pick up where we left off. I'm asking if you even want me in the same house. Not as your husband, fuck, I know I forfeited that... but as the kids' father. As someone who wants to earn a place again."

She was quiet. I imagined her pacing the kitchen, arms wrapped around herself, her eyes blurry and red-rimmed.

"I could be home when you are working. Someone to stay with the kids. I know Liam is old enough but ..."

I trailed off, not knowing what to say. I knew that Sloane had survived on her own in my previous life; what right did I have to impose upon her now? Would she find it presumptuous of me that she even needed my help?

"Thank you, Levi. But ..." She paused for an agonizingly long time before she said, "Honestly? I don't trust you."

My chest caved in, my breathing ceased, and I grasped the steering wheel so hard my fingers screamed. Every muscle in my body seized.

Of course she didn't trust me. She shouldn't trust me after what I'd done. It wasn't shock or anger that triggered such a violent reaction in me, but an earthquake of conflicting emotions: revulsion with myself, reverence for her, shame of who I had been, and finally pride at who she was.

How I managed not to cry in that moment, I couldn't say. I choked out the words, "I know. And I understand."

"You hurt me, Levi. You humiliated me. And not just with her... you were gone before she ever touched you. You checked out. Every time I asked for help, you gave me either silence or resentment."

"I know... I was a selfish bastard and I didn't even see it until you were already standing in the wreckage I'd created."

Another pause. "Since when have you been so poetic?"

The truth was that I had twelve years of hindsight and regrets tempering my words. I had twelve years worth of wondering how many different ways I could forge an apology that could encapsulate my regret, my sorrow, my shame.

I couldn't tell her that, though. So instead I said, "Ever since I realized how desperately I need to earn your trust back."

I could hear her scoff through the phone. I could almost see her pull back to stare at the screen from the audacity of my words. I knew it was bold, but it was honest. I needed her to know how much I meant what I'd said.

"I am not saying yes." Her voice was low, as if she didn't want the kids to hear. "But I'm not saying no, either. The kids... they need you. They miss you. I might be willing to let you stay the nights I'm working. *Might*." Her voice sounded stern.

I closed my eyes and held back the swell of emotion rising in my chest. "Then I'll wait," I whispered. "I'll do whatever you need me to. If it's a rental, fine. If it's the guest room, fine. I'll sleep in the garage if that's what it takes."

"You don't get to charm your way back in," she warned. In her stern tone she used with the kids she said, "If you come back, which is still a very big *if*... it will be under *my* rules. One wrong move, and you're gone. For good."

"Understood," I said. "I'll be good." I had to stop myself from saying *'a good boy.'*

I started to wonder if the New Me had come back as a masochist. Good God, I fucking loved listening to her reprimand me and I was grateful in this moment that she had stood up for herself. She had answered the phone and that alone felt like a crack of light through the darkness of my soul.

She said, "I'll talk to the kids. And I'll think about it."

"Thank you, Sloane."

She didn't say a word of thanks. No goodbye. The line went dead, leaving only silence behind.

I sat there, my chest tight with each painful breath, as I replayed our conversation over and over and over. I would celebrate every victory, no matter how small, as I battled my way back. And this?

This was my first win.

Chapter 8

That night I stayed in a hotel room. The frigid air cut through the thin sheets as I lay awake, replaying not just the events of the day but... everything that had happened in my previous life. How the Old Me had tried to build himself back up, but never succeeded. The divorce. The twelve years of regret and anguish that ended in a car crash. I died when I was a few years short of fifty, and the struggles of the Old Me felt so distant and irrelevant now. My life had taken some unexpected turns. Brutally painful ones, honestly.

After the divorce and after the world had started to crawl back from the virus, I had fought to remain relevant in the building world despite having to start from scratch. I'd worked myself to exhaustion, to the point where the drive to stay important was an obsession, despite the fact that those accomplishments didn't bring me peace. How could they? How could anything bring me peace after all that happened?

Liam got incarcerated. Violet, my baby girl... she had disappeared. Both of their absences left gaping holes so vast and incomprehensible that neither Sloane nor I knew how to recover.

A few years after our divorce had been finalized, Sloane remarried someone from her work. She'd found a guy who worshipped her, fawned over her, doted on her. It ate me alive knowing how much of a perfect match they were. How much he helped her heal. How he loved her in ways I didn't know how. He did all of the things I could never do right. It sickened me, but I couldn't be angry at him much less at Sloane. All that anger, all that bitterness... faded into more pity, loathing, and regret.

It took countless therapy sessions filled with harsh truths to untangle the knots of my narcissism and to finally understand the scars I'd left on Sloane. The worst part was how long it had taken me to realize that I was the one who had fucked everything up by not being a real father, or even a good partner. I'd spent years working on myself before I'd made any meaningful breakthrough. And by then? It was far too late. By the time I'd started trying to pick up the pieces of the life I had shattered, there was nothing left to repair.

Then Sloane's husband committed suicide and her world crumbled all over again. The fragile threads of her life unraveled in front of me, and I wanted so desperately to help keep her together. What little grace I had been granted in her eyes, I grasped at with desperation.

In this new chaos, I was the one who was closest to her, and I couldn't let her go. I focused on her, on her hurt and on the pieces of her that were breaking again. In her devastation, I saw an opening, a chance to inch closer. I wanted to be the one to help her heal this time.

I'd known it was selfish; to enjoy being needed by her. But I hadn't felt important to her in such a long time, I could not help myself. I was grateful for that time we had spent together. It felt like some god out there had actually listened to my decade of groveling and given me a second chance to be near her again.

For a year before the car crash, she leaned on me. I was dutifully there for her. I became the stable rock she needed, using every bit of the therapy I'd done over the years to support her. She clung to me, and there was a twisted satisfaction in it. I was there for her and, in a way, it felt like redemption.

Maybe it was my narcissism snaking back in, but I believed I was the only one who truly understood her heart. We suffered through the shattering of everything we had built, lost so much we had both cherished and we'd survived it. I convinced myself that no one else could see her the way I did. That my familiarity with her pain gave me the tools I needed to help her heal. I thought that maybe, just maybe, I could rewrite our story with a happy ending.

After everything, after all that had happened and the rising affection growing between us, I finally texted her one day. Simple and straightforward.

> Hey, can I visit for lunch tomorrow? We need to talk about a few things. About us maybe?

> Sure Levi. I'll be waiting.

When she agreed, my stomach flipped. It was like a flicker of light, a beacon that I had a chance to be part of her life again.

I'd stopped by a jeweler. A knot of anxiety tightened in my chest as the sales rep led me through the selection. As she showed me a variety of glittering jewelry, the pit in my stomach deepened. When she finally pulled out the ring, a 2-carat emerald cut, it felt like a symbol of every damn thing I still hoped for: a second chance for reconciliation and a future with Sloane.

The drive up to her house was surreal. Joy buzzed in me so fiercely that I must have lost myself in it... must have also lost sight of the road.

I'd been so focused on the idea of starting over, of making things right, that I didn't see the nightmare red truck barreling through the red light until it was too late. The impact was instant. A violent, blinding flash of metal.

Then nothing.

But now that I was back, here and in this moment, I had to accept that I had been given a strange gift. I knew that I could spend every moment of the rest of this life pondering the how and the why of it all, and I would never have an answer. So, neither the how nor the why mattered. Not really. Not to me. All that mattered was that I was given a chance to fix the worst parts of what had gone wrong not only in my life, but in the lives of my loved ones.

Would it have been better if I had come back before I had ever met Angie and made the worst mistake of my life? Obviously. But that wasn't the hand I'd been dealt, so I had to focus on the positives: Sloane hadn't started dating her future husband yet in this new life; Violet hadn't vanished; Liam hadn't started using; and Rufus, that damn dog, was still alive. The Old Me would have only focused on the pain he'd caused and wallowed in his self-loathing before spiraling into one self-destructive habit or another.

However, the New Me? I found myself grateful that I had this chance.

I stared out the window of the hotel room, letting the lights blur into a haze. I knew I wasn't the man I used to be and I wasn't sure if Sloane would ever forgive me... I didn't know if I even deserved her forgiveness. But I knew one thing: I was determined to do anything and everything to earn it.

The next morning, I sent Sloane a message asking if I could stop by for lunch. My fingers hovered over the screen longer than they should've, each word typed with the caution of a man who'd learned too late what carelessness could cost.

When she replied with a short "That's fine," I exhaled, tension still coiled in my chest.

The irony wasn't lost on me as I backed out of the hotel parking lot and eased into traffic. Every intersection I approached, I slowed... looked twice, thrice. My knuckles whitened around the steering wheel. I kept seeing the crash in my mind: the warped metal, the flash of light, the finality of it.

Only it hadn't been final.

Now, every green light felt like a dare. Every yellow was a warning. By the time I pulled onto Sloane's street, the weight of the second chance I'd been given pressed down hard. I took a few grounding breaths and did my best to visualize what I wanted. Redemption.

I knew she was waiting and I had to walk in there not as the man who left, but as the one trying, desperately, to stay.

I used my key to let myself in. Anxiety laced my steps as I rounded the corner into the open-concept kitchen and living room where the smell of homemade bread hit me: warm, welcoming, and filled with memories.

Sloane's eyes flicked up when I walked in, noting my clean shaven appearance and gave a small nod toward the living room.

"Hey," she said as she curled into the corner of the couch. She skewered me with a scrutinizing gaze as she hugged a pillow, as if it was a shield to protect her from me. "You wanted to talk Levi?"

I sat on the edge of the couch, far enough to not crowd her. I could hear the kids' faint laughter in the background upstairs. Good. They didn't need to hear this.

"I pulled out of the Key West project," I said.

She raised an eyebrow but didn't look away. "That deal was worth millions you said?"

"A little over two after everything," I said. "I told Jose we're not expanding. We're going to focus on local builds. Smaller scale. I already called the lawyers."

"Didn't you say you already had investors?"

"I did."

"Won't they be pissed?"

"They will."

She leaned back against the cushions, squeezed the pillow in her arms. "That's pretty goddamn ballsy of you. Why are you telling me this?"

I knew I had to be honest. "Because it's not just about the business," I said. "It's about what I've been using it for. I buried myself in it. Avoiding home. Avoiding us. I was chasing some version of success that kept me from sitting still long enough to see what I was destroying."

Her mouth twitched like she was biting back a bitter laugh. "And now what? You think scaling down means I should let you back into this house?"

I fucking loved her snarky attitude. She was everything I'd ever wanted in a woman. She wasn't afraid to call me out when I was fucking up, but she could still uplift me when I was drowning in my own mess. It was a balance the Old Me never fully appreciated.

But I did. I knew that she didn't just put up with me, she challenged me. She made me face myself, even when I didn't want to. The Old Me resented her for it, but the New Me understood how I *needed* that.

I shook my head. "No. I don't think this buys forgiveness. I just... I want you to know I'm not hiding anymore. Not behind work. Not behind excuses. I'm done feeding my ego and calling it ambition."

She didn't blink as she studied me. I could see a conflict of emotions. "You spent years coming home late and ignoring the mental load I carried. Then, when I finally couldn't hold it all up anymore, you didn't ask how to help. You found someone else. Am I supposed to thank you?" It wasn't anger in her voice. It was a truth spoken simply that carved me open.

My chest tightened, constricted by the brutal accuracy of her words. I had to tell her this next truth, even if she wasn't ready to hear it and even if I wasn't ready to say it. She needed to know. "I did not cheat because you were not enough," I said. "I cheated because I wasn't man enough to face my own emptiness. Angie wasn't a person. She was a broken mirror I let convince me I was something more than the selfish liar I'd become."

She looked down at her lap, her fingers absently working a loose thread on her sleeve. When she finally looked back at me, her eyes were dry, but I could see how weary she was behind them. "So what now, Levi?"

What now? *I could kiss you.* The thought hovered as I stared at her lips, unable to look anywhere else, as the urge burned harder with every second. I wanted to throw myself before her, press my lips to the hollow of her neck where her pulse beat beneath the sensitive skin there, and whisper the words I knew she needed to hear. Sweet devotions that should have been said long ago with promises I had failed to keep. The urge was overwhelming, a tide of longing that threatened to drown me but I knew better than to act on it. Not now. Not when the space between us was so fragile.

"I'm going to add you to everything," I said. "The accounts, the business, all of it. No more hiding things. No more leaving you in the dark. And I am going to face myself Sloane."

She didn't respond, but I saw the flicker of surprise in her eyes.

"I will find a rental to stay at that's not too far away," I continued. "I show up when I say I will. I go to Violet's and Liam's games. I help with school projects, with packing lunches, with homework, with bedtime routines. I show up as their dad. The dad I should've been from the start." My throat tightened, but I didn't stop. This next part was going to be the hardest. "I give you space. Real space. No guilt, no pressure. And if somewhere down the line you still want me gone…" I swallowed hard. "I'll go. Without pushing back or fighting you. If you tell me to fuck off? I'll fuck off. Forever."

My voice cracked on that last part, but I kept my eyes on hers. I was no longer aiming for control, for comfort, or for a shortcut back to her heart. I was simply desperate to be worthy of standing in front of her again. I hoped that Sloane would see this for what it truly was; not a plea for forgiveness but a vow that I was ready to finally grow the hell up.

She didn't respond at first. We sat in silence for awhile before she said, "Fine. You can stop asking for one more chance and just… change. Don't talk about changing. Change."

The small opening I needed. I nodded. "I will."

I stood, my legs stiff and nerves frayed. "Tell the kids I'll see them later. I just wanted to talk about the business with you."

"Levi, why tell me now? You never liked talking to me about the business." She sounded resigned.

The question hit me hard. In that moment, I saw it all: how I'd kept her at arm's length, and how I'd built walls around everything that mattered. My pride and arrogance had made me blind to how much she had contributed. How much she had built with me and I felt the sting of the realization, sharp and bitter.

The Old Me had been a narcissistic asshole. Too consumed with his own image to see how much she'd poured into our lives. I swallowed hard as I recalled her attorney's voice arguing during the divorce: *"She deserves half. She helped you get to where you are."*

Damn right she had. This woman had poured everything of herself into those around her and I wasn't going to let her slip away, unnoticed in the chaos I'd created.

"You helped me build it: both the business and this life we have. Hell, Sloane... nothing is mine and everything is ours. I couldn't have done any of this without you," I said.

Sloane nodded, a brief acknowledgment of something she had known all along. "Thank you for that."

I smiled and said goodbye.

Chapter 9

After that conversation with Sloane, I knew I had to do more than just show up now and then. I had to earn back what I'd broken.

I started with flower deliveries to the house. When I called a local florist, the warm voice of an elderly lady greeted me and introduced herself as Margot.

"Now, are these for a special occasion?" she asked. "A birthday, perhaps? Maybe an anniversary?"

"No," I said. "They're for... forgiveness."

There was a pause on the line before she said, "Blue hyacinths, then, are a good start. You see, they mean sorrow and regret. What else would suit?" I heard her clucking her teeth as she thought. "White roses, I feel, are a must if seeking forgiveness."

"Do they mean something, too?"

Margot laughed at that, a hearty and warm sound that reminded me of my grandmother. "Oh, dear. All flowers mean something. Yes, white roses are for sincerity and, sometimes, also new beginnings."

"Then that's perfect. Blue hyacinths and white roses. Every week."

The day after that first delivery, I asked Sloane if I could swing by the house to walk Rufus during my lunch breaks. Thankfully, she consented. In reality, it was just an excuse to ensure the house was clean before she got home with the kids: counters wiped down, floors vacuumed and mopped, dishes put up, laundry folded and put away, snacks for her and the kids prepped and waiting in the fridge. Dozens of things the Old Me had never thought about to do on my breaks despite the business being only ten minutes away.

A week passed by and we fell into a new familiar pattern that I was appreciative of. I went to board game night with Violet and on quiet drives with Liam. I cooked celiac safe dinners for both Violet and Sloane. I helped both of the kids with their school projects, relishing every second as if they were precious treasures.

Because they were. They always had been. Old Me was just too self-absorbed to see it before. It sickened me to remember all of the time Old Me had thrown into the gym, or a bar, or some inane meeting.

Despite those moments of respite, there was something else looming. Something only I knew was coming: the virus, the shut downs, the panic, and the chaos that approached. So between late nights at the business and early mornings checking numbers, I was making moves: fast and calculated ones.

I went to an estate attorney I'd worked with before, the one who had helped me and Sloane write up our wills. I told him exactly what I wanted: two revocable trusts, one for Liam and one for Violet. That part was easy for him. When we began discussing asset allocation, however, the conversation got tense.

He raised a brow as he scanned the portfolios I had already built for the kids: a struggling e-commerce company, the smallest of the pharmaceutical giants, a biotech penny stock, and a tech start-up that nobody had ever even heard of. "This is a risky mix, Mr. Shaw. Especially for your children's futures. Are you sure these are the companies you want to invest all of this money in?"

"I'm sure."

He paused, clearly wanting to ask more questions, but he didn't. He finalized the paperwork and I headed to the bank next.

As I turned out of the lawyer's office, I couldn't help but laugh. I was sure he would tell his friends about the crazy client he saw today who'd insisted on pissing away half a million dollars. I understood the man's hesitation. All of the companies I picked were either complete unknowns or were currently struggling to carve a place for themselves in today's market. However, what I recalled from the upcoming pandemic was how much these select few stocks had soared. The growth potential was astronomical. By the time Violet was in college, both her and Liam's accounts would easily be eight figures.

At the bank, I placed the trust documents in a safety deposit box, the key to which I'd planned to give to Sloane. While I was there, I added her name to the accounts: all of the accounts. What Old Me had used as a wall between him and Sloane, I had hoped to turn into a bridge. Giving her complete access to everything felt less like surrender and more like the kind of honesty I'd been starving for. It was strangely liberating to lay everything bare.

That evening as Sloane and I sat on the couch, I expected her to view all of this with suspicion. She was so accustomed to Old Me keeping his finances private, separate, and shutting her out of the innerworkings of the business. I mean, Sloane wasn't stupid. She knew we were well off. Old Me had constantly kept at least five thousand in our joint checking at any time, so she could pay the bills; how magnanimous of the asshole.

So she was aware that I had money saved up... but when she opened the banking app and saw the totals, she gasped.

"You have... how much?" she asked, gaze lifting to mine. The look on her face was equal parts disbelief and quiet confusion. "Levi, this is excessive. How do you have this much?"

I could feel the edge in her voice, a sharp flicker of anger for being kept in the dark. Old Me had locked her out for so long with excuses and lies. She had every right to be angry.

"I don't have this much, Sloane. We have this much. And if you look here, this one's the business account. I've already told the accountant you have full access. He's sending over a company card for you, too."

"Company card?"

"Yeah. As a business partner, you have the right to know where everything's going and the freedom to make calls on expenses, vendors, whatever you think we need." I let that sink in before I said, "Obviously, I don't want this to conflict with your current career, but Master Builders is here if you ever want to join me."

She stared at me then, still looking at me with that same confused skepticism. "Levi... you didn't."

"I did. He's sending the operating agreement this week. You and I are fifty-fifty now. Full partners. The way it should have been from the start."

She didn't respond right away. I could see her processing before she laughed and said, "Levi I don't know the first goddamn thing about running a construction company. How the hell am I supposed to be a partner?"

Her expression shifted. I saw years of tension melt away. I knew she was trying to reconcile this version of me with the one who left her holding everything alone.

"Sloane, this isn't just about the money. It was about finally letting you all the way in where you've always belonged. I'd been too proud or too blind to see you were the reason for my success. I wouldn't be here without your own hard work and sacrifices."

Her eyes brimmed. She blinked hard, but one tear slipped down anyway.

"Thank you," she said and then, just as quickly, she laughed a little incredulous. She wiped at her face and let out a small snort. "Well fuck, Levi... I didn't realize we had *millions*."

I smiled, tension breaking in my chest like the first crack of sunlight through storm clouds. "Well, technically, Master Builders has millions. But yes, Sloane. We, as in you and the kids, are financially safe."

She nodded. "I'm still mad at you."

"As you should be."

There was a pause as she took a few deep breaths. Then she arched a brow and asked, "But just to be clear, I still get half if I kill you, right?"

I coughed out a laugh. "Yes, but uh... can we maybe hold off on that until after tax season?"

She smirked. "I'll try my best."

"There is one other thing."

"What, do we also own a yacht?"

I laughed and said, "Sorry. They were all out of yachts last time I was at the store."

"Damn."

"Sloane," I said as I held my hand out, "may I see your phone?"

Her eyes narrowed for a moment, but she handed it me. I sat our phones down next to each other on the coffee table and proceeded to work. She said nothing as she watched my fingers fly across the screens, but eventually her curiosity got the better of her and she leaned over.

"All done," I said as I handed over her phone.

"With?"

"I set it up so you can track my phone's location with this app. See?" I showed her how it worked and explained that it was only one-way; she could track me, but I couldn't track her. Not unless she decided to turned it on.

She didn't look very impressed. "Okay, Levi... but what stops you from just turning it off?"

I smiled, because I expected this exact reaction from my ever cynical wife. "I won't be able to. The GPS settings will be locked by a password that you will set and keep to yourself."

I watched it all sink in, saw her process the implications of the evening. It was, I imagined, disorienting for her to reconcile this man in front of her with the secretive Old Me she was accustomed to.

After a moment she nodded and said, "Well, this makes me want to kill you a little less."

"Only a little?" I asked.

"Only a little."

Afterward, Sloane was cordial in all her texts. Polite. Like I was a colleague arranging a lunch meeting, not the man who once shared her bed and ruined her capacity to trust. She let me know the time and place with clinical precision, and I never pushed. I didn't have the right to.

But those brief moments of banter between us fueled me as I tried to be present in their lives.

I signed a short-term monthly lease on a small two-bedroom house in the same neighborhood so I could be close. I told myself it was only for a month or two, just enough time to get my head on straight and give Sloane the space she needed. But the moment I stepped through the door to that rental, I knew I had made a mistake. It wasn't home. Hell, it wasn't even shelter in the emotional sense. It was a shell. Beige walls and thin carpet that smelled faintly of someone else's regrets, pets, and cigarettes.

You don't realize how loud life is until it's gone, until the silence slams into you. Violet's constant stories. Liam's stomping down the hall with his headphones blaring. Sloane's voice in the kitchen calling out that dinner was ready. All of it... evaporated.

I was in exile.

This is my penance for betrayal.

Angie hadn't reached out since I first came back; that night I'd fled, panicked and nauseous, from her house. From her. I'd blocked her on everything: phone, email, socials. However, even though she was gone, the stench of what I'd done still clung to me like the cigarette smoke on those rental walls.

I couldn't even pass the gym without feeling sick. That building had become a testament to the worst mistakes Old Me had made. It was where he'd fed his ego, let it grow until it devoured his common sense. Now it stood there every morning like a reminder: *This is what you chose over them.*

Then every night I came back to that empty house and it whispered the same truth: I lost my family the moment I stopped appreciating them. Getting them back, earning the right to be with them again? That was all that mattered.

Chapter 10

The next morning, I visited my local health clinic. I needed a full STD panel and a referral to a urologist for a vasectomy. Old Me hadn't contracted anything from Angie in my previous life, so I knew I was clean. But Sloane had no way of knowing that, and I needed her to see me taking intelligent and reasonable steps forward.

The clinic smelled of antiseptic and something faintly floral, like lavender trying to smother the stench of bleach. I sat on the paper-lined exam table, its crinkle loud in the sterile silence, until a quiet knock broke through.

The door opened and a doctor whose badge read Laura Taylor, M.D stepped in. She looked like she belonged on a park bench with a sketchbook rather than working at a clinic in a white coat: red curls pulled back into a ponytail, freckles scattered across her pale face, and eyes the color of a forest in spring. Her appearance was disarming.

"Good morning," she said, offering a gentle smile as she sat on the rolling stool across from me. She opened my chart. "Looking over your intake… a referral to a urologist shouldn't be a problem." She flipped a page. "And I see you're here for an STD panel. Married but... separated?"

I cleared my throat, already feeling the heat rise to my face. "Uh... yes. There was a new partner, and I want to make sure everything's clean before I do anything else stupid."

She nodded, professionalism intact. "Absolutely. We'll get that going for you today. It shouldn't take long. Is there anything else you'd like to talk about while you're here?"

I hesitated, then pushed the words out before I lost the nerve. "Do you have any recommendations for couples therapists in the area?"

Dr. Taylor tilted her head. "We do, yes. Depends what you're looking for."

I glanced at the floor. "Infidelity," I mumbled the word like it was gravel in my mouth. "I cheated. It's for my wife. I'm worried about her."

The room shifted into a strange stillness. When I looked up, Dr. Taylor was staring at me as if she were measuring something invisible in the air between us. Her brow furrowed. "Usually," she said, "it's the betrayed partner who asks about therapy resources."

"It seemed like the right thing to do," I said.

She crossed her legs, setting the clipboard aside. "Tell me – what exactly are you hoping for? Because if your wife isn't open to couples therapy, individual counseling could still be beneficial for her. Or for you."

I nodded. "I agree. I want to give her every tool she might need to get through this. Even if," I struggled and took a breath, "even if I'm not in the picture anymore."

She studied me for another long moment, before she gave a small, noncommittal shrug. "A loving spouse," she said. "Well except for the obvious."

I huffed a short, bitter chuckle. "Yes, well... hence the STD test and the vasectomy. I know that I messed up."

There was no judgement in her reaction, just the quiet matter-of-factness that I imagine comes from years of hearing confessions in a clinical setting. "Well, the STD test is a smart step towards ensuring you don't cause more harm. I recommend condoms until you get the test results."

"Yes, ma'am."

She stood and jotted something down on her clipboard before turning back to me. "Look, I'm not a therapist, but I do want to mention something you may not be aware of. Have you heard of hysterical bonding?"

I blinked. "No. What is that?"

"It's a psychological response that sometimes occurs after betrayal," she explained. "A kind of emotional whiplash. Despite the pain, the betrayed partner may suddenly feel intense intimacy toward the person who hurt them. Sometimes, it's sexual. Often, it's confusing. It's not inherently healthy, but it is common."

"So..." I trailed off, unsure how to even ask, "we shouldn't have sex at all?"

She gave a quiet sigh. "I'm not saying that. But you need to make sure it's something *she* really wants. Not just her trauma trying to keep her safe. You've been married for how long?"

"Seventeen years this year. We were high school sweethearts." I swallowed the lump forming in my throat.

Dr. Taylor's expression softened, the clinical edge in her tone losing a bit of its sharpness. "Then keep this in mind: she is going through a traumatic experience. Right now, her body and brain might not be on the same page. If she seeks out physical closeness, it doesn't necessarily mean she's forgiven you. It might be her survival instincts; her nervous system reaching for familiarity, for comfort." She paused, watching me carefully. "That push and pull you might feel from her? The hot-then-cold? That's not manipulation. It's not cruelty. It's her trying to make sense of something senseless. Trying to reclaim control in the only way she can. And that confusion is not her fault."

I nodded slowly as the doctor's words settled.

She said, "Given how long you've been together, how much history you share, it's almost impossible for you two not to react to each other. That bond doesn't just vanish, even when it's broken. Especially when you still love them. Your job now isn't to interpret what every touch or glance from her might mean. If you want to earn her trust back, your job is to give her what she asks for. To be safe, consistent and honest. It's up to her to decide what closeness means, if it means anything at all."

I nodded again, this time with a little more understanding.

"If the two of you do decide to reconnect physically, make sure it's mutual, clear, and without pressure. Have the conversation first. Protect her peace, not just her body."

My voice barely above a whisper I asked, "Are you sure you're not a therapist?"

She laughed at that as she handed me a pamphlet, a referral slip, and a lab order form. "I know the path back is a long and hard one," she said as she opened the door. "But sometimes it's not about the return. It's about the path you take and the choices you make along the way."

I left the clinic feeling better than I had when I'd walked in. I placed the pamphlet in the passenger seat and thought about how to broach the subject of couples therapy.

Just then, Sloane texted if I could watch the kids; she was going to be stuck at the clinic until late that night. I didn't hesitate. I was already reversing by the time I replied, "Of course." Not because it was the right thing to do, but because I missed them. I missed being needed by them.

I took Violet with me to pick out groceries for dinner, relying on the Gluten Free app on my phone to help me navigate the shopping. Old Me had never gone grocery shopping and would have been clueless on how to find anything celiac safe.

On our way to checking out, Violet asked, "Can I pick out flowers for Mommy? Some that match the ones you sent to her?"

"She'd love that," I said with a smile.

So, when we returned home, Violet was excited to set daisies and lavender in a mason jar on the kitchen table, right next to the blue hyacinths and white roses. It was a small gesture, but it mattered to Violet. Her eyes lit up and it filled my heart to see her so happy.

While Violet helped me put away the groceries, she chattered away about the two large projects she was working on for her school's science fair: a diorama of the solar system and the classic baking soda volcano.

"I want you to help me build them," she said, tugging at my sleeve. "Mom said I could do it on my own, but it's more fun with you! You've helped Liam before with his."

My throat went tight. *Damn, this kid is amazing.* I nodded. "Of course, baby girl. I'd love that."

Violet beamed and skipped off to gather the materials for her projects. Liam, who had been hovering quietly near the fridge, finally broke his silence. "You don't have to act like everything's fine," he said, his voice flat and guarded.

Ah, yes. There is my angsty boy.

I turned to face him. The noise of the kitchen seemed to fade, and all I could hear were his words echoing in my head. "I'm not," I said. "But I'm trying." It was the truth I knew they were tired of hearing.

He shrugged, arms crossed over his chest, a wall of indifference rising between us. His face was unreadable beneath that mop of dark hair, the years of silence and distance written in the slump of his shoulders, in the way his eyes refused to meet mine.

"Whatever," Liam said before he slinked away upstairs.

Violet hummed in the background, a sweet carefree melody that pierced through the stillness. I knew the song well. Sloane used to sing it to her as a baby and I felt the pang of longing to hear her sing it one more time as Violet's voice carried into the kitchen. The tune was a reminder of how much I missed her, how grateful I was to still have her here, even though the cracks in our family were too large to ignore.

I still didn't know what had happened to Violet in my previous life. I had never understood how she'd... vanished. One day she was there, then the next? She'd disappeared after meeting someone from an online game.

The memories of her disappearance, of losing her, of the years of never knowing what happened to her... those memories still tortured me. The police had found chat records between her and several other online friends, one of whom called themselves Prince_Harming.

That was who she had gone to meet.

This Prince_Harming person had given Violet a location and time. When the police followed the address, it took them to an abandoned warehouse. The only thing they ever found there were tire tracks and signs of a struggle. It had been one of the first, one of the last, and one of the only clues in what faded away into a cold case.

I still had nightmares of losing Violet. Even now, over a decade later, I asked myself: *did I cause it? Is it my fault she'd been driven away?*

But I was with her in this new life. And here with Liam. I was together with them and for a moment, I felt drunk on the simplest thing: gratitude. Gratitude that I was given this chance to heal the damage that Old Me had done, that his countless fuck-ups hadn't completely destroyed this family, yet.

While Violet gathered everything she needed for her science fair projects, I climbed the stairs. Liam had taken refuge in his room after our tense exchange, a silent barricade that felt familiar. I stood outside his door, the hallway dim, the upstairs quiet but for the creak beneath my feet. I took a few deep breaths to collect myself before I knocked; a gentle tap, enough to say *I'm here.*

He was thirteen now. Caught in that brutal, restless in-between stage of boy and man. The sharpness in his eyes lately wasn't teenage moodiness; it was weariness. A kind of mistrust that didn't grow overnight.

The truth was, he'd grown up too fast and I knew exactly why. My mistakes had seeped into the floorboards of his childhood. The lies, the fights, the absences? My wreckage had left fingerprints on his life.

And now I stood outside his door, hoping that it wasn't too late to repair the damage that had already been done. I needed to show my son that he didn't have to bear the burden I'd given him.

"Yeah?"

"Hey," I said, pushing the door open a fraction.

He was laying on his bed, headphones in, lost in whatever storm raged inside his head. His eyes flicked up, but he didn't pull the headphones off, didn't speak. That silence, that cold, distant silence, was more painful than any angry words he could've thrown at me.

"Mind if I sit?" I asked. He shrugged, the closest thing to permission I was going to get.

I sat on the edge of the bed, unsure how to start. What could I say?

I really fucked everything up, Liam. Your mom is broken and I destroyed the trust you have in me?

No, I couldn't say anything like that. He didn't need me to pile more weight onto his shoulders.

Instead I said, "Violet's excited for the science fair." I tried to sound casual, tried to bridge the gap with something neutral. "We're going to start working on her projects. You wanna join us?"

Liam barely moved, but I saw his lips twitch. He probably remembered the countless times I'd helped him with his own school projects. I used to be there for him. Hell, I used to be there for all of them.

"Yeah, maybe," he muttered. "I don't know." He yanked the headphones out, tossing them onto the bed, then sat up, crossing his arms.

"Do you still like Echo Forge?" I asked.

For a second, something shifted, a flicker of connection between us. Liam's gaze sharpened, a hint of curiosity breaking through his usual indifference. "Yeah. Why?"

"Wanna try to catch a show together? I think they're touring near us soon."

I felt awful for offering the boy something I knew would never happen. His favorite band was on tour, and they did plan to come through later this year; but I knew that the world would shut down in a matter of weeks. Everything was on the brink of collapse right now.

But, in that moment of us being father and son, I said it anyway. Because the concert wasn't what it was about. It was about the offer.

It was about showing him I gave a damn. It was about wanting to be near him, about hearing him laugh, about remembering how to have fun together. Above all, it was about my son not flinching every time I entered a room.

Liam watched me like he was trying to figure out if this was real or another moment that would fade. When he spoke, I thought I heard the tiniest bit of hope in his voice. "Yeah, okay. I'd like that. You should check out their songs."

I nodded, my heart aching because I already had. In my previous life, Liam had clung to that band like a lifeline: angsty, bitter lyrics shouting about broken families and lost futures. It was the soundtrack to his downfall, a reflection of everything I failed to protect him from: drugs, crime, prison sentences.

The truth was, I had failed him. Over and over. He'd been a kid once, before the constant indifference and carelessness of the narcissistic asshole that was Old Me broke him. A lengthy series of reckless decisions led to a version of Liam I couldn't recognize anymore... and Old Me had stood there, barely watching, aggressively pretending he wasn't the cause or catalyst for any of it.

This time, I would do better. This time, I'd be different. I refused to make the same mistakes Old Me had made. I wanted to be there for him, hear those songs with him, hold his hand, and show him that not all families are beyond repair... that we could heal together.

I watched Liam for a moment, trying to read the way his eyes shifted and listen to everything he didn't say. He was too damn much like me. I could see the walls he'd built around himself; walls I had no idea how to break down.

"I'd love to," I said, "Maybe you'll show me a few of their newer songs? I can take a look at tour dates."

Liam nodded. "Only if you aren't too busy."

I leaned back, trying to hide the ache that had taken root in my chest. I loved him so much it burned. I was grateful, maybe even to the point of madness, for the cruel twist of fate that brought me back and gave me this opportunity. Being here with him, with all of them... it was the only thing that mattered anymore.

But even as I had that thought, I felt the weight of it, the suffocating responsibility of fixing a broken past.

"Of course," I said with a nod. " I'll make as much free time as you need me to. I'm here and I'm not going anywhere."

Liam stared at me for what felt like an eternity. His gaze searched for something in my face, some proof, I was being honest. I kept my expression as neutral as I could while he studied me.

An irrational part of my mind feared that being haunted by the specter of knowledge would show. That Liam could see in my eyes the memories of a life unlived, of twelve years of horror, of a future already unfolded.

"Why?" he asked. His voice was low and hesitant, as if he was afraid to push too hard.

I opened my mouth, but nothing came out at first. Honesty is best here Levi. "Because I don't want to give up on this," I said, gesturing to the empty space between us. "On you. On Violet. On Mom. I know I fucked up, Liam. But I'm still here. And I promise to continue to do everything that I can to be a better father... a better person. For all of you."

We sat quiet for a moment before the door creaked and Violet poked her head in. Her usual excitement lit up her face as her eyes flitted between me and Liam. "Hey, Daddy," she said, "can we work on my project now?" Her voice, high and bubbly, hit me like a wave.

"I'd love to, baby girl," I said, standing up to ruffle her hair. She giggled, the sweet sound contagious and I couldn't help but smile back.

Liam rolled over on his bed, his eyes flicking to me for a second before he grabbed his phone from the nightstand. He didn't say anything more. But Violet? She bounced off to her project in a flash. I watched her skip down the hall, the innocence of a child still untainted by the mess I'd made of everything.

I followed her to the dining room where she'd set up her project, an elaborate display of graphs and diagrams she'd clearly put a lot of effort into. There were colored charts and tiny plastic models lined up, each one artfully crafted. She had an intense fire in her eyes, the same one that made me fall in love with her mom before Sloane had ever spoken a word.

"Is Liam okay?" she asked.

I nodded, even though I wasn't sure myself. "Yeah. He's got a lot on his mind, but he's okay."

Violet beamed. "I'm glad. We're a family again, right?"

"Yeah. We're a family again." I said it with all the certainty I could muster, but even I wasn't sure if it was true yet.

Violet bounced over to the table, "I was thinking I could make a cool display with glitter for the solar system! Then I have to show volcanos over here in this other project," she said, her little hands working quickly to arrange the planets and plaster figures.

"Sounds awesome," I said, pulling up a chair next to her. I wanted to feel like me again, like the dad who would've done this without hesitation. The dad who didn't walk out. I cleared my throat, unsure how to tread through the waters. "Hey, kiddo, what's your favorite planet?"

She looked up at me, eyes wide, then burst into a smile. "It's gotta be Mars! It's so red and... fiery! Almost like a volcano." She paused for a second, her face turning more thoughtful. "Why?"

I shrugged, giving her a smile that didn't reach my eyes. "Just wondering. We're a team now, right? You think we can make these projects amazing?"

"Uh, obviously! I've got the best Daddy ever!" Her excitement was enough to pull me back in, back to the feeling of purpose I used to have.

I helped her arrange the planets while she talked, asking me about different colors she could use and if I could help her with the measurements for the presentation. And though I answered as best as I could, part of me was distracted, wondering if this was enough. If my presence, even now, could begin to heal the cracks in her perception of me. Would she look back at this moment and remember that I tried? Or would she remember the time I wasn't around?

As Violet put the finishing touches on her volcano, I sat beside her, my hands restless, my mind stuck in a loop I couldn't cease. There was a question that had been burning inside me ever since I woke up in this new life, and I had to ask it. I kept my voice casual, even as my pulse drummed violently against my ribs.

"Hey, Violet... have you been playing any online games lately?"

She didn't look up right away, simply shrugged, twirling a marker between her fingers. "Yeah, I started this new one. You build stuff and make your own worlds. You can even share them with friends. It's called *Robot Blocks*."

The name sent a jolt through me. It sounded harmless. But it had sounded harmless in my previous life as well. My throat tightened, but I forced a smile as I said, "Oh yeah? How do you talk with these friends?"

She grinned. "There's these public chat rooms. Liam helped me make my own account. I only play on the weekends, but there's this girl in my class who's helping me build a dinosaur world. It's awesome."

"That sounds awesome," I lied. I was unraveling. *This* was it. This was the rabbit hole she'd fallen into in my previous life: a game, a stranger, a trap that I had been too distracted, too selfish, too absent to see coming.

Not this time. Not this life.

But how could I stop it without sounding paranoid? Without coming across as crazy, without scaring Violet, without revealing the unbelievable truth of what I'd already lived through?

Step one: be a cool dad.

"Maybe we could play together sometime?" I offered, as casually as I could.

She laughed, scrunching up her nose. "Daddy! You're way too old."

I laughed with her. But in my mind I was already planning firewalls, account monitoring, lockdowns. Whatever it took. She was still here. I would keep her here.

And that "friend" of hers? The one who took her away from me? Prince_Harming? I would find that monster, no matter what name they used, no matter what mask they wore. And when I did, I wouldn't call the cops or look to the system for justice. I would bury them myself, pour their screams into concrete, and let them rot beneath the foundation of my next project.

A fitting tomb for the kind of monster that tears little girls from their families and leaves nothing but silence behind.

This time, they wouldn't get the chance. Not with mine. Not again.

Chapter II

After we made a lot of progress on her science fair project, Violet helped me cook dinner. I opened all the windows to let in the cool autumn air. That night, we sat together to eat the gluten free spaghetti we'd made, as well as some delicious homemade garlic bread Sloane had baked earlier in the week. Violet kept the conversation going and Liam even cracked a small smile at one of her jokes. I didn't try to force anything. I listened and took it all in.

The kids were already fast asleep by the time Sloane came home. I didn't need to hear more than the way the door clicked shut behind her to know she'd had a brutal shift. I heard it in the way she trudged into the living room, her movements slow and defeated. She rubbed at the back of her neck like the weight of the whole damn world had settled there. She didn't say much; a low "Hey" before heading straight to the shower.

While she was gone, I ensured the kitchen was spotless from mine and Violet's earlier cooking. I threw together a small charcuterie board and poured Sloane a glass of red wine, a vintage I remembered she used to love before life got too loud and bitter. I didn't do this out of romance, but genuine care; something to take the edge off if she wanted it.

When she came out, her hair damp and skin pink from the scalding hot shower, she paused in the hallway. The shirt and jeans she wore clung to her in all the right ways as her eyes flicked from the glass to me. Her gold flecked hazel eyes nearly distracted me from the fact she was still not comfortable enough to be in her night clothes around me. Not that I could blame her. It stung, but it was fair.

As I stared at her, I knew this wasn't her trying to punish me. It was her protecting herself. She was drawing a line in the sand that said we're not there yet. Maybe we never would be again?

Fuck me, I missed that version of her. The way she'd shuffle out of the bathroom in soft cotton shorts and one of my old T-shirts, hair tangled from the shower, eyes heavy with sleep. That was when she was most beautiful, unguarded, effortless, and *mine*.

Now, she wore her clothes like armor and I was the reason for it.

"Hi," she said, voice soft, almost uncertain. "Did you have a good night with the kids?"

I nodded. "Yeah. They were really great." My voice cracked slightly at the end, and I hoped she didn't notice.

She smiled. "Yeah. They are."

I gestured to Violet's backpack on the bench. "I signed her field trip form. Slipped some cash in for lunch. I hope that's okay. There's pasta in the fridge and I made sure to grab the brand you recommended. Honestly, it wasn't too bad though I think we had better luck with lentil pasta than the chickpea."

I was rambling about other items, about mundane things that didn't matter; bills or groceries or the chance of rain tomorrow. When I turned to look at her, I found her standing in the doorway, arms crossed, staring at me with something unreadable on her face. I replayed everything I had said in my head, worried I'd blurted out something stupid. "Um... Sloane?"

"Who are you?" she asked, her voice filled with playful accusation.

"What?" I asked, taken aback by her mischievous tone after weeks of stoicism.

She shook her head and let out a short laugh. "You're... different." She sounded out the word deliberately, as if she knew it wasn't the most accurate word but couldn't think of a better one. "I don't know if this is all a facade or an act, or if you've hit some kind of wall, or, fuck, Levi... it's like someone swapped you out for a better version of yourself."

I took a deep breath as my heart thundered. She'd practically hit the nail on the head and I was thinking of how best to reply. "I'm not faking it. I know that I've made mistakes. Huge mistakes. And if I lose you all ag-" I stopped myself from saying *again*. My voice shook as I said, "I think I would die if I lost you all."

There was the faintest curve at the corner of her mouth despite the fact I'd laid bare my heart before her. "You dying would save me the trouble of killing you," she said, lifting a brow ever so slightly.

I laughed and looked down at my hands, stared at the worn indent on my ring finger that hadn't yet faded. My ring was in my wallet, tucked into the smallest pocket like a secret I didn't deserve to bear. I hadn't worn it since the affair and I wasn't sure if I'd ever earn the right to put it back on. Not until Sloane told me to. Not until she looked me in the eye and said I could.

I smirked in spite of myself. "Yeah. I suppose that's true."

She stretched then, her arms lifting above her head, fingertips brushing the side of the doorframe. The movement was unthinking and natural but it undid me. Her shirt lifted ever so slightly to reveal a sliver of her taut stomach, one of my favorite places to kiss her. Her body curved effortlessly into the stretch, and heat rose in me. Sharp and immediate.

I had the violent intention, the reckless, hungry urge, to close the space between us. To press her back against the doorframe, pin her there with my hands at her waist, and kiss her until the past fell away. I could see it. Feel it. Taste it in the space between us... but I didn't move. I couldn't. Not when everything between us was still raw and fragile. Not when one rash movement could snap the delicate threads I was weaving.

Instead, to focus my attention elsewhere, I said, "I would do anything for you and the kids."

"Oh, Levi... I've heard that song before."

"What?"

Then she let out a small sound; a half sigh, half laugh that drove me wild. "Well," she said, her voice laced with irony, but softer than before, "You have some common songs you sing. That one is practically a greatest hit by now."

I swallowed hard, grounding myself to the floor beneath me. Her tone was playful with an edge to it; a glint of memory and of hurt dressed up as humor. She was teasing me, yes, but also reminding me: she'd heard it all before. The compliments. The apologies. The promises that had turned into dust.

I asked, "Are you compiling them into an album?"

"Oh, no. I stopped keeping track somewhere between 'I'll Do Better Next Time' and 'You're the Only One I Want.'" Her voice was light, taunting.

That made me laugh. Fuck, this woman would be the death of me. It was the same magnetic current I remembered from all those years ago, before kids, exhaustion and silence started crowding the space between us. I had forgotten, somewhere in the haze of growing up, of losing ourselves in the routines and responsibilities, how much I enjoyed bantering with her. How her sarcasm had always been flirtation in disguise, how she wielded wit like a blade and laughed while she cut me barely enough to keep me craving more.

Right now she wasn't twisting the knife of everything I had done. It was a quiet reminder that what fragility lay between us was still there, and my sinister little wife relished watching me squirm. I was the one stumbling through the minefield while she got to stand steady, clearly amused at the wreckage I made trying to put everything back together. There was a malicious beauty in it. How calm she was in that moment. How much power she had in her silence, in the small curve of her lips that told me she knew. She knew what she was doing. She knew exactly how much I still *burned* for her.

Control.

Balance.

She knew I loved the chase. The way she'd narrow her eyes as if she could see right through me, daring me to pursue. I used to live for that look, the fiery heat of challenge in her eyes, before we'd melt into one another once I closed the distance. Not just claiming her but earning her. Her fire, her body, her trust.

I smiled and took her invitation. "Then maybe it's time for a new track."

She raised an eyebrow at that, gaze meeting mine across the space like a dare. "Hmm... we'll see if it charts."

I grinned. "Good to know we're both still pretty lame."

Her laughter, unexpected and unguarded, spilled into the kitchen, and my breath caught. I'd forgotten how much I missed that sound. Not just the laugh, but the ease behind it. The glimpse of the woman I used to fall asleep beside, the one who could meet my sarcasm beat for beat, roll her eyes, and still somehow soften the air in a room simply by being in it.

Then she stepped into the kitchen and brushed past me so close that I felt the heat of her skin right before being hammered with her unmistakable scent: lavender, warm honey, and sharp citrus. Her scent was one I had known for nearly my entire life; I was convinced I could sniff her out like a bloodhound. Yet, somehow, this time it caught me off guard. My body responded before my brain could catch up. Every nerve sparked to life. I watched her move, watched her hips sway in that familiar rhythm, and I felt the pleasurable ache of my cock hardening.

I cleared my throat and said, "I really didn't understand you back then."

"Hmm," she murmured, amused, disappointed. "No. You really didn't."

She paused near the counter and placed her hands against it as if she needed it to anchor her. The air between us grew taught and electric with the unspoken. With desire. With need.

She looked back at me over her shoulder and said, "The kids are lucky to have you." Casually, almost like an afterthought. It wasn't sarcastic... only her quiet truth and maybe even reluctant admiration.

I looked at her, really looked at her: tired eyes, hair loose, a crease between her brows that hadn't been there years ago. I basked in her radiance. "No Sloane... they're lucky to have you."

I took a timid step closer, afraid to ruin the moment of connection I felt we were building. I opened my arms, the unspoken invitation between us. She didn't move at first as she stared at me. But then, cautiously, she leaned into me, her body soft against mine. She fit into all of my hard lines as her warmth seeped into my soul. Her body molded to mine as if we were built to fit. All the hollow places within me had been waiting for her to fill them.

I wrapped my arms around her and pressed my cheek to her hair. Her scent and heat drove the air from my lungs and I trembled as I held her. To feel her against me for the first time in what felt like years?

Fuck, for me it had been years.

Her breath was shaky and stuttering against my chest, and I felt her trying to hold herself together, trying to stay strong. Those earlier moments of heat dissipated... faded like steam.

"Thank you," I whispered. "For letting me back in. For the chance, no matter how small, to show you that I can still be the man you need. For allowing me to be near you again, after everything... this is more than I deserve."

Her voice cracked as she said, "I know you probably think I'll let you come back for the kids. But honestly, Levi, you don't get to decide that." She let me hold her, even as her tears soaked through my shirt. "This wound... it's still so fresh. Most days, I feel like I can't breathe. I barely eat. I put on a smile for Violet and Liam, but inside I'm unraveling." Her fingers clutched at my shirt and she trembled. "I know our marriage wasn't perfect. We both did things, said things, we shouldn't have. But what you did, Levi... there was no justification for that."

"Sloane," my voice was hoarse as I struggled to not break down, "I know I destroyed everything. I know a lifetime of apologies cannot erase what I've done. I think about it every day," I whispered. "What I did to you. What I threw away. I *hate* myself for it."

She pulled back enough to look at me, her angelic face furious and fragile all at once. "Then why did you do it, Levi? Why her? Why Angie?"

The name scythed through the air and I flinched. "I was selfish. I was self-centered and entitled. I had lied to myself for so long about who I was and what I deserved, I thought she was something that I needed... but all I ever needed was you."

"You didn't just hurt me," she said with a shaking voice. "You made me question everything. My worth. My sanity. The way I looked at myself in the mirror. Do you understand that? Can you ever understand that?"

I nodded, but it wasn't enough. It could never be enough to understand the true pain she endured, the suffering Old Me had dragged her through. Her trauma would twist how she looked at herself and force her to question her self worth.

She was a wife, a mother, an advocate for animals; constantly on the front lines for those that needed her, even when she didn't have the strength to give. I saw it in the lines under her eyes, in the way she sprinted from one responsibility to the next without pause. Always giving, always being there for everyone else, while no one was there for her. Not the way she needed.

She stepped away from me and folded her arms. "I'm not saying I don't still love you. That's the worst part... I wish I didn't. I wish I could hate you and move on. But loving you doesn't mean trusting you. And I don't know if I can ever trust you again."

"I'll earn it back," I said without thinking. "Whatever it takes, Sloane. I'll earn your trust back. I'll stay. I'll show up. For you, for the kids, for-"

"Don't promise me things, Levi. You've already broken too many promises." She wiped her cheeks, straightened her shoulders, and looked up at the ceiling. I knew she was thinking of the kids asleep upstairs. "I'm not making any decisions tonight," she said. "But don't confuse this, us, standing in this room, crying in the dark... with a second chance. This is not that."

If only she knew what I knew. If only she knew how wrong she was. "I understand. For as long as you'll let me, I'll do whatever it takes and I'll let you lead. You call the shots now."

That earned the tiniest lift of her lips. "Well! That's a rare sight. Levi Shaw surrendering control?"

I let out a low groan as I caught the edge in her tone. "Is that a jab at my bedroom habits?"

She arched a brow, but said nothing. Still, the challenge was there in her startling eyes and in the sharp pull of her mouth that I desperately wished to kiss.

I lowered myself to my knees in front of her, deliberate and slow, never breaking eye contact as I kneeled before her. "A man can change, Sloane. Hell, especially for the woman he's spent seventeen years failing to deserve... just like I have. If you'll let me," I whispered, "I'll bend the knee every damn day... not in apology but in worship." My breath caught as I watched heat fill her eyes and my voice was gravel as I continued my confession, "I would offer love with tongue and adept devotion, until your doubts forget how to breathe."

Her breath hitched as the air between us shifted back to what it was earlier: thick, electric, and laden with the raging inferno of desire we shared. I watched her eyes as her gaze trailed down my body, then my mouth went dry when I saw her nipples grow taunt underneath her cotton jersey.

But as quickly as the feeling swelled between us, she stepped back. She tightened her jaw and swallowed hard. "I still want you," she admitted. "God help me, I do despite everything."

My heart thudded painfully against my ribs. Hope flared, uninvited and reckless. She needed time. I can't forget what the doctor said about hysterical bonding.

She looked away, distancing herself from the heat that crackled between us. "Don't mistake my body's betrayal for permission to come home." The ache in her words cut deeper than any rejection.

I nodded again as I stood. "I won't. You need to make that decision without me here." I wanted to touch her. I wanted to apologize all over again. I wanted to gather her into my arms and convince her that I can still be the man she once believed in.

Instead, I took a small step back, the space between us stretching wider. Because wanting her had never been the problem. It's what I did when I had her that tore us apart. And now? All I could do is prove I wouldn't make the same mistakes again.

"Good boy," she said.

Chapter 12

It was late that night, close to midnight, when we finally made our way to bed.

Sloane and I tried to watch a show together; a small, simple gesture that felt like a rickety bridge between us. Despite the show's ominous nature, it was a chance to share something again, something that didn't carry the weight of everything else. She chose one of her favorite true crime series she loved to binge late at night, long after the kids were in bed.

Because watching a documentary about a scorned wife nearly getting away with murdering her husband isn't foreboding as fuck.

I never understood why so many women were fascinated by stories about murder, betrayal, and survival. There seemed to be a special draw to the ones where wives killed their husbands. It used to make me uncomfortable in a way I couldn't explain, this flirtation with the macabre for entertainment.

But that night, sitting beside Sloane while the screen flashed with blood-stained headlines and cold forensic narration, I understood it in a way I hadn't before. It wasn't about entertainment. It was about *safety* and about *learning*. It felt like it was about giving her control in a world that had taken it from her.

When the show ended, we both realized how late it was and there was a quiet pause between us as we measured what came next. Sloane gave me a look, and without much more than a nod, she motioned toward the guest room.

"You can stay," she said.

I blinked. I hadn't expected that. Honestly, I didn't think she'd want me there. The idea that she could tolerate me under the same roof, even if it was in the guest room for one night, felt both strange and impossibly tender.

"Hell, I'm kind of afraid now after that episode," I said with a half-smile.

Her laugh filled the room like a song. "Well, it would be too obvious if I did it tonight."

"But it is on the table. Noted."

She rolled her eyes, but the corners of her mouth twitched again like she was trying not to smile. "I know you weren't planning to stay, but you do have some old clothes bagged up in the garage."

"The garage?" I asked. "Seems like an odd place to put them, since that's where we keep our sentimentals."

"It's also where we keep the trashcan," she said with a wry smile as she stood.

We padded into the kitchen, our footsteps barely making a sound against the floor.

"Goodnight," I said.

"Night." She veered toward her room - what had once been *our* room - without another word.

After I'd rummaged through a bag of my old clothes and found gym shorts and a t-shirt, I headed up to the guest room. I grabbed a quick shower and crawled into bed. I expected that I'd be too on edge for sleep, too bursting with everything that had happened throughout the day, but I must have drifted off at some point; I awoke to the unmistakable creak of the hallway floor outside the guest room.

I jumped out of bed to find Liam standing there in his faded band shirt and pajama pants, eyes rimmed red behind his shaggy bangs.

"Couldn't sleep?" I asked.

He shrugged. "You were talking in your sleep. Kinda loud. I could hear it next door."

I tensed. "I'm sorry, bud. What did I say?"

"Something about not letting us die this time?"

Fuck. Mental note: I needed to ball gag myself. Maybe Sloane would be into that?

Focusing on Liam, I stepped back and opened the door wider. "Wanna sit?"

He hesitated, then shuffled in. He sat on the floor with his back against the wall, knees up, arms hugging them as if he was bracing for bad news.

"You okay?" I asked.

"I dunno," he muttered. "You're acting... different."

"Yeah," I said with a feeble laugh. "Your Mom said the same thing."

He shrugged.

"Well," I asked, "Is it good different or bad different?"

"Weird different. Like... old man wisdom and sensitivity crammed into a guy who forgets my birthday."

"Old man wisdom?" I asked. "I guess that's a compliment, right?" I did my best to sound amused, but fuck me this kid was a lot more perceptive than I'd ever realized.

The smallest smile flashed across his face before he turned solemn and said, "I don't get you, Dad. I don't get why you left."

Ah, there it was. The festering wound beneath all the others. I felt his words slam into my stomach, harsh gut punches of honesty.

He looked down at the floor and his voice wavered as he continued. "Mom, she... she's hurt. I'm hurt, too, but I don't know how to tell her that. Or how to feel about you anymore." His words were loaded with suppressed anger and confusion.

He was just a boy of thirteen. Yet, he was being torn apart by a storm he didn't know how to weather. I knew he was desperate to keep his mom safe, but also trying to find a way to connect with me despite everything I had put them all through.

I sat across from him on the floor. "Those feelings make perfect sense. I was disgustingly selfish, Liam. For a long time, for far too long, I thought everything revolved around me. My work, my success, my image." He sniffled while I spoke, but he didn't look up. "I don't expect you to forgive me, son. But I want you to know that I see it all now. I see all the pain I caused. I see all the weight your mother carried. I see all the times you and Violet hurt while I wasn't there."

Liam whispered, "I hated you."

I nodded, my voice patient with understanding. "And you had every right to."

"So why now?"

Because I've seen the world end once already, and I know what a lifetime of regret tastes like...

But I obviously couldn't say that, so I told him the truth that made the most sense. "Because I wasted so many chances. I don't want to waste anymore."

Liam finally looked up. He stared at me for a long while. Then, slowly, he shifted and crawled forward. He leaned in and rested his small, shaggy head against my shoulder. "You still have a lot to prove."

My throat closed around the swell of emotion that threatened to break free as I rested my hand on his back. "I know. And trust me buddy, I will."

I felt his tears soak into my shirt and heard my son sniffle. Pride swelled beneath my guilt, strange and unexpected. My son had stood his ground, called me out, and defended his mother without flinching. He had every right to hate me, and yet all I could feel in that moment was a twisted kind of awe. He was strong. Stronger than I had been at his age. Stronger than I had raised him to be and as much as it hurt to hear the truth from his mouth, a part of me was so very proud of him.

I patted his back. "It's okay son. Let it out."

I had not held Liam while he cried since he was a toddler. The Old Me would have told him to toughen up, that real men don't cry, and all of that other toxic masculinity bullshit he'd espoused. I knew this one night, this single moment, would not reverse all of that, but I also knew it was a step in the direction he needed to heal. I wanted him to feel safe. I wanted him to feel safe with *me*.

After Liam had cried himself dry, I walked him to his room and sat on the edge of his bed. I promised I'd leave once he fell asleep. He gave me this sheepish roll of his eyes, the kind only a thirteen-year-old could pull off; equal parts *Dad, you're embarrassing me* and *please don't go*.

The truth was, I didn't care if he thought I was being silly. I wanted to be with him. After everything that had been breaking and bending in our lives lately, sitting with my son felt like the only solid thing I could do right in that moment.

He eventually turned over, curled into the blankets, and within minutes his breathing deepened.

I watched him sleep. Even in rest, his face carried the weight of everything he'd been forced to shoulder. His brow twitched every so often, some invisible worry still lingering in his dreams.

I leaned down and kissed his forehead, brushing a curl from his temple like I used to when he was small... back when the worst thing in his life was a scraped knee or a forgotten math test. I knew full well he would groan or roll his eyes if he caught me being so sentimental, but I didn't care. He'd grown taller and sharper around the edges, but he was still my boy.

"I've got you," I whispered, though he was already far from hearing.

The hallway was dim as I slipped out and pulled the door closed behind me. I nearly collided into Sloane.

"Christ, Sloane... hey."

She gave me a smile. "Hey."

"I know you said you weren't planning to kill me tonight, but you very nearly gave me a heart attack just now."

She didn't miss a beat. "I heard what you said in there."

The tone of her voice set my heart to fluttering. Heat rushed to my face and I rubbed the back of my neck. "Yeah... I meant every word."

"I know." Her voice cracked.

And then she looked at me, or perhaps it would be more accurate to say she looked *into* me. I stopped breathing as I watched my wife decide my fate.

Hell, this was not a casual look done in passing, nor in the detached, cautious way she had studied me over the past two weeks. She was weighing my soul like Anubis.

Her hazel eyes locked onto mine and they still held that fire that drew me like a moth to flame. Even in the dimness of the hallway, there was a golden flicker in her hazel eyes as her gaze drifted lower and scoured over me in a way that drove me wild. It wasn't lust. It was grief, longing, and the rawness of everything.

The moment we shared earlier that night still burned through me and left me painfully desperate. Despite how much I wanted to ravage her right now, I meant what I'd said: she was in control.

During her inspection, my treacherous body betrayed me and made it undeniably clear how much I desired her. I saw those predatory eyes narrow and her breathing quicken when her gaze settled on my hardened cock straining beneath the gym shorts.

My heart thundered in my throat, my breathing fast and shallow as I felt the weight of her stare.

"Couldn't help it," I said, feeling embarrassed as I adjusted myself. My words sounded silly even to me.

She closed her eyes for a moment, as if gathering strength, then nodded. A small laugh escaped her. "It's okay. Good to know everything still works."

When she opened her eyes, they held a flicker of heat. Calculated, curious, possibly a test I wasn't sure I was passing and just like that, my brain short-circuited. I swallowed hard as the vivid image of her lips wrapped around my cock rammed into my head. I shifted and tried not to make it obvious that every muscle in my body had remembered exactly what her touch felt like.

Down, big guy. Fuck.

This wasn't the right moment. But tell that to the part of me that didn't care about timing; only proximity mattered to my most carnal urges.

She cocked an eyebrow, clearly noticing the shift in my posture or maybe she was reading my mind like she always could. "Jesus, Levi," she said, voice dry as bone. "You look like you are about to ask me to bless you and defile you in the same breath."

I held up my hands in mock surrender, a sheepish grin tugging at my lips. "Hey, not my fault. You looked at me like that. You know what that look does to me."

"Right," she deadpanned. "I forgot your self-control has the structural integrity of wet paper."

I laughed, the sound a little too raw, a little too real. "That's fair. I've never been great at... delaying gratification."

"Understatement of the year."

There was silence for a beat and then I let the smile fall. "But I'm trying now. Really trying to be better. Not just about that, but... about everything."

"I see you trying."

"I'm gonna screw up again," I said honestly. "Not like before. Nothing like that *ever again*. But I know I'll still get in my own way sometimes."

"That's what marriage was always about, wasn't it? Enduring each other's nonsense and choosing to stay anyways." Her voice held both hurt and love as she said those words.

My heart ached at that. I reached for her hand, tentative, and when she didn't pull away, I looped my fingers through hers.

"I love you," I said. There was no way I could not tell her as we held hands in the hallway of our home. I didn't soften it or package it in apology or wrap it with a bow of pretty promises. I let the words fall from my lips how it used to.

"I know, Levi." She looked away from my face, down to our interlocked fingers. "Honestly... I should be more stern with you. I should be more angry." She glanced back up at me, her eyes teary. "But I'm not. Not right now. And I don't know if that makes me weak or... tired of being angry."

She stepped closer, hesitating inches away. Her auburn hair was still down, loose waves falling over her shoulders and curling slightly at the ends. I felt the heat radiating off her skin. Her eyes searched mine, wary but open, and for one agonizing second, I thought she might turn away.

Then she leaned up towards me, her hand flat over my chest, grounding me. I let her close the gap.

The kiss was cautious, a brief brushing of lips and the familiarity of it, the ache of it, sent a shiver through me. It was a tenderness that felt like a question and a forgotten promise all at once.

Her lips parted slightly and I followed her lead, hesitant, unsure if I had the right to taste the depth of what we once shared but she didn't pull away. Instead, she tilted her head, a quiet invitation, and I couldn't resist. The kiss deepened, her tongue meeting mine in a slow, tender dance.

"Oh, fuck Sloane." I growled.

She was my home. My everything. I felt it in the core of my bones as we kissed, every inch of me waking up to the truth Old Me had been blind to. In the gentle press of her body against mine, I could almost taste the life we had before it all went wrong. Every mistake, every betrayal felt distant now, fading into the background as I held her. Her presence was a quiet haven, her love so strong and forgiving that I felt both weightless and anchored all at once. She wasn't just the woman I loved. She was the center of everything I'd ever wanted, even when I hadn't known it.

"You taste like heaven," I said, the words spilling out before I could stop them. My voice was low, unsteady.

I felt her heartbeat against me, the rhythm so steady, so full of life, reminding me of the times we'd sat together on the couch, talking about everything and nothing, feeling invincible in our own little world.

"Levi."

My name, but not like before. It came out as a plea: quiet, desperate, and trembling with too many emotions. Everything we had been and everything we had lost crashed together between our lips.

Each time I broke the kiss, it was only because I had to breathe but even that felt like too much time apart. I couldn't stop. Couldn't hold it in. Every brush of her lips against mine ripped another truth from me, a confession I had carried like a stone in my soul for far too long. "I want you... all of you Sloane."

She was my everything: my anchor, my storm, my salvation, my punishment. And in that moment, with her mouth against mine, her body molded to me like we were created in tandem. I felt *alive* in a way I hadn't in over a decade. She gasped against my lips, her hands tangled in my shirt, her breath catching in that way I remembered so vividly as she held on to me tighter. Desire burned through me, raging like a wildfire, fast, relentless, implacable.

"My only thoughts when I wake up are of you," I said, the confession spilling out. "You. Always you. Every morning, every goddamn night, you're there. In my mind. In my heart. Only you." She had no idea how many mornings and nights I meant with those words... hundreds upon hundreds. I was desperate for her now. Each kiss bruising and brutal. I broke apart long enough to growl, "Do you go to bed thinking of me? Haunted by it? Consumed by desire and love, Sloane?"

I kissed her harder then, as if my breath had been punched out of me and the only way to survive was through her. There was no hesitation in it, no gentle testing of boundaries. Simply raw, uncontrollable need.

"Please Levi." Her breath came out ragged every time our mouths parted. She held herself from the edge, desperate not to fall, yet already slipping. Her lips lingered on mine, clung to me, refused to release.

The intoxicating taste of her, like sweet honey and strawberries, was both familiar and new all at once. Memory and magic. My hands slid around her waist, pulled her tighter, steadied myself in the feel of her, in the reality of her.

A panicked part of me feared this was a dream and that I'd wake up in an empty bed, sweating and full of sadness.

I didn't deserve that moment. I knew that. I had taken her trust and shattered it. Yet here she was, letting me in, reaching for me despite everything the Old Me had dragged her through. I knew, *I knew*, that if I grabbed her and scooped her up that she would wrap her legs around me, that I would carry her across the hall to the guest room, that we would ravish one another in a hundred different delirious ways...

The words, hysterical bonding crashed through my fantasy like a freight train.

I pulled back a fraction, my forehead resting gently against hers, both of us breathing a little heavier, a little more uncertain. "Sloane," I breathed, barely more than a whisper.

Her eyes fluttered open, and for a moment, she stared at me, something unreadable in her gaze. Was it hurt? Love? I couldn't quite tell. It was like she was weighing the same question I had been asking myself.

What happens now?

The kiss had been a spark, the kind that flickers before it bursts into an inferno. I could see the possibility of us together, shining through the cracks of everything that had fallen apart.

She didn't speak. She held my gaze in that silence and everything paused. We were both afraid to move, afraid that a single word might sever the delicate thread between us. Her cheeks were flushed. Pink crept down her neck. Her lips, fuck, her lips were kiss-bruised and trembling.

But it was her eyes that undid me. There, in the soft burn of her gaze, was something feral and aching... unfulfilled desire, sharp and flickering beneath all the restraint she was clinging to.

"I..." I started, but the words felt too heavy, too much to say all at once. "I don't want to do anything until you are ready."

We breathed together for a long time. Her fingers grazed my cheek, her touch soft, like she was memorizing the feel of me again. "We don't have to figure everything out tonight," she whispered. "But I felt it too. I... I do need more time, Levi." Her body was already speaking in tremors and unspoken pleas as she held her ground.

I closed my eyes, trying to keep myself from reaching for her. "I understand. Take all the time you need."

Chapter 13

The next morning, I left early, before either the kids or Sloane awoke. I didn't want to disturb them and I knew I would linger if I saw their faces.

I had a full day of chasing down lost revenue, and trying to brace for the inevitable. The pandemic was weeks out and I felt it in the tightening air, and heard it in the background noise of every radio host who couldn't stop talking about the outbreak overseas being a hoax. The truth was too stark for most of the United States to accept. A virus in China and Europe with thousands already dead? No one over here took it seriously. Not yet.

That night, I barely touched dinner. I microwaved something I didn't taste and dropped straight into bed after my shower. The silence of the rental house was unbearable. I thought I'd appreciate the quiet after a day of numbers and stress, but it felt like a punishment. Sloane and the kids had left for the impromptu trip and I had until the next morning before I needed to check on Rufus. I'd thought about just staying at the house, but Sloane didn't offer and I didn't ask; it seemed presumptuous.

I glanced at the clock and watched time crawl. I didn't realize how much I'd miss them until they were gone.

Thankfully, a storm rolled in at some point and the steady sounds of wind and rain lulled me closer to slumber. I felt myself drift. Despite the cold, clammy sheets pressed against my skin, and the painful longing for the comfort of Sloane's scent, I did eventually sleep.

And dream.

I stood in our home and it was rotting from inside. Not in the walls or the foundation... no, this rot came from deeper within. It floated through the air, like mold on the soul. The place still stood, but it was hollowed out, its insides eaten alive by everything I had done.

The worst part? Sloane was gone.

No note. No trace. Just... gone. Like she'd never even been there... simply erased.

The hallway stretched: long, unnatural, unending. Each footstep felt like trespassing. I passed the mirror in the entryway and I didn't dare look at the reflection. In that surreal nightmare logic, I knew that it would be Old Me staring back. His shadow writhed with wrecked lives, his weak and trembling hands struggled with the zipper on his jeans that he could never close.

I ran through the house looking for Sloane, but all I found were empty rooms stripped of her laughter, her light, and her scent. The place we'd built together had become a carcass and I was its maggot. I screamed soundless apologies that nobody was there to hear before a cackling laughter thundered through the house, shook the broken glass of the windows, and reverberated into the darkest pits within me.

Angie.

I whispered her name in the dream, fearful and timid as if saying it too loudly might conjure her. I ran faster then, but I'd stopped looking for Sloane. I knew she was gone, forever gone from this accursed place. No, I ran from Angie.

But she found me anyway.

Her smile scythed through the darkness and her voice coiled around my guilt, but I couldn't understand the words that slithered off her tongue. Disgust crawled up my throat as she drew nearer. I turned to vomit.

I woke with a gasp. Sweat coated my body as I turned over and dry heaved. The bedroom in the rental felt sterile, unfamiliar, and cold. The silence of the rental tried to return, but the rain outside still fell in a steady patter.

What in the hell?

No one ever tells you about this part. After the rubble settles from what you've destroyed and you're still breathing? Still waking up despite every wish to just disappear? The quiet becomes a living thing that feeds on your regrets. It whispers every *what if* you tried to bury. In my previous life, Old Me had convinced himself that he'd chosen the right path. But this time? I knew what a complete fucking idiot the Old Me had been, and reliving through his mistakes was giving me cataclysmic PTSD.

I should have stopped when Angie had said hi to me. I should have admitted to myself that she was nothing more than an insecure wound I never should've opened.

I reached for the bottle of water on the nightstand, remembering how the Old Me in my previous life would have been reaching for a bottle of scotch. Or bourbon. Or anything, really.

There were several years when the Old Me hadn't been picky, just needed to wrap himself in a drunken blanket for any chance of sleep. I wasn't an alcoholic, not in the clinical sense, but Old Me had developed a severe dependency not long after this point in his life. Yet one more thing that nearly a decade of therapy had helped me with.

The doorbell rang. I froze, water bottle in hand. No one knew I lived here other than Sloane, who was in another state. I got out of the bed, threw on a shirt, and walked to the door. I pressed my ear against the wood, but heard only the sound of rainfall on the other side. I opened the door a crack.

There was no one there. *Weird.*

Then I looked down and saw it: an envelope, white and pristine, sitting on the welcome mat. I flipped it over to see just one word written in red lipstick:

LEVI

Fuck me. I stared at my name: sharp and accusatory lines bled into the paper. I turned the envelope over. My fingers trembled as I opened it. Inside, a single photo slipped out and my breath caught as I realized what it was.

Sloane.

I could tell it had been taken through our living room window. The distinct white border of a Polaroid camera framed the image. Sloane was sitting on the couch reading. Her face was calm, untouched by makeup, her legs tucked under her. She looked peaceful. She looked serene. She looked... *watched*. The photo reeked of invasion, obsession, and malice. How the fuck had somebody gotten so close without anyone seeing her?

On the back of the photo, scrawled in the same red lipstick, was a warning that made my world tilt:

> If I can't have you, no one will.

Angie.

This crazy bitch. I looked up and nearly jumped out of my skin. Across the street, she was standing in the rain under a flickering streetlight.

Are you fucking serious?

Her blonde hair was slicked back, she wore a long black trench coat she'd buttoned up to her throat, and her blood red lips curdled into a too-wide grin. She stood next to the cherry red sports car her daddy had bought for her, its lights off and engine idling. She raised her hand and waved as if we were old friends; as if she hadn't been the driving catalyst for Old Me to destroy his life.

How did she find me?

I stood frozen on the porch.

Your company truck is in the driveway, you fucking idiot.

I should have slammed the door and called the police, or at least tossed the note out like the trash that it was. But something held me back; a gut feeling that if I made any moves then things would get a hell of a lot worse.

Without taking her eyes from me, that manic smile still scrawled across her face, she slid into the driver's seat with a methodical and eerie calm. She revved the engine, winked at me, then drove off into the night like a shadow melting into the road. I watched her taillights vanish.

Cause that's not freaky as fuck.

I retreated back into the rental, my heart thundering against my ribs. Each floorboard whined under my weight as I paced and I knew I couldn't sleep now. My pulse hammered in my head. My guilt clawed the walls of my ribcage as it gnashed its teeth and howled through my thoughts. My sin stalked the streets smothered in red lipstick.

I paced from room to room as if I was trying to outrun something that I didn't have the courage to name, but I knew what it was: fear.

Fear of the unknown variable in this new life. This Angie... she was not the woman I remembered, not the woman from my previous life. She was some darker thing now, calculated and cruel, a warped reflection of the Angie I knew.

I was desperately trying to recall my time with her in my previous life, scraps of memories that could have hinted she was this unhinged, when I saw my phone buzz on the counter.

I'd blocked her number. I know I did. It was one of the very first things I made sure to do when I decided to get this new life in order. I picked up my phone, saw that it was an unknown number, and answered it anyway.

Road noise, rainfall, and obscenely heavy breathing came through the other end before Angie's voice, eerie and euphoric, drawled my name out. "Leviiiii. Haven't you missed me, baby?"

I could never miss you, is what I wanted to say. But I didn't respond, didn't engage. She made her little pouting noise, the one that the Old Me had thought was so damned adorable and preceded him giving her anything she'd wanted.

After I gave her nothing but more silence, she said, "Oh... I have missed you. I have missed you so much. I'm glad I could finally see you, but you looked like a ghost, baby."

Yeah, bitch. You fucking scared me half to death.

Angie breathed a giggle into the phone as I stayed silent. I was caught in the tight space between fear and fury, my thoughts snarling too loud to form words.

"I liked that shirt on you," she said. "Sloane never appreciated your body the way I did. She never looked at you the way I did. You do remember that... right?" The last word was enunciated before the line clicked.

I stared at the phone, my chest tight with indignant rage. Fragments of our past arguments flashed through my mind; memories of how Angie's entitlement oozed from shrieked demands and shouted desires. Her tantrums had always been those of a spoiled princess who'd been denied a shiny thing. That's just who she was: a bratty, vain, selfish, spoiled princess.

Or that's who she had been... in my previous life. But now? I didn't know what the hell Angie was other than goddamn creepy. She was watching me. Fuck me, she was watching Sloane.

Clutching my phone, I went into survival mode as I locked every door and window, closed all of the blinds and curtains, and turned on every outside light. The problem was, she wasn't just outside; she was squirming inside my head. I reminded myself who I was and what mattered, all that mattered in this new life was Sloane, the kids, and our future.

Eventually, the roaring waves of adrenaline settled and were replaced by unnerving ripples of nausea. I stumbled to the bathroom, gripped the edge of the sink, and stared into the mirror. My reflection looked unfamiliar and sickly: drawn, gray, taut. My eyes were ringed with exhaustion, regret, guilt, and anxiety.

My phone rang again as the blood drained from my face. I clicked on *Block* but a few minutes later it rang again.

This wasn't just an obsession. This was a warning. A promise. A sick game I was already losing, but I needed to win in order to protect my second chance.

Fuck this bitch. It's on.

Chapter 14

Early the next morning, I walked the perimeter of our home to double-check the gates and fencing. Rufus followed at my heels, tail wagging, unaware of the new weight I carried in my chest. I needed to ensure everything was secure and safe for all of us.

My initial instinct had been to install the most sophisticated security system a civilian could legally purchase, with full 360-degree motion sensor infrared cameras monitoring every inch of the house and surrounding lots...

But Sloane would want to know why we needed the added security, and I refused to lie to her about Angie ever again. As much as I was ashamed by the situation, as much as I wanted to handle it myself, as much as I didn't want Sloane to worry more than she already did... I refused to keep this from her. I needed to talk with her before I did anything rash.

Besides, this was Sloane's house. Me peppering it with spyware gadgets and hidden cameras without so much as consulting her was not a winning strategy for regaining her trust.

No, I had to find the right time to tell her about what happened after she returned with the kids. Then we could combat it together. As a team.

After pacing the entire property thrice and debating if it was too soon, I pulled out my phone and texted Sloane.

> Hope the kids are having fun. Tell them I miss them.

I didn't expect a reply right away but a few minutes later, her message came.

> They miss you too. Violet wants your help painting her project when we get back.
> Thank you for watching Rufus.

Her texts had been simple and cordial. But I read what she had woven between the words, and I clung to that frayed thread of hope as if it could save me from falling.

I threw myself into work at Master Builders for the rest of the day. While on the job site, I barked orders at my guys like a grizzled drill sergeant. Jose gave me a few wary glances, but he didn't ask any questions. We had been a team for long enough that he knew when to push and when to let me simmer.

That night, I sat outside the rental on a rickety lawn chair that wobbled with every movement. The sky above was bleeding into indigo. It was the kind of quiet dusk that should've felt peaceful... but nothing inside me was quiet.

I lit a cigar I didn't even want and thought about the house I'd built for Sloane: our home. Every inch of it had been designed with her in mind. The wide kitchen windows so she could watch the kids play. The deep tub because she loved long baths. The walk-in closet she never filled because she always put the kids first.

Tomorrow, I would set about getting it ready for their return.

My phone buzzed.

> Violet wants to FaceTime. You free?

> Always

The screen lit up with Violet's name and a little heart emoji she must've added herself. I answered immediately, my heart thudding with excited anticipation.

"Daddy!"

Her face filled the screen, eyes wide, hair wild from the humidity. Behind her, the hotel curtains fluttered with outlines of the theme park's mascot and Liam was bouncing on one of the beds, clearly hyped from a day of overstimulation and sugar.

"Hey, sweetheart," I said, trying to keep my voice steady. "How's the trip?"

Violet launched into a full report as if she were giving a school presentation. "We saw the fireworks and I met so many princesses and Liam got a churro that was bigger than my arm and I rode the big swirly coaster and Mommy said I can keep the princess cup if I don't lose it! And Daddy? They have so much gluten free food here!"

I laughed. "Well, sounds like you're livin' the dream."

She beamed for a moment, before looking up. Her hand shifted, then all I could see was the hotel ceiling.

"Violet? Sweetie?"

There was a moment of silence, then her voice came back in a whisper. "I miss you, Daddy. I wish you were here, too."

That kicked me in the chest. "I miss you more," I whispered back, "but I'm really glad you're having fun with your mom. That's important."

The video shifted and Liam appeared then, his grin half-crooked. "Hey, dad. I beat that laser ride score."

"You *didn't*," Violet snapped, shoving his shoulder. "Your gun stopped working.'"

"I *still* beat it after I fixed it!"

The phone jostled wildly between them, spinning in dizzying angles as their laughter erupted into full-blown chaos. Somewhere in the mix I heard, "Give it back!" and, "Stop sitting on me!" before the screen tilted sideways and all I could see was a blur of carpet and limbs.

Violet's frantic voice shouted, "We're trying to find the phone! Don't hang up, Daddy."

I smiled until my cheeks ached. *Good God I missed them.* Every loud, ridiculous second of being with them.

Then Violet's upside-down face popped back into view, her hair flying everywhere. "Found you!"

Sloane's voice came from somewhere offscreen. "Okay, guys... say goodnight."

I stiffened as my heart stuttered from the sound of her voice. I wanted to ask how her day was, to see a glimpse of her face. But I knew the rules: she was in control. If Sloane hadn't shown herself on the call, it meant she didn't want to. And... I would have to accept that.

Violet frowned and pulled the phone close again, her voice urgent, "Wait, wait! Daddy, can we work on my project when I get back? It's due next week and I want to paint it with you."

Oh, my sweet, darling Violet. I have missed you so much for so long.

I swallowed against the lump in my throat and forced a smile. "I wouldn't miss it," I said. "We'll make it awesome. Pinky promise."

She raised her pinky to the camera and I did the same as we forged our digital vow.

"Love you," she said around a yawn. "Night, Daddy."

"I love you, too. G'night, bud," I added as Liam gave me a lazy wave.

The screen went dark and the quiet rushed back, but this time it didn't feel quite as oppressive.

The next morning at Sloane's, sunlight poured through the kitchen windows to cut sharp angles across the counter. I stood barefoot on the cold tile, coffee in hand, staring at the new curtains I'd hung up throughout the house as if they might offer answers. That was a project Old Me had promised Sloane he would complete over a year ago, but he'd been too busy seeing how far he could shove his head up his own ass to get it done.

Rufus padded into the kitchen, his nails clicking against the floor and gave me that look of half expectation and half judgment.

"You think she'll notice the curtains?" I asked him.

He tilted his head, almost voicing his opinion that I was an idiot for even asking.

"Yeah, you're right. Of course she'll notice them. She notices everything," I said as I scratched behind his ears.

Over the next few days, Rufus watched me with quiet patience as I worked on small repairs and renovations. Aside from the curtains, I tackled a dozen little odds and ends around the house: tightened wobbly doorknobs, oiled squeaky hinges, fixed the loose towel rack in Liam's bathroom, installed a new garbage disposal, cleaned the gutters, adjusted the pantry shelves, patched, sanded, and painted the holes in the drywall.

All of it gave me an excuse to spend more time at the house, and I needed a series of projects to ease my anxiety after that fucked up night with Angie.

After three agonizing days without them, I'd run out of things to fix. Thankfully, Sloane texted me that morning they were on the road and what time they'd be home.

Fuck me, thank God. I was about to start building a goddamn gazebo in the backyard.

I spent that entire day riding waves of anticipation and anxiety while preparing the house. I didn't just clean. I cleansed. As if I could erase guilt from scrubbing grout lines. Every surface was spotless, polished, and shiny. I ensured there were freshly washed sheets on every bed. I lit new vanilla and cedar candles, Sloane's favorite, throughout the house. I stocked both the fridge and pantry with everybody's preferred snacks. I even rearranged the furniture in the living room the way Sloane had asked me to over six months ago. I moved the clumpy old dog bed Rufus preferred, the only dog bed we could ever get him to sleep in, near the window.

"Don't mind me, boy... just rearranging your kingdom."

Rufus sniffed the old bed in the new location, then flopped down with a groan. He approved.

"Good boy," I said while ruffling his ears. He let out a huff. "I know. I can't fix everything with elbow grease and clean floors. But hell... I gotta start somewhere, right?"

He didn't answer. *Obviously.* But it felt therapeutic to say my thoughts out loud.

That evening, as I prepared dinner, I heard the car doors slam followed by Violet's high-pitched giggle. The front door opened and Liam was in the middle of a sarcastic quip about a spilled slushie in the back seat. Sloane's melodic voice, tired but patient, rose to calm them both.

My heart filled with trepidation and joy. I was a man on the outside of his own life, unable to move forward without their permission. Rufus sat at my feet, ever patient for the three days I cared for him, almost as if he truly understood my rambling one-sided conversations with him.

Violet burst in first, already launching into a story about the roller coaster that made her scream so loud it gave Liam a headache. She clung to me like she hadn't seen me in a month, and I soaked it in.

"Daddy! Oh man, what did you do to the house?"

I laughed and said, "Thought you might appreciate the change. Hope that's okay."

"It looks *fabulous*, Daddy!" She gave me another hug before bolting upstairs to unload her luggage.

Both Sloane and Liam stepped in together and my lungs forgot how to work when I saw Sloane. Her auburn hair was pulled up in a loose pony tail, wisps framing her face. She looked especially beautiful, even with dark circles under her eyes.

I watched them pause to take in the new curtains and the rearranged layout of the living room. I knew it was a big adjustment. I worried that I'd gotten it wrong, that I'd swapped where Sloane wanted the couch and the loveseat. Part of me worried she would see it as just another thing that the Old Me had neglected, one more request of hers he'd ignored. Now it stood there like an overdue apology.

Thankfully, Liam at least gave me a small smile and quick nod before heading off to his room.

Sloane didn't speak. Her gaze moved back and forth across the living room, her brow lifting slightly. Then she walked past me, dragging a bag in behind her into the walk-in pantry. I followed her and saw she was already unpacking snacks, mechanically, as if she was trying to ground herself in a routine.

I contemplated my next words. I needed to tell her about what had happened with Angie, but not with the kids still awake.

Her voice broke through my thoughts. "Dawn says hi and she's sorry she couldn't help with Rufus." She watched me out of the corner of her eye, probably gauging how I'd react to the mention of my over-the-top sister-in-law.

"She shouldn't be sorry. I enjoyed my time with him. Gave me an excuse to avoid people."

"He probably preferred you to Dawn anyway. She's all bark, no patience."

"Yeah, well, Dawn's idea of 'helping' is usually showing up at the door in leopard-print pajamas and telling everyone to relax while blasting old rock albums. Not exactly the calming energy for a dog with a sensitive stomach." I paused, imagining Dawn on one of her 'Zen' days, trying to coax Rufus with essential oils and unsolicited life advice. "I'm pretty sure Rufus tolerates me more than her."

Sloane chuckled, but I could see her holding something back as she turned to face the window.

"How is Dawn, really?" I asked, already bracing myself for the answer.

She shrugged and avoided meeting my eyes. "My sister? Still loud. Still eccentric. Probably wore a tiara to her last therapy session. Told me I should've kicked you out years ago when things first started to go bad."

I winced. "Yeah... can't really argue with her there. I know she's never been my biggest fan, but I've always liked her." She was a loving sister who was fighting for Sloane's peace. How could I not admire her?

Sloane didn't respond. She kept staring out the window as if she were searching for something.

"I moved those shelves down like you wanted," I said, pointing toward the reinstalled pantry rack. "And I added those bins for the kids' snacks... figured it might help mornings go smoother."

"I can see that. Looks like you also rearranged the living room." She still had her back to me.

"Yeah. I remembered you said it felt too cramped with the ottoman in the middle. I figured more open space might feel less chaotic."

She hummed a noncommittal sound as she went back to putting away snacks in the pantry. "And the lighting?"

"Yeah, I went out and got new bulbs. Warm tone. You always said the old ones felt like a hospital waiting room."

She paused with a bag of popcorn in her hands, finally turning to look at me. Her expression was thoughtful and measuring as she said, "I didn't think you were listening back then."

"I wasn't. Not the way I should've been. But I am now."

She stared at me, searching my face for a moment, then turned to place the popcorn in a bin and continued to unpack. When she spoke next, her tone was lighter, yet still layered in fatigue. "Well... it doesn't feel like a frat house anymore. So, that's something."

I smirked. "High praise. I'll take it."

She gave a barely-there smile. I handed her a box of granola bars as I stood by her side.

"Did you sleep okay while we were gone?" she asked casually, like it was an afterthought.

I hesitated, unsure if I wanted to burden her with the truth. "No. No, not really."

She didn't look at me, but I saw the twitch in her jaw. There was a part of her that still cared for me, even when she wanted to bury it. She nodded. "Me neither."

"Yeah... I'm noticing that." I reached out to gently touch her cheek, brushing a thumb over the soft skin under her dark circles. "You sure it wasn't all those rope drops and early hours running to the rides that got you?"

She did look at me then and her face softened for a second, as if I'd managed to penetrate her armor. I stared into her eyes, those perfect hazel eyes flecked with golden embers that danced in the sunlight when she laughed.

She said, "I'm sure." Then her gaze fell to the dark circles I knew were under my own eyes. "You had a rough time."

"Yeah, I did." I was struggling and she knew it. I was desperate to tell her about my nightmares and what had happened with Angie, but it had to wait.

Fuck me, she looks exhausted.

"These last few days have been hard. A hell of a lot harder than I thought they'd be," I said, my voice rough with truth. "I've had a lot of time to reflect. I've missed you three so much... I've missed you more than I know how to explain. I've missed how *right* you make everything feel just by being near me. You are my everything, Sloane. You, the kids... hell, even Rufus."

The words spilled from me into the space between us. All these things the Old Me had never been brave enough to say, that he'd buried under layers of pride, shame, and denial. Things I was afraid to face.

Sloane watched me with crossed arms and an unreadable face. Her silence was palpable enough to strangle me.

Desperate to break the mounting tension, I said, "I took care of everything around the house you've been asking for... do you like it?"

Then, finally, she spoke. Her voice was calm when she asked, "Do you think handling the things that I asked you to - mind you, a year ago - cancels out how much of an asshole you have been, Levi?"

Her words hollowed me out, carved out a cold pit where my heart had been. I stared at her, open mouthed and dumbstruck, before I realized she hadn't asked a rhetorical question; she was waiting on an answer.

I wish she was strangling me instead.

"Hell no," I said, shaking my head. "Absolutely not. Of course it doesn't." I floundered, desperate and drowning. I grasped at something, *anything*, my frightened mind thought could help in that moment. "I also did all of the cleaning, dinner is in the oven, laundry is done, and I made the kids' school lunches for tomorrow... I wanted to knock out as much as I could before you got home."

This, however, seemed to infuriate her even more. Her nostrils flared, she squeezed her crossed arms and her nails dug into her skin.

"Sloane, I wanted to show you that I'm trying to fix things. I'm trying to-"

"*Fix things*? You think you can *fix* that you shoved your dick in Angie?"

I flinched and turned, so sick with shame that I couldn't look at her. Nausea roiled my stomach and panic pounded my head as I struggled to breathe. "Sloane," I somehow managed to choke out her name between rasping breaths. "I know... this can't make up for... nothing can make up for that."

In glacial tones she whispered, "Then don't expect me to throw a goddamn parade because you cleaned the house and made dinner. I've done that every single day for years. Without backup. Without applause. Without gratitude."

Tears blotted my vision. I blinked them back, humiliated and wrecked. The truth of her words stripped me raw. I thought of all the small signs of normalcy I'd tried to create: crisp clean sheets on the beds, laundry folded, dishes done, bookbags packed and lined up for the kids. All of it felt meaningless now.

But the nearly endless tasks, both large and small, were not meaningless. They never had been. However, I had allowed myself to believe they were somehow more meaningful because *I* did them.

Because I'm an idiot.

I heard Sloane sigh. "Levi, I do appreciate the effort. But I am trying to help you see why this is such an adjustment for me. I have always done these things because it's what needs to be done. Not because I want to be rewarded or recognized."

"You're right," I said, my voice rough. "I am sorry, Sloane. I wasn't trying to earn a gold star. I... I wanted to show you that I care. That I've always cared, even when I was too selfish or blind to act like it."

She arched a brow. "Well... I will admit, it was a pleasant surprise. But this whole thing is going to take time for me to acclimate."

"What whole thing?"

She waved her hand up and down, a gesture to encompass all of me. "This. This new Levi you keep bringing to me."

I cleared my throat and struggled to regain my composure. "My priorities are different now. It's not about me anymore. It's only you and the kids. That's it. That's all that matters to me. I can't say it enough and I won't stop saying it until you believe me."

She didn't reply to that. She stood there and dissected me with her startling eyes and unyielding gaze. It was the same quiet, assessing look she skewered me with anytime I'd done something heinously stupid. I mentally berated myself as I replayed everything I'd said.

What dumb thing came out of my mouth to cause her to look at me like this?

She stepped closer, and her scent overpowered me. Right there, cramped in the corner of the walk-in pantry, my knees trembled as she approached.

Sloane had always possessed this power over me, a quiet ferocity that could either pull me in with desire or push me away from fear. Sometimes both. But in that moment, as she drew nearer with the ominous intensity of a storm cloud, as the chaos of my mistakes rumbled between us, I had no clue which way the wind would blow.

Is this how I die?

I didn't breathe as my wife, like the predator I knew her to be, stalked her prey. She was now only inches away, radiating heat and fury. I was so fucking aroused and scared at the same time.

I'm a good boy. Good boys get rewarded.

For one irrational moment, when my panicked mind saw her hands moving, I thought she would castrate me. But instead, she rose onto her toes and pressed a soft kiss to my cheek, warm and fleeting.

Then she brushed past me like it hadn't happened, like we hadn't stood on the edge of something fragile and real, as the heat of her lips lingered on my skin. I stayed frozen for a moment, afraid that if I moved I'd lose the last trace of her touch.

She kissed me. Sloane initiated contact and kissed me. Why?

Eventually, I followed her out of the pantry to help with the rest of the unloading. As I hurried to catch up with her in the driveway

I asked, half-laughing, half-terrified, "How close was I to dying just now?"

She replied in a deadpan voice, "Did you know the femoral vein runs along the inner thigh, from the groin to the back of the knee?"

"Oh... that's, uh, good to know. So... really close to dead, then?"

Popping the trunk of her SUV, she turned to look at me; her eyes glinted with something that could have been amusement or mischief. She held her thumb and forefinger up, barely a millimeter apart. "Yep. This close. Thank God you're cute and the father to my children."

I laughed. It was impossible not to. The way she could deliver those casual, lethal remarks with zero emotion still caught me off guard every time, even after all our years together. I watched her, trying not to smile too much.

She's lowering her guard with me. Thankfully.

"So, I'm cute, huh?" I asked, grateful that this was the moment we'd landed on.

"Cute enough to survive," she said with a shrug. Her lips curled into a grin that reminded me of everything I loved about her.

I watched her as she pulled out suitcases and set them in the driveway between us. She was perfect. Perfect in a way I didn't deserve. Yet here she was, still standing in front of me, still making me laugh

"Damn right I am cute," I said, as I lifted her suitcase and headed back towards the house.

I'm fucking adorable.

Chapter 15

That night, after the kids were asleep, we sat on the couch together decompressing. I turned to her and said, "I know the kids had fun, but be honest... did you have a good time?"

She shifted, pulled the throw blanket over her legs and nestled into her corner of the couch. I watched her snuggle into the cushions and was, for the first time ever in my life, furiously jealous of a couch cushion.

"Yes," she said with a large exhale. "It was a much-needed break. The kids loved the hotel, and the pools were actually relaxing. I even got to read for a bit."

"That's rare," I said, trying in vain not to stare at her. "What book?"

"Some thriller Violet picked out for me. It was terrible in a fun way." She smiled, then looked over at me. "You'd have hated it."

"Probably." I chuckled. "And the rope drops?" I teased, nudging her foot gently with mine, hoping for a spark of our old rhythm.

She rolled her eyes with a smirk. "Don't get me started. Liam practically dragged us out of bed before dawn like he was the one paying for the goddamn trip."

"Sounds about right. The boy has military precision when it comes to coasters and churros."

She actually shivered. "Ugh. I hate the lines for the rides the most. I saw a grown man nearly trample a toddler to be first in line. Honestly, I don't know how people can plan all that."

I laughed. "Yeah, well... it's supposed to be a magical place."

She rolled her eyes. "More like a mental place. PTSD from the dining reservations, the color-coded itinerary, and the fact that I needed a PhD to book a quick pass. I was setting alarms at 6 a.m. just to get a reservation for a restaurant where the gluten free waffles cost more than my dignity."

"Are you sure you had a good time?" I asked with playful, mock concern.

She took a deep breath and nodded. "I did, yes... despite the stressful parts."

We sat in silence for a moment. I looked at her. I found her so adorable, the way she sat curled on the couch like a cat, and my heart ached to hold her and be held by her in turn. I thought of a hundred different ways to tell her how much I loved her.

Instead I said, "I'm grateful the kids still have you."

She frowned and her gaze narrowed. "They have you too, Levi. Don't talk like you're already halfway out the door again."

Halfway out the door again.

I jolted upright as my voice flooded out in a rush. "No! Not that, never again that."

Her gaze scoured my face as she pondered my words. I knew she was discerning my sincerity, and the moment between us was taut with silence before she said, "Good boy. Because that would contradict all the groveling you've done over the last few weeks."

Those two words filled me, nearly to bursting, and I felt my heart explode with joy from her praise.

I'm a good boy.

She seemed to struggle with what she said next. "When things first started to fall apart... you filled my head with so many hollow excuses and empty promises. You lied about you, about us... goddammit Levi, I can't help but hear the echo of those lies every time you talk like you're vanishing."

I scooted closer and said, "I know I've given you every reason to doubt me and I can't erase what I've done... but I'm here. For real. This time, I'm not simply saying the right things. I'm doing the right things. Every day."

She didn't speak right away as her fingers absently rubbed the edge of her sleeve, an anxiety sign I knew as her way of processing emotions too heavy for words.

After a minute, she said, "The kids notice, you know. That you're trying. Violet asked me if you were 'back-back.' I didn't know what to say."

My chest clenched at that. "You tell them whatever you think is best, Sloane. I know we're trying our hardest not to involve them in our issues, but I won't stop being a parent for them regardless of how this turns out."

"That's oddly mature of you," she said.

"Thanks. Always trying to impress."

That earned the barest flicker of a smile before she continued, "You know what really scares me, Levi?" She looked down at her hands for a moment, then back at me. "It's not that you cheated. I mean, goddamn, that was hell. But what scares me more is how easy it was for you to forget us while you were doing it. Like we... stopped existing to you."

Her words sliced into me with surgical precision. Not out of cruelty, I knew, but out of the harsh honest truth of her pain. Tears swelled in my eyes as I struggled to find the right words.

"I didn't forget you," I said in a rasp. "I buried you. I buried us. I buried everything good about my life under whatever lie I needed, just so I could fool myself into feeling justified."

She didn't flinch. She sat silent and listened.

"I see it now," I said, "how I made you invisible in your own home. How I walked around like I was the victim, because life didn't feel worth living anymore. And you... you were working such long shifts, always taking care of the kids, doing your best to hold it all together while I tore it all apart."

She blinked and I knew she was also fighting back tears as she said, "I used to pray you'd notice. That you'd look up one day and see how tired I was... but when you finally looked up, it wasn't at me. It was at her."

A brittle and aching silence sat between us on the couch for a time.

"I know I don't deserve your forgiveness," I eventually said. "But I'll earn your trust back, even if it takes the rest of my life. Even if you never love me the same way again. I still want to be someone worth loving. Someone the kids can look up to. Someone you can rely on."

Sloane let out a shaky breath, tucking her knees up and wrapping her arms around them as if she were holding herself together. "You broke me, Levi. You shattered me to pieces and I don't know if I can be fixed."

"I know," I whispered, almost whimpering.

"But you're not leaving me to hold those pieces alone and... that's something."

What I said next came with such force, such intensity, it caused her to jump. "Sloane, I will *never* leave your side again. Not until you tell me to go."

Her eyes met mine. They were wet, but unwavering. I knew the fragile honesty we'd shared had done more to bridge the chasm between us than any amount of groveling, gifting, or apologizing either had or could.

Her lips parted, like she wanted to say something, but nothing came. Then, with a timidness that was uncharacteristic of my wife, she reached out and brushed her fingertips across my hand. Our fingers interlocked, warm and tentative.

That was the second time she'd touched me that day. The simple feel of her delicate fingers intertwined with my own spiraled my mind to an unimaginable height, where I lost all sense of place and time. We held hands on that couch for either five minutes or five hundred years; I could not say for certain.

Sloane withdrew her hand and, for the briefest moment, my heart ceased at the loss of her touch. But then she slid her fingertips up my arm, slow and deliberate, tracing the curve of my shoulder.

I didn't move. My breathing was shallow, my mouth dry, my pulse pounding. I feared a single word might sever this delicate thread binding us together, so silence reigned between us.

Her fingers slid from my shoulder, to my neck, and then lower. When she flattened her palm over my chest, I feared the thundering beat of my heart was enough to bruise her. I placed my hand over hers, pressing it against me to anchor her touch to my skin.

I felt like a drowning man breaking the water's surface, gasping a desperate breath of air.

She looked at me, her gorgeous eyes searching mine, unsure but willing. I leaned in to brush my lips over hers with graceful care, with tender gentleness, as if she were made of the most delicate filigree.

"Levi, wait. Please." Her voice was small, timid.

I felt her quickening pulse under my fingers, and the way she shifted away told me she wasn't sure of where this was going. Or where it should go.

"Sloane," I whispered, "I don't want to do anything unless you're sure."

She said nothing with her lips, but her eyes were full of questioning uncertainty.

"I mean it," I said. "No blurred lines, no pressure, no risking that you'll change your mind halfway through. No regrets. If this is just a moment, then let it pass. If it's comfort, I'll be here for that and nothing more. But I refuse to take what you're not ready to give." I hesitated, waiting for her to process, then added far more awkwardly than I'd intended, "Also, I don't have a condom... if you wanted to use one."

She arched a shocked brow. The corner of her mouth twitched like she wasn't sure whether to laugh or roll her eyes. "I don't want to use a condom. But thank you for checking?"

"I'm clean," I said. "I got tested. I wanted to make sure... in the off-chance you wanted to... I mean, I wanted to ensure you were safe."

She gave me a long look, her expression unreadable. Then she gave a short, unimpressed hum. "Hmm. Not exactly romantic, Levi."

I smiled. "No, I know... but still important. Romance is giving flowers. This is... basic human decency."

"Look at you. Evolving."

"I'm a work in progress," I said as I watched her. "But for once, I'm not rushing the ending."

"That goes against your previous nature."

"Funny," I muttered. "I walked into that one, didn't I?"

She shrugged. "I mean, you used to rush through everything. Conversations, conflict resolution, foreplay, sex."

I winced. "Hell, okay... ouch."

Her eyes flickered with the tiniest glint of amusement. "I'm saying... this is new. The slowness. The awareness."

"I am trying," I said. "It's like emotional yoga. I am sore in places I didn't know existed."

"You have changed," she said as a wicked grin crept across her face. "But let's see how much." She leaned in close then, her hand now clutching my chest through my shirt. She brought her lips close to my ear, her hot breath against my neck, as she whispered in the sultry tone she knew drove me wild, "I bet this... still hardens your cock, doesn't it?"

Fuck yes it does.

My body responded instantly. She looked down at the unmistakable bulge rising between my legs and she let out a short, playful laugh. "Still works, huh?"

Her nearness, her heat, her scent, her nails digging into my chest, her cockiness, her mastery over my body, her voice, *that* voice, all came together to overpower me. I had never, in this life or my previous one, ever swooned before. But I sure as hell did just then. Words failed me, so I did the only thing I could think to do.

I brushed my fingers against the back of her neck on *the spot*. The one place that always made her shiver, always weakened her legs, and often made her whimper. Like it did in that moment.

Her breath hitched, subtle but undeniable.

I grinned. "Still works, huh?"

She shot me a warning look, trying and failing, not to smile. "Don't get cocky."

"Too late," I said. "That ship sailed the moment you said 'cock.'"

She rolled her eyes, but didn't move away. "You're impossible."

"But slightly improved," I said as I moved closer.

"Debatable."

"We can debate later," I kissed her throat once, tentatively.

"You're not making this easy, you know," her voice a mixture of warmth and warning.

I paused, a slight laugh escaping me. "What do you mean? I'm... remembering."

"Remembering what?"

I traced the edge of her jaw with my thumb. "The way you feel. The way we used to be. I never forgot, Sloane, not really. But I've... missed this." I lowered my hand from her neck to her back gently. "May I?"

She nodded. We let the silence speak where words would have fumbled, moving slowly as our clothes eased away, barriers dropping with each careful motion. Her warm skin beneath my hands, sun-kissed and soft in a way that felt like home. I removed her bra, my breath catching in my throat as the fabric slid off, my eyes tracing the swell of her breasts and all the familiar contours of her body that I once took for granted.

I took my time, memorizing all of her again, each freckle, every curve, as if I was tracing a memory that time had taken from me; her body was familiar and new all at once. We explored each other, unspoken but understood, with each brush of fingertips, each sigh, each shared glance that lingered, swollen with longing.

Her breath shook underneath me, her chest rising and falling in shallow, uneven gasps as I took her nipple into my mouth. A tremble rippled through her as I teased the sensitive bud.

My hand slid to her side, thumb tracing the curve of her ribs, and I kissed the beauty mark beneath her left breast as if it was sacred. To me it was.

Lower still, I followed the path of her navel with my tongue, then paused at the delicate dip of her hips.

I looked up at her from where I knelt. Our eyes locked. "Can I keep going?" I asked, my voice quiet, sincere.

She nodded, slow and sure, then reached for me, threading her fingers through my hair. "Yes," she whispered. "Please."

When she said *please*, it lit a fire inside me. I kissed the inside of her thigh with tender reverence. Her fingers tightened in my hair, a quiet plea. I answered by settling between her thighs, parting her gently with my tongue, and devouring her as a growl escaped from deep within my chest.

"Fuck, Sloane," I breathed against her. "You taste divine."

She gasped, one hand rushing to her mouth to muffle her moans.

I stayed there and savored every reaction, transfixed by every flicker of emotion that crossed her features. Her stuttered breaths. How her hips lifted instinctively, inviting more. The way she bit her lower lip anytime she wasn't covering her mouth drove me mad. I took my time and drummed a steady rhythm against her with my tongue until her legs trembled around me, until I felt her body grow taunt like a drawn bow string.

"Fuck, Levi, fuck, I'm gonna... I'm gonna..." Her whispered mewl edged me as I listened to her desperate cry for release.

"Come for me, Sloane." I growled as I slid my fingers inside her silky heat.

That was enough to push her over the edge. She muffled her strangled cry into the couch pillow she bit into as the orgasm tore through her, sending her whole body into quivering tremors.

Only when she stopped convulsing did I pull back, kissing my way up her body. Her skin was slick with heat, her breath shallow, eyes heavy-lidded and drunk with pleasure.

I hovered over her, brushing a strand of hair from her face as I murmured, "That was so hot, Sloane. You're such a good girl, coming all over my fingers like that."

Her eyes opened, still glazed but sharp enough to catch my cocky grin. She took a few heavy breaths, but when she spoke her voice was a velveted challenge, laced with teasing that quickened my pulse. "You like listening to yourself talk, don't you, Levi?"

I laughed, genuinely caught off guard. "Is that what it is? I thought I was offering praise where praise is due."

She raised an eyebrow, lips twitching in a smirk. "Mm-hmm. If this whole builder thing doesn't work out, you could always become a phone sex operator. You really commit to the dialogue."

I leaned in, brushing a kiss against her cheek, then her jaw, then her throat, letting my voice dip into a whisper. "Only for you. I live for your five-star reviews."

She huffed a laugh, body still trembling beneath mine. "Shut up and kiss me."

You don't have to tell me twice.

She pulled me up to meet her mouth. Her kiss was frantic, needful, hungry. Her hands moved down to wrap around my cock. I groaned into her mouth as she gripped me and guided me to her. Our foreheads pressed together, breath mingling.

"Levi... I'm... " Uncertainty cracked her voice as I positioned myself at her entrance. The heat radiating off her drove me nearly insane.

"Give me your permission, Sloane," I whispered, my voice raw, barely above a breath. "Your choice. I'm here. I'm never leaving again."

The vow reverberated between us. Her breath came in shallow, uneven gasps, her body tensed at the weight of the choice she was about to make, the vulnerability she was allowing, the grace she was granting.

She reached up. Her fingers gripped the back of my neck to pull me closer. "Yes."

The word was a thread between us, a lifeline. I slid into her slowly, so very slowly. I savored her divine warmth as it enveloped me inch by languid inch. The world fell away. There was nothing else in that moment but us.

She gasped again, the sound trembling through her body, and her arms locked around my neck to pull me against her. "Oh god, Levi," she whispered. Her voice wavered with the heat of our connection.

Some unfathomable feeling beyond desire, something primal and frightening, tightened within my chest. "You're a goddess," I breathed, unable to stop the words from escaping. "You deserve worshipping."

I kissed her deeply as I moved in and out of her, as if I could somehow show her, with every kiss, every breath, every thrust, that I was there. That I was hers, fully and completely.

We moved together. Our bodies rediscovered our secret rhythm as we rocked back and forth, remembering what it meant to belong to one another. Her legs wrapped around me, anchoring me to her. Her name broke from my lips and her breath hitched when my hand slid under her thigh, pulling her closer, deeper, needing all of her.

"Fuck, Sloane... you feel so good. So damn wet and tight."

She moaned, deep and guttural. "Levi... please don't be gentle." Her nails dug into me, urging me faster.

I felt the heat of her skin, felt every inch of her body drawing me deeper, pleading for more. My control, my sanity, was slipping away, lost in the sound of her voice, and in the desperate need between us.

"Anything for you," I whispered between ragged breaths as I gave in to the overwhelming pull of her.

There was no room for hesitation now. No space for the doubt that had lingered between us. Just her, just us, consumed by the need to reconnect, to feel alive again in each other's arms.

I leaned close, whispering into her ear, "I'll fuck you until you scream my name, Sloane. Brand it across your lips, seal your own into my skin. I can't live without you, fuck, can't live unless I'm inside you." I bit her neck, right beneath her ear, and relished the gasp that mingled with her moans before I whispered, "I'm yours. Only yours."

Her cunt tightened around me and I almost came. She whimpered against my neck, "God yes, Levi. Faster. Fuck me harder."

My heart thundered, driven by a deep, uncontrollable hunger for her, to feel every part of her. The urge was indomitable as my thrusts hastened, harder and faster, to bring her the release she craved. Her breaths came quicker as we both teetered on the edge of this raw, vulnerable precipice.

"Fuck, Sloane. I'm close."

Her gasp came out torn, "Me too... can you? Please?"

I reached down, my fingers finding her clit, edging her until her release crested when she called out my name again and again. I buried my face in her neck, unable to hold back any longer as I followed her over the edge, every nerve alive, every part of me unraveled and remade in her arms.

Afterwards, I didn't move. I couldn't move. We lay tangled together, breathing heavy and deep, hearts racing.

Her fingers brushed through my hair. "That was..." her voice broke off as she touched my chest. "That was really *you*, wasn't it? All those things you said... felt so true."

"Yeah... I meant it before, during, and after." I kissed her fingertips. "I'm not going anywhere, Sloane."

We stayed there for a while, wrapped in each other's arms as our breathing steadied. We traced soft patterns on each other's skin.

The world outside felt distant, almost non-existent, as if time had paused for the two of us. Eventually, Sloane shifted, breaking the moment as she murmured that she needed to use the bathroom.

Heavy with reluctance, I pulled away and got dressed. The possibility that the kids could come downstairs seemed more real now than it had when we were in the height of passion. Sloane returned from the bathroom and I was handing over her clothes when it happened.

Rufus growled; a low, primal sound that vibrated through the quiet.

We both jumped. I forced a laugh to cover the creeping unease. "Rufus? Hey boy, what's wrong?"

He didn't wag his tail or return to his lumpy old bed. Instead, he padded through the foyer toward the front door, his nails clicking against the floor. His whole body was stiff and alert. He stopped, looked over his shoulder at me, then whined deep in his throat. Protective.

My heartbeat kicked up. "Rufus?" I called again, moving toward him.

He growled once more, low and warning, then pawed at the doorframe.

I followed him through the foyer, reached for the doorknob, muscles taught with caution, all the hairs on the back of my neck stiffened. Sloane stood behind me, silent but watchful. I opened the door a crack.

But there was nothing there other than the night air and a gentle breeze. The only sounds were cicadas and a distant dog barking.

Then I looked down and saw it: a folded piece of white paper, taped to the door. I pulled it free.

Sloane leaned over my shoulder. "Levi? What is it?"

I unfolded it to see letters scrawled in red lipstick.

> You think you can erase me? I'll remind you exactly who you are.

My stomach lurched. The handwriting was familiar, looped, and feminine.

Peeking over my shoulder, I felt Sloane's presence as she read the note. I turned to explain as I felt the shift in her posture. A stiffening. A wall going back up.

Rufus whined again and nudged my leg. I crumpled the note in my fist, pulse hammering in my ears as I looked down at my hand. "No more hiding," I said.

"Levi? Hiding from what?"

I turned to her.

How do I explain this?

I struggled to find the words. "I was planning to tell you after the kids went to sleep."

The second it left my mouth, I knew it was the wrong thing to say. Her face hardened, jaw clenched. "Another lie, Levi?"

The sight of her fury building struck me with panic. "Hell no, not a lie. Sloane, it's not what you think." I closed the door. "Please, let me explain."

"Then explain it," she snapped. "Because if this is more of the same, you can forget *whatever* that moment between us was."

I stepped towards her, my hands trembling as I showed her the crumbed note. "It's Angie. She's been stalking me... us. She took a picture of you on the couch and left it for me the other night at the rental and now? She left another here."

Sloane's face shifted from anger to disbelief, and then, beneath the surface, I saw it: fear.

Fuck, I never wanted this to happen.

She stared at the note in my hand as she whispered in a tone of restrained fury, "You need to handle this, Levi. Do it the right way with the police. Before she hurts someone."

"I will. I promise," I said. "Sloane, I wanted to tell you. I wasn't hiding this from you. But I didn't want the kids to hear."

At that, anger flashed back across her face and she crossed her arms. "Then instead of fucking me on the couch, you should have been talking to me. You should have told me about this."

I opened my mouth to defend myself, then...

Fuck me. She has one hundred percent of my balls right now.

"You are absolutely right," I said.

"You're goddamn right I'm right."

"Sloane, I was not hiding this. I was... caught up in that moment with you. On the couch. Nothing else in the world mattered. Only you."

She glared, arms still crossed, brow furrowed.

"Sloane... I don't want to lose this," I said as I gestured to the space between us.

"That's not for you to decide, Levi." Her tone was accusatory and firm. She turned and headed towards the kitchen.

Even as I locked the door, I knew the peace I'd been building had been shattered. Again. I followed her into the kitchen. "Sloane - "

She held up her hand without looking at me, an old habit of hers that used to be cute. Right then it felt like a warning flare. I stood there, stiff with the fear of disappointing her again.

"Don't," she said. She opened the fridge and grabbed the wine I'd picked up for her. She poured a glass, then set it down untouched. Her fingers wrapped around the rim, knuckles white. I worried she would break it.

"Sloane, please. Let's talk about this."

She turned then, hazel eyes sharp with clarity and resolve. "I need you to listen to me, Levi. If she escalates? If she comes near the kids? Then this is over."

My mouth went dry. "I know. She won't. I've blocked her in every way I can. I've cut her off completely."

"Clearly that wasn't enough," she snapped, then caught herself. She closed her eyes and exhaled through her nose. "I don't care what she wants. I care about *my* peace. My *children's* safety. And right now? Right now, she is a threat to that."

I nodded, guilt twisting my guts. "I'm going to deal with it. I'll file a police report. Talk to a lawyer if I need to. I'll make sure she goes away and stays away."

She tilted her head and watched me. "Good. But understand this, Levi... this isn't a warning for her. It's one for *you*. I let you back into our lives because I believed you had changed. Because I saw the man you are trying to become. But if your past bleeds into our present?" Her voice broke before she continued. "I won't hesitate to cut you out for good."

"I don't want you to cut me out," I whispered. "I want to *earn* being here."

My wife stood there and picked me apart with her analytical gaze. She closed herself off, every inch of her a fortress. "Then clean up the mess you made. All of it."

Rufus let out a soft whine at our feet, sensing the tension.

She picked up the wine glass and finally took a sip, eyes never leaving mine. "We deserve peace, Levi. Do not let her steal it from us."

She turned and walked down the hallway toward the master bedroom, a room we once shared, leaving me alone in the kitchen with the note still crumpled in my hand and an inferno of determination and fear raging within my heart.

Chapter 16

Back at the rental, I started sleeping with the lights on. Not because I believed they'd protect me; hell, I knew they wouldn't. But because it felt like the dark made Angie stronger.

The crazy bitch wasn't just watching from the shadows anymore. She was in the walls. In the hum of the fridge. In the creak of the floorboards. Sometimes I swore I could feel her crawling under my skin, whispering through my molars like radio static.

For the first time since I woke up in this new life, I wondered if there was a cost to being pulled backward through time. Some invisible toll taken on the soul.

Whatever cruel and sadistic god decided I was worth dragging out of that wreckage hadn't done it for redemption. No... it was clear they wanted carnage, and I was their chosen puppet, spinning in the center of the chaos like a coin.

Was I losing my mind? I pondered at a dozen different explanations for Angie's behavior, for her obsession, for why she was so erratic and different in this new life. Had I truly changed her this much with my choices? Had the fact that I had been inside her when I woke up in this new life done something to her, broken her mind somehow? Had I brought some *thing* back with me that just looked like Angie?

The questions chased each other through my skull, relentless, looping, and snarling. I paced the rental's halls like a trapped animal, each step echoing too loudly, each shadow stretching too far. The house felt off-kilter, as if the bones of it had shifted in my absence.

There was a new crack in the hallway mirror, jagged and crooked like veins. Was it new? Or had it always been there, and I'd never noticed it until I was so on edge and hyper aware that I was noticing everything?

Two nights after the envelope was left at Sloane's, I saw Angie.

It had been a long day with the kids, and Sloane asked for some space. Reluctantly, I headed back to the rental: away from my home, my kids, my wife. I showered and was getting ready to lay down when I saw movement outside the bedroom window. With my pulse pounding despite frozen veins, I pressed my back to the wall, slid to the edge of the window, then peered out through the glass.

Angie stood close to the rental, her face blank and emotionless. She was holding... something? Another note? A gun? My bedroom was dark, I knew she couldn't see me, so I moved further into the window to get a better view of whatever was in her hands.

A camera. But not just any camera. Sloane's camera.

The old Polaroid I'd given her on our third anniversary. The one she used to capture the quiet moments: sun-drenched Sundays, sleepy-eyed smiles, the kind of peace I'd destroyed.

How does the bitch have Sloane's camera?

Had Angie broken into our garage? Gone through our things? Rifled through our memories as if they were simply junk to pawn? My fists curled into tight knots as I stood there, unable to blink or breathe.

Then Angie lifted the camera, aimed it at the rental house, and took her time to adjust the lens. That's when I knew the bitch wanted me to see her. She wanted me to know that she was in control of the situation.

The bright flash felt alien in the dark moonless night. My vision filled with spots.

She stood there, her face still a mask of emptiness, as she shook the Polaroid picture. When she examined it, her eyes widened and her lips curdled into that same, crazed, too-wide grin from the other night. Her head snapped up from the photo and she looked directly into my eyes with an obscene intensity that caused me to step back from the window.

I could still see her. See the way she giggled, waved, then turned to walk away. No hurry. No fear. As if she owned the night.

I drew a shaky breath as cold air bit against the dampness of my skin. I didn't even realize I had been sweating until Angie was gone.

Gone? No, she wasn't gone. She had momentarily receded like the tide, but she would be back.

My phone buzzed and I jumped. No caller ID. A private number this time. *Ah, fuck.* I answered.

Angie's voice slid through the phone, as sweet and unsettling as poisoned honey. "Levi... let's skip the formalities. You picked up knowing it was me." A shuddered breath from her as she continued, "By the way, do you know the little gray sweater? The one with the tear at the sleeve?"

My throat clenched, mouth dry, and I couldn't bring myself to speak. I knew that gray sweater well. It was Sloane's emotional armor: soft, frayed at the cuffs, stretched at the sleeves. She wore it after our worst fights, the kind where we didn't talk for days but still passed each other in the hallway like strangers. I remembered her curled up on the couch in it, silent tears soaking the collar, refusing to look at me even when I begged her to. She wore it when she was pregnant with Liam and again with Violet. When her body hurt, when her back ached, and when the weight of motherhood was crushing her.

I'd given her that sweater casually, thinking it was just another soft thing to warm her. But she had treasured it for years. Hell, she'd worn it through everything.

"She wears it when she cries," Angie went on, savoring the words. "Did you know that, Levi? Last night, she curled up on the couch in it. The poor thing was shaking. Whispering your name like it hurts her." Angie let out a soft, mocking *tsk*. "Then she tossed it out in the garage like it was trash. That pathetic little cunt."

My vision went red and the line went dead before I could respond. To hear her disparage my wife, to call one of the most selfless and thoughtful people I'd ever known a cunt? If Angie had been in front of me, I would have ripped her to bloody pieces. A decade of therapy would not have saved her from my bloody knuckled rage.

Deep breaths, big guy. In and out.

I forced myself to breathe, to slow my heartrate. Anger was what Angie wanted me to feel. Anger meant I would do something rash, something stupid. I waited until I'd calmed myself before I sat on the bed to think.

The garage. Obviously, Angie had gotten into our garage. It wouldn't be that hard to slip in for someone as unhinged as she was. The garage was where we kept the things too sentimental to throw out, but too painful to keep close. The in-between space. Our memories in storage bins. Sloane's childhood keepsakes, the kids' old toys, that damn sweater folded neatly beside a box of anniversary cards we'd stopped reading years ago.

It's also where we keep the trashcan, smart ass. Maybe she was throwing it out.

In the wake of her taunting phone call, a suffocating silence settled over me. I'd heard her words, but it was what Angie didn't say, what she'd left unsaid, that I kept playing over and over in my head: "I'm watching her Levi and there's nothing you can do about it."

A deep ache gnawed at my chest, threatening to consume me.

Angie had gone too far. The thought of her filthy, greedy hands touching anything of Sloane's disgusted me, of course. But the worry that Angie might be dangerous? That she might actually try to hurt Sloane? I hadn't considered that a real possibility until then. Something about Angie breaking into our garage made me realize that she wasn't just a scorned lover anymore. She was a genuine threat.

Sloane deserved better than this. She deserved to feel safe, to feel secure, and I wasn't going to let some psychopath ruin that.

This bitch doesn't realize who she's dealing with.

No one hurt Sloane. I would bury Angie under concrete if she did.

I let out a breath through clenched teeth. I shot a text to Sloane, my fingers zipping over the screen.

> Do you still have your gray sweater with the torn sleeve?

I was met with silence. *Obviously, you idiot. It's past midnight.* I doubted Slone was awake.

Desperate for an ounce of control, I paced the room while I cataloged the years I could remember I'd spent with Angie.

She'd left me two years into our relationship, right around the time mine and Sloane's divorce had settled. Master Builders Inc. and our home had been sold, the proceeds split down the middle, and I paid a lump sum of alimony towards Sloane.

I had tried to start anew with Angie. She was already gorgeous when I'd met her, but she'd transformed herself into an absolute bombshell. Her body was built in a surgeon's office: carved, sculpted, and suctioned into existence with my money I pissed away. Every time we fought, I imagined those stacks of cash I'd burned to pump fat into her ass and freeze it under her skin. Her forged beauty became a grotesque monument to every stupid, disgusting choice I'd ever made. Her fake lashes fanned dramatically, drowning her eyes in plastic glamour. She became a parody of seduction.

Was she always this fucking crazy, though?

Had there been signs? I ran through every moment, every interaction I could recall with Angie. The flirtation, the smiles, the fights, the hints that I was too blind to see her for what she was. In my previous life, was she really this unhinged and the Old Me had never noticed? Or had some fragile thing snapped in her after I woke up in this new life? Is she this insanely obsessed because of how I fled, terrified, from her?

I couldn't shake the unease gnawing at me. The pieces were all there, scattered and jagged, coming together in a way I could no longer ignore.

Our last interaction burned in my memory, sharp and unforgiving. We were staying at her Dad's place in preparation for a party. Angie had lost her shit on me because I couldn't take her to Key West for our anniversary. After two years of gifting her with anything and everything she'd ever asked for, with that one cancelled trip the carefully painted facade of our relationship cracked open to reveal what had always been underneath: sex, control, and money. I gave her what she wanted, when she wanted it, and if I couldn't? What use was I, then?

We screamed at each other, her mascara streaming black tears down her face as rage coiled in every syllable. That fight stripped everything between us bare. I saw myself in the shattered mirror of that moment, standing in the wreckage of a life I had built on ego and lies. I had nothing. No dignity. No home. No family that trusted me.

But it was her final words that branded themselves into my spine.

"You are nothing without me, Levi," she spat. Her voice shook with a furious hunger. "You are mine and if I can't have you, then believe me... no one will."

She slammed the door on her way out. I stared at it for a long time, listening to the silence crawl in around me before I packed my stuff and left. I blocked her, cut her out of my life, and made sure I would never hear from her again.

After Angie, I abstained from alcohol and other women. That's around the same time I'd started therapy. Hell, I did everything I could to turn my life around.

I finally saw Sloane for the miracle that she was and, for the first time in a long time, I tried to live a life worth living. After I'd lost Violet and watched Liam bounce in and out of juvenile detention centers, I'd desperately wanted to lead a more selfless life.

There were a few women who came and quickly went for the remainder of my years, but never more than one or two dates at the most. It was as if they could sense the rot within me, the sins I'd committed, the wreckage I'd left in my wake. If there had been a world record for 'number of times ghosted' I would surely have held it.

I stayed single for the rest of that life and was content being a friend to Sloane whenever she'd let me.

A bing sounded as my phone lit up, pulling me out of my memories of my previous life.

> I think it's in the garage. Everything ok?

I tried to be calm. I didn't want to alarm her.

> Missing you madly and wishing I could see you. I hope you haven't had to wear it recently.

Silence greeted me after that, the implications of my words evident to us both: *I hope I haven't made you cry recently.*

I buried my face in my hands, the pressure doing nothing to stop the downward spiral in my mind. Angie was bleeding into every corner of my life, our home, my marriage. She was a parasite feasting on our suffering.

Then, a knock. Not at the door, but from the bedroom window. Three soft taps.

Anger surged, flooding my veins. I remembered her voice over the phone earlier, calling my Sloane a cunt, and I clenched my teeth until my jaw ached.

I am going to murder this bitch.

There in the darkness of the bedroom, I sat with my arms wrapped around my knees and listened to my breath turn ragged. I practiced my deep breathing, rocking back and forth on the bed, fighting to contain the boiling rage within me as I repeated a mantra over and over in my head.

She wants you to snap. Don't go out there. If you go out there, you will kill her. If you kill her, you will lose everything. Do this the right way. For Sloane.

At 4 a.m. I found the envelope on the patio table.

The handwriting had changed, become more erratic and almost illegible. The red lipstick smeared across the paper; each letter evoked its own sense of screaming.

> I still want us to go to Key West.

What in the actual fuck?

I stared at it as a flicker of confusion teased at the edge of my memory. Had I already invited her to come down to Key West with me? Had we already discussed vacationing there?

Then the stench hit me, that cloying, sickly-sweet perfume of Angie's. It clung to the paper thick and chemical, crawling up my throat. I gagged, stepping back instinctively, bile rising. My hands shook as I held the note away from me, like it might burn through my skin.

This wasn't simply stalking. It was an obsession.

I took a deep breath and forced myself to sit still and stay in control.

But fuck me, she was crazy. So crazy, I think it was time to get the police involved before I did something irrevocably stupid.

Chapter 17

The next morning, I drove straight to the police station. The sky was overcast, that dull gray that feels like the world is holding its breath. Even the air felt suspended, thick with unspoken warnings.

The police station stood stark against the sky, its brick facade washed in shadows, cold and unmoved. I pulled into the parking lot and killed the engine, but didn't move. I sat there in silence, gripping the steering wheel with both hands like it was the only thing keeping me grounded. My knuckles whitened.

The note Angie left replayed in my mind on a loop, her handwriting sharp, slanted, almost manic. Her handwriting burned into my memory.

It might get worse. The thought chilled me. I wasn't going to wait for her next message.

Inside, the fluorescent lights buzzed overhead as I approached the front desk. The officer behind the glass barely looked up. "Help you?"

I nodded, holding up the notes in a clear zip lock bag. "I need to file a report. Someone left this at my home. It's a threat."

That got his attention. He took the bag, read the notes, then motioned for another officer. Twenty minutes later, I was sitting in a small, windowless room going over everything: who she was, what had happened between us, the affair, the blocked calls, the obsessive texts, and now this.

I didn't hold anything back. I couldn't afford to.

"I'm not pressing charges yet," I told the officer, "but I need this on record. I've got kids in the house and I need a restraining order."

The officer nodded. "You've done the right thing coming in. If you've got any old texts, emails, voicemails, anything, send them to us. Keep this note. We'll make copies. And keep your security cameras on at home."

I left the station with a weight lifted and a folder full of paperwork, documentation, steps for filing a restraining order, and the contact info for the officer assigned my case. I called my lawyer next. I wanted everything airtight. Angie had been a crack in the foundation of my life, and I wasn't going to let her become a fault line again.

Back at the rental, I installed a pair of security cameras, one for the front porch, one for the back. I texted Sloane the update, but kept it brief.

> Filed a report. Getting restraining order next. You and the kids are safe. I won't let her near you.

She responded a few minutes later:

> Thank you. For handling this the right way. I didn't want to have to bail you out of jail...

> That was one time Sloane. I can be a good boy.

162

I hoped that gave her at least a chuckle. Reading her words gave me something I hadn't felt in weeks - a sense of control. Hell, it was starting to finally feel like I was doing the right thing. Not just talking about change but proving it.

Baby steps, big guy.

I wasn't only protecting them from Angie. I was protecting them from the man I used to be.

So when Sloane continued our conversation, I was elated.

> Hey... I've been feeling off the past few days. Think something's going around the clinic. I'm exhausted.

> I'm sorry to hear that. What do you need?

> Would you mind taking the kids tonight? I took off from work and plan to stay home today. I need to rest. Maybe sleep without anyone knocking on the door.

> Of course. I'll pick them up after school, take care of dinner, Liam's soccer game, homework, bedtime routine, whatever they need.

> Thank you.

> And thanks again for handling the Angie thing. I've been sleeping better knowing you took it seriously.

> I meant what I said… I'll protect you and the kids no matter what.

> Let me know if you need anything else. I plan to bring extra security cameras to set up over there. I don't want her anywhere near you guys.

The private school pickup line felt longer than usual, or maybe that was the knot of nerves twisting in my chest. Both kids would be getting out around the same time, which had been a simple but major selling point when we picked that school; staggered release times were always inconvenient, and often impossible, for working parents.

I spotted Violet first, her hair bouncing as she waved and backpack slung half-open like always. Liam followed behind already in his soccer uniform, his cleats slapping against the pavement.

"Hey, you guys hungry?" I asked as they piled into the truck.

"Daddy, I am starving," Violet groaned dramatically. "I barely made it through math."

"Can we stop for sandwiches?" Liam asked, buckling his seatbelt.

"Done. Let's go."

Dinner was fast and easy. I let Violet pick the music in the truck while Liam scarfed down his sub in record time. The conversation drifted from school to YouTube to whatever new project Violet wanted help with. It felt… normal.

By the time we got to the soccer field, the sun had dipped low and the floodlights buzzed overhead. The air held that early autumn chill, enough to make me grateful I'd remembered to grab their jackets.

Sloane had always been the one to show up early, set out the folding chair, make sure Liam had his water bottle and extra socks. I used to brush it off, thinking it wasn't a big deal. But now, holding Violet's hand while we crossed the grass, it hit me. It was a big deal. Every tiny moment was a huge moment.

"Dad," Liam said, running up before the game started. "You'll stay the whole time, right?"

I placed my hand on his shoulder and met his eyes. "I won't miss a second."

He nodded and tried to act cool, but I saw it: relief.

Violet and I cheered loud. Maybe a little too loud. She stood on the bench, screaming her brother's name. I found myself yelling too, guilty of coaching from the sidelines, even though I didn't know a damned thing about soccer. Parents side-glanced at us, but I didn't care. Liam played hard. Scored once. Missed a second shot. But he smiled through all of it.

Once we got back home, I let them watch one episode of their favorite show while I folded laundry and prepped a small dessert. I texted Sloane a picture of Liam's muddy jersey with the caption:

> Victory stains. One goal, one near fight, three grass stains.

Her reply came a few minutes later:

> Thanks for being there tonight. It means more than you know.

Once they were tucked in, Violet with her favorite stuffed fox and Liam already snoring, I walked downstairs with Rufus in tow. The house was quiet except for Rufus's tail thumping against everything we walked by.

I got to the bottom of the stairs and I saw it. A folded piece of paper slid halfway under the front door. I picked it up knowing who it was from.

Same red lipstick, same scrawling letters.

> You think you can cut me out? You're still mine. They'll never see you the way I do. I've seen you at your worst.

I stared at it for a full minute while my heart pounded like a war drum.

This wasn't going to be over unless I started being more proactive. I snapped a photo and sent it to the number the police station gave me, the one they said to use if things escalated. A confirmation text buzzed back: a case number, cold and clinical, followed by a promise that someone would be in touch within twenty four to forty eight hours.

It wasn't fast enough. Not for the way Angie moved, but it was a start. I needed to stay ahead of her and gather all I could: every photo, every call, every spoiled breadcrumb she left behind.

Angie might not be the same as she was in my previous life, but like hell if I was going to let her ruin this life for me. I wasn't only protecting myself anymore. I was building a case strong enough to bury her.

I folded the note and slid it into my back pocket. Rufus sat near the door, ears up and eyes sharp, on high alert. He must've either heard her or smelled her perfume.

I checked the locks twice and turned off the porch light before I made my way towards the master bedroom. Sloane's door was cracked, soft light spilling into the hall. She had slipped out during the final countdown with the kids and given them brief kisses before heading to shower.

I stared at the soft outline of her door, what used to be our door, and I felt a pang as I raised my hand to tap.

"Yeah?" she asked, her voice tired but gentle.

I pushed the door open and stepped inside. She was propped up in bed, book in hand, a mug of tea on her nightstand. She looked pale. Her eyes were shadowed with fatigue.

"You okay?" I asked, hovering near the edge of the room.

She nodded. "Tired. Headache won't go away."

"Want anything? Water? Ice pack?"

"No, just sleep. I already took something earlier."

I hesitated before I crossed the room to sit on the edge of the bed. I didn't want to disturb her, but I hungered to be near her, hear her voice, see her face.

"The kids are finally down," I said. "Liam crushed it tonight. One goal and tons of attitude. Violet wants to paint her sneakers tomorrow."

Sloane gave me a faint smile, as if that was the exact update she'd needed.

"Thanks for being there, Levi."

"There's nowhere else I'd rather be. I'm glad I could help." We sat in silence for a moment before I asked, "What are you reading?"

"Oh, a romance. Why?"

"Just wondering. I, uh…" I started, then paused, rubbing my palms together. "There's something I've been meaning to ask you. Or maybe… bring up."

She glanced at me over the edge of her book. "Levi, if this is about trying any of the things in this book, I should warn you: this hero does Pilates, rescues dogs, and has the stamina of a Greek god. You cannot compete."

I blinked. "Okay, well, I was going to ask if you wanted tea, but now I feel personally attacked."

She smirked. "You walked into it."

"This is why men stick to talking about weather and traffic."

"Well, Levi... you are tragically real."

"Great. What every man wants to be: tragic and real."

She put the book down. "You were not going to ask me about tea. Stop delaying. What's wrong, Levi?" Her expression didn't change much, but I saw her posture shift, guarded, bracing for bad news.

"I know it's soon. I know things are still raw and I want to respect your space, your boundaries." I met her eyes. "But I'd like to come back. Home. Not only crash in the guest room occasionally, or help with the kids. I mean really move back in. Start again."

Sloane blinked as the silence between us stretched.

"Levi..." she whispered, "I don't know if I'm ready for that."

"I get it. I do. I'm not asking for an answer tonight or tomorrow. It's just... being here, helping with them, being around you..."

Her lips parted like she might speak, but no words came. A slow exhale.

"I'm not asking you to forget or forgive," I said. "Maybe... consider."

Finally, she nodded. "Let me sleep on it."

I stood and brushed her arm with my fingers before leaving. "Of course. Do you mind if I crash in the guest room again? So I can help with the morning routine?"

She nodded, "Sure. Goodnight, Levi." She gave me a tired smile and went back to reading her book. As I walked towards the stairs to head up to the guest room, I saw Rufus at the front door still. Staring. Guarding.

And in my back pocket, the note from Angie burned against my leg.

Chapter 18

The next morning I was up before the rest of the family, silent in the kitchen, preparing breakfast for the kids: eggs, toast, some fruit if they remembered to eat it.

Sloane hadn't said anything last night beyond *let me sleep on it* but her voice had lingered in my head. She'd sounded soft and uncertain. I replayed every syllable, every pause.

I heard the creak of the hallway floorboards and turned to see her step out of the bedroom, wrapped in a robe. Her face was still pale, even paler than it was last night.

"Hey," I said.

She didn't answer. Instead, she froze, eyes wide for a second, then bolted straight to the bathroom.

I dropped the spatula and followed her without thinking, but hesitated at the doorway. The sound of her retching sent a chill through me. Rufus whined behind my legs.

I knocked lightly. "Sloane?"

She didn't answer for a second, then managed, "I'm fine. I need... a minute."

I backed off, but didn't go far.

A few minutes later the door creaked open. Her face was damp with sweat and her hair stuck to her temples. But what stunned me wasn't her condition, it was the haunted look in her eyes: guilt, fear, and something I couldn't pin a name to. She walked past me and leaned against the hallway as I waited.

"I was going to tell you," she said, voice hoarse. "I needed to be sure."

I stared at her as my heart beat faster. "Tell me what?"

Her gaze found mine. "Levi... I'm pregnant."

Everything in me went still. The walls, the floor, my body, it all blurred as if the world had tilted on its axis. Gravity didn't exist.

Well, fuck me. Getting that vasectomy is pointless now.

I swallowed. "How far along...?"

She grimaced. "Weeks. I was hoping maybe it was the flu, but... I'm definitely pregnant."

"Weeks," I repeated. "Are you sure?"

"Yeah, Levi. I'm sure. After the awful fight we had over you missing Liam's birthday party? I think it was after that fight... that must've been when it happened."

Our last toxic rage fuck.

How in the hell am I this fucking stupid? Obviously, she was already pregnant by the time I came back in this life.

I tried to defend myself for failing to do the mental math: I was operating off of twelve year old memories from a stressful time of my previous life; I was worried about the impending pandemic; I was focused on groveling my way back into Sloane's life; then Angie had turned into a fucking creepy, ever-present, boogeyman. It was not an exaggeration to say that I'd had a lot on my mind.

But still... I felt like the biggest fucking idiot on earth in that moment.

I nodded as her words squeezed the air from my lungs. I struggled with what to say next, but it was my wife who broke the silence: my beautiful, snarky, sarcastic wife.

"We'd always been trying for a third," she said with an irreverent smirk.

I laughed because it was true. We'd dreamed of a big, loud house filled with little feet and crayon-covered walls. We never used condoms because... well, between the struggle to conceive and our shared hope, it had never seemed necessary. And now? Now it felt like another thread tangled in the knot I'd created.

I ran a hand through my hair as my guilt crushed me. "Yeah, a third and a fourth and a fifth... we dreamed big."

She didn't say anything as she stared at a fixed spot on the wall, arms wrapped tightly around her middle as if she were already protecting the baby.

While I stared at her, memories from my previous life assaulted me. How our divorce had dragged out because of this exact pregnancy. How the virus ravaged the country that winter, killing hundreds of thousands before Christmas. How Sloane had miscarried in a hospital bed, alone, while her sister stayed home with the kids.

And what was the Old Me doing? Oh, he was down in Key West, trying and failing to keep his development project together. He'd chosen to chase money instead of hold Sloane's hand. The entire country had been shut down and quarantined, so the Old Me couldn't have driven home to Sloane if he'd wanted to. Which he didn't. He was too busy fucking Angie, lying to himself that he could drown his self-hatred between her legs.

I let out a stuttering breath. "Fuck me, Sloane. I feel like an idiot for not connecting the dots sooner. If I'd slowed down. If I'd been paying closer attention..."

She glanced at me, the smirk on her face still there. "If you'd done emotional yoga sooner?"

"Yeah, if only I had."

Sloane's breathing steadied. She didn't see me spiraling, but I felt the clock ticking faster than I wanted it to.

I refused to lose sight of what the Old Me had been too blind to see. This time, I would not lose Violet or Liam. I would not lose Sloane. I would not lose this baby. Not again.

"Okay," I said.

Sloane blinked and her wry smirk turned into a look of shock. "Okay? That's it?"

"No," I said as I stepped closer to her. "It's not just okay. It's everything. And if you'll let me, I will be here for every second of it. The morning sickness, the cravings, the uncertainty, the fear. All of it."

Tears welled in her eyes. "Are you sure?"

"Absolutely. You and the kids are my everything Sloane. This new addition... this doesn't change that. If anything, it reminds me how much I still want this. All of it. Us."

Her bottom lip trembled and she looked away.

"This wasn't how it was supposed to happen," she whispered.

"I know," I said. I placed my hand, gently, on her shoulder. "But maybe this is how it needs to happen. I know this isn't perfect, but fate is real." And I felt that deep in my core as I stood there with her, being granted this second chance to be at her side.

She let out a shaky breath and wiped under her eyes. "God, Levi... you screw up everything with fireworks, but then show back up like some reformed Hallmark husband."

"I'm still working on the Hallmark part. I haven't figured out how to chop firewood in slow motion while wearing a flannel. Yet."

That earned me the smallest, most precious snort.

I saw the relief hit her then. "About last night," she said. "I was going to say yes. To you moving back in. Not because I need help or need your money. But because it will be good for the kids. And maybe... good for us."

Fuck, I love her.

I didn't hesitate. I reached for her, pulled her into my arms, hugged her. "Okay, my love. I am a slave to your whims. Tell me what you need and I'll be there."

Tears clung to her lashes and soaked my shirt, her voice shaky as she said, "Levi, I don't know if I can do this, if I can ever forgive you... but I miss you. Goddamn, I miss you."

That was all it took. My lips found her cheeks, her jaw, the corners of her eyes where tears had streaked like falling stars. The faint scent of mint on her breath told me she had brushed her teeth despite battling the nausea that tore up her insides. Even in her weakest moments she held herself together, refusing to be seen as unkempt or vulnerable.

But in that moment? She lowered her walls, invited me to see her, and let me in. For the first time since I had woken in this new life, it wasn't simply me chasing Sloane and groveling before her. She chose to open her arms and ask for me.

It wrecked me, how much I missed her. To think of all the intimacy I'd thrown away by chasing validation in the wrong arms sickened me.

"Sloane," I managed in a guttural whisper. Then the following words tumbled out of me, desperate and bare. "I want to kiss away your pain I've caused. I adore you, cherish you, desire you, admire you." My breathing quickened and shook, bursting with things I should have told her years ago. "I used to want control. I thought I needed it. But now... all I want is to surrender. To you. Completely."

My thumb traced the curve of her jaw as I turned her face to me.

She startled, flinching enough for me to pull back. "Levi."

"Fuck, I'm sorry, Sloane," I said. *Did I say too much?*

She shook her head, her eyes shining. "No. I... I want you, too."

Those simple words broke my resolve and we met each other halfway. Our mouths collided with a hunger that bordered on starvation. My tongue brushed against hers, exploring at first, then deeper, more urgent as she leaned into me. Her body pressed against mine. The soft gasp that escaped her lips, followed by a quiet, aching moan, ignited something primal in me. It wasn't only lust. It was need, raw and tangled in regret, in longing, in everything we'd lost and everything we still might have a chance to reclaim.

Her fingers curled into my shirt, clutching me like she was afraid I'd vanish if she let go. I felt her tremble from the kiss that wasn't a kiss; it was a reckoning. Betrayal and silence squeezed into the heat between us.

I ran my hands along her shoulders and back, relishing and remembering her curves. She let me in, if only for this moment, and I refused to take it for granted.

She broke the kiss first, breathing hard, my forehead resting against hers. Her voice was barely above a whisper. "Goddammit, Levi. I don't know how to forgive you."

My throat tightened. "Then don't. Not yet. First, let me try to be worth forgiving." I brought my hand to her neck and my fingers felt her pulse quicken. Her skin was warm, flushed.

She didn't pull away as she said, "I see your ego still has no limits."

"Only because I know you were made for me, as I was made for you. I want you, Sloane. I want you trembling and shaking beneath me as I worship your body with my tongue."

I felt her shiver at my words.

"But then there's the darker part of me that wants to tie you up and fill you with my cum until you can taste it."

When I kissed her again, it was rougher. Intentional. Both silent apology and carnal promise wrapped in every motion.

Her lips parted beneath mine. The heat between us simmered, then surged. My hands slid beneath the hem of her robe, feeling the familiar terrain of her waist, her ribs, the delicate rise of her back as she arched into me.

"Sloane," I whispered between kisses, "I'll fuck you so hard, your knees will stay weak for weeks."

"Oh, fuck, Levi." She let out a breath that was half-sigh, half-moan.

"Hopefully, you'll say that too." I winked at her and guided her toward the bedroom as she laughed. I closed the door behind us and moved her to the bed.

The backs of her knees hit the edge and she sat, drawing me down with her. She reached for my shirt, her fingers trembling as she peeled it over my head. I caught her wrist and held her. Not to stop her, but to anchor her.

My next words came out tight, strained even to my own ears, but I needed her to hear them. "This is your choice. You need to be sure."

"I want this," she whispered. "I want you… don't disappear on me again. Don't make me regret this."

"I won't," I breathed, kissing her knuckles before guiding her hand to my chest. "I'm right here. I'm not going anywhere."

Our clothes came off in hurried motions. There was hunger, yes, but it was still laced with a desperate and anxious grief.

She felt familiar and sacred. How she gasped when my mouth moved down her collarbone then past her breasts, how her fingers tangled in my hair as I kissed her hips, how her thighs trembled when I settled between them. All of it tethered me to that moment.

"Levi, you don't have to." Her voice was gentle, but there was a tremor in it, a vulnerability that hit me harder than anything else.

I kissed the crease of her inner thigh with a tender slowness. "I want to."

Her breath caught and I felt her hesitate. Despite our previous coupling on the couch a few nights past, a part of her still braced for disappointment; for the familiar letdown.

The Old Me had been convinced of his sexual prowess and consumed by his need to remain in control and dominant. He had no desire, or even capability, to provide the kind of thoughtful devotion Sloane needed. He was a child pretending to be a man; a man who understood nothing of love.

He had been so focused on his own ego, his own desires, that he'd failed to see how much Sloane had given and how much she deserved to be worshipped. He'd ignored the drawer full of toys she kept hidden as a quiet reminder of the nights he'd had been absent, both physically and emotionally. So many nights the Old Me had chosen to chase empty dreams rather than satisfy her… to ignore her needs as a partner.

And that knowledge gutted me. The Old Me had made her feel invisible, as if her desires were inconvenient and her longing for connection was too much. When really, he was the one who wasn't enough for her.

Fuck that guy.

As I rested my forehead against her skin I whispered, "I want to please you, Sloane." I meant it. With every part of me that had finally woken up. "Can we use one of your toys?"

Her eyes widened at that, laced with disbelief. "Wait, what?"

I nodded toward the nightstand. "The toys I used to be jealous of. Let's use one."

"But... you always said it was demeaning."

I kissed the inside of her thigh, "Yeah, and I was a fool. A very insecure fool who was too wrapped up in proving something to care about what *you* liked."

She didn't move as she stared at me, caught between confusion and caution.

So, I stood and walked to the nightstand myself.

"Levi, wait," she said, panicked. "Really, it's okay."

But I didn't stop. I opened the drawer and stared at the small collection she kept tucked away. A low whistle escaped me. "Well, fuck me, Sloane. I've seen a smaller inventory at boutique shops."

Behind me, she groaned. "Oh god..."

I turned, grinning, and held up a sleek silver one like it was a relic. "Is this battery-operated or possessed? Be honest."

"Levi." Her voice was sharp, but I caught the flicker of a smile beneath her mortified expression. "Put that down."

"Both. Got it." I nodded solemnly, as if conducting a serious study. Then I picked up something that looked like a rose. "What does *this* do? Pollinate?"

Sloane's face flushed deep with embarrassment. She reached for it as she said, "You really shouldn't-"

But I held it out of her grasp with a crooked grin. "Uh-uh. Now, I have to know. Is this decorative or weaponized?"

She failed to suppress a smile as she said, "You're insufferable."

"I know." I stepped closer to her, wrapped an arm around her waist, and gently pulled her down onto the bed with the toy caught between us. "I want to know everything about you. What makes you laugh, what breaks your heart. What brings you pleasure... and what doesn't." I looked into her eyes and lowered my voice. "I want to learn your body. Understand the notes it plays when it's touched right. When you feel seen."

Then I kissed her and she held nothing back. She melted into me.

"I'll only agree if you do this seriously," she said, eyes locked on mine.

I attempted to look as stoic as I could and said in the most deadpan voice I could manage, "Ma'am, I am always serious."

She rolled her eyes. "Goddammit, Levi. This is already embarrassing enough. The last time I asked for us to use a toy, we fought. Now you want to include them?"

"Consider me on the path to enlightenment," I said as I kissed her neck, "with your consent of course." I turned the toy over in my hands and curiosity lit up inside me. It was delicate, almost elegant in design; nothing like what my ego had imagined. It was... something meant to bring her joy.

Sloane let out a light and shy laugh as she pointed to the toy. "Here... this is how it turns on." Her finger brushed mine, and the toy came to life with a quiet hum. "It has a suction feature, and this button here changes the intensity."

I glanced at her, my voice teasing. "You could teach a class."

She blushed and gave a little shrug. "Well... when you're alone a lot, you learn what works."

That hit me hard. Not with jealousy over the toy, but a guilty ache that she'd been lonely in the first place.

How many nights did I leave her by herself?

I leaned in and kissed her temple as I held the toy between us. "Teach me, Sloane. I want to know what works. Let's do this together. Do you feel up for it?"

There was a pause. A few breaths of hesitation. Eventually, she nodded. "Only if you are willing to be an attentive student."

I kissed her forehead, then guided her to lie back against the pillows. I settled between her legs. My thoughts rushed out dark and unfiltered, "Attentive? My love, I want you coming all over me day in and day out. I want you drenched and soaking our sheets. If we need to use a toy to achieve that, then I will scour every brick and mortar and online store to ensure you are gushing all over my cock."

She trembled beneath me. The intensity of my words, my desires, and my intentions seemed to disarm and arouse her. I held her gaze as I brought the rose-shaped toy between us. A whimper escaped her lips. "Levi... oh, fuck."

"I crave you Sloane. I want you. Everything and anything about you. But if we do this, I want it to be about you. No shame. No hiding. You're beautiful when you're unguarded, Sloane. Let me earn the right to see that part of you."

Her eyes softened as she reached for my hand and guided my fingers over the toy. "It's... gentle. Meant for the clit. You don't have to... do much."

I met her eyes. "I want to take my time and watch you unravel for me. Can you do that, Sloane? Can you be a good girl and show me what has always been mine?"

I turned it on the lowest setting. A soft hum filled the quiet space between us, and I felt her chest rise with anticipation as her gaze heated.

Her legs parted wider, and I kissed her stomach. "That's my good girl. Tell me if you need me to stop," I whispered. I never took my gaze from her face. I wanted to watch her unravel, not only from pleasure, but from being *seen*.

Her lips parted in a soft gasp, and she reached out blindly, clutching at the sheets. "Levi... I don't know if I can," she said. Her voice trembled with the rawness of vulnerability. "It's still... weird. New."

"Sloane," I murmured, my fingertips tracing slow patterns along her hips. "Let go. You don't have to hold back. Not here. Not with me."

She looked at me and I knew she was trying to believe my words.

"You are art, Sloane. Every inch of you." I leaned in to kiss the space above her navel. "I'm here. If you want to stop, then tell me," I whispered. My hands traced lazy, reverent lines down her inner thighs. "Hell, Sloane, you have no idea what you do to me. My balls ache when I think of you. My cock twitches every time you are near me. I would die over and over again just for the chance to be near you."

A soft whimper tore from her lips, raw and unguarded. Whether it was from my words or the toy finally coaxing a response, I couldn't say. Her body responded in small, trembling pulses as her breath hitched in her throat.

I kissed her ribs, trailing upward, worshipping every delicious, beautiful curve. Her collarbone, delicate and exposed, begged for attention. I pressed my lips there, feeling her shiver beneath my touch. Finally, the place right beneath her ear, the spot that always drove her mad. I nipped gently, savoring the shudder that followed, a silent surrender to the moment.

Her voice came out in a surprised whisper, as if she were shocked to say, "I'm gonna... fuck, I'm gonna..."

"Sloane, eyes on me," I commanded, the words slipping out before I could stop them. I needed to see it, the way she came undone, how she let go. I wanted to witness the moment when she surrendered completely.

Her gaze met mine, and in that instant, I saw something break open in her both fragile and beautiful. Her release wasn't simply physical; it was everything she'd been holding back, everything she'd hidden from me. Her back arched, the tension in her body a silent plea, the tautness of her muscles trembling beneath my fingertips. I watched her unravel, piece by piece, as the toy pushed her to the brink and then beyond.

She had surrendered. She trusted me with a part of herself she'd kept buried for so long. In that moment, I wasn't just seeing her as a woman; I was seeing her heart laid bare, vulnerable, as she lowered the walls she'd built around herself.

Afterward, the waves ebbed from her body and her breathing gradually returned to rhythm. Her chest rose and fell like a settling tide and I held the silence with her, taking in what I'd learned.

"Good girl," I said with admiration in my voice. What she'd shown me had left me in awe of her, how she had opened herself to me and let me in. "You're incredible. You are so much more than I ever deserved."

She gave a shaky smile. Her eyes glistened with unshed tears. "You still couldn't give up control, huh?"

I couldn't stop the grin that spread across my face. "Still a smart ass ever after that? The toy didn't do its job well."

She rolled her eyes, but the corner of her mouth twitched fighting back a smile. "Don't push it. I usually use a few per night."

Surprise flickered through me as I glanced over at the open drawer. Curiosity tugged at the corner of my mouth as I reached for another. "Well shit, Sloane. In that case," I said, my voice dropping to a conspiratorial whisper, "let's use another."

Her laughter spilled out, light and joyfully breathless. "Oh god," she sighed. "I don't know if I can do it again with you."

"I'm pretty sure we can find something in this warehouse of yours."

"You've definitely changed," she whispered. Her voice held a mixture of surprise and something else I couldn't name.

My chest tightened as a lump formed in my throat, but I pushed it down to focus on her; on that moment with her. I reached for another toy, my hands steady but my thoughts scattered. "I am changing," I said.

"I know, Levi. I see it." She put her hand on her stomach. "My nausea is better."

"So an orgasm is the cure? Well, I can absolutely make sure that keeps happening."

I rifled through the drawer with mock seriousness. "Okay, this one's purple... and this one is ribbed?" I turned it over in my hand with a playful arch of my brow. "Do any of these come with a user manual or a 'how to not mess this up' guide?"

Sloane laughed again, freer now, as we settled on a toy together; something designed for deeper pleasure. An insertion toy. Her nervousness lingered, but she didn't retreat.

I looked up at her, slowing things down again. "Tell me if anything feels too much, okay? Because I'm flying blind here."

She nodded, fingers finding mine and squeezing gently before letting go.

I turned the toy on, again choosing the lowest setting. Its quiet vibration hummed between us as I slipped the tiniest tip of it inside her. She shifted slightly, her breath catching, anticipation coiling. I moved slowly, in and out of her opening, teasing the toy inside her with care. I never took my gaze from her face: how she parted her lips, fluttered her eyes, gasped each time I went slightly deeper.

"Good?" I whispered.

Her nod was barely there, but her voice, breathy and trembling, said, "Yes... good. Good boy. I am so close. I'm gonna..."

Just like before, her body responded as pleasure curled her toes, one hand gripped the sheets, the other dug her nails into my back. She was so close I could taste it. I adjusted the toy's setting higher and she gasped. She bucked her hips and arched her back, as her body trembled beneath the rhythm I kept. The soft gasps, low moans, and heavy breathing that escaped her were music to me, thickening my already swollen cock.

"Fuck me, Sloane. I might come from watching you."

I don't know if she heard me as the second orgasm took her. It wasn't just her sound that undid me; it was her face. I don't think I was ready for me to witness her in her full glory.

The realization that I must have been a lousy lover punched me as I watched her come down.

I have never made her come this fast or this hard.

I relished in all the little twitches of her body as I held her tightly.

"That was intense," she murmured and nuzzled closer.

I chuckled, brushing my fingers through her hair. "Sounds like I've got steep competition."

"Shh," she whispered. "I love it when you do it too."

"Glad to know I made the top contenders. I'll take bronze. Maybe silver."

"You're gold, you idiot," she murmured against my neck.

I pressed a kiss to her temple, then to her cheek. "Do you want more?"

She looked up at me with her sleepy eyes as she reached down to wrap her hand around my pulsing cock. "I want this."

"Your wish is my command." I entered her gently, as slowly as I could, fighting my every urge to thrust as deep and hard into her as possible. I cradled her body against mine and as we moved together, she curled into me as if she'd been waiting all this time for me to come home.

Her thighs trembled against mine as her breathing turned ragged.

"You okay?" I asked. My voice was rough. I was barely hanging on, my balls already tight.

"Yes... don't go slow."

Whatever restraint I still had was shattered in that moment, swept away by the whirlwind of her voice, her heat, her body, her trust. I held her tighter, kissed the slope of her shoulder, and thrusted into her with a desperate urgency, the rhythm fast and punishing. Her body yielded to every movement with breathless and ravenous need.

"I'm going to fuck an imprint of my cock into you."

Her nails dug into my shoulder, clinging to me as if she were drowning under the waves of pleasure. "Fuck me, Levi. Fuck me so hard that I think of your cock for days."

The sound of our skin meeting was overlaid by her whimpers, which turned into moans, which were punctuated by screams.

Ah, it's too much.

My hips ached as I thrusted mercilessly into her.

"Fuck, Sloane," I groaned against her neck, my lips dragging over the damp heat of her skin. "I won't last long."

"Don't care," she whimpered. "Come with me."

That was all it took.

Her body clenched tight around me and I lost it. My release hit hard, every muscle locked as I buried myself deep, a guttural sound ripping from my throat as if it had been imprisoned for years.

I held onto her, forehead pressed to her temple, arms curled around her. "Fuck," I breathed, "You've ruined me," Still inside her, still connected in every way that mattered. Her legs trembled around me as I murmured, "You're mine." My lips brushed her cheek. "And I'm yours." The words were not a command but a vow.

She let out a sound, something between a laugh and a sigh, then pulled me closer.

We stayed like that, entangled and trembling, our breathing uneven while our hearts thundered. Our sweat-slicked skin cooling as the intensity of the moment ebbed to leave only love in its wake.

Sloane let out a long, contented breath, her body heavy and boneless in my arms as she blinked up at me, eyes hazy with sleep. "I think I need... a nap."

I smiled, brushing a damp strand of hair off her forehead. "You've certainly earned it."

She was already drifting. I kissed her lips before I eased out of bed and pulled the blankets over her shoulders. She curled into them with a happy sound, like the warmth was permission to let go.

I stood there for a while watching her sleep. The softness in her features, the calm that had settled where stress used to live. I felt it too; a happiness I hadn't known in years.

I snuck a clean pair of sweats from the garage and headed quietly to the bathroom. The shower was quick, enough to wash off the sweat and to steady myself as the water ran over me.

Cold shower. Like a factory reset.

By the time I padded out, the house was already stirring. Liam was at the kitchen table, eyes glued to his phone. Violet sat cross-legged on the floor with colored pencils scattered around her like confetti.

"Morning," I said, ruffling Liam's hair as I passed.

He grunted in that half-asleep preteen way, barely glancing up. Violet gave me a beaming smile.

"Where's Mom?" she asked, looking around me.

"She's resting," I said. "She had a long night."

Violet wrinkled her nose. "Is she sick? Again?"

"No," I said as I grabbed eggs from the fridge. "She's tired. I told her we'd handle things this morning."

Liam looked up now, suspicious. "You made breakfast?"

"Don't look so shocked."

He smirked. "Last time you tried, the toaster caught fire."

"Unrelated incident," I muttered, cracking eggs into a bowl.

Violet giggled. "What are we having?"

"Scrambled eggs, toast, maybe fruit if it's not furry."

"Ewww," they said in unison.

"Oh, so you would prefer your fruit to be furry?"

"Nooo," they exclaimed together.

As the pan sizzled, the smell of butter and eggs started to fill the kitchen. The house remained quiet. Sloane was safely asleep and I was here: cooking, parenting, trying. Not for show. Not out of guilt. But because I was being given the chance to do things the right way.

I flipped the eggs with a bit of flair. Violet clapped.

"Oh, by the way... your mom's pregnant."

They both squealed in unison. I grinned. Small victories.

Chapter 19

Over the next few days, I stayed in the guest room, making myself useful to Sloane as she struggled with nausea. I kept her comfortable, brought her water, and did everything I could to help ease her discomfort. The kids didn't ask questions, they simply adapted with a resiliency that only the young possess.

I called the rental company to cancel my lease. There was no hesitation, no second thoughts. My home was wherever Sloane was.

In the meantime, I promised her I'd slip back into the guest room one morning this week before the kids woke up. We didn't want to confuse them. Or worse, give them hope we couldn't live up to. The thought hurt, but I understood it. We were rebuilding trust brick by brick, not rushing it. Not pretending everything was fixed just because we remembered how to touch each other.

It was a few days after Sloane had told me she was pregnant when I found the medication.

It was early in the morning, still a few hours before the rest of the family would wake. I was in the kitchen. I set a pot of coffee to brew, letting the rich scent fill the kitchen. I prepped Sloane's mug the way she liked it then set it beside the kettle with a peppermint tea bag; in case her stomach felt unsettled when she woke up.

The small things mattered now. They always had, but the Old Me had been too selfish to notice before.

I grabbed a sticky note and scribbled a quick message:

Drink some tea if you need it. Text me if you're craving anything. Anything at all. I mean it. - L

I stuck it to the cabinet where she'd definitely see it.

Looking over to grab the creamer, something caught my eye. Tucked just behind it, barely visible, was a prescription bottle. My hand froze mid-reach.

It wasn't mine and it definitely hadn't been there before their trip to the amusement park.

I slid it out from its hiding spot, the plastic cool against my fingers, and turned it in my palm. Alprazolam. The name didn't register.

Curious, and already feeling the stirrings of unease, I pulled out my phone and searched it.

'Used to treat acute panic attacks and generalized anxiety disorder.'

My stomach dropped. I looked again at the label, my eyes zoning in on the name printed across it. *Sloane Shaw.*

The kitchen blurred for a moment, and the ground tilted. I braced myself with a hand on the counter, trying to stop the sudden pounding in my chest. The bottle in my hand weighed a hundred pounds.

Oh fuck Sloane.

Anxiety coiled in my chest, a steel band tightening with each breath. Fuck, she'd never told me. Not about this. Not about the panic attacks. Not about needing medication just to function.

While I'd been busy chasing my guilt and playing the role of the man trying to fix what he broke, she had been surviving in her way. Quietly. Secretly.

Damn it Sloane.

I scanned the warnings. Dosage. Then down to the bottom where a line caught my eye.

'Not recommended for individuals who are pregnant or may become pregnant.'

I stood there, the hum of the refrigerator suddenly deafening, and for a second, I forgot how to breathe. My eyes locked on the sentence like it was written in fire. My pulse roared in my ears, my heart stopped as I read it again and again.

Finally my brain scrambled, latching onto panic and possibility. Was she...? Had she... been taking this while unknowingly pregnant? The implications twisted like a screw.

How long had she been on this? Was this why she couldn't sleep? Why she looked so tired all the time? The dark circles, the sudden long showers, the silences?

How many times had I missed this? Misread her? Assumed she was just "moody" or "withholding," when really she'd been hurting?

Guilt suffocated me. She had been trying to tell me how much she was drowning. Worse, I convinced myself that things were getting better. I had ignored the years of negligence for a few good days, some shared laughter, and two nights of intimacy thinking it could undo the war still raging inside her.

I let my own selfish hope drown out the truth: she was still struggling and she had been for a long time.

Who knows how long she had been fighting panic attacks alone. Her nights of taking medication hidden behind a creamer bottle, hidden from me because I hadn't been a person she could trust.

Fuck me. I really am fucking worthless.

I hadn't been a safe place for her to bring her pain and she had to stop now knowing she was pregnant.

I made a silent vow to myself as I placed the bottle back exactly where I found it with a trembling hand. I didn't want her to know I'd seen it. Not yet.

Sloane, I will do better. I promise to be your safe place.

I made a plan to talk to her about it. I had to think of a way to explain how I wasn't snooping, and that I wanted to support her regardless of what she was going through. Therapy could be a good start. Right. Therapy.

Regardless of how hurt I felt for her, I knew this meant holding the truth of who she'd become in my absence and that I needed to learn how to stand beside her in it. If things went well, maybe I would earn the right to be the person she could leave her prescription bottle in plain sight of.

The walk out of the kitchen felt heavy. But clarity, I was learning, always came with that type of weight.

Later that morning, I met with the agent for the rental as we did our final walkthrough. The move out was easy. I gathered my clothes and threw a handful of things into my one suitcase. I made sure to snap some photos that I'd left the place in good standing, everything neat, no damage aside from the broken mirror. The agent promised me my deposit back, and I knew I'd played my part in fulfilling the terms.

After the walkthrough, I planned in my truck. Worried for Sloane, I placed an order for N95 masks using the company card. Along with them, I added boxes of emergency medical supplies, toilet paper, gloves, antiseptics, and a few pregnancy items I knew she would need, like a body pillow and ginger chews.

Staring at the list, it felt excessive. Maybe even paranoid. But the last thing I wanted was to be caught unprepared when it came to Sloane and the kids. I knew that the pandemic was going to be awful, but I wasn't sure how different things were going to be with me in the picture this time. This was the beginning of a dark time, and I wanted to be the one who had thought ahead for once.

For the first time in a long while, I wasn't acting on impulse or guilt. I was acting to protect something. Even if I didn't know whether I still had the right to do so.

Coming home that night, a quiet sense of peace settled into my bones, as if the weight I'd been carrying for so long was finally lifting. While I subtly moved more of my things into the guest room, I felt a stab pang of uncertainty. I didn't want to assume I had the right to stay in the master with her. Not yet.

The bed in the guest room was cold, but I welcomed it. It was a reminder that, right now, I had to earn my place beside Sloane back.

The next few days, Sloane barely moved from the couch. She took time off from work to rest, the blanket tucked up to her chin, her cheeks flushed with the fatigue only early pregnancy could bring. She tried to reassure me it was just the usual nausea and exhaustion, but I could see it wearing on her; she was pale, her eyes dulled at the edges.

I brought over peppermint tea and the ginger candies she liked, kneeling beside her as Rufus settled by her feet with a huff.

"You don't have to hover," she murmured in a groggy voice.

"Too late," I said with a smile. I brushed a stray curl from her temple. "I'm officially a hoverer."

She gave a tired smile and leaned her head against the cushion again. I kissed her forehead and stood to adjust the curtains...

And I froze.

A figure stood across the street, half-shadowed behind the skeletal frame of a dying tree. I knew it was her by the tilt of her head, the way she stood too still, too long. Watching. Waiting. My chest tightened with a bubbling anger.

Fuck you, Angie. You aren't getting to Sloane. Not when she is like this. Not ever.

I glanced over at Rufus. His ears were perked but he didn't bark. When I looked out again, she was gone.

Fuck me, am I seeing things now?

No, she was there. My gut knew full well she had been. That cold crawl down my back and the wrongness in the air?

"Everything okay?" Sloane asked.

I forced a grin, even though my pulse still thundered in my ears. "Yeah. Everything is going to be okay."

I didn't lie to her. In that moment, I believed that everything *was* going to be okay. I refused to allow anything to happen to my family, to my Sloane. My thoughts were centralized on one thing: *You are mine to protect.*

Later that night, after I finally coaxed Sloane into bed and she drifted into a restless sleep, I sat in the kitchen and did my deep breathing exercises.

Silence clawed at me, wrapping its fingers around my throat as panic curled in my chest. *Could I really protect my family?* A vicious, gnawing fear ate at me.

It wasn't just about me anymore. I could fight Angie on my terms, drag her into the light and tear her apart if I had to. But I knew the cost of doing that. That kind of war would leave shrapnel in everything I'd tried to mend with Sloane and the kids. One wrong move, and it could all come crashing down.

Fuck, maybe I need to take one of Sloane's pills for my anxiety.

The thought had me chuckling as I secured the house and headed for bed. I laid there, eyes staring at the ceiling, heart thudding in my chest, unsure if sleep would ever come.

Chapter 20

The nightmare hit around 3 a.m.

I was standing in a delivery room, but there was no sound. Sloane was screaming with no voice. Nurses moved in slow motion. I looked down and my hands were covered in blood.

When I woke up, drenched in sweat and gasping for air, I thought I was still dreaming. Rufus had his chin on the bed, watching me, his big brown eyes like anchors to reality as he made a little huff noise.

"Hey boy. Thanks for watching over me."

I sat on the edge of the bed and put my palms over my face as I tried to stop the tremble in my fingers. This wasn't sustainable. I needed an outlet. Somewhere for the truth to go that wouldn't hurt her.

That morning, I bought a leather-bound journal. I didn't write anything poetic, only the facts. The series of events. The details I didn't want to forget.

Day 47. Angie is watching. I'm losing sleep. Sloane is pregnant. I remember when the miscarriage happens. I'll fix it this time. I have to.

I slammed the cover shut and hid it in the bottom drawer beneath my undershirts.

The next few days blurred into a quiet rhythm. I focused on Sloane, meals, handling the kids, reminding her of vitamins, long walks with Rufus when she needed space. She was tired but stable, her body adjusting in small, brave ways. Every time she smiled through the nausea or let her hand rest on her belly, I felt both awe and guilt gnawing at me.

I didn't tell her about Angie or how her shadow had reappeared at least three more times: once near the grocery store, once at the kid's school pickup, and again outside the job site as I reviewed plans with Jose. That fucking psycho stayed distant, making sure to show me that she was always watching.

Truthfully, it felt like it was hard to pin anything on her. She never approached. That was the part that made it worse because I knew she wanted me to wonder when she'd get closer.

Each time I saw her, I wrote it down in the journal. I kept it updated, tucked in the dresser drawer, pages swelling with inked desperation. I snapped pictures of her with my phone anytime I could.

Day 53. Angie was at the gas station across from the clinic. She didn't even look away when I saw her.

Day 54. Angie was in the same grocery store, a few aisles down. I heard her singing.

At night, my panic attacks were subtle, well-disguised, neatly timed. If I felt it building, I excused myself and pretended I had a call to take or needed to walk Rufus.

And Rufus... he knew. I swear he did. That dog barely left my side. Slept by the front door guarding it and watched the windows; alert and expecting. He was the best dog in the whole goddamn world.

It didn't help that the news was ramping up every day, inching us closer to the shutdown I knew was coming. First it was whispers, then footage, hospitals in chaos, people collapsing in the streets, body bags stacked outside clinics like sandbags before a flood. Radio stations called it a scare tactic, a giant hoax that we needed to squash. Despite all the negativity, I listened, knowing the truth of what was to come.

I almost hit my breaking point in the middle of one of Liam's soccer games.

I had been sleeping and eating less, taking care of the household and supporting Sloane more. Honestly, I don't know how my woman fucking did it, because I was tapped out. I admired her strength to have managed this for so long and I grit my teeth in silence. I had no right to complain when she had done this for *years*.

On this particular day, Sloane came to watch Liam play. Her energy was still low but fuck me, she was as gorgeous as ever. She sat on the bleachers in one of my old hoodies, legs tucked beneath her, a thermos of peppermint tea clutched in her hands. Her hair was in a messy bun, loose strands teased by the breeze. Despite the fatigue in her face, the sight of her still robbed my breath.

Hell, that hoodie hugged her in all the right places. I didn't mean to stare, but I did.

I made my way up beside her, leaned in close enough that only she could hear. "Pretty sure that hoodie was mine," I murmured as my gaze slid down to the curve of her ass. "But you certainly wear it better. I might have to let you keep it."

She glanced at me, her cheeks flushing a pretty pink, then rolled her eyes. I caught the ghost of a smile tugging at her lips. "Levi," she warned under her breath, "everything you own is mine."

"Well hell, Sloane. I'm simply admiring the view, but you still have to put me in my place like that?"

"I've got a leash and collar waiting for you at home if you keep this up."

My balls tightened at the thought of her leashing me, commanding me, praising me. A growl curled in my chest. "We could leave the kids here. They're old enough."

She burst out laughing, her head falling slightly against my shoulder. "Levi!"

That laugh? I'd live a hundred lifetimes just to hear it again.

These were the kind of moments I used to take for granted. Now, it felt like a privilege to sit beside her, to earn a blush, a smile, or hell, a joke at my expense.

I looked out at the field where kids ran in uneven formations, limbs too long for their coordination then back at her.

"Thanks for coming out today," I said, quieter now, meaning every word. "I know it wasn't easy."

She didn't look at me but her voice was steady. "I wanted to try. Pregnancy or not, I don't want to miss any games."

My chest tightened with something fierce and fragile all at once. I didn't deserve her, but I loved everything about her. She was my eternity.

Then, Violet came bounding up beside us, face painted in smudged pink and blue. "Bathrooms are so gross," she announced with her usual flair.

I chuckled and gave her a hug. "Next time, stick with the house."

"Yeah, right." She scoffed like a mini version of her mother. She was already hopping with energy, gearing up to scream every time her brother kicked the ball.

I stood up behind them, arms folded, eyes flicking between the field, the bleachers, and the creeping sky above. Dark clouds were rolling in fast.

Then I saw her.

Third row on the opposing team's side, sitting alone on the end of the bleachers. She wore a baseball cap and sunglasses, but I'd know that posture anywhere, one slender leg crossed over the other, head tilted slightly, bored smile tugging at her garishly red mouth.

My stomach dropped. She looked directly at me, the edge of her lip twitching like she was daring me to react.

Sloane turned to me, sensing my tension. "You good?" Her hazel eyes squinted in the fading sun.

"Yeah," I lied. "Just looking at those storm clouds. Hoping we don't get rained out."

She nodded and looked back toward the field.

I pretended to do the same, though my pulse beat too loud in my ears. Angie was still there but now she wasn't watching me. Her gaze slid with subtle precision from my son's sweat-slicked sprint down the field to my daughter's bouncing form beside me. It was chilling. Then Angie smiled. A full, slow, twisted smile.

Oh fuck no.

My vision swam with rage and fear, but I didn't move. She wasn't doing anything technically, but this level of stalking and obsession had to count for something with the police.

Fuck, this promise to Sloane is going to get us killed. I want to bury her myself.

My hand tightened around my phone. I slid it out and snapped a quick picture, pretending to scroll through photos. With the distance and the lighting, I knew it'd be hard to prove... but it was something.

Maybe it wouldn't hold up in court, but I'd be damned if I didn't document every moment of her intrusion that I could.

I felt Sloane watching me from the corner of her eye. She didn't say anything. Probably thought I was being one of those proud dads grabbing a photo of their kids mid-game and I let her think that. I didn't want to crack the fragile peace of this moment with the fire clawing at my gut.

"I'm gonna head down to meet the boy," I said. "You good here?"

She took a sip from her thermos then curled tighter into my old hoodie. "Yeah. I've got tea and comfort. What could possibly go wrong?"

Everything.

I smiled. "That's the spirit."

When the final whistle blew and the crowd erupted, Liam jogged toward me: cheeks flushed, sweat-matted hair wild, grin wide. I clapped him on the back and did my best to channel normalcy.

"Hell of a hustle out there, bud. Elite stuff, champ."

His eyes flicked to the stands, searching. "Did Mom see it?"

I nodded, nudging him with my elbow. "She did. Looked like she was gonna toss that thermos in the air."

He laughed, pride blooming across his face. I kept my voice light, playful but I made damn sure my body stayed between my family and the stands.

By the time the game was over, though, Angie was gone.

I didn't say anything to Sloane. What could I say? That the woman I'd wrecked our life for was now orbiting us like a ghost, slipping in and out of view, leaving dread in her wake?

No. Not yet. Instead, I wrote it down.

Day 57. She was at the game. Watching Violet and Liam. Watching me. Smiling like we shared a secret no one else knew.

With a shaking hand, I underlined the last part twice.

Chapter 21

Sloane and I hadn't connected for a few nights, which made sense with everything going on. Due to her pregnancy and my own stress of the looming pandemic and constant presence of Angie, a distance formed between us, a lingering exhaustion that we couldn't bridge.

It wasn't just reality that wore me down; it was the nightmares. Nightly nightmares that tore through me without mercy, and I was almost thankful I'd stayed in the guest room. They came for me with relentless cruelty. Each one left me gasping for air, my heart thundering against my chest, each one a smothering blanket when I'd wake. Every time I closed my eyes, I saw Angie and Sloane's faces; the psycho's malignant smile and my wife's silent scream.

Sweat clung to my skin as I turned in bed, my body heavy with the weight of the night's haunting images. I reached for my phone, the screen lighting up in the dark room.

Ten missed calls. My stomach dropped as I scrolled through the call log.

Better screenshot this, too. One more log to throw on Angie's pyre.

The case was moving forward, and I already had a mountain of evidence to bury Angie under. Every call, every message, every note she left behind was a twist of the noose tightening around her neck.

I clenched my jaw, anger simmering within me. The idea of her voice creeping into my life again, like some kind of infection, made my skin crawl. She thought she still had power over me. She thought she could still manipulate, control, or break me.

I had promised Sloane I would do this the right way and I meant it... otherwise that bitch would be in a concrete tomb.

Angie's name flashed, the number I'd deliberately unblocked at the detective's recommendation. I didn't want to answer it, but I did.

The voice that wormed through sounded unhinged and calculating. "You really think you can fix this, baby?"

I'm not answering this crazy bitch.

I pressed record on my phone with the new app I'd installed.

She continued on unaware. "You don't get it, baby. She's not coming back to you. She won't. You know why, right? You already lost her. And you... you're mine always." She let loose a low laugh, a sound I once thought was sultry and sexy.

Bile rose in my throat as she said, "You think you can fight this, but you can't. You need me." She paused, breathing into the phone. "If you won't talk to me, then I'll go to Sloane."

Her words sliced into me as Sloane's face flashed in my mind. I clenched my fists, the simmering anger rising to a boiling rage. "Leave Sloane out of this Angie. All of this needs to stop."

Her next words sounded amused. "Oh, Levi... I'm not going to stop." She was enjoying my discomfort, feeding on it. "I have been patient, you know. But you don't seem to understand something, baby. You can't fix this. The damage is done."

I heard her breathing more heavily into the phone and I hoped that if I kept her talking for long enough she would say something incriminating, maybe threaten me or Sloane. Hell, she might be crazy enough to threaten my kids.

Come on you fucking psycho. Give me something more to send to the police.

She said, "And don't think I don't know what's coming next, baby. The world is about to fall apart. Your precious little business, everything you've worked for? The pandemic is going to ruin you, ruin everything. It's going to be chaos, Levi."

My heart sank as panic twisted my insides.

Angie sounded more manic and crazed, her words coming out in a rush. "I could destroy you. Everything you've worked for? Everything you've rebuilt? All I have to do is tell Sloane everything about us. *Everything*, Levi. Do you understand? And I will tell her. Make no mistake, baby. You can't outrun me. Not now. Not ever."

Then she hung up.

I didn't feel the impact of the floor when I dropped to my knees. I was shaking, my entire body trembling as the rage, guilt, shame and helplessness consumed me.

There wasn't anything Angie could tell Sloane that I hadn't already told her, so her threats were hollow. But it was the venom in which she delivered them. The crazed hostility.

I can't let that psycho get anywhere near my Sloane.

I felt my resolve waver... but I stood up regardless, my palms slick with sweat. I pulled up the recording on my phone and sent it to the number the detective had given me. The weight of everything I was carrying felt crushing, but I focused on the evidence. It was all about the evidence now.

Angie had tipped her hand too much this time. She was unraveling. I could practically see her deranged grin through the phone. She would only be seen as a raving lunatic to the police, desperate and unhinged. Between the photos I'd managed to snap of her appearing throughout my life and this recording, I had enough to expose her for the psycho she was.

The next day, the shutdown happened faster than I'd anticipated.

The news outlets had been buzzing for weeks, rumors of a viral outbreak in China, scattered reports of hospitals overwhelmed with the sick. But when the announcement finally came, it rushed through like a tidal wave. Everything shifted in an instant.

I was sitting in my truck outside the office when the alert came through. A breaking news banner flashing across my phone, the bright red letters leaping out at me.

PRESIDENTIAL ADDRESS: NATIONAL EMERGENCY DECLARATION.

I clicked the video, and my stomach twisted as the familiar face of the president appeared on the screen. He was flanked by experts, doctors, scientists, advisors, each of them with grim faces, holding back the severity of the situation as best they could. But their eyes told a different story.

The president spoke first, his voice steady but tense, laced with the weight of the moment.

"My fellow Americans. Today I am announcing the activation of a nationwide lockdown in response to the spread of a dangerous respiratory virus. After consulting with our nation's top health experts, we have come to the difficult conclusion that these measures are necessary to protect our lives and the lives of our loved ones."

Despite knowing this was coming, it still felt surreal.

"Starting tomorrow, all non-essential businesses will be closed. All public gatherings of more than ten people are now prohibited. Our health officials are strongly urging everyone to stay home. This virus spreads quickly, and the only way to mitigate its effects is through social distancing."

The air in my truck felt suffocating as I processed the gravity of it. The incoming economic collapse, the forced isolation, and the immediate halt to everything that kept the world spinning. Then came the directive that made the entire situation real for me.

"Masks are recommended for anyone entering stores or public spaces. I cannot stress this enough: we are all in this together, and this is our chance to prevent a crisis from becoming a catastrophe."

The man's voice cracked as he said it. The shutdown wasn't a temporary inconvenience: it was a total reset. A forced pause on everything we had known, everything we had taken for granted.

"Please," the president added, "stay home as much as possible. For your safety and the safety of your loved ones, remain inside. We will get through this, but only if we act quickly and responsibly."

I sat there for a long time, staring at the screen long after the address ended, the echo of his words lingering in my mind: *stay home, wear masks, don't go out unless necessary.* I thought about Sloane, about the kids, and about the business.

The world was shutting down and no one had any idea how long it would last except me.

I forced myself to focus. Things were about to change. And they were about to change fast.

Chapter 22

Later that day, the sky was overcast as I pulled into the school parking lot. The presidential announcement was still rattling through my mind. The line of parents in the pickup line stretched farther than usual, cars idling, faces drawn with confusion and fear. Teachers and staff rushed to hand out papers, calling out names, ushering kids into vehicles as if we were evacuating for a hurricane rather than just going home.

But this was a storm. Just a different kind.

Violet was the first to spot me. Her tiny frame seemed even smaller under her huge backpack, which sagged with hastily packed folders and books. She wasn't smiling. Her mouth was pinched tight, and her eyes were glassy as they darted around. I knew she was trying to make sense of the senseless chaos her school had erupted into.

Liam trailed behind her, earbuds tangled in his hand, face pale and distant. He didn't even try to act cool like he usually did. Just climbed into the passenger seat silently while Violet buckled into the back.

"Hey, guys," I said as I put the truck into drive. "How was school?"

"Scary," Violet said without hesitation. "They made us clean everything. They said we weren't coming back for a long time. Like, weeks."

Liam snorted, a bitter sound for someone so young. "They said maybe after winter break, but they were lying. Mr. Caldwell looked really freaked out. He kept staring at his phone during class."

I glanced at them through the rearview mirror and kept my voice calm. "It's going to be okay. You'll do school from home for a while. Your teachers will send stuff online, and I'll help where I can."

Violet looked like she might cry. "But I don't want to stay home. What about art class? And Mrs. Ortega said we might not have our recital."

I felt my chest tighten. I wanted to fix it. To promise them this was temporary... but I knew better. I'd lived through this pandemic once already.

"I know it sucks, sweetheart," I said. "But we'll make the best of it, okay? We'll do projects at home. I'll set up a space just for you guys to work. You'll still talk to your friends. You'll see."

Liam scoffed, not mean, just tired. "Dad, it's not going to be the same. They're saying people are dying. Mom's pregnant. What if she gets sick?"

That blasted the wind right out of me. I gripped the steering wheel tighter and chose my words carefully. "She is being careful. We are all going to be careful. That's why they're sending everyone home... to keep you and her safe. To give the hospitals a chance to catch up."

Violet sniffled. "Will we get to see you?"

I glanced at her through the mirror again. Her eyes looked so big, full of questions no kid should have to ask.

"I'm not going anywhere," I said. "I live as the golem in the guest room, remember?"

A small chuckle from the kids and then no one spoke for awhile.

I looked at their faces in the rearview: scared, uncertain, on the edge of something they didn't understand yet. I knew I had to hold it together, even if the world outside was cracking apart. This was just the beginning. But the kids had me now. And I'd be damned if I let them go through this alone.

As we turned down the winding road toward home, my phone buzzed against the console. I reached for it at a stop sign, glancing down at the screen.

> Hey, I'm stuck at work. We're short-staffed and slammed. Can you help the kids with their assignments and dinner tonight? I might not be home until late.

I stared at the message for a beat longer than I needed to. She must not have seen the announcement, too caught up in the clinic. I didn't want to cause more stress for her.

The weight of everything, the shutdown, the fear in the kids' eyes, Sloane throwing herself right back into her job settled in my chest like wet cement. I should have felt burdened or overwhelmed, but honestly? I welcomed the responsibility. I needed it.

> Of course. I've got them covered. Don't worry about a thing. Just get through your shift.

She didn't respond right away, but I imagined her in that cramped breakroom at the clinic, rubbing the bridge of her nose, exhausted and overworked, trying to shield her growing nausea from coworkers who probably hadn't even heard the news in full yet. She was carrying more than I could fathom, and this time, I refused to let her carry it alone.

I put the phone down and glanced at the kids. Violet had her forehead pressed to the window, watching the wind jostle the trees. Liam was scrolling through his phone, but his eyes were glossed over as if he wasn't really seeing anything.

"Change of plans," I said and I injected warmth into my voice. "You guys are with me tonight. Mom's stuck at work. How does burgers sound?"

Violet perked up slightly. "What about gluten-free pizza? Can we build a pillow fort? Can Rufus sleep with us?"

Liam gave me a sidelong glance. "Do you even know how to make burgers? Or are we ordering pizza?"

I grinned. "Watch it, boy. You're about to witness greatness in the kitchen. I might even break out the garlic bread for our buns."

That earned a small smile from both of them. A flicker of light in all the uncertainty.

As we pulled into the driveway, Rufus barked with excitement through the window by the front door. I stepped out into the cool, heavy air and helped the kids get their stuff inside. Rufus immediately shoved his nose into Violet's hand, then circled Liam before trotting up to me with a snort.

"Yeah, yeah," I muttered, rubbing behind his ears. "I know. It's going to be a long night."

Inside, I started pulling out the meat while the kids unpacked their school bags at the kitchen table. I didn't know what tomorrow would bring, or exactly how long this would all last... but tonight, I had this moment.

Sloane had trusted me. The kids needed me. And for the first time in a long time, I felt like I was exactly where I was supposed to be.

The kids were in the living room, half-watching cartoons with plates of half-eaten burgers in their laps when my phone vibrated on the counter: an unknown number. I stared at it, heart stuttering in my chest.

I dried my hands on a dish towel, the scent of lemon soap still clinging to my skin, and stepped out onto the porch. The late evening air had cooled, but it did nothing to stop the burn crawling up my neck.

"Hello?" I answered, cautious.

The voice on the other end was low and clipped, the kind that didn't waste time. "Mr. Shaw? Detective Harlan."

My stomach tightened. The air suddenly felt like it was pressing down on me. "Yeah. Speaking."

"We believe we have enough evidence to move forward on Angie Collins."

I didn't speak. I should've felt relieved, grateful even... but instead, a slow, sour twist settled in my gut. Like hearing the gun cock before the trigger's pulled. My throat tightened. "What kind of evidence?"

"We've connected the threatening notes to her handwriting," he continued. "The home footage, your wife's witness statements, and now we've got a neighbor's Ring camera that shows her casing your property multiple times. It's enough to push for a warrant."

My mouth went dry. I stared out at the quiet street, the comforting hum of crickets suddenly hollow.

The detective continued, oblivious to the rising discomfort in my silence. "We're finalizing the paperwork, but I wanted to give you a heads-up. When we move on her, it could get loud. We don't know how she'll react. Based on her behavior so far, we've seen that she's been erratic and obsessive. This may not be clean."

I exhaled sharply through my nose. "So, what does that mean for us?"

"It means keep your doors locked. Keep the kids close. And don't let your wife be alone, if you can help it."

There it was, the dread. I felt bile creep up my throat, burning my chest.

I rubbed a hand over the back of my neck. "That's going to be difficult. Sloane works."

There was a pause before a measured response. "Then inform her supervisor. Have them keep an eye out. Let the workplace know to contact the police if anything unusual happens: strangers lurking, phone calls, a woman showing up uninvited. This isn't paranoia, Mr. Shaw. It's precaution."

"Yeah, you're right. Precaution. Thank you, detective."

"You've got a family, Mr. Shaw. The goal is to keep everyone safe. We'll do our part. You do yours."

I thanked him and hung up, standing still on the porch for a long moment.

Across the quiet street, a single car sat idling, lights off. It could've been nothing. Could've been a neighbor. But I knew better than to dismiss anything now.

The door creaked open behind me. Violet's voice, soft, "Daddy?"

I turned, quickly pasting on a calm expression. "Yeah, baby girl?"

"Can Rufus sleep in my room tonight? I feel... weird."

I glanced down and saw Rufus already pressed against her side like a shadow. He was alert, ears twitching.

"Yeah, of course," I said, forcing a smile. "Rufus is on night duty."

She smiled, then vanished back into the house.

I stood on the porch a moment longer. The night felt... swollen, expanded, as if it were holding its breath. Somewhere out there, Angie was watching. Waiting.

But so was I. And this time, I wasn't anything like the Old Me who ran from consequences or responsibilities. I was a man who protected his family.

Even if it meant burying a few bodies.

Chapter 23

After the call with the detective, I decided to wait for Sloane to discuss our next steps with the world and with Angie.

In the meantime, I spent the night quietly with the kids. Liam disappeared into his room to video chat with the band guys he liked to practice with, while Violet was already setting up her game.

I lingered in the hallway outside of her room for a moment, listening to the soft clatter of her keyboard, the faint hum of her computer. Then I walked in, trying to sound casual.

"Hey, Violet. Wanna play together?"

Her face lit up before a flicker of suspicion crossed it, as if my sudden interest raised a red flag. "Sure, Dad. But that's pretty sus."

I couldn't help but laugh. "Fair. But let's play anyway. You can show me around."

She nodded and scooted over to make space. I logged in beside her with my work laptop, and for the next couple of hours, we built a castle together out of digital blocks in a virtual world. She taught me the controls, the map, the quirks of the server. I made sure to ask questions to get her talking. But I also kept an eye on the voice channel, listening for anything out of place; conversations that dipped too far into the personal or any other red flags.

I always had my eyes scanning for that one specific username: Prince_Harming.

It was just a game. But I knew how people could use 'just a game' to worm their way in.

That night, I memorized every detail I could. Not only the layout of the castle or the crafting recipes, but the way her voice softened when she felt safe, the ease in her laugh when I struggled to move my character.

It was surprisingly relaxing and maybe a little ironic that I was both a builder in real life and now, also, in my daughter's digital world. There was something therapeutic about it. Placing blocks, crafting walls, creating shelter out of nothing. Violet and I worked side by side, and for a while, it felt like the world outside that glowing screen didn't exist.

Eventually, bedtime rolled in. I glanced at the clock and gave the gentle reminder that had somehow become routine again.

"Alright, you two. Time to start winding down."

Violet groaned but logged off without a fight, which I took as a small miracle. Liam was already tucked into his audiobook, earbuds in.

I made the rounds, turned out the lights, checked the locks, felt myself linger a second too long at each of their doors.

Damn, that was a good night with the kids.

Sloane walked into the kitchen around midnight, her hair pulled into a messy bun, face pale and pinched from another long shift. She didn't notice me at the dining room table at first; she had immediately focused on reviewing the kids' school packets on the counter. The low swish of the dishwasher filled the silence.

I sat there, watching her. She was the center of this fragile, reclaimed peace we'd built and I was about to shake it.

"Sloane," I said, my voice low.

She spun, startled, holding a stack of papers in her hand. "Jesus fuck, Levi... hey." She managed a small laugh at herself. "I thought you'd have gone to bed already."

"Sorry to disappoint."

She made her way over to the table next to me. "Thank you for handling the kids tonight."

"Don't mention it. We had a blast." I saw the lines etched across her face, the worry, the uncertainty. "Are you okay?"

She didn't answer right away. She let out a shaky breath and shook her head. "No. Not really." Her laugh was brittle. "Everything going on... it's too much. The kids I'm sure were anxious, there's no word on how long school is going to be virtual, and-" She cut herself off, lips pressing into a line. "I still can't believe everything the president said."

I felt it then, the truth itching at the back of my throat.

If only you knew how bad this is about to get, my love.

I wanted to tell her everything. How I wanted to not only unburden the part of me that was hiding this unbelievable secret, but also to tell her what I knew about this pandemic.

But I couldn't.

I took her hand in mine and said, "Listen... we need to talk."

I felt her flinch, as if she were about to snatch her hand away. She stopped herself and instead went stiff. "The last time you said that, you left. What is it?"

I glanced toward the hallway and listened for any sounds of the kids coming downstairs. I wanted to ensure they weren't within earshot. Rufus was already laying in his lumpy old bed after he'd tucked Violet in earlier.

"It's about Angie," I said.

Sloane's entire body went rigid and I could have sworn I heard her teeth clench. "What now?"

"The detective in charge of the case, Detective Harlan, called me tonight. They have enough. They're moving forward with a warrant."

She didn't say anything, just sat there, blinking slowly while she processed.

"They linked the notes, my call logs, our security footage, the sightings from neighbor's cameras," I continued. "She's been watching the house. Closely. Maybe even tonight."

Sloane pulled her hand out of mine and rested it lightly on her stomach. "Levi, why didn't you tell me sooner?"

I dropped my gaze. "I was trying to protect you. I didn't want to bring her name into our home, into our lives... again. I didn't want her to taint what we've been rebuilding."

She was silent, but her breathing had gotten quicker, shallower. I could see her anxiety stirring under the surface.

"I should've told you," I said. "I know that and I'm sorry. I was wrong. I knew you were handling-"

"You don't get to decide what I can handle, Levi." Her voice was tight, fury building, her eyes shining.

"I know."

Her next words were like a hammer striking an anvil. "I am pregnant. Our children are in this house. She is your responsibility. This is your fault."

This is your fault, big guy... you fucking idiot.

"I know, Sloane. I do know all of that and I hate myself for it."

Sloane pressed the heels of her palms to her eyes. "Goddammit, I thought the worst was behind us."

I reached for her, slowly, palms up. Her anger caused my words to gush out in a rush. "I know, so did I, and I am so sorry it's not. This has been eating at me, the stress and the guilt of it, I've even been keeping a journal every night, trying to work through it all." I took a deep breath then before I elaborated. "My nightmares, my panic attacks, fear of losing you, of losing the baby. I am trying to keep my head above it, but I feel like I'm drowning."

She dropped her hands and met my gaze. "Nightmares? Panic attacks? Levi, why wouldn't you tell-" She took a deep breath and checked her rising anger. "Why would you keep something like that from me?"

"I wasn't hiding it. Not exactly," I said. "I didn't tell you fast enough."

Her laugh was short and sharp. "That's not better."

"I know." I reached out for her hand again and she took mine. "I didn't want to burden you, Sloane. You already have so much... too much. I didn't want you to see it as a sign that I couldn't handle being here, being your partner."

"I wouldn't have seen it as anything if you'd just told me," she snapped. But she winced at her own words and tone, her shoulders drawing with regret at her sharpness. "Damn, Levi. I don't need you to be perfect. I never did. I need you to be honest. That's always been the bare minimum." She looked at me for a long time before letting out a long sigh. "So, what now?"

I squeezed her hand. "Now... we wait for the police to do their jobs. In the meantime, we stay alert and keep the kids close. I'm not letting her anywhere near you or the baby."

Her lips trembled. Her eyes were darker now, rimmed with unshed tears and something colder: fear.

"Okay. I agree with you. We let the police handle it. Levi, Listen..." She paused and I saw she struggled with what to say next. "I didn't tell you everything either."

I felt my mouth go dry. "What do you mean?"

She swallowed. "Angie's been calling the clinic. Leaving voicemails. Threatening ones."

"What?" I leapt up from the table, the chair clattering to the tile. Rage coated my next words. "I am going to go kill her, Sloane."

"Levi, no!" Sloane's desperate plea helped me stay grounded. She stood, reached up, and put her cool hands on my hot face as she looked into my eyes. "You promised me you would do this the right way, didn't you?"

I broke my vows to fuck that bitch. What's one more broken promise? I will kill a thousand Angies to keep you safe.

I didn't say that. Instead, I saw my wife through a haze of red... and I took a deep breath.

"Please," she said, "stay here with me and listen."

I picked the chair up, sat back down with her, and we held hands as she spoke.

"Angie would call and say things like, 'You'll never know him like I do,' or, 'He will always be mine,' or, "I'll never let you steal him from me.'"

My knuckles popped as my fists clenched. Angie was trying to unravel everything I had been carefully working towards. "Sloane, why didn't you tell me?"

"For the same reasons you didn't tell me. I suppose that's why I can't be too angry with you." She took a deep breath before she said, "Also, I was scared of how you would react."

With the thoughts of my hands wrapped around Angie's throat still fresh on my mind, I had to concede her point. "I am sorry you didn't feel safe sharing this with me. What did you do?"

She exhaled shakily. "I deleted them before anybody else could hear them. She only left them when my shift started, so I think she was watching the clinic. Plus, I didn't want anybody at the clinic to see me as... fragile."

I cupped her face with my hand. "You are not fragile, Sloane. You're stronger than anyone I know. But no one should have to be strong alone."

She didn't pull away and nestled her face against my palm, but her jaw stayed tight. "The kids cannot know about this."

"I know."

Her voice turned hollow. "She knows where I work, Levi. Where our kids go to school. And now we're supposed to sit here and just... wait?"

"No," I said. "We take this to the detective. Every detail you can recall needs to be sent to Harlan. Plus with the shutdown, the kids will be here at home, I've called off all jobs at Master Builders, and I don't plan on leaving this house unless it's for necessities."

Sloane nodded with glistening eyes. "Okay." Her shoulders slumped. "I am so tired, Levi."

"I know. But we're going to end this. I swear. I will do it right and let the police handle it. Alright?"

"Okay. I am choosing to trust you on this."

We sat in silence for awhile, unpacking everything we'd said and still wanted to say. Then she reached for me.

I didn't hesitate. I opened my arms for her to fall into, the warmth of her body seeping into me. I kissed her temples, felt her breath hitch as I nuzzled into her neck to inhale the scent of her: comforting, familiar, delicious, everything.

"Fuck, I missed you today," I whispered, my voice hoarse, raw with emotions I didn't know I had left to give.

I felt the faint curve of her smile against my chest as she let out a long breath. "I missed you, too."

She peeked up at me, the gesture so cute that I couldn't help but lean down to kiss her. This woman was my world, my love, my life. She was so damn strong, so damn beautiful, and I was overwhelmed with gratitude every damn day she allowed me to be a part of her life.

I felt her hands tighten on my arms as her body pressed into mine; her body pleaded for more as my tongue explored her mouth. We pulled away, our breathing heavy.

"Move this to the room?" she murmured, her voice low, but certain.

"Fuck, yes, Sloane," I breathed, barely able to control the surge of need that swept through me.

I didn't wait another second. I stood and scooped her up, her surprised laughter drawing a smile on my face as I carried her to the bedroom.

"Careful you don't throw your back out, old man," she said between laughs.

"For you, I'd throw my back out a thousand times if you'd let me."

While holding her in my arms, Sloane's eyes locked onto mine. I saw her hesitation, the lingering uncertainty under the surface. But I also saw her hunger, the insatiable need within her. I felt it too, the scars we both carried and the burning intensity of our love. She was here. She was with me, and that meant everything. She was trusting me with her body and soul again.

Once we reached the bed, I laid her down, but never broke her gaze. The world outside disappeared. In that moment, all that existed was her and me. I leaned down and brushed my lips against hers, not a kiss, not yet.

"All I could think about today was you," I whispered, our lips barely touching. "Only you." My words were raw with honesty.

She whispered, "How often do you think of me?" Her voice shook as her hands wrapped around my neck.

My response came out low, possessive, a primal force I could no longer contain. "All the time, Sloane." I nipped at her bottom lip, savoring the shiver that ran through her. "I think about your laugh. Your smile." I kissed the corner of her mouth as I placed a hand to her hip. "I remembered when you came, your screams, your face."

Her breath hitched as I kissed her deeper, then pulled away. "Your little noises when I find the spots that make you fall apart." I bit her lip harder and heard the sharp intake of her breath.

I couldn't stop myself. Each word, each touch, was a confession. In the space between kisses, I unraveled as I realized just how much I did think about her, how much I needed her in ways I hadn't fully understood before.

I growled, "And let's be honest... I think about how your tight, wet cunt fits perfectly around my cock."

Her fingers dug into my shoulders, pulling me back to her lips as if she couldn't get enough of me. I kissed her harder, again and again, every movement becoming more urgent, more hungry.

We undressed, Sloane mumbling about needing to shower but I desperately needed her in this moment. There was something else in the air now, an unspoken invitation to explore, to trust each other in ways we hadn't dared before.

I paused, breath shallow, and met her gaze. Her eyes were dark with anticipation, and I couldn't stop the smirk that tugged at my mouth. "Maybe I could become one of your book boyfriends," I teased. "They seem to get you pretty hot and bothered."

Her laugh rang out, that soft, musical sound I craved.

"Levi! Don't make fun of my boyfriends," she said between laughs.

With a mock growl, I lunged and tossed her to the far side of the bed, careful but dramatic. "I can be aggressive too, you know," I said as I crawled over to her. I kissed her collarbone, letting my voice dip low, teasing. "I can growl and whisper filthy poetry in your ear."

She laughed again, her eyes sparkling, but there was something else behind them: vulnerability, quiet and sincere. She didn't look away. "Are you sure?" she asked softly, breath catching. "Some of them have wingspans."

That made me laugh. "The Halloween store has wings. Say the word."

We broke down laughing together, tangled in the sheets and breathless. When the laughter faded, she looked up at me. She looked... shy.

"I trust you, Levi."

Trust.

Not just affection. Not just lust. She was handing me something delicate and hard-earned, a precious treasure that the Old Me had never cherished. I stared dumbfounded into her eyes, clueless on what to say.

"So, Levi... are we doing this? Otherwise Mama's got a date with a shower and a bed."

I laughed. "Didn't realize my competition was a loofah and hot water."

"The loofah always listens. Doesn't interrupt. Great for exfoliation and post-breakdown therapy. Very low maintenance."

I said, "Well, I guess I'll have to work harder than the loofah."

She raised an eyebrow, her voice dry. "Levi, we both know you're always harder than a loofah."

"Why thank you for noticing," I said cordially as I pressed myself against her. "You have this effect on me. It's a constant problem."

"Mm-hmm," she muttered with a lazy smile. "It certainly doesn't feel like a problem."

"Oh, Sloane," I murmured as I kissed her forehead, "you haven't felt anything, yet."

I pressed my lips against her skin, lingering, grounding us both in that moment. Then I reached over and opened the drawer, pulling out one of the toys we'd talked about the other day along with the restraints.

This was all new territory for the both of us. We didn't move fast with these things. Every decision was deliberate, a brick in the foundation we were rebuilding together.

"Tonight's item," I began, holding up the sleek toy with faux announcer flair, "is a very special purchase. Five-star reviews. Promises of intensity, transcendence, and mild spiritual awakenings."

Sloane arched a brow. "Spiritual, huh? Should I light a candle first?"

"Only if it's peppermint. That's my scent of focus and performance," I deadpanned.

She rolled her eyes. "God help us."

I smiled, letting the performance drop as I settled down beside her. "Jokes aside... this is about you. What you want. What you feel safe with. That's all I care about tonight. That's all I care about every night from now on."

Her smile faded into something softer, deeper. "I know," she whispered. "That's why I said yes."

"We don't have to do this tonight," I murmured, my fingers brushing gently along her wrist. "I want you. Desperately. I want to know what it feels like to have you choose me again. Not only in the quiet moments, but like this too. To know you trust me with every part of you."

She nodded, breath shaky, but her eyes didn't waver. "I want this. I trust you," she repeated.

That word again.

"Okay," I whispered.

With deliberate care, I secured her wrists first, the soft leather fitting snugly but gently around her skin. I checked each one twice, brushing kisses to her knuckles as I did. Then her ankles, binding her to the corners of the bed in a way that left her exposed but not powerless.

Her body was splayed open beneath me, her chest rising and falling faster now, but her eyes never left mine.

She was beyond stunning. She was utterly devastating in her vulnerability.

I reached for the blindfold next, but paused with my fingers resting lightly on her temple.

"You remember the safe word?" I asked.

She gave a soft scoff, trying for humor, but I could hear the nerves in her voice. "Yeah… I remember. Wait, can we use a new one?" She paused for a moment before whispering, "I'm nervous, Levi."

I kissed her gently, my lips brushing hers like a promise. "That's okay. Being nervous means it matters. But you are in control, Sloane. You always are. I'll stop the second you need me to. Say the word, and we're done."

She took a deep breath, then gave a subtle nod. "Okay."

"Say it once for me now so we both know it," I said, brushing a strand of hair from her face.

"Loofah."

I smiled and kissed her again. "I see what you did there."

"Complaints?"

"None. It's perfect."

With that, I began as I slipped the blindfold over her eyes.

With her vision gone, her other senses sharpened. I saw it in the way her lips parted, the slight arch of her back as she adjusted to the loss of sight, the quiet exhale that left her.

I let my hands wander first, tenderly tracing every curve and dip of her body as if I was memorizing her all over again. Then I reached for the items I'd gathered for different textures and sensations: a soft feather, a velvet glove, a silk handkerchief, a loofah.

She gasped, squirmed, and moaned. She laughed at the rough edge of the loofah. Her body arched and trembled beneath the blindfold, and I watched it all, my own body tense, aching, alive with every reaction she gave me.

"You're so beautiful like this," I said as my lips trailed along her skin. "So perfect."

Her thighs trembled, restrained, and she let out a low, needy sound. "Levi... please."

I paused, nose brushing right below her navel. "Please what? Tell me what you want, Sloane."

A moment passed as her breath hitched. "I want your mouth," she whispered, raw and pleading. "I want to feel everything."

Fuck yes.

I spread her thighs wider, placing a kiss to the inside of each before letting my tongue finally meet her heat. And good fucking god, I gave her everything I had.

She cried out, the sound sharp and unguarded, her hips jerking hard against the restraints. I licked slowly at first, teasing, letting her build again, her legs trembling in my grasp as I held her writhing body.

She was ravishing like this: exposed, trusting, unleashed. I loved her more in that moment than I ever had before.

She gasped, her fingers digging into the bindings, and I felt her body tense again. "Levi," she whispered, her voice trembling "It's... so much."

I kissed her softly, pulling back enough to tease her, my breath warm against her skin. "We can stop anytime," I reminded her, my thumb brushing over her clit. "Say the safe word."

But she shook her head, her breathing coming faster, more desperate. "No. Don't stop." Her voice was low, but there was no hesitation in it. "I want this. I want all of it."

"I am yours to command." I chuckled darkly before grabbing the next item, "And I'm the only one who will ever get to hear you beg like this."

When I added the toy, she moaned so loudly I thought she might cry or wake the children. I pressed my hand to her mouth, "Such a good girl, letting me hear you. But we can't wake the children now, can we?"

She shook her head, my hand falling down to wrap around her throat as I slipped the toy inside her deeper, letting it hum to life, low and deep.

"That's right. You will obey, won't you?" Her body shuddered at the words, the audible sound of her soaking the sheets as the toy pushed her body to the edge. I leaned down, curling my tongue at the same time over her clit.

"Come for me Sloane. Let me hear my name on your lips." I felt her pulse, erratic under my fingertips as I applied pressure.

The reaction was instant. She stiffened, then broke. The orgasm hit her hard as her body came apart beneath me, her head thrown back, fingers clenched into fists. Her moans tore from her throat like confessions. As much as I knew I should silence her, I was desperate to hear her cries.

"Yes, yes, Levi, oh my god-"

I didn't stop using the toy. Her legs trembled and soon she was begging, more laughing breathlessly onto another impending orgasm, her voice breaking. "Stop - please - fuck, I can't-"

"Are you sure Sloane?" The words slipped out low and devilish. "If I stop now, we are done for the night."

She couldn't stop her body from convulsing as she pulled against the restraints, her cries desperate, 'No. Please, I want you inside of me. I'm gonna-"

"Ah, fuck. To hear you beg." I pulled back, kissing her thighs, her stomach, her chest and as we'd agreed, I entered her. She cried out my name and the sound tore through me. "Fuck me, you feel perfect."

I furiously thrust into her, kept her teetering on the edge, wave after wave. Her body writhed beneath mine, each gasp, each shudder a plea and a surrender all at once as the thick of the orgasm broke, her body already trembling from the revelation.

"Yes. Take this cock and come on it Sloane. Let me hear you soak the bed." I gripped her thighs, my fingers bruising on her skin as the sound of flesh hitting flesh echoed in the room.

She sobbed as I moved within her, the overwhelming pleasure, too much, too fast, too deep as she drenched the sheets with her release but she never used the safe word. Never asked me to stop.

When I finally came, it was guttural, like something breaking open inside me. I held her as I unraveled, my balls tight and empty against her ass, bodies tangled, breath ragged, hearts pounding in sync.

The silence that followed was deafening as I removed her blindfold. "You okay?" I whispered, tucking her hair back and checking in on her.

She nodded. Her breathing shook. "That was... fuck."

I smiled, kissed her temple, and whispered, "Good fuck?"

Her laugh was weak, but real. "You think?"

I undid each restraint, slow and careful and she curled into me the second she was free, limbs trembling, chest still heaving.

"You've made me feel more than I thought was possible," she whispered, her voice barely audible.

I kissed her forehead, my hand brushing down her back. "My soul only belongs to you."

And it was true. I felt at peace.

There was a pause, soft and full of afterglow, then she added dryly, "You know, it won't be like that every time."

I laughed, catching the teasing lilt in her voice. "Well then, we better celebrate this rare phenomenon accordingly."

She raised an eyebrow. "With food. Obviously. I'm starving."

I reached for my phone like a knight drawing a sword. "Book boyfriend accepts the quest. Retrieval of sustenance is underway!"

She snorted. "What's the ETA on said heroic delivery, my champion? Because I'm imagining pancakes."

I pretended to scroll with great importance. "Our options are limited, milady, but your champion shall secure the fluffiest stack in the kingdom. Thank goodness for delivery services."

Sloane's quiet laugh filled the room, warm and unguarded. "God, I missed this."

"Me too," I said, glancing over with a smile. "Especially being called a champion. Might put that on my résumé."

Chapter 24

We talked softly in the kitchen, the quiet, intimate sound a stark contrast to the late hour, both our hair damp from the recent shower.

It was nearing 2 a.m. and the faint glow of the oven light cast long shadows across the room. I was in the middle of grabbing a bowl of cereal after our failed food delivery. Sloane didn't think she could handle any of the greasy food options and instead chose to nibble on some crackers, her tired eyes still carrying a trace of warmth from the night we'd spent together.

"I knew you'd go for the cereal," she murmured, a small smile tugging at her lips.

"It was either this or those weird freezer-burnt fish sticks the kids pretend to love."

She arched a brow. "You could've made toast."

"I thought about it," I said, pouring the cereal into a bowl, "but then I remembered we're out of butter. And I wasn't about to disgrace your toaster like that."

She chuckled under her breath, a sound that did dangerous things to my cock. "How considerate."

I leaned against the counter, spoon in hand. "You doing okay?"

She paused, chewing slowly. "I think so. My body feels... sore. But not in a bad way."

I swallowed a laugh. "Emotional yoga?"

She rolled her eyes. "You and that metaphor."

"It's accurate. You're stretching parts of your heart you haven't used in a while. Probably wondering if I'm going to drop you mid-pose."

She gave me a long look, equal parts fond and skeptical. "That was almost poetic. Who are you and what have you done with Levi 'Avoidance Is a Coping Skill' Shaw?"

I smirked. "He's still here. But he's been benched. The new guy's giving this whole accountability thing a try."

She broke off another cracker. "Dangerous."

"I like to live on the edge," I said, crunching my cereal dramatically. "Next I might try budgeting."

"Slow down, Casanova. One wild fantasy at a time."

We fell into a comfortable silence after that. Just the sound of soft chewing and the occasional creak of the house settling.

Then, the knock came.

The sound cut through the air, sharp and unexpected. Both of us froze, our hearts skipping a beat. Rufus, usually so calm, growled low from the hallway, his hackles raised.

Sloane's voice was barely audible, a fragile thread of panic. "Don't answer it."

I didn't need to ask who it could be. The tension in the air, the way the hairs on the back of my neck stood at attention, told me everything I needed to know.

Angie was outside.

Sloane and I stood frozen in the kitchen. The knock came again: three slow, deliberate raps. Rufus snarled low in his throat as he crept toward the front door.

"Don't," Sloane whispered again, clutching my arm now. "Please don't answer it."

I nodded, slowly backing us both out of view from the windows.

"Sloane. I have to..."

I reached for my phone and texted the detective immediately with the number they provided for emergencies.

Fuck, I feel like a sitting duck.

> She's here. At the house. Knocking.

The soft bing of the text being accepted was the only noise as we waited. Minutes passed. The knock didn't come again. Instead, the sound of footsteps crunching across the gravel.

Rufus bolted to the window and barked. I hushed him as I peeked through the blinds. I heard the unmistakable sound of glass breaking.

All I saw was the blur of a figure disappearing down the sidewalk, hoodie up, posture unmistakable. It had to be Angie.

I turned to Sloane. "Stay here. Don't open the door for anyone. I'm going to check outside."

She looked like she wanted to argue, but her fear overrode it. She nodded.

I grabbed one of Liam's hockey sticks and slipped outside through the back, circling the house. Everything looked normal until I turned the corner to Sloane's SUV.

The windshield was shattered. Glass glittered across the hood like ice shards. Car doors smeared with red lipstick scrawled in thick, erratic strokes:

> BITCH HE'S MINE. WE BELONG IN KEY WEST

My nostrils flared as my fist clenched at the scene before me. I turned around to scan the street, but saw nothing.

I'm going to bury you in Key West, Angie.

Back inside, I locked every window and door while Sloane stared at me with the question already in her eyes. "What did she do?" she asked quietly.

I paused, running a hand over my face before I answered. "She vandalized your SUV."

Sloane blinked. "Goddamn."

"Yeah."

We stood in the dark silence of our kitchen, the situation and all of its implications churning between us, before we looked into each other's eyes. It was a testament to how long we'd been together, how perfect we truly were for one other, that we wore matching grins.

Incredulous, Sloane asked, "The cunt couldn't have gone for the expensive company car? The one with full coverage?" She shook her head in mock disbelief. "Nooo, she had to go after my piece of shit."

"So inconsiderate of her," I said with exaggerated seriousness.

"Inconsiderate and illogical. Destroy the most valuable thing you can. Isn't that basic Stalker 101?"

"My love, I don't think logic was the driving force here."

She stared at me, deadpan. "Of course it wasn't, Levi. After all, why process your emotions like an adult when you can vent them out on someone's SUV?"

"Maybe she was attempting to turn it into a modern art piece?"

"I love modern art." Sloane looked thoughtful for a moment. "Is it at least... a good attempt?"

I tried not to smile. "I think she was going for 'rage graffiti' as a genre."

Sloane huffed. "Great. Let me guess. Something real subtle? Like 'homewrecker' in spray paint?"

I suppressed a laugh. "It's in lipstick, actually."

"She wrote 'homewrecker' in lipstick?"

"No," I said, "if she'd tried, I bet she would have spelled it wrong. 'Homwreckur.'"

She closed her eyes and muttered, "She's out here threatening my life and she doesn't have the decency to use spell check?"

I shrugged. "Unhinged and illiterate. She also broke the glass."

Her eyes widened and her gaze drilled into me. "Levi, I swear to God, if she touched Violet's Taylor Swift bumper sticker, this is war."

I held up my hands in surrender. "Swift is intact. She must have known better."

"Damn right she did," Sloane said as she marched toward the kitchen. "Even psychopaths know there are lines you don't cross."

"I don't think the kids woke up thankfully." I followed her, "Sloane?"

Sloane pressed her lips together and exhaled shakily, holding her stomach instinctively. Our moment of levity, of using sarcasm and humor to keep the panic and fear at bay, had passed. The shadows seemed darker and the night felt closer.

"So what now, Levi? That could've been me. That could've been the kids."

"It won't be," I said. "Detective Harlan said they had enough for a warrant before she went this far. The cameras would have recorded her smashing your window. She just made this so much easier for us, Sloane."

I reached for the kitchen chair and sat down hard. Rufus stayed tense as he paced the kitchen.

Sloane sat across from me, tired and pale. "We need to tell the kids something. They're going to notice the broken windshield."

"I'll get it cleaned up before they wake up," I said. "I'll figure out what to tell them. You rest."

She didn't respond right away as she looked at me with an expression that was equal parts relief and dread. "I'm scared, Levi."

I reached for her hand. "Me too. Get some rest Sloane. You need it."

She nodded in agreement, "Okay."

Sloane went to bed as I stayed up cleaning the kitchen, anxiety high. Light filtered through the blinds in weak, gray sickly shadows across the kitchen floor.

My phone rang. An unknown number again. I answered on instinct hoping that it wasn't Angie.

"Mr. Shaw, this is Detective Harlan. I apologize for calling so early."

You can call me anytime, I almost said as relief coursed through me.

I sat back down at the table, heart tightening as I hoped to hear the words I wanted. "Please tell me you have enough."

A pause. Then a sigh, heavy and frustrated. "We did. But we're on hold right now."

"What?"

"The department's operations changed overnight. You saw the announcement, didn't you?"

I had. The president on every channel last night, speaking in that somber, measured voice no one trusted anymore.

My mouth went dry. "You're telling me she's free to do whatever she wants now?"

"She's not free. She's... not the department's priority. Not right now. Our resources are limited, Mr. Shaw, and the entire government's focus is on the public's health. We can't move on her until we have full clearance from a judge. And with the shutdown-"

"I have kids," I snapped. "I have a pregnant wife under this roof, and she's stressed out about everything. You can't seriously expect us to believe that the police can't do anything?"

"I understand your frustration, but this goes above my pay grade." There was a pause and his tone was lower, "Listen. I'm not saying to stop documenting everything. Continue providing evidence, because the more we have and the more she escalates? The sooner we can act. But you need to keep your family safe. Don't confront her. Don't engage. For now... bunker down."

Bunker down. Like this was a war zone. Maybe it was. With the world going to shit and Angie circling us like a shark, it felt like a dystopian nightmare.

I thanked him stiffly and hung up.

The phone buzzed again immediately. This time, not unknown. Angie's name flashed bright.

I hit *Reject* and waited expectantly. Three seconds later it rang again. And again. And again.

Voicemail pinged. I played it with trembling fingers.

Her voice slithered through the speaker, sugar-sweet and venom-laced. "I saw the news. Cops have their hands full don't they? Which means it's just us now, baby. You, me, and the truth you're too scared to tell Sloane."

As I listened, I saw the ping for another voicemail then another.

My call log read like a horror story. Twenty missed calls. Fifteen voicemails. All in the last few minutes.

My fingers ached from the constant forwarding, each tap of the screen sending another piece of evidence to the detective I'd just spoken with. I could feel my resolve building with each message, the weight of everything piling up.

I need them to take this more seriously. If something happens to Sloane or the kids, I will never forgive myself.

I thought about Rufus then.

Yeah, I will strangle the bitch if she touches my dog.

I texted Detective Harlan again, the words burning with urgency.

> She's not going to stop, and the car was vandalized last night. Check the video I uploaded.

> Detective Harlan here. I'll get this in front of a judge ASAP.

Footsteps broke my thoughts as I looked up. Sloane had walked in quietly, still in her robe, one hand resting against the counter.

"Did you sleep?" she asked gently.

"No."

Her eyes scanned my face, reading the words I was not ready to say, "You okay?"

I forced a smile. "Yeah. Just... the detective called."

Her eyes searched mine. "And?"

"They've put the case on hold."

She blinked. "What?"

"They said the shutdown changed everything. Limited staff. Focus is on public health now."

Sloane stared past me for a long moment, something in her hardening. "So, she gets away with it?."

"Not forever," I said, standing. "We're not going to let her scare us. I'll do whatever it takes to protect you and the kids. Pandemic or not. I sent over last night's video and the voicemails she left me. It's got to be enough, and Harlan said he's going to try to get it in front of a judge."

She nodded, "Okay."

My phone buzzed again on the counter. I silenced it and flipped it over.

But we both knew that didn't stop her.

Chapter 25

An hour or so later, fueled by coffee and anger, I cleaned up Sloane's SUV as much as possible before the kids woke up. I obviously couldn't replace or repair the broken windshield, but I at least got rid of the lipstick and shattered glass.

I called a guy that owned a local body shop who owed me a few favors. He joked that I might be his last customer for awhile, given the mandatory shutdowns, but he assured me that he could have Sloane's car towed in, windshield replaced, and dropped back off by tomorrow. I thanked him and told him that we were even.

It pained me to remember that his business didn't make it through the pandemic in my previous life. I couldn't even remember if he had.

With Sloane's SUV squared away, I planned to head up to the Master Builders Inc. office to shut it down and lock up for the coming weeks. On my way to the door, Sloane asked me if I'd run by the grocery store whenever I finished.

I kissed her neck and murmured, "I would do anything for you, Sloane."

"Hmm... that's great and all, but I really just need eggs, milk, and meat."

I pressed myself against her as I said, "Meat and milk, huh?"

After she called me an idiot with a laugh and a playful slap, I headed out to my truck. The roads were mostly empty on my drive up to the office.

I double checked the place was locked up before I sat alone in that empty building to hold a conference call with Jose and our accountant; we needed to finalize the paychecks and ensure my people would be taken care of while the world shut down.

"That's a lot of outflow without any revenue, jefe." Jose's voice was sharp with doubt after he heard the accountant announce the amount needed to pay everyone. "Are you sure about this?"

"Yeah," I said. "The guys have earned this break. That includes you, Jose. Take the money, rest up. When things open back up, we'll hit the ground running. Trust me."

Jose's breath came through the line, a heavy pause before he said, "Okay. I trust you."

I thanked him and the accountant, told them both to take care, and then the line went silent. I sat there in the dark and empty office for a time, thinking.

I was used to being the one who was in control, the one who gave orders... but at that moment? I was trying to keep everything from falling apart.

According to the news and my memories of the first time I'd lived through this pandemic, it would be at least three weeks before the national lockdown was lifted; three weeks before society attempted to claw its way out of this chaotic pit, back to some semblance of normalcy. Three weeks hadn't been long enough, as the death toll continued to rise.

The first strain of the virus had been the deadliest; practically melting people's lungs into liquid shit. There was no way in hell I was letting Sloane go outside without a mask. In my previous life, she had gotten sick, causing her to miscarry in a hospital alone. This time might be different, but I didn't dare risk it. Not when the world felt as if it was teetering on a razor's edge.

Come on, big guy. We're done here and we need to get back to Sloane.

I finished up at the office and headed to the grocery store. The place felt like a scene from some post-apocalyptic zombie movie. The shelves were nearly bare. The store had been stripped of toilet paper, bread, hand sanitizer, milk, eggs; as if society had collectively agreed that these were the first things to hoard when the world began to crumble. I adjusted my N95 mask and ignored the wide, uncomfortable stares of the people around me. I kept my head down and focused on the task at hand, but it seemed impossible to escape the tension in the air.

That's when she appeared.

An old woman shuffled over to me, eyes wild and bloodshot with some kind of fury I couldn't place. "Are you one of those bastards?" she screeched, her voice shrill and vibrating with hatred. "This is all a sham. There is no virus!"

Her words slapped me as spit flew from her mouth.

I raised my hands in front of me, my pulse quickening. "Ma'am, I don't want any trouble."

She raised her voice even louder. "Trouble is all you bigots bring us! Sheeple! Cowards! Poisoned by your screens and your science! You think this is real? You think they're not watching?"

I was between backing away and calling 911 when she threw her arms in the air like she was summoning lightning.

"The Four Horsemen ride again! The virus isn't real. It's death in disguise! You've opened the gates! You've let them in!"

The old woman was not angry; she was unhinged, her entire body vibrating with raw, unrestrained emotion.

"They want your blood. Your babies. Your souls," she said, pointing at random people in the store. "And you're standing there. Watching. Like it's all normal!"

I saw the manager rushing over, moving as quickly as he could, but he was too far away to stop the old woman from grabbing the front of my shirt.

She yanked me toward her. "Get back here, you coward!" she spat, eyes wild.

The manager was finally at my side, trying to pry the old woman off of me, his voice apologetic. "I'm so sorry, sir," he said, his hand on the woman's arm, trying to pull her away.

I shook my head, forcing a calm I didn't feel. "No problem," I muttered, backing away as fast as I could, avoiding any more confrontation.

Fuck me, what in the hell was that?

The fear, the aggression, the sheer lunacy of it all, left me rattled. I felt the adrenaline buzzing in my veins as I waited to check-out.

My hands shook while I scanned the items: pantry staples, extra slabs of meat for the freezer, anything that would last us through the coming weeks.

The Four Horsemen ride again.

The thought kept going off in my head as I stood there processing my payment. The encounter with the old woman had set my head to spinning. I knew something of the Four Horsemen, how each one represented a different thing: war, death, famine, and... plague?

With everything going on, with me being reborn, that old lady might be right.

The world was breaking down and there was nothing I could do to stop it. The people around me, some of them desperate, some of them in denial, were all struggling to survive in a world that seemed to be slipping away from us. That old woman was not the first to crack under the mounting pressures of this pandemic; she wouldn't be the last.

The moment I walked into the house with the groceries, Sloane could tell something was off.

She watched me in silence as I brought in bag after bag, my every movement quick, mechanical, and frantic. Once I'd gotten the groceries in, I beelined straight for the laundry room and closed the door behind me.

I stripped off my clothes and tossed them into the washer as if they were radioactive, like they might hold some contagious germ of the madness that had unfolded at the store.

Sloane's voice, gentle with understanding, floated through the door. "We do the same thing when there's a parvo case at the clinic."

Her words, while I knew they were meant to comfort, didn't reach me fully. I was too busy struggling to breathe, my thoughts swirling in chaotic spirals.

I poured detergent into the washer with shaky hands, the sounds of the liquid mixing with the hammering of my heart in my ears. My memories, my knowledge of what was to come, clawed at me. It was a constant, oppressive presence in my mind.

My next words erupted from me, jagged and heavy. "It's going to be bad, Sloane," I said, my voice trembling as I gripped the edge of the washer. "It's so deadly that five million people will die."

She opened the door, placed her hand on my arm, and stood with me. She didn't say anything right away, just... stood with me, her presence grounding me. When she spoke, her voice was a soft balm against my burning mind.

"Levi... it will be okay."

I want to believe that, my love.

Fuck, I really did. But I couldn't shake the gnawing, aching worry in my bones. My eyes were haunted as I met hers, my voice barely more than a whisper. "I don't think it will, Sloane."

I saw the concern on her face. She stepped closer then and wrapped her arms around me. I let her. I allowed myself to relish her warmth, her steadiness.

The world outside was crumbling, but at that moment, she was all that mattered. She was the only thing that felt real, the only thing that made me feel real.

Later that evening, I pushed everything down and pretended my worries didn't weigh ten thousand pounds. We all watched a movie together as a family, the kids bickering over the popcorn, the soft sound of their laughter filling the room.

I indulged in some chocolates with Sloane and tried to savor the simple pleasure of the moment, despite the dark clouds lingering at the edge of my mind. I knew the kids sensed something was off after our brief conversation about the vandalized car, but they let it go. For a little while, it felt as if things might be okay. Maybe we could hold onto what little normalcy we had left?

Sloane took my truck to exchange books with her sister Dawn; a quick late-night coffee run and a brief chance to socialize before her late shift. I knew Sloane was excited to get out and see her sister, even if she pretended it wasn't a big deal. It was an escape, even if only a small one.

The rain had just started when it happened. Fat, heavy drops slammed the windows like impatient fists. The house was dim. Quiet. I had finished setting up Violet's tablet for her virtual class tomorrow morning when I heard the sound.

Glass shattering.

I was down the hall within seconds, adrenaline spiking. Rufus barked from the living room, deep and guttural; this wasn't a fallen tree limb or debris from the storm.

It was Angie.

I heard the sleepy steps of my kids as they ventured down the stairs. I rushed to the foyer and yelled up, "Stay in your room. Lock the door. Do *not* come out!"

I heard Violet burst into tears, Liam's voice comforting her, their receding footsteps as he pulled her into his room, followed by his bedroom door slamming shut.

Good job, son.

I turned the corner from the foyer into the kitchen and saw Angie.

She was stepping through the broken sliding glass door, a jagged edge clinging to her coat. Her eyes were wild, smeared with mascara and rainwater, hair plastered to her face like a drowned ghost. She held a metal rod in her hand, her face filled with a determined fury. But when she saw me, her scowl was replaced with a manic grin.

"You can't hide from me," she breathed, soaked and panting. "I've always known where you live, baby. Always."

No shit you crazy bitch. You've been stalking us for months.

Before I had a chance to speak, Rufus lunged. His ferocious barking was cut short as Angie swung her metal rod and cracked him in the ribs.

A sickening thud, a pained yelp, my best boy cowering with his tail tucked. I snapped.

I am killing her now.

The finality of that realization should have unnerved me, but I felt nothing other than incandescent rage. I strode over to her. Anger, fear, and a dozen other raw emotions fused into something monstrous, something unrelenting. Something no longer within my control.

Angie must have seen it on my face because her too-wide grin faltered as she took a step away.

"You break into *my* home? You hurt *my* dog? You threatened *my* Sloane?" I charged, slamming into her with the full weight of everything I'd buried since this nightmare began. She dropped her metal rod as we crashed through the coffee table, the wood splintering around us. I mounted her amid the wreckage of the shattered table and she clawed at my face.

"You don't get to erase me, baby," she shrieked then laughed. I wasn't sure which sounded more horrifying.

Kill her. Break your promise to Sloane and kill her.

I wanted to. Fuck me, I did...

But I didn't.

It took every ounce of restraint for me to wrap my hands around her wrists instead of her throat. I pinned her down, easily overpowering her. Breathing hard, my mind and body were at war between my desire to hurt her and my devotion to keeping my promise to my wife. I took a deep, stuttering breath.

Even if I did decide to kill her, I couldn't do it here; not with my kids upstairs... but, fuck, I wanted to grab a glass shard and ram it into her.

Still laughing, she writhed and bucked under me, gyrating her hips as if this was all twisted foreplay.

I squeezed her wrists as I leaned down and growled, "What in the actual fuck is wrong with you? Did you really think you would get away with this, you crazy psycho bitch?"

Like flipping a switch, her laughter spiraled into crying and her manic anger melted into hysterical delusions. Between sobs she said, "I wanted them to see me. I wanted to show you I still matter."

I heard sirens in the distance. I was grateful one of the neighbors, or maybe Liam, must've called 911.

"I told you to stay away," I hissed.

"I love you!"

"I *never* loved you," I said with a vicious honesty that I hadn't even realized fully until that moment.

I had never loved Angie. The Old Me had loved the fantasy she gave him. Nothing more.

"I never loved you... ever," I added. I was unsure if I'd said it to her or myself.

Those words froze her as the front door burst open, the lock ripping from the wall at the forced entry. I glanced over to see the cops.

Fucking finally. And goddammit, I just changed that lock.

Flashlight beams and shouted commands filled the house. Within seconds they had Angie in cuffs. She was sobbing. One of the officers yelled at me to stay still so I waited.

"Tell Sloane," she wailed as they dragged her out. "Tell her the truth, baby. The whole truth!"

The police were quick, dragging her outside with harsh authority. The loud, sharp calls of, "Clear," echoed throughout the house.

My chest ached from my thundering heart, adrenaline still spiking as an officer walked over to me. I raised my hands, desperation in my voice. "Please, I have kids upstairs."

"You live here, sir?"

"Yes, I've been working with Detective Harlan."

The officer gave a short nod, his eyes flicking over me before he turned to his shoulder radio and relayed the message to his team. A response came back and he motioned for me to get up. "Detective Harlan will be here soon. Go on ahead. Go to your kids."

He gave me the all-clear and I bolted to the stairs, took them three at a time, and found Liam and Violet standing in the hallway, both pale and trembling. Liam had a baseball bat clutched in both hands. Violet's stuffed fox dangled from one arm.

"I-I tried to protect her," Liam whispered.

I knelt down. Wrapped them both in my arms. My body shook. "You did good," I said as I kissed the tops of their heads. "You both did so good."

All together we walked downstairs, careful of the broken glass, aiming for the kitchen so the police did their work. As we passed the living room, Rufus whimpered nearby.

Oh fuck. Rufus.

I rushed to him, thankful to see him alive. His breathing was heavy and he was curled up... but he was alive. Liam and Violet stood off to the side, holding onto each other near the kitchen table.

Violet's voice broke through, "Is he okay?"

Worry lined my voice but I held steady. "Yeah, baby. He will be."

I heard my truck pull into the driveway, the door slam, then Sloane yelling at the police. It sounded as if the cops were trying to keep her out of the house... which I could have told them was about as useful as a toothpick in a tornado. I had never heard such an inventive use of curse words until that night, as my fierce and tenacious wife went on a verbal rampage towards us.

She burst through the front door and stormed into the kitchen. When her gaze landed on me and the crying kids, she dropped to her knees without asking a single question. Her hands went straight to them, pulling them close as they clung to her, still trembling from the chaos.

"Oh thank god you two are okay. I love you. It's going to be okay. You're safe." She looked at me then, tears streaking her face, "Levi?"

I didn't know how I looked at that moment, but I gave her the smile she needed to see. "I'm okay Sloane."

She reached for me then. I walked over to them, held them as my heart ached from the catastrophe I'd created. Of what we'd just survived. I could feel the heat of Sloane's tears against my cheek as I whispered to her, "Rufus is hurt. We need to take him to your work."

She nodded quickly, her voice hoarse with emotion. "Okay. Okay. Let's - get your shoes, kids."

I barely heard her as I turned and saw who I assumed was Detective Harlan entering through the busted front door, his face drawn with fatigue. "Mr. Shaw." His voice was gruff. "I hate to meet in person under these circumstances."

I shook his hand, forcing a tight smile, trying to hold it together. "Thanks for coming. I understand she's officially arrested now, right? After all, she seems like a threat to public health."

A weary smile tugged at the detective's lips. "Yes. We'll take her into custody, Mr. Shaw. You don't need to worry about that anymore."

I nodded with relief, but it didn't take away the dread that was still crawling through my chest. "That's all I can ask right now. Is there anything else you need from us?"

Detective Harlan glanced around the house, his eyes sweeping over the broken window and the mess. "Honestly, we'll need to take some pictures of the point of entry. We'll have a team come help board up the window. Shouldn't take long."

I exhaled, trying to process everything, trying to keep myself from falling apart. "Great. Unfortunately, our family dog was injured. We need to take him to the vet. Are we okay to leave?"

The detective nodded. "Of course. Take care of what you need to. We'll be here for a few hours unfortunately, but in touch if we need anything."

Turning, I made my way to the kitchen, where Rufus was huddled on the floor, his body trembling. His fur was matted with dried blood. He looked up at me, eyes wide with confusion and pain.

"Easy boy."

I crouched down beside him, gently running my hand through his fur. His breathing was shallow, and I could see how badly he was hurting. I swallowed hard, trying to hold it together for the kids, for Sloane but all I could think about was getting Rufus the help he needed.

"We're going to get you fixed up, buddy," I whispered, my voice hoarse.

I carried Rufus out to my truck where Sloane and the kids waited, then we sped off to Sloane's work.

Chapter 26

Ten minutes later, we were at Willow Creek Emergency Animal Clinic.

With my heart in my throat and Rufus's limp form cradled in my arms, we marched through the front doors.

The clinic had always been a place of routine. Vaccines. Checkups. Preventative care. But now it felt sterile and surreal, as if the walls were holding their breath with me.

Sloane, calm but firm, said, "Kids, go to the playroom down that hallway. You'll find a room full of consoles and games, okay?"

Violet headed off, but Liam lingered. My son's brow furrowed as he glanced at me, then at Rufus.

"Go ahead, bud," I said gently, keeping my voice steady. "We'll be right out here."

He gave a small nod, cool and composed, every bit the teenager trying to be brave. But I saw his hand subtly brush Violet's back as she turned a corner, guiding her protectively like he always did when he thought no one was watching.

Sloane's gaze shifted between Rufus and me. "We'll get him examined. Hold on, Levi."

I nodded, but my throat was tight. The weight of Rufus in my arms felt heavier by the second, as if my guilt had seeped into his fur. I pressed my cheek briefly to the top of his head, murmuring a soft, broken, "Hang in there, boy."

The scent of antiseptic, the soft hum of fluorescent lights, and the clack of distant keyboard taps filled the air as we continued to the front desk.

"Sloane? Oh no, tell me what's going on."

The voice came from the old receptionist who'd worked here as long as I could remember, seated behind the desk. She stepped out, her reading glasses still perched on her head, silver curls slightly frizzed like she'd been caught in the rain earlier. Her face softened the moment she saw Rufus cradled in my arms.

Without asking, she leaned in to peek at him, her hands practiced as she reached to gently lift one of his paws, careful not to jostle him.

Sloane's voice cracked, the events of the day bleeding into her words. "We have a bit of an emergency, Sarah. I'm so sorry to barge in like this, but could you please let Dr. Monroe know we need him?"

"Absolutely," Sarah said, her tone shifting from concern to calm authority. "Let's get this boy checked in." She gave a reassuring nod and disappeared down a different hallway, her footsteps brisk.

A vet tech appeared just moments later, clipboard in hand as she took information down. Sloane stayed close to Rufus to whisper soothing words as the tech took his temperature. I sat nearby, elbows on knees, heart drumming.

And then *he* walked in.

He wore navy scrubs and a quiet authority that compelled the other staff to nod as he passed. Tall. Broad-shouldered. Confident.

I knew this man from my previous life. Blonde, early 40s, eyes a calm steel-blue that flicked across the room until they landed on Sloane. My stomach churned and my world spun.

Charlie.

The man that Sloane had remarried after our divorce.

Why the fuck is he here? Now?

I racked my brain and scoured my memories from my previous life. Had Sloane and Charlie already met by the time the Old Me left? I remembered that they both worked here at the clinic, but I never knew when precisely they'd met; I'd always assumed it was after our divorce.

Based on the brief exchanges I had with him in my previous life, I knew Charlie was a kind, dependable, faithful, secure rock for Sloane after everything I put her through. I hated him for it... and respected him, too. Because I hadn't been those things for her. Not for a long time.

"Sloane," he said warmly. "You are in awfully early. We were not expecting you for hours, yet. Is everything okay?"

Fuck me. There's no way she doesn't already have feelings for this guy. What woman wouldn't? He looked like a Greek god.

I saw the blush rise on her cheeks as she said, "Char- I mean Dr. Monroe. Our dog, Rufus, has been through a traumatic event. Blunt force trauma with a metal pipe. Is it too busy to rush him in for an emergency exam?"

Charlie glanced down at the dog, his expression shifting from concern to quiet resolve. He crouched beside Rufus, gently offering the back of his hand. "Hey, big guy," he murmured, then looked up at Sloane. "Of course. We will get him registered under the nonprofit."

Sloane started to say, "Oh, you don't have to do-"

"It is done," Charlie said with firm finality.

"Thank you, doctor." I saw tension melt from her shoulders as relief touched her face. I hated that I was not the one to make her feel that way.

He stood and his tone softened. "Well, he is part of the family, right? That makes him our priority, okay?"

Sloane nodded, her lips pressed together. I could tell she was trying her best not to cry again.

Then Charlie, always one for lightening the mood from what I remembered of him, said with a half-smile, "But to be clear, Rufus is not allowed to unionize with the other animals. We are already dangerously close to a goat rebellion in the barn."

A small laugh broke from Sloane as she looked down at Rufus. "You hear that, buddy? No starting revolutions."

Rufus gave a single, low tail thump, which Charlie pointed at dramatically. "That will be one warning."

The technician took Rufus and began heading towards the back.

Charlie's gaze shifted over to me as I stood and forced myself to appear as calm and affable as possible under the circumstances.

Time to play nice.

I offered my hand and said, "Levi. I'm Sloane's-"

"This is Levi," she interrupted me. "The kids' dad."

Right. Not her husband. Not her partner. Just the kids' dad.

It hurt. It hurt far more than it should have, but I managed a tight smile anyway.

Charlie's face didn't change. He just offered a single, polite nod, his body language calm and unreadable. "Dr. Charles Monroe." He looked away, already dismissing me, "Sloane, let us go take a look at Rufus, okay?"

He turned without waiting, and she followed. I watched as he adjusted his pace to match hers; subtle but unmistakable.

What a considerate, perfect-ass bastard.

My jaw tightened as they walked down the hall together. I couldn't look away, watching her move beside the man I knew she had come to trust and love in my previous life.

Feeling light-headed, I sank back down into the chair in the waiting room and stared at the floor as if it might anchor me. My hands wouldn't stop shaking.

How could I have either forgotten or not known Charlie was already part of her life? How had I not even considered the possibility that she'd already met him?

Because you're a fucking idiot.

While I didn't disagree with my self-deprecation, I knew it had to be more than just that. When it came to most things, I was about as sharp as a bowling ball. But this had to go beyond mere stupidity.

I was so hyper focused on winning Sloane back, preparing for this pandemic, dealing with Angie's crazy ass, keeping tabs on Violet's online activity, being a better father and more present partner that... yes, I had forgotten all about Charlie.

Because you're a busy idiot.

I told myself that Charlie being in the picture didn't change anything. I was still here. My priorities hadn't changed. But in that moment, I was acutely aware that if I fucked up the second chance I'd been given and shattered my marriage again? Charlie would be there to pick up the pieces.

Fifteen agonizing minutes later, Sloane returned alone. She looked exhausted, her arms folded tight across her chest.

"Rufus has two fractured ribs," she said as she sat next to me. "Nothing punctured, thank God. They're giving him pain meds, monitoring his breathing. He'll stay overnight."

I nodded, swallowing the knot in my throat.

I tried and failed to keep my tone light and teasing as I said, "You never told me you worked alongside one of your book boyfriends. Does Dr. Monroe also do Pilates?"

Sloane didn't laugh, her face grim. "Levi, you've never wanted to talk about my work at the clinic. You said it was too depressing, hearing about all the animals we have to put to sleep."

Fuck, the Old Me was such an asshole. Come on, big guy... dig yourself out of this one.

"I did say that... didn't I?"

Sloane just scoffed.

I placed my hand on her shoulder. "That was unkind of me. I see that now. I am sure this place, the clinic, the stress of it? I know it weighs on you. I should have been there for you to talk to about it."

"Yeah," she said with a voice of stone, "you should have."

We sat together in silence for a moment. I tried to keep my tone neutral and steady, hoping not to betray the worry that raged within me. "I'm glad I finally got to meet him."

Sloane glanced over. "Dr. Monroe?"

I took a chance with what I said next. "You mentioned him once before. You said you admired him."

Her tone shifted, softened. "Yeah. He's one of the good ones."

I nodded. "Yeah... I know."

"I'm amazed you even remembered." She looked at me, as if she were analyzing an abstract painting.

"I know, right? Your idiot husband actually remembered something," I said as I stood and brushed off my jeans. "We should check on the kids. Since when has the clinic had a game room?"

Sloane led the way down the hall. "Since Charlie's nonprofit paid for it. I thought it was really considerate of him. Some families can't leave their kids behind, have to bring them up here, and so they have different consoles to choose from. With the parents' consent, of course."

"Yeah," I said, as an uneasy edge crept into my voice. "He really thought of everything, didn't he?"

She made a noncommittal sound.

As we walked down the hall, I tried to shift the conversation before I lost my nerve, before the sight of our kids distracted me. I kept my voice low and delicate, as if speaking those next words too loudly would shatter what we'd been rebuilding together.

"Sloan, I want to work on our marriage. I want you back."

She stopped. Her hand stilled on the doorknob, eyes lifting to meet mine, wide and stunned. "Levi..." she breathed, her voice somewhere between a warning and a wound.

I didn't look away. I couldn't. I held her gaze as I said, "I know I'm the last person you should believe right now. But I mean it. I've meant it every day since I realized what I stood to lose."

Sloane swallowed hard, blinking fast. "You can't just say things like that out of nowhere. You said we could take small steps. And I haven't forgiven you." I heard how torn she was, trying to stay quiet and firm.

Trust, yes... but not forgive. She's still hurting.

"It isn't out of nowhere," I said as I brushed my fingers against her cheek. "It's been building for weeks. We've been trusting each other more and more... and I miss you. I miss us. The real us. Even the messy parts."

She looked away then, back down the hallway like she was searching for an escape.

God, I wanted to grip her waist, pull her close, kiss her hard enough to erase everything but that one moment. A bruising kiss, one that said *don't go looking for someone else when I'm right here, Sloane. Still yours. Always yours.*

The game room buzzed faintly beyond the door, our kids laughing inside. The normalcy of it made everything else feel all the more fragile and alien.

"I know we said we would do what we'd been doing. The sex-" I paused, realized I was stumbling. "Sorry... I'm trying, Sloane. And I'm here for this new chapter of our life. I want to be with you. I want to be with the kids. I want to earn my place back."

Sloane looked away, blinking hard. "Levi. This is neither the time nor the place for this. Let's... please, let's take care of Rufus first. Then we can take 'us' one day at a time."

I nodded, swallowing the disappointment even though I knew she was right. "Of course. Right now, Rufus comes first."

It was the right answer. The only answer. Focus on what mattered now which was her healing, our children, and the dog. Those things had become the glue holding this fractured version of us together.

But Charlie... he lingered like a ghost in the corner. A shadow I couldn't shake. A reminder of all the things I had never been for my wife before.

Sloane is mine. I will not lose her again.

Chapter 27

That night, the house was quiet and still. We'd dropped the kids off at Dawn's. It may have been irrational, but we felt uneasy having them sleep at home when there was a boarded up hole where the glass backdoor should be.

I'll replace the door first thing tomorrow morning.

Sloane hadn't spoken much since we got back from the clinic. She was in her room, her door cracked just enough for me to hear her moving around; slow and mechanical, like a clock ticking down the moments she had left. There was no warmth in her steps, no rush to anything. She was simply existing.

I was a nervous wreck from the evening. Considerate Charlie had given her the night off, telling her to text him if she needed an extra day. Apparently, they had each other's numbers already. Which, I tried to remind myself, was fine. They worked together. Her having his number, him having hers? That was fine.

I stood at the kitchen sink, washing a dish that was already clean. The water scalded my hands, but I didn't care.

Charlie kept invading my thoughts.

The man was steady. Calm. Uncomplicated. Everything I wasn't. Everything I hadn't been when Sloane needed me the most.

I thought about my previous life, the one where I had failed her completely. I remembered the soft, tender grief in her eyes when she told me she was moving on. That she couldn't wait for a man who kept choosing the wrong things. I saw the way her shoulders finally relaxed when someone else treated her like a woman instead of a burden.

I gripped the edge of the kitchen counter, my muscles straining, as if I could uproot the damned thing from the floor.

"Not this time," I vowed with resolve. I forced the words past the lump in my throat, but doubt didn't heed vows. Doubt didn't care about second chances. Doubt was a poison, creeping slow, and I felt it crawling through my veins.

I dried my hands, walked down the hallway, and entered the guest room. I pulled my journal out from its hiding place, and flipped through the pages littered with messy handwriting. I had spilled my mind out into that book; every ounce of guilt, regret, and truth I didn't dare speak, along with Angie's menacing behaviour.

I sat down, picked up the pen, and wrote:

Charlie would take care of her. I know that. And she would have let him, if I hadn't been given this chance. That's what this is. A second chance. Not a reset. A test. And I'm still not sure if I'm passing.

There's a version of me that she doesn't love anymore; that our kids tiptoe around; that invited Angie into our lives, even when the tiny, quiet, good parts of me screamed not to. And that version? He's still in here. Lurking.

I'm terrified he's stronger than I am.

I heard a soft creak behind me and I froze.

Sloane stood in the doorway, her robe wrapped around her, one hand resting on the frame, watching me like she could see into the depths of my secrets.

"You okay?" she asked, her voice quiet.

I nodded too quickly. "Yeah. Just... writing. Trying to get it all out of my head."

She stepped closer, but didn't look at the journal.

"That's good," she said, her voice weary, "Do you want to talk about it?"

"Yes. I'm scared," I admitted.

She tilted her head, watching me carefully. "Of what?"

"That I'll ruin this again," I whispered, my throat tightening. "That I'll lose you. That someone better... someone like Charlie will take my place and do it right."

Her expression shifted then, a flicker of softness breaking through the guarded mask she wore so often. "I'm not looking for someone better," she said. "I'm looking for someone honest. Someone who doesn't make me feel alone in my own house."

My throat tightened, and I felt the sting of tears I refused to let fall. "And if that's not me?"

She shrugged, the movement small but deliberate. Her eyes never left mine as she found the courage to say what she needed, even if the words threatened to tear us apart. "Then I'll survive. But it's my choice, Levi. I can choose to be with you, or I can choose to be alone, or I can choose to explore what I have with Charlie."

Fuck me. She said "have" not "could have" or "might have."

"So there is something there."

Sloane shrugged, "Maybe? He gave me his number recently. We laugh and work well together. But it's not as if I've moved on, Levi."

I closed my eyes for a few seconds, tasting the bitterness of regret and hope tangled together. "I know. I want to respect your decision and give you freedom. I have no right to say anything else after all I've put you through."

Her lips curved into a small, genuine smile. "No, you really don't," she said, "but honestly? I am proud of you for accepting that."

I managed a weak, crooked smile. "Well, if you do decide to explore what you have with Charlie, at least promise me you'll ask if he's good at taking out the trash. Because, I was always way better at that than I gave myself credit for."

She laughed. "Is that your big selling point? Trash duty?"

"Hey," I said, grinning despite how rotten I felt, "it's the little things that keep a marriage alive, right? Plus, I make a killer gluten free grilled cheese. Can Charlie do that?"

She rolled her eyes but there was a warmth in her gaze. "No one makes a grilled cheese like you, Levi."

"Okay, I'll take that. Grilled cheese and trash disposal. I am such a fucking catch."

She shook her head, still smiling. "You're impossible."

"But you love me anyway."

"I do... and sometimes that's hard for me to admit." She sighed. "I'm going to bed. Try to rest, okay?"

I nodded, swallowing the lump in my throat. "Sure. Go get some sleep. I love you." The words jerked out, like a reflex.

She paused in the doorway, a flicker of surprise in her eyes before her smile widened ever so slightly and softened her features. "I love you, too. Good night, Levi."

She turned and left me sitting there, alone in the doorway of my own mess.

Chapter 28

Sleep came for me quickly and, for the first time in a long time, nightmares did not plague me. The soreness throughout my body from the spiking then falling adrenaline, the emotional whiplash that left me raw, led to slumber's firm grip.

Once I woke the following morning, I ambled into the kitchen. Sloane was already in the living room, sitting with her back to the boarded up, broken glass doors. The rough wooden planks filtered the sunlight into a dull, hazy glow.

The floor had been swept clean, but I still sensed the remnants of last night's chaos. Tiny shards of glass clung stubbornly in the corners, hidden from plain sight but impossible to ignore once you knew they were there.

What was missing was even more noticeable. The distinct absence of the coffee table I'd slammed Angie into. A lumpy, old dog bed that sat empty by the window.

It all screamed that Angie had been there. She'd broken in. Crossed a line.

I slid onto the couch beside Sloane, needing to be near her. Last night had driven a wedge between us and I feared any amount of distance from her; physical or emotional. "Hey," I said, my voice hoarse.

"Hi." She was quiet and thoughtful as she cradled a cup of coffee, her hands wrapped around the warm mug. "Rufus is doing better."

"Good. Did they do X-rays?"

She nodded, her gaze flickering back toward the window, her mind still seemingly far away. "Yeah, the clinic did everything they could: bloodwork, X-rays, you name it."

"That's great," I said. I pondered how I could ask what was eating at me without it sounding odd or out of place.

Fuck it, just ask.

"Did they find anything else?"

Sloane looked at me, her eyes narrowed and lips parted, but she didn't speak.

"Sloane?"

It took her a moment before she said, "Yeah... they did, actually. Cancer."

Oh, thank fuck they found it.

I did my very best to act surprised and shocked. "Cancer? Seriously?"

"Seriously," she said with an exhale. "It's a miracle that Charlie found it. It's very small. Operable. They anticipate he'll make a full recovery."

My jagged memories of losing Rufus in my past life, of not even being in the same state when he died, collided with a wave of relief flooding through me. My old boy was going to make it. He was going to be okay.

I nodded, tears in my eyes, and cleared my throat. "Cancer on top of everything else? A good boy like Rufus doesn't deserve that."

Sloane saw the emotion on my face and reached a hand out to touch my cheek. "Levi, this is good news. We caught it in time. There are so many pet owners that aren't this fortunate."

"I know. You're right."

She gave a dry laugh. "Honestly? That damned dog is super lucky to have gotten hurt when he did. Otherwise, we probably wouldn't have known until it was too late."

I leaned into the comfort of her palm against my face, her hand hot from holding her coffee.

She said, "And to top it off, Charlie's nonprofit is going to cover his treatments."

What in the actual fuck?

The night before, I had been far too exhausted, too distracted, too panicked by the relentless onslaught of events, I hadn't given much thought to those words.

Charlie's nonprofit.

Did Charlie have a nonprofit in my previous life? I honestly didn't know. That doesn't seem like a thing I would forget... but it also wasn't a thing that the Old Me would have paid any goddamn attention to.

You were too busy shoving your head up your ass and your cock into Angie to notice much else.

I had to stop spiraling and say something. I don't know what was on my face at that moment, but Sloane looked concerned as she watched me process this oddity.

"Wow," I said with genuine shock and mock gratitude, "I didn't realize his nonprofit could cover that much."

"Benefits of being an employee, I suppose." She withdrew her hand from my face, sipped her coffee, then continued. "Charlie only started the nonprofit recently. He had some really well-timed investments skyrocket. He made enough to found the nonprofit and buy out the clinic's previous owner." She trailed off, but her voice sang with relief and admiration.

I forced a smile that probably looked like cracked plaster smeared over a hole. "Wow," I repeated like an idiot, "what a lucky guy."

Thankfully, Sloane didn't see how unhinged I had to look. She stared off, appearing wistful, as she let loose a soft laugh. "Yeah, it was like he'd won the lottery. He barged into the clinic and lifted me off my fee- " She stopped. Her words twitched between us, like a thread waiting to be pulled.

Fuck me, when was this? How long ago?

I didn't say anything, though. I didn't trust myself to say anything. Instead, I gave her time and space to speak.

She shifted on the couch, her eyes wide and fearful. She was expecting me to explode, to rage, to break things; the Old Me would have.

When she spoke, her voice was filled with trepidation. "Levi... nothing happened. He gave me a hug. A spinning, affectionate, and 'inappropriate for the workplace' hug. But that's it."

Sloane has never lied to you. Not in this life or the previous one.

I nodded as I tried to quell the rush of confusion and dread rising inside me. "My love, you're preaching to the choir over here. In what reality do I have the right to be angry over a hug? Really... it's okay."

Relief evident in her posture, she relaxed, "I think anybody would have had that reaction, right? Being able to quit working for somebody else and focus on your own dreams?"

"Of course."

We fell into silence for a time.

My thoughts were a chaotic mess, each one tumbling out faster than the one before it. I didn't know how to process these feelings, these revelations. It was all too much to unpack in that moment.

"When can we get Rufus?" I asked. The question felt out of place, but I needed something to ground me, distract me.

Also, I missed my old boy.

Sloane leaned into me, resting her head on my shoulder. Her scent threatened to overpower me: lavender, honey, citrus. She murmured, "They'll call us. But hopefully soon."

I felt Sloane shift. The tension in her body told me she was still processing everything that had happened. She was so strong holding it all together, but I could see it in her eyes. The fear of what might be unfolding that none of us could fully understand yet.

"Levi," she whispered, "what if this... what if all of this is bigger than we think?"

I wrapped an arm around her, pulled her against me. I wanted to reassure her, but the truth? I didn't know how to. I could plan and place pieces in hopes that things would go my way, but nothing felt certain anymore. Nothing felt solid, not even the ground beneath me. The world had become this swirling mess of possibilities, and I was just grasping at whatever I could hold on to.

I looked into her hazel eyes, those fierce, fiery, stubborn eyes, and in that moment, all the chaos faded to the background. Even with the world broken and laden with uncertainty, there was no one else I would rather be facing this mess with. No one else I wanted beside me as we tried to find a way forward.

Gently, I cupped her cheeks in my hands, my thumbs brushing her soft skin. "It will be okay. We will work as a team. Together."

She smiled, though it didn't quite reach her eyes. "I just don't know if I can handle anything else, Levi. Everything... everything's too much."

I leaned forward, pressed my forehead to hers, and closed my eyes as I felt the connection between us. I reminded myself why I had to keep going. I whispered, "You don't have to handle it alone. Not anymore. Never again."

She didn't pull away when I kissed her, delicate and reverent, letting my lips linger at the corner of her mouth before trailing down to the warm hollow of her neck. Her breath shuddered into me, her body tight with all the things she was still holding in.

"I know a few ways to help you relax, my love," I whispered, the words slipping out like a promise.

She chuckled, low and unexpected, the sound curling around my ribs and anchoring itself deep inside my chest. "Since when have you been so quick to offer?" she asked, voice teasing but eyes still watchful.

"Since I realized I can't live – hell, I can't even breathe – without you."

That earned me a real look. She peeked up through thick lashes, her cheeks tinted rose, lips parted just slightly. "You are such a sneaky devil," she said softly, the edge of a smile ghosting across her face.

"Only for you." I brushed my thumb across the bottom of her lip, enjoying the way her lips parted for me.

"Does Charlie really scare you?" she asked.

The question, sharp and serrated, sawed through my ribs, twisted my heart in barbed wire. I jerked away, face hot, stomach sick.

I was afraid of Charlie because of what he represented. What I could lose her to if I wasn't careful.

I exhaled a slow and shaky breath. The truth ached in my chest. "I will not lie to you, Sloane. I am afraid to lose you. Terrified of losing you."

She pressed her lips together, and I felt a pang of longing. I wanted to kiss her. Bite her bottom lip. Suck until she gasped my name. I wanted her to feel how much I meant every word.

"I know you, Levi," she whispered. "I know you like I know myself. Or at least, I thought I did until you fucked everything up." There was no accusation in her voice, just the quiet certainty that came from years of scars and secrets.

I chuckled under my breath, heeding her tone and knowing she meant no harm. "That you do. As I know you, Sloane... and I can tell by how hard your nipples are, talking isn't what you want to do right now."

She rolled her eyes. "Stop with the jokes. We're having a serious conversation."

"Yeah," I said with a heavy breath, "it's just hard to be serious when all I can think of is how badly I want to taste you right now."

Her breath hitched, barely, but I caught it. That little tremble. That tiny falter in her resolve. The thought of my tongue working at her was under her skin.

"Sloane," I said, my voice low, "can we not talk about another man right now? Not when you're right here, looking like sin itself, and I'm starving for you."

She arched an eyebrow, a challenge simmering in her gaze. "What are you suggesting?" she asked.

I leaned in, brushing my lips along her jaw. "I'm saying... you could sit on my face and let me remind you what it feels like to be worshipped."

Her lips parted in shock then amusement. I smirked.

"Or," I whispered, "you could open that pretty mouth and let me forget everything else for a while."

Her breath caught again, this time sharper. I felt the heat building between us, undeniable and raw.

But I didn't move in yet. I waited.

Let her come to me. Let her choose.

Time crawled tortuously while she contemplated her next action. I waited, ever patient. Slowly, her tongue darted out to wet her bottom lip.

She moved forward without a word, her hand trailing down my chest, over the firm lines of my stomach, until her fingers brushed the waistband of my sweatpants. Her touch was tentative at first, like testing a bridge that had once collapsed. I didn't rush her. I didn't dare breathe.

Her fingers dipped beneath the band.

I swallowed hard, my eyes locked on her, burning with the quiet plea I couldn't voice: *Let me be enough for you again.*

She leaned in, close enough for her breath to warm my jaw. "Don't you dare move," she whispered in the low and sultry tone she knew shattered me. She was in control, then. Completely.

Her fingers undid my fly with practiced ease, like muscle memory, like she hadn't forgotten.

She pulled my pants down and wrapped her hands around my hard cock. And then she sank to her knees.

Good fucking god.

I gripped the edge of the couch as she looked up at me, her lashes fluttering like velvet against her cheeks, lips inches away from the part of me that throbbed in her presence.

"Still think denial is funny?" she whispered, teasing. But there was something else there; something darker. Need? Power?

"No," I choked out. "Not anymore."

Her mouth brushed the tip of my head, a feather-light kiss, and I shuddered.

Then she opened her mouth.

Heat exploded in my spine. My hips jerked but her hands were already there, pressing me back down, setting the pace at her command.

Languid. Torturous. Intentional. She was in complete control and we both knew it.

She hollowed her cheeks and sucked deeper, her leisurely rhythm maddening. Her fingers curled around my base, twisting as her mouth worked me over, and I couldn't hold back the groan that tore from my chest. I braced one trembling hand on her head, not to guide her but to anchor myself. She didn't stop. She didn't flinch.

Fuck, she is magnificent.

When her eyes flicked up again, locking on mine, it nearly undid me. I saw the challenge there. Her eyes screamed, *"Do you still think you're in charge?"*

I didn't. Not anymore.

"Sloane," I gasped, fingers tightening in her hair, my body pulled tight like a bowstring. "You – fuck – you feel like heaven."

Her tongue flicked along the underside, her pace unrelenting now, deliberate and devastating. She didn't let up. And I knew she was punishing me by owning me with pleasure. By reminding me exactly who the hell I belonged to.

And, gods, I let her. Because she did own me. She always had.

When I finally came, it was with her name ragged on my lips, my vision blurring as my body folded around the storm of her.

And even then, even in the release, there was something unspoken between us: Sloane held the reins of whatever fragile thing was left of us.

Chapter 29

Angie was taken in, but it wasn't long before her family's wealth and influence came into play. Just one of the many perks of having a filthy rich dad who came from old money.

Within a day, she posted bail and was free.

I envisioned her striding out of the jail with a smug expression plastered on her face. I feared she would be a true agent of chaos after her brief incarceration, and it did not take her long to turn my fears into reality.

I was in the backyard with Rufus, who was finally showing signs of recovery, his limp disappearing as he trotted around the yard. Charlie had done a good job.

Sloane came to the back door with an envelope in her hand.

Moving toward her I asked, "What is it?"

She was pale and I saw the envelope was addressed to her in neat handwriting. She looked into my eyes and there was the shadow of fear upon her face. She handed it to me without a word.

I opened it to find a short note inside; far too short to contain all of the hatred and jealousy Angie had festering within her. But the message was clear:

> He is mine, Sloane. He always was and he always will be. You'll pay for stealing him.

My throat tightened. I wanted to destroy the paper in my hands, throw it into a fire and watch it burn. But something about this note? It felt like an omen. Angie was planning something dark, something sinister.

Sloane's eyes were cold. A look of quiet resolve settled over her face. "She's not going to stop, is she?"

"No," I said, shaking my head. "She isn't."

We didn't talk about it further. There was nothing left to say.

I called Detective Harlan, who arrived wearing an N95 mask that barely hid the weariness etched into his face. The tension in the air was thick, not just from Angie's escalation, but from the suffocating reality settling over the world as the pandemic began to sink its claws in.

He took the note as evidence with gloved hands, nodded solemnly, and assured us that the paperwork for new warrants was being processed.

"Once the judge sees this, it'll be clear this woman is a threat and issue a permanent TPO," he said, voice muffled by the mask. "It's only a matter of time."

I wanted to believe him, but I couldn't shake the sense that time was the one thing we were running out of.

Over the course of the following week, life felt as if it were on the edge of shattering again, but this time the tension came from a different place. I'd kept my head down, to focus on repairing what was broken around the house and pushing away the fear that Angie might come back to hurt us in some other way.

While Rufus had been given the greenlight to come home, he still needed daily visits from a veterinarian, which would have been difficult given the pandemic and shutdowns. However, Considerate Charlie, ever the professional, had offered home visits for his closest patients. And since we were only ten minutes away from the clinic?

Charlie had been in and out of the house every day that week.

On the surface it was to check in on Rufus's recovery. But each visit lasted a little longer than the previous one, and led to more frequent and deeper conversations between him and Sloane.

That would have made me uncomfortable on its own, but it was the added fact that Rufus's cancer treatment was being fully paid for by Charlie's nonprofit. He didn't have to do that; he knew he didn't have to. Anybody who took a single glance at our home would recognize we weren't hurting for money.

Then there was the nonprofit itself, funded by Charlie's lucky investments. It ate at me that I had either forgotten entirely, or possibly was never even aware, that the man had his own nonprofit in my previous life. It was a painful reminder of just how little the Old Me noticed anyone or anything that did not directly benefit or hinder his daily life.

Yet despite all of those unsettling pieces, the part that caused me the most unease was that first visit when Charlie came to check on Rufus.

I'd opened the door to let him in, and his composed mask of confident competence cracked a fraction; he was shocked, perhaps crestfallen, to see me standing in the house I had built. I knew Sloane had told him about our separation, but it was apparent she hadn't mentioned I'd moved back in.

That first visit, he sat down with me and Sloane to talk through Rufus's treatment plan, and ensure we didn't have any questions. During our conversation, Sloane asked if I could grab pen and paper from my room. When I returned, I saw the realization sparkle in his eyes and the ever so subtle upturn of a smile; he knew I wasn't sleeping in the master bedroom. The man's face was almost unreadable, but there was a hungry hope there that never left my mind.

Despite the obviously tense situation, he and I remained cordial.

After that first week, with Rufus nearly recovered from his initial injury, Charlie's visits grew sparse. He came less frequently, only popping in a few more times for check-ups. Until one day when he showed up at the front door with a different look on his face. It was subtle, but it was there... a shift in his demeanor. There was something in his eyes, something more certain, more intentional.

When I opened the door to him that afternoon, he didn't offer his usual easy smile. Instead, his gaze was firm, calculating, as if he'd made up his mind about something. It was disarming, and elevated the tension between us.

"Levi... how is Rufus holding up?"

"Better," I replied, keeping my voice neutral. I held the door open for him, trying to appear welcoming. "A little more energy, but still on the mend."

He nodded as he stepped inside, but he lingered in the doorway... almost as if assessing the space between us. He studied me for a moment before he spoke again, his voice lower this time.

When he spoke next, his tone was casual, but there was an edge beneath it. "You know, I have been thinking about a few things. About you and Sloane."

I froze, my fingers clutching the front door knob as every muscle in my body turned rigid. "What about us?"

His eyes narrowed. "Sloane told me what you did."

Bullshit. Sloane isn't the type to gossip about our problems.

But I knew he was telling the truth. This was the man she married in my previous life, the man she grew to love and trust. That relationship did not start in a vacuum; it started with her sharing the parts of herself with him that she felt she couldn't share with anyone else.

I took a deep breath before I said, "And?"

"And I know you are trying to do the right thing this time. But the truth is, I have seen the way things are between you two. We both know how this plays out-"

You don't know shit, buddy.

"So do you agree that you should do what is best for Sloane?"

My face was a furnace as I clenched the doorknob. I wanted to rip the front door from its hinges and beat the smug prick with it.

Instead I asked, "I suppose you know what's best for Sloane?"

He shook his head. "No, Levi. Only Sloane knows what is best for Sloane. I am asking you... are you capable of allowing her to decide what that is?"

Sloane came up behind me, her voice full of surprise and warmth. "Charlie!" She greeted him like an old friend, her tone inviting and genuine.

I excused myself with a slight nod and stepped into the kitchen to busy my hands with the dirty dishes. It gave me the distance I needed, allowing me to stay out of their line of sight... but within earshot.

Because eavesdropping on your wife is a great way to rebuild trust, you idiot.

From the kitchen sink, I heard how they interacted with each other; the warmth in her voice, the laughter, the easiness in how she spoke with him. It was torture, exquisite and unbearable, to hear her laugh at another man's jokes, to accept another man's compliments, and to know there was love kindling there.

It was subtle. Nobody else in the world besides me, or perhaps Sloane's sister Dawn, would have heard it. She had feelings for him.

Charlie, for his part, seemed to understand that he didn't need to rush her. He wasn't pushing or making any overt moves. He was simply... there. Listening, being present, offering a shoulder without expectation. I knew he wasn't trying to force anything; he was patient, giving her space to figure things out on her own.

It gnawed at me, the quiet undercurrent of their interactions. I sensed the shift in her, the slow pull of something that might turn into more. And despite how I tried to shut the thoughts out of my mind, I couldn't help but wonder what would happen if Charlie's patience turned into something more than just friendship.

I didn't have to wait long.

He cleared his throat. "I was thinking... maybe we could go grab dinner sometime? I know you have been through a lot, but if you are up for it, I'd really like to take you out. No pressure, just... a chance to unwind."

There was a moment of hesitation before I heard Sloane's reply. "I think I'd like that, Charlie. Thanks."

Jealousy and anger simmered under my skin.

Don't be a hypocrite, big guy. You did a hell of a lot more than take Angie out for dinner, remember?

I had already done enough damage to Sloane. If she could find solace in someone else, maybe that was the best for her?

Maybe Charlie was what she needed.

I swallowed hard and focused on the dish in front of me, but I couldn't ignore the cold knot that settled in my stomach.

Rufus padded into the room, sitting down beside me with a low whine, as if he could sense the shift in the air too. I scratched behind his ears, "It's okay boy."

I heard the door close and Sloane's soft footsteps on the stairs to check on the kids.

I guess she will tell me whenever she's ready.

Later that night, as I sat alone at the kitchen table, silence lorded over the house. The kids were upstairs, tucked away behind closed doors, their laughter from earlier in the evening already fading into dreams. Rufus was asleep at my feet, tail twitching against the floor. I stared into a cold cup of coffee I had no intention of drinking.

Sloane came in and stood by the counter for a moment, her arms crossed, a mug clutched in her hands. She looked tired but clearer, too, as if something inside her had settled into place.

"I need to talk to you," she said softly.

Well fuck. Here goes.

I straightened in the chair. "Okay."

She didn't sit next to me and instead stayed by the counter, a safe distance away. "I'd like to go out with Charlie," she said. "On a date. A real date."

I stared at her. My teeth clenched hard enough to crack a diamond. I hadn't prepared for the honesty of it, not like this. She wasn't asking for permission. She was informing me.

"Good for you, Sloane." I kept my voice light because, in a bizarre and fucked up way, I *was* happy for her. I knew how difficult this had to be for her, to process these emotions and share her desires with me. I was proud of her.

She cleared her throat. "Did I hear you correctly? Or did you forget to add sarcasm to that?"

I chuckled into my cold coffee. "I know he's a good man. I can see that about him. It seems you two have a good friendship. He makes you laugh."

Sloane nodded, her gaze not leaving mine. "That's not why I said yes. I said yes because I need to know if this," she gestured vaguely between us, "is something I want to fight for... or something I'm just used to surviving."

I swallowed. My mouth tasted like ash, "Can you explain more?"

"I'm not trying to hurt you, Levi," she went on, her voice steady but gentle. "But I don't trust this new version of you, this new version of us. Not yet. I don't know if what we had can exist anymore without all the hurt in the middle. And I don't want to feel like I only let you back in because I didn't want the kids to be without a father."

"You're allowed to figure that out," I said, though god fucking damn it pained me to say it. "You deserve to know what it's like to be... happy."

Her eyes softened, but she didn't move closer.

"This isn't about revenge," she added, "or some weird kinky polygamy plan."

I blinked. "Well, that's oddly specific."

She cracked a small smile. "Just wanted to cover all the bases. In case you thought this was some long game where I show up one day with a boyfriend and a spreadsheet titled *'Polyamory Pros and Cons.'*"

"That'd actually be the most organized emotional disaster I've ever been part of," I said, trying to smile through the ache.

She shook her head, the amusement evident in her voice. "This isn't about making you feel what I felt when you cheated. It's about finding out if there's still a version of me that can breathe, without the weight of everything you and I have been through."

"And... if there isn't?"

She shrugged. "Then I guess I suffocate quietly in a well-decorated apartment with Charlie and a rescue dog named Peanut Butter."

I surprised myself with my own laugh; it felt foreign in my throat. "At least name the dog after me if that happens."

"Only if he is a leg-humper who needs constant validation," she shot back with a smirk.

Good fucking god, I love this woman.

"Ouch."

She turned to leave the kitchen, pausing in the doorway. "I'm not shutting the door on us, Levi. But I need to do this." And with that, she was gone, back into the room we used to share.

I looked down at the table, down at my hands; my thick fingers and scarred knuckles. Those were the hands of a lifelong carpenter, mechanic, mason, builder. Those hands were meant for creating... yet they had destroyed so much.

Some things had to be broken before they could be rebuilt. But damn if it didn't hurt to be the one holding the hammer.

She will come back. You are doing everything you can to prove you are worth coming back to.

Chapter 30

Sloane was finally past the worst of her nausea, looking more herself again, more human. Meanwhile, I juggled virtual classes with the kids and stayed glued to the news, watching the world unravel by the hour. Cities were locking down. Hospitals were flooding. People were scared and so was I.

The next few days were hell for me as I struggle to maintain a sense of normalcy with my family.

That afternoon the weather was too nice to ignore, so I fired up the grill. Steaks hissed over the flames while Rufus lounged on the deck, his head tilted toward the sun. The kids shrieked and laughed in the backyard, running wild through the sprinklers. It was a brief, precious break from the hum of online school and the weight of the world.

Sloane stepped out onto the porch, shielding her eyes from the light. She inhaled, a soft smile tugging at her lips. "Smells amazing," she said, walking over. "Too bad I still can't really stomach it."

She looked beautiful, hair pinned up, a touch of makeup, dressed in a way that made me ache inside. A pit formed in my stomach before she even spoke again.

"I was going to go out for a bit," she added, her tone casual, like it didn't carry a thousand pounds of implication. "You okay to stay with the kids?"

I nodded. "You know they're still asking people to stay home, right?"

She shrugged, half-apologetic. "I wanted to walk in the park. Charlie's meeting me there and we'll keep our distance from others. We'll be safe."

The tension between us grew taut like the slow draw of a bowstring. She was going on a date. I had promised I'd be understanding and I meant it... even if it hurt.

"Okay," I said, voice even. "Can you... text me when you're on your way back?"

She smiled and nodded, but it didn't settle the unease gnawing at me.

"Mommy, you look so pretty!" Violet came barreling toward us, dripping wet, hair stuck to her cheeks. She wrapped her arms around her mom's waist, admiring her styled hair and pink-tinted lips.

Sloane laughed, hugging her back. "Thanks, Violet."

She waved to Liam who was crouched at the edge of the yard, refilling a water gun. He gave a nod and shouted, "You look nice Mom."

"Thanks, kids. I'll be back. Listen to your father." And then she was gone. The door shut behind her, and I was left with unease crawling under my skin, refusing to quiet.

I spent the afternoon trying to focus on the kids. We ate out on the deck, and when evening rolled around, they showered and curled up for a movie. I'd baked a new batch of gluten-free brownies, this time using sweet potatoes instead of that awful black bean recipe I'd tried before.

Violet took one bite, grimaced dramatically, and slathered it with hot fudge. "Needs more sugar!" she declared, giggling like mad as she added a tower of whipped cream.

Liam hovered nearby, eyeing the brownies like they might bite back. "So... they're bad?"

Violet made a noncommittal shrug. "Hmmm... they're okay." She turned to me, "Wanna build another base or castle later, Daddy?"

I laughed as I started on washing the dishes. "Absolutely, baby girl. I have this idea for an automated chicken egg collection assembly line."

Her face lit up, "Oh that sounds awesome!" Then she ran off, sugar tower in tow.

And if I'm lucky, we'll bump into a new friend.

I had still been on the hunt for my monster: Prince_Harming. He was out there, somewhere, lurking in the anonymous darkness of the internet. It was only a matter of time before he attempted to make contact with Violet in this life, and I was going to be waiting there when he did.

"You okay, Dad?" Liam asked. His tone was thoughtful and too grown for his years.

He'd been watching me scrub dishes and plot a murder, and I had no idea what expression was on my face.

I'm fine, boy. Just torn between strangling or stabbing your sister's kidnapper.

"Yeah, bud," I said with a nod. "Just happy to be home."

And that was not a lie. Despite the fucked up state of the world, the looming threat of Angie, Charlie being a thorn in my plans... I was happy. Being there, being with them, that part never stopped feeling like a gift. He gave me a small smile and returned to the couch.

Time crawled.

When Sloane finally came home after texting me she was on her way, night had already settled. She walked in, looking tired but peaceful in a way I hadn't seen in a long time. She helped tuck the kids in, humming under her breath as she moved through the motions.

"We grabbed takeout and watched the sunset," she told me later, leaning against the counter, her voice dreamy. "It was nice."

Simple. Romantic. Thoughtful.

Fuck, why hadn't I thought of something like that?

I knew corporations and businesses were willing to stay open during this turbulent time and could have tried ordering us something one night.

She reached for a brownie, took a bite, her expression twisting as she thoughtfully chewed. "Maybe more honey next time?"

"You can say they suck," I muttered, half-laughing.

She smiled, licking a crumb off her thumb. "No. I appreciate that you try. Especially the gluten-free thing. It means a lot."

"Of course. It's important for you and Violet and since I'm not eating gluten either..." I trailed off, not needing to finish the thought. We both knew why I was being careful. Those stolen kisses. The lingering closeness.

I rubbed the back of my neck, heart hammering. "Sloane?"

She looked up. "Yeah?"

I stepped toward her and my voice caught on the jagged edges of my fragile confidence. "I've been thinking a lot about us... about everything. I know I screwed up and I know I put you through hell but I was wondering... would you be willing to try virtual marriage counseling?"

I was taking a shot because I felt like I was going to lose her if I didn't.

She froze in that quiet way she does when she's deciding how much of herself she can safely show me.

"I'm not asking you to forgive me," I continued. "Not to promise anything. I... I want to talk. I want to work on this. Even if we don't know where it's going yet."

She looked away, biting her lip. "I don't know, Levi."

"I get it," I said quickly. "It doesn't even have to be marriage counseling right away. There's individual therapy as well. After everything we've been through, your anxiety, the shutdown, the stress... maybe it would help to talk to someone. You deserve that support."

The hesitation lingered but then she nodded, slow and cautious. "It's not a bad idea."

Relief surged through me, almost dizzying.

"I actually researched a few therapists," I said, grabbing my phone. "I can send you a list with reviews. You can pick whoever feels right. This one has great reviews and has been practicing for twenty years, but this one could do in-person sessions if you are masked, and this on-"

She touched my arm and I stopped rambling.

"You can send it, Levi," she said gently. Then she kissed my cheek, and I felt it all the way down to my toes. "Thank you. For handling the kids, the house, and for thinking of this. Even if it's not something I wanted to admit we might need."

I pulled her close, burying my face against her neck. "Anything for you. Anything to help with your mental load. I mean that."

When I pulled back, I looked into her eyes and saw all the pain... all the history and hope too. Despite the date she had with Charlie, she was here with me in that moment. I searched the deep hazel of her eyes, admiring the golden flecks as I cupped her face. She leaned into me and I felt her body sigh.

Despite how much I wanted her to be free, to make her choices and find out what she wanted, I was terrified of losing her. As we watched each other, I think she knew. I could see it in the way she looked at me, and I poured every ounce of love in my hands, my eyes, my body towards her.

Delicately, she kissed my palm and I leaned down to kiss her softly, hovering long enough to let her change her mind.

She's the one who gets to choose, big guy.

Instead, she leaned in and we melted into each other, clinging onto each other like survivors. I lifted her gently onto the counter, my lips trailing along her neck, toward the edge of her blouse, where her breath began to catch.

Her legs parted instinctively as I stepped between them, her knees brushing my hips. I was careful with my hands, tentative, reverent, as I touched her thighs, trailing my palms upward as I reacquainted myself with her sacred heat.

She didn't stop me, the open invitation a balm to my existence.

My mouth found hers again, slower this time, deeper. Her hands moved to my hair, fingertips curling, holding me there like she needed the closeness as badly as I did.

The tension that had stretched between us for months, the uncertainty, melted into the heat building in our shared breaths, building on the previous connections we had allowed ourselves to share. It didn't erase what we'd been through, didn't make things whole, but it was real.

It was everything.

I slid my hands under her blouse, feeling the warmth of her skin, the slow rise and fall of her chest. Her breath caught when my thumbs grazed beneath the lace edge of her bra.

"Sloane…" I whispered against her mouth, asking her silently with every inch I crossed.

She responded with a kiss that was all tongue and emotion, pulling me closer by the front of my shirt, anchoring me to her. I didn't need more permission than that.

I kissed down her throat, pausing at her collarbone, letting myself feel the way her body responded, tense at first, then gradually giving in. I paid attention to her breathing, ignoring the strain of my cock, balls so tight I felt like I would come any moment.

I was desperate to be in her, feel the connection of our bodies. I wanted to ravage and worship her all at once. My hands moved around her back, unclasping the bra with a muscle memory I'd honed from all our years together, and when I pulled the fabric away, she was stunning, bare and vulnerable in a way that stole my breath.

I took my time, allowing myself to simmer in the self-inflicted torment. As much as I wanted to ravage her, I couldn't ignore the slow, undeniable pull of our bodies drawing together. I wanted her to feel pleasure in ways I had never given her.

I traced my tongue along her breastbone, kissed the soft curve of her chest, felt her tremble against me as her fingers curled around the back of my neck. She let out a low, shaky breath as I brought her nipple into my mouth, sucking gently, hands keeping her steady. I chuckled at the way she squirmed under my teasing.

She gasped, her head falling back, exposing her throat. My name spilled from her lips. "Levi…"

My name from her lips? Good fucking god it undid me.

I lifted her, cradling her against my chest, and carried her into the living room where the lights were dim and the house was quiet, save for the soft hum of the dishwasher, swish of the ceiling fan, and the distant sound of sirens.

We didn't speak as I laid her down gently on the couch, her blouse undone, her jeans pulled slowly from her hips. She looked like a siren, no, a goddess, and for a moment, I forgot how to breathe.

Her brow furrowed, a flicker of concern in her voice. "What's wrong?"

"You're beautiful," I said, barely able to get the words out.

A soft, shy blush bloomed across her cheeks. Then she reached for me, urgent, tugging at my clothes like she needed me bare, needed me near, needed *me*.

Our hands trembled, betraying the need that burned beneath our skin as we kissed each other with the kind of hunger only desperation brings.

"Levi, skip the dirty talk tonight. I want you."

"Whatever my mistress desires."

She chucked at that. When she reached for me through my boxers to pull me out, I felt the last of my control unravel. Breathing through my restraint, I entered her slowly, feeling everything in that moment of longing, my heart aching for her.

Her eyes stayed locked on mine, dark with want then darker with need. Moving in and out of her, I leaned in and kissed her, slow at first, but she met me with urgency, arms wrapping around my neck as her tongue slid into my mouth. Her kiss felt like a question, asking if I was real, if I was there, if I was hers.

I kissed her back with all the answers, telling her in ways only our bodies could understand that she was my everything, I was hers, she was mine.

"Mine," I growled.

She laughed, the sound loud in the quiet of the room, "Yes my primitive mate. Yours." Her voice curled around the word like a tease.

I groaned against her mouth, "Even your mockery gets me off."

She tilted her head back, smiling beneath me, and I caught her mouth again, swallowing the sound of her amusement as it dissolved into something heavier and hungrier.

"I want to feel all of you, Sloane," I murmured into the heat of her skin. "No more distance. No more pretending."

I moved inside her with a forced slowness as my forehead rested against hers. Our fingers locked above her head as our breaths synced: shallow, shared. We moved together in perfect harmony for a long while, each thrust a promise, a needful benediction that I never wanted to end. Eventually, the pressure built, more and more, nearly too much to contain.

"Levi, can I come?" The way she asked, the submissiveness of her request... I lost the last shred of control.

"Fuck yes, Sloane," I growled, my voice hoarse with need. "Come all over my cock. Let me feel you lose it for me."

She shattered beneath me, her body trembling as release tore through her. Her body clenched around me, tight and pulsing, drawing me deeper, dragging me over the edge with her.

Her cry was lost in a kiss we crashed into, and only then, only when I felt her fall, did I finally let go and fall with her.

Inside that moment together, we weren't husband and wife. We weren't betrayer and betrayed. There was no past, no scarred life to trip over. We were simply two people who had once belonged to each other, meeting again at the edge of something half-remembered and holy.

After, we collapsed together, tangled and exhausted. The room was quiet; the dishwasher had long ago finished its load. The only sound was the soft swishing of the ceiling fan and the steady rhythm of our breaths.

She curled into me, her head resting on my chest, one leg hooked over my hip as if she needed the contact to believe this wasn't a dream.

I held her close, my fingers tracing slow, absent-minded patterns along her arm, grounding both of us in a silence that didn't need to be filled.

"I love you," I said, a vow to her.

The silence stretched and finally, *finally*, her voice broke through, soft and fragile.

"I love you too, Levi."

Chapter 31

The light filtered in through the living room windows in soft golden streaks, painting the couch and floor. The blanket had slipped halfway off during the night, and I stirred first, opening my eyes to silence.

Sloane curled around me, her leg draped loosely over mine, one hand resting where my chest rose and fell. Her face nestled in the crook of my shoulder, her hair spilled like silk across us both.

I lay motionless, soaking in the faint whir of the fridge, birds chirping outside, the muffled sounds of Liam and Violet moving upstairs.

This moment? I know I didn't deserve it. But I cradled it, held it close to me, knowing how fragile it was.

Fuck, she is beautiful like this. Peaceful. I could stay here forever, just watching her breathe.

She shifted, eyes fluttering open. A moment of confusion crossed her face before her gaze locked with mine. Her lips curved upward.

"Morning," she said, voice rough with sleep.

"Morning," I replied, tucking a strand of hair behind her ear.

We remained there, not rushing back to reality. No awkwardness, just calm. A stillness between us that had been missing for so long. Not empty. Just... quiet.

"I didn't mean to fall asleep down here," she murmured, stretching slightly without moving away. "The couch isn't exactly luxurious."

"Best night of sleep I've had in weeks," I admitted.

She smiled faintly and nestled her head back on my shoulder, fingers tracing my shirt seam. "I didn't think I'd ever feel okay waking up next to you again," she whispered. "But I do."

My breath caught. I stayed still, silent, giving her space to continue.

"I know we've been with each other multiple times," she continued, eyes fixed on my chest. "But last night... for the first time, it felt right, almost perfect."

My hand found hers, squeezing gently. "It was perfect in every way."

She exhaled slowly and finally met my gaze. "I want to try, Levi. Not just counseling. I want to try *us*." She paused. "But I need to go slow. And I need you to be honest with me. Every time. No matter what. I've laughed with you more than I ever have. I know we've explored so many new things in the bedroom and I've trusted you with myself. I want all of you Levi. The Good. The Bad."

After everything I've done, she's willing to give me another chance. Don't you dare fuck this up.

I nodded, throat tight. "You'll get nothing less."

Sloane leaned up and pressed her lips to mine.

We stayed tangled together until footsteps thundered down the stairs, Violet's laughter mixing with Liam's groans: "She's hogging the bathroom again!"

Sloane's laugh vibrated against my neck and it felt like sunshine breaking through clouds.

"I should make breakfast," I said, not budging.

"You should," she agreed, equally still.

Eventually we peeled ourselves off the couch, took showers and brushed teeth before bumping hips in the kitchen as we cooked gluten-free pancakes and scrambled eggs, cartoons and sibling bickering filling the house.

Later that afternoon, I walked in to find Sloane at the dining table, her laptop open from her virtual therapy session. The kids occupied the other room; Violet working on an art project while Liam scrolled on his tablet.

Sloane looked up with red-rimmed eyes but a peaceful expression. The usual tightness in her face had softened.

I approached carefully. "Hey... how'd it go?"

She offered a small, tired smile. "It was good. Hard. But good."

I sat across from her, hands folded, waiting. Pushing would only make things worse.

Sloane gazed out the window briefly before turning back to me. "She said something interesting. The therapist. She said sometimes people can't say what needs to be said, especially when there's hurt. So she suggested I try writing."

"Like journaling?" I asked.

She shook her head slightly. "Love letters. But not the sweet kind. Letters filled with everything. The pain. The betrayal. The confusion. The love that still lingers. She said if I write to you, even if I never give them to you, it might help me process everything."

My throat dried. "Will you... give them to me?"

Every wound I caused, inked out in black and white.

Letters about how much I had hurt her. I was terrified to read them, but I knew I would need to... if she would allow me the privilege.

Sloane studied me, weighing whether she trusted this version of me. I couldn't blame her hesitation. It was a leap of faith.

"I might," she finally said. "If you're willing to read them without getting defensive. Without trying to fix or explain away every emotion I have."

I nodded. "I won't defend myself. I won't interrupt your truth."

She raised an eyebrow. "Even if it hurts?"

"Especially if it hurts," I said, voice low. "Because I caused that hurt. And I can't rebuild anything with you unless I face it all."

Sloane glanced away, blinking rapidly. "Okay," she said softly. "Then I'll start. One letter at a time."

Liam appeared in the doorway, hovering uncertainly. His expression mixed curiosity with protectiveness. I knew he was still figuring out my place in his mother's heart.

Sloane noticed him and smiled gently. "Hey bud. Want to come sit for a sec?"

He joined reluctantly, sliding into the seat beside her.

"I did a therapy session today," she said, running her fingers through his hair. "And I talked about how everything's been affecting me. And about your dad."

Liam nodded slowly. "Was it... weird?"

"A little," she admitted with a soft laugh. "But good. My therapist suggested I try writing love letters to your dad. Not mushy ones. Real ones. About what it felt like. What changed in me. What still hurts."

Liam turned to me, eyes narrowed. "You gonna read them?"

I answered before Sloane could. "Only if she wants me to. But yeah, I'll read every word. As many as she writes. I'll even let you write me letters as a freebie."

He laughed before his expression sobered. "You really are trying your best dad."

My son. My boy. Fuck, I almost lost him too.

"I'm trying," she said. "And that doesn't mean I've decided everything. It just means I'm willing to explore what healing could look like."

Liam sat back, quiet for a moment. Then he said, "That's cool." The teenage equivalent of approval.

I chuckled. "Well, maybe therapy is something we can all use, to build the tools we need to emotionally regulate and process."

And I meant it. The tools I had learned from years and years of therapy in my previous life were one of the main reasons I was able to admit my mistakes and grow. It's one of the traits that separated the Old me from... me.

Tears welled in Sloane's eyes as she pulled him into a hug. "I love you." Her words carried so much raw emotion. I saw the strength she'd built in herself. I loved her even more for the woman she'd become, desperate to join her on that journey.

Chapter 32

Dear Levi,

I don't know how to start this, or where it's supposed to go. The therapist said I didn't need to make sense, but I needed to be honest. So here it is. My honesty.

You broke me.

And I hate how cliché that sounds, but it's the truth. You shattered something I thought was unbreakable between us. For so long, I carried the weight of our life… our kids, my job, the appointments, the emotional labor you never saw and I did it gladly, because I believed we were a team. Even when we drifted, even when I was exhausted, I believed you were still with me.

But you weren't. You were with her.

And I felt it, you know? Long before I knew the truth, I felt the distance growing like a void I couldn't name. I blamed myself at first. Thought I wasn't enough. Maybe I was too tired. Maybe I'd stopped being the version of me you wanted. Maybe if I'd been more… more attentive, more sexual, more everything? Maybe you wouldn't have looked elsewhere.

It took me months to realize: your betrayal wasn't about me being less. It was about you not seeing me at all.

I hate you for that.

Yet I still love you.

That's the part I can't wrap my head around. That love and rage can live together in my chest like warring beasts, both tearing me open. You're the father of my children. You make Violet laugh until she snorts. You make Liam feel safe enough to talk. You know how I take my coffee and that I can't fall asleep without the fan on. You're my person, even when you failed me in the worst way.

And yet, I don't know if I can ever fully let my guard down with you again.

When you say you want to rebuild, I believe you want to try. I do. I've seen the changes. The presence. The effort. And it scares me how badly I want to believe this version of you is the one I get to keep. But I'm afraid. Afraid that if I let myself love you again completely, I'll be opening a door to another fall I won't recover from.

You've made it clear that my comfort, my peace, my safety? They matter to you. Whether it was setting up the GPS tracker on your phone, giving me full access to your emails, or doing whatever I felt was necessary to rebuild the trust you shattered, you did it and I want to thank you because I see the effort. I see the remorse. I see *you*.

So I'm here. Writing this. This means something, doesn't it?

I'm not writing to forgive you. Not yet. But I'm writing because I need you to understand the storm you dropped me into. I need you to hold it without trying to fix it or justify it or minimize it. Just... hold it with me.

Because despite it all, I want to see if there's still something left in the ashes worth growing.

– Sloane

Chapter 33

Society was unraveling by this point, chaos flourishing in a world of climate emergencies, global pandemics and government-imposed lockdowns. It wasn't healing, it was rotting like meat left out in the sun. The virus moved through every street, every town, every cracked corner of humanity. The elderly died first, many alone and forgotten. Nurses zipped them into body bags in silence while politicians spat blame across podiums, their words as hollow as the churches now locked and echoing. No one took accountability. Everyone bled.

But inside our walls, there was a fragile illusion of control that I'd carved out with scraped knuckles and obsession. Grocery trips had become surgical missions. I'd strip at the door, bleach containers, scrub fruit like I could scour death off the skin.

Sloane's work had shifted to curbside handoffs. No one entered the clinic unless they were family and even then it was kept limited, though not managed well. People wept in their cars as their pets slipped away without them.

And the kids, those amazing fucking kids, they adjusted like children always do. School through screens. Laughter through static.

We were surviving until the call.

It came from an unknown number. I was sitting behind Violet during her virtual class, half-listening as her teacher enthusiastically outlined next semester's options. Apparently private schools were their own strange ecosystems, full of jargon, expectations, and things like "block scheduling," which sounded more like a prison term than a fourth-grade curriculum. I nodded politely, pretending to follow, while my mind wandered toward what I would cook for dinner.

Then the phone buzzed again and again. Its vibrations against my leg grew insistent, no longer just a mild inconvenience but a pulse of dread. I fished it out, silencing it once more with a thumb swipe, but it buzzed again almost immediately. Relentless.

My chest tightened. That low, dull certainty started to settle in my gut and I knew that something was wrong. Deeply wrong.

When Sloane's name lit up, I was already standing, picking up the call expecting to hear her. "Sloane what's wrong?" Shock hit me when it wasn't her voice that answered.

Charlie said, "You finally picked up." He was breathless, as if he'd been in a marathon.

My pulse stuttered. "Charlie? What's going on?"

His voice cracked. "Sloane. She was attacked. Paramedics are with her now. We are on the way to the hospital."

The air left my lungs.

"She might lose the baby," he added, barely audible.

A noise tore out of my chest, something between a growl and a scream as I shoved through the hallway toward the kitchen. "What the *fuck* happened?"

"Angie," he said, and the name landed like a curse. "She showed up at the clinic. She told the front desk she had an appointment and was insistent she wait in the lobby. When Sloane came around the corner, Angie went straight for her. No hesitation..."

"I swear to fucking God-" I stopped myself, turned sharply as Liam appeared, alarmed. "Watch your sister. Don't ask questions. I have to go."

He nodded, eyes wide. My son. Always steady. I hated the fear I planted in him now.

Climbing in my truck, I barked into the phone. "Which hospital?"

Charlie gave the name. I didn't say goodbye. I didn't even hang up. I threw the phone into the passenger seat and drove like Hell was chasing me.

When I pulled into the ER lot, it was bedlam.

A sea of suffering people lined up in masks, eyes glassy, coughing into the crooks of their arms. Nurses moved like ghosts in gowns. Stretchers rolled past. A man screamed for help while another slumped against a wall in the corner, either asleep or dead. It was war. It was madness.

I forced my way to the front desk, ignoring the signs to stay back, ignoring the way the nurse flinched when I leaned in.

"My wife," I said, voice shaking. "Sloane Shaw. She was brought in a few minutes ago. Pregnant. Attacked."

The woman frowned, clicking slowly through her monitor, her fingers too calm for the storm raging in my chest.

"Please," I said again, quieter this time, like begging would make her faster. "I need to know if she's okay."

The nurse finally looked up, her eyes bloodshot behind fogged glasses and the crease of an N95.

"She's in Room 312. Third floor. You'll have to be quick. Only one visitor at a time, and it has to be brief." Her voice was flat, clinical, but something in her gaze lingered on me, a flicker of sympathy. She knew I was breaking apart in front of her like so many others in this waiting room.

I didn't wait for more. I shoved past the line, ignoring the protests, the temperature checks, the signs screaming *Do Not Enter Without Clearance*. My legs carried me on instinct, my heart thundering behind my ribs, shaking everything inside me loose.

The elevator took years. The hallway smelled of bleach and sorrow. Machines beeped in distant rooms like soft, fading heartbeats.

Then I saw the number.

312.

I pushed the cracked door slowly, afraid of what I might find... and there she was.

Sloane. My wife, pale and still. Unconscious on a hospital bed, wires running from her arms to machines that whispered in cold rhythms. Her face was bruised, the side of her jaw swollen and tinged with a sickening violet. An oxygen tube rested beneath her nose. Her hands, God, her hands, so small on the white sheets.

Beside her sat Charlie, a bandage above his eyebrow and dried blood at his temple. His scrubs were smeared with something dark and his posture was wrecked, like someone had folded him in half with grief.

He looked up when he saw me. I was shocked to see him crying, though perhaps I shouldn't have been. Exhaustion and regret were etched across his face and his expression screamed *I couldn't protect her*.

"I stayed until you got here," he said quietly, voice thick.

My throat felt raw as I stepped closer, one foot at a time, afraid I'd collapse if I moved too fast. I couldn't tear my eyes away from her. I had never seen her look this fragile. Not even during labor. Not during her hardest nights when anxiety kept her pacing the halls.

"What did the doctors say?" I asked, my voice gravel.

Charlie stood then, his eyes on her as well. "They are monitoring her. The baby is still... there. But they are watching for signs of trauma. Placental abruption. Bleeding."

The words didn't land right, scattering inside of me.

"I should have seen her coming," he added, pain bleeding into every syllable. "I should have- "

"Stop," I said, too tired to be angry now. "You called me. You stayed with her. Thank you."

Charlie didn't reply to that. He nodded once and slipped past me, out the door, leaving me alone with her.

Exhaustion tore through me as I dropped into the chair beside the bed, my fingers hovering above hers, afraid to touch her.

"Sloane," I whispered, but she didn't stir.

My eyes burned and I blinked hard, reaching at last for her hand. It was cool against the crisp sheets of the bed. Instinctively I wrapped both of mine around it as if I could will her to wake.

"I'm here," I said, not knowing if she could hear me. "I'm here now. I swear to any god who will listen, that I will never leave your side again."

Her hand didn't squeeze mine back. I stayed there, rooted to the spot, whispering promises into the sterile air, clinging to the hope that somehow, despite all the damage, I hadn't already lost everything.

The room quieted again, except for the gentle beeping of the monitor and the soft sound of Sloane's breathing. I stayed still, not daring to move, as if any shift might undo the fragile thread tethering her to peace.

A quiet knock at the door broke through the stillness. I straightened up as a doctor in hunter green scrubs stepped in, clipboard in hand, a plastic face shield over his mask. His eyes, visible above the PPE, were calm but tired. I recalled this weary look from my previous life on the face of every frontline worker.

"Mr. Shaw?" he asked, keeping his voice low.

"Yes. That's me. And my wife?" I said quickly, standing. My hands were shaking. "Is everything okay?"

He took a step further into the room, glancing at Sloane. "We've reviewed the scans and lab work. She has a mild concussion and several bruised ribs, but no internal bleeding. The baby..." He paused, eyes softening, "...the baby is fine. The fetal heartbeat is strong. No signs of placental damage or distress. That's rare, given the trauma she experienced. She's lucky."

The breath I had been holding all came out of me in one ragged exhale. My legs went weak, and I gripped the edge of the bed to steady myself.

"Thank God," I said with a shaky exhale. I looked over at Sloane again, pale and still but alive, intact, and carrying our child.

Still carrying our child.

The doctor nodded. "She'll be groggy for a while, but we'll continue to monitor both of them closely. We'll want to keep her for observation for at least twenty-four hours. And she'll need rest. No stress."

I nodded. "Right. Yes. Whatever she needs."

He took a step back toward the door. "You can stay, but one visitor only, due to current restrictions. If anyone else tries to enter, they'll be turned away."

"No one else is coming," I said, my voice dark with meaning.

The doctor studied me for a moment, then gave a quiet nod and left the room.

The door clicked softly shut behind him, and I sank back into the chair, this time cradling my face in my hands. Relief pulsed through me and the storm that had been raging inside me felt as if it was finally breaking. She was okay. The baby was okay. For now, that was enough.

Sloane shifted faintly in her sleep, and I leaned forward, brushing her hair back from her face.

"I'll be right here," I whispered.

I didn't know how long I sat there.

The hospital lights dimmed slightly as the evening settled outside the windows, gray and quiet, as if the sky itself was holding its breath. The machines beside Sloane murmured on, steady, rhythmic, cruel in their patience.

Then, the smallest movement. Her fingers twitched.

I jolted upright and leaned closer, unsure if I imagined it. But then her eyelids fluttered, slow and heavy, as if waking cost her more than she had left to give.

"Sloane?" My voice cracked.

Her eyes opened, bloodshot and glazed with confusion. She blinked at the ceiling, then turned her head slightly toward the sound of my voice. Her lips parted, dry and trembling.

"Levi?" she whispered.

A sound left me, part sob, part prayer. I pressed her hand tighter. "I'm here. I'm right here."

She blinked again, eyes focusing now, face flinching as the pain set in. Her free hand drifted to her stomach, instinctively. I didn't stop her.

"The baby?" she asked, voice brittle as glass.

"They said everything's stable," I said gently. "They're monitoring. You're okay. You're both okay."

A long silence passed between us, broken only by the quiet hum of the IV pump. And then, her eyes filled, not just with pain, but something else. A terrible, heartbreaking tenderness.

"I thought she was going to kill me," Sloane said, her voice barely audible. "I looked in her eyes, and there was nothing there. Like she was empty."

My heart twisted, every muscle in my body screaming for revenge I couldn't act on.

"I am so sorry," I whispered, resting my forehead on the back of her hand. "If I hadn't... if I hadn't brought her into our lives- "

"No." Her voice, despite the circumstances, came out firm.

I looked up at her, startled.

"This is not your fault," she said slowly, clearly, even as her throat worked to get the words out. "You made a mistake. A terrible one. And I hated you for it. But *this*... what she did... this is on her. Not you."

Tears slipped down my cheeks. I shook my head. "You don't have to say that," I rasped. "You don't have to make me feel better."

"I'm not," she said, her fingers squeezing mine this time. "I'm saying it because it's the truth. I need you to stop carrying every ounce of this pain like it's your punishment. That doesn't help me. Or the kids. Or us."

I couldn't speak. Couldn't breathe. The knot in my chest twisted tighter, threatening to break me open.

Her eyes softened. "She came at me with a knife," she added, like she was still processing it out loud. "And I somehow blocked it with the chart I was holding. Whacked her a few good times too."

My brows lifted. "The patient chart? Like a clipboard?"

She nodded. "Yep. Smacked her like I was swatting a fly."

Despite everything, a wet laugh escaped me, half-sob, half-hysterical. "That's... honestly, kind of badass."

She winced. "Well, not badass enough. It didn't stop her from wailing on me with her fists. She acted like I'd insulted her botched boob job."

Fuck me, how is this woman cracking jokes right now?

"She always had a temper."

"Mm-hmm," she said, shaking her head. "If she'd spent half as much time working on her self-control as she did on her eyeliner wings, none of this would've happened."

Another shaky laugh bubbled out of me, and for a moment, the weight in the room felt a little lighter.

"Hell, Sloane," I breathed, rubbing the heels of my hands into my eyes. "How do you do it? Find humor or good in everything?"

I looked at her, bruised, exhausted, her hair a tangled mess, and yet somehow she still managed to carry this impossible grace. I couldn't stop this pain from spreading, from tightening in my chest like a vice. It was admiration and guilt and awe all tangled together.

She shrugged lightly, though her lips curled into a crooked smile. "Honestly? Because I know good people."

I blinked, unsure how to respond to that.

She tilted her head and said, "Charlie came to my aid, remember? And it's a good thing too, because goddamn, Levi... that woman is freakishly strong Like, Amazon warrior-strong." Then in a deadpan voice she added, "I'm surprised she didn't break your dick off. Or Charlie's in our throw down."

I choked on a half-laugh, half-wheeze. "Fuck, that took a turn."

"She *was* aiming low," Sloane said, trying and failing to look serious with the wires and bandages. "You should thank your lucky stars she was wearing heels and didn't have better footwork otherwise Charlie would be suing us for endangerment."

I chuckled, shaking my head. "You're unbelievable."

"Why? Because I'm not falling apart like you expected me to?"

"No," I said softly. "Because even after everything... you're still here. Cracking jokes. Making me laugh. When I least deserve it."

She looked at me for a long moment, then reached for my hand again. "I'm not laughing for you, Levi. I'm laughing for me. Because if I stop, I'm afraid I might break down all over again."

Tears pricked my eyes. "You can break down Sloane. I'll be your foundation, your rock, and everything I couldn't be before."

"You stayed," she whispered, her voice cracking. "That's all I ever wanted, Levi. Not the perfect man. Just one who was honest and would stay when things got ugly or hard."

I leaned over and kissed her knuckles. My lips trembled against her skin. "I'll stay forever if you let me."

Her breathing deepened and she nodded, slow and weary, eyes already beginning to close again.

"Then we start over," she murmured. "I'm ready."

"I'll wait. It's no rush. We have all the time now," I promised.

And as she drifted back into the heavy haze of exhaustion, I sat there, still holding her hand.

Chapter 34

Sloane would need to stay overnight and I intended to stay with her. But, I had to figure out what to do with the kids and Rufus.

Thank fucking god Dawn is one of those weirdos who actually answers her phone whenever anybody calls.

I knew Sloane would be sleeping for the next couple of hours. As much as I didn't want to leave her, I had to take care of the dog, the kids, call Dawn, and call Detective Harlan.

I kissed her forehead, whispered a fevered combination of, "I'm so sorry," and, "I love you," a dozen times into her hair, and left.

As soon as I stepped out of the hospital, I called Harlan. By now, he would have received the hospital notes I'd asked the nurse to fax him.

"Detective," I said, my voice raw.

"Mr. Shaw," Harlan said, grave but steady. "I got the report from the hospital and Charlie's statement. I'm sorry. I am really sorry this happened."

I swallowed hard. "You told me you had a warrant. That she'd be found. Now my wife's in the hospital with stitches and bruises, and we almost lost the baby."

"I know. I know, and I won't feed you excuses. We've been short-staffed. We didn't prioritize the threat she posed. That was a mistake, and it's mine to own."

"She walked right into the fucking clinic," I said, teeth clenched. "No disguise. No hesitation. That's not someone unraveling. She's intentional. She's escalating."

"You're right," Harlan said. "And that escalation gives us leverage with the judge now. Attempted assault with a deadly weapon, premeditation, violating no-contact orders... we have what we didn't before."

"So what now?" I asked, heading to my truck. "You going to tell me she's disappeared again?"

"She can't stay hidden for long," he said firmly. "We've flagged her ID, plates, everything. There's an interstate warrant, and we're coordinating with surrounding counties."

I exhaled slowly. It didn't help. "She's already done enough damage."

"I know. And saying we're trying isn't enough. So here's what I *can* say: we've assigned units to watch the clinic and your home. If she shows up again, we'll be there."

I said nothing. My jaw throbbed from clenching.

"Listen... I've got a daughter," Harlan said quietly. "She's a nurse. Pregnant. When I read the report, Levi... it hit hard. I can't undo what happened. But I'll do everything to make sure she can't hurt anybody else."

The sincerity in his voice cut through my anger. "Just find her," I said, voice thick. "Before she finishes what she started."

"We'll stop her. You have my word."

We hung up, and I climbed into my truck, fists clenched the entire drive back home.

When I stepped through the front door, the day's weight crushed me. My clothes reeked of antiseptic and hospital cold. The house was quiet. Liam peered around the hallway, eyes wide with worry. Violet curled on the couch, clutching her stuffed fox like she already knew something was wrong.

I took a breath and crouched beside them. "Hey," I said gently, my voice breaking.

"Where's Mom?" Violet asked, sitting straighter.

"She's okay," I said quickly, taking her hand. "She's safe, and so is the baby. But something happened today. She got hurt at work."

Liam stiffened, connecting dots. "It was her, wasn't it? Angie."

Fuck, they don't deserve this.

I nodded slowly. "Yeah. She came to the clinic. They didn't recognize her, and before anyone could stop her, she... attacked your mom."

Violet gasped. Liam's jaw tightened, his body rigid. I reached for both of them.

"She was taken to the hospital. The doctors took good care of her. She was unconscious briefly, but she woke up. She's strong and going to be okay." I struggled to keep steady. "The baby's okay too. We are going to be okay."

Violet buried her face against my chest, trembling. I held her tight, stroking her hair. Liam sat beside me, silent but radiating anger. I knew that feeling. It had nowhere to go.

"I don't want her near Mom again," he said quietly.

"She won't be," I promised. "The police know now. The attack gave them what they needed. They'll find her. When they do, she's done."

Violet looked up, eyes red-rimmed and frightened. "Can we see Mom?"

"Soon, baby girl. She needs rest for now, but she's coming home tomorrow." I kissed her head and stood. "I need to call your Aunt Dawn."

I pulled out my phone, stepped into the kitchen, and called Sloane's sister. It didn't ring twice.

"Levi?" Dawn's voice cut through, sharp with worry. No hello, just alarm.

"I need help," I said, barely holding together. "Sloane will be okay, but she's in the hospital. She was attacked today at the clinic. The baby's okay, but Sloane needs time. Rest. And I need to be with her."

A pause. "Holy goddamn shit," Dawn whispered. I heard movement; a door closing, maybe a bag unzipping. "Sloane didn't even mention she was pregnant. Are you fucking serious, Levi?"

Ah yes, a family of sailors and strong women.

"I know. I didn't know how else to say it." My throat tightened. "I need help with the kids. Just for a while."

But Dawn being Dawn, didn't let me spiral.

"I am on my way," she said as she shifted to logistics. "I'll pack and be there tonight. I'll bring gluten free snacks, Liam's favorite card game and Violet's weird-ass glow-in-the-dark fox demon I won for her at the fair. I've got it covered."

Relief flooded me. "Thank you," I breathed. "Really. Thank you."

"I'll handle the kids," she said firmly. "You focus on Sloane. She needs you... which is a thing I have not said out loud in years, so soak it up, Levi."

A tear slid down my cheek, but I managed a weak laugh. "Soaking."

"And Levi?" Her voice dropped to her no-nonsense tone. "If you screw this up *again*, I will personally make your life a series of unfortunate events, starting with hiding your car keys in jello and ending with something far more serious, unpleasant, and final for you. You smell what I'm stepping in, Levi?"

A choked laugh escaped me. "I smell it, Dawn."

"I love my little sister," she said. "Even when she's wrong. Even when she's stubborn. And she's been both of those things, *a lot*. But she is *everything*. You get me?"

"I get you," I said, swallowing hard. "Probably now more than ever."

"Good. Gimme fifteen. Text me hospital details. I need to know where to send the emergency caffeine and sarcasm supply."

I sent Dawn the information and collapsed on the couch. I didn't remember falling asleep, but I remembered when Dawn arrived; a force of nature in a Patagonia vest and mom jeans, sweeping through the door without questions or judgment. Bags in hand, orders ready, voice calm but eyes steel.

Within twenty minutes, Liam was brushing his teeth, Violet was being bribed to sleep, and somehow the dishwasher was running.

I watched her from the hallway like she was a magician. Her presence wrapped the house in a calm it desperately needed. The panic in my lungs finally eased enough to breathe.

"You look like hell," she said, passing me to collect laundry. "Go. Be with my sister. Try not to cry in front of the vending machines again."

Low fucking blow, Dawn.

She was referring to when the kids were born. The Old Me was too embarrassed to be seen crying, because, "Real men don't cry," or whatever macho-bullshit I had always told myself. Yet after both births, I had snuck off to find a secluded place to weep joyful tears in private.

Both times Dawn had found me. She never said anything either time, just pretended that she needed a candy bar at that exact moment.

Convinced Dawn had everything at the house handled, I sped back to the hospital and rushed up to room 317. The world outside was quiet, washed in gray-violet. Sloane slept, her chest rising steadily.

I sat in the hard plastic chair beside her bed, the armrest jabbing my ribs. Every few hours, a nurse checked her vitals, rustling curtains and murmuring politely, startling me awake. Each time, I'd blink toward Sloane, confirming she was still there, that she was okay.

Eventually, she stirred.

Her eyes fluttered open, blinking against the sterile light. I sat up as she turned to me, the smallest smile touching her lips. In her hospital gown, she looked oddly radiant... fragile but resilient.

She whispered, "You look like hell."

Sloane echoed the same words her sister, making me laugh.

"So I've been told," I said with a smile.

She asked about the kids and I put her mind at ease, explaining Dawn had the house under control. I brought her up to speed with my conversation with Detective Harlan and there was a determination that settled over her while I spoke.

A different doctor came by, though she looked no less tired than the one I'd spoken to yesterday. She reiterated to us what the previous doctor said and that Sloane could go home.

Discharge took time; the paperwork, whispered instructions, the nurse side-eyeing me when I asked to carry Sloane to my truck. She refused, and instead rolled Sloane out in a wheelchair while I pulled my truck around.

As we drove home, Sloane stared out the window.

"You okay?" I asked gently.

She nodded without looking at me. "I think so. I'm... absorbing it all. I keep waiting to wake up... like this is still part of a nightmare. But I'm not asleep. This is just life now."

I gripped the steering wheel. "It won't be this way forever. Hell, Sloane, it won't be this way for much longer."

"I don't want to live in fear," she said suddenly. "Not of her. Not of the past. Not of us."

"You won't have to," I said. "They are going to catch her, and we won't have anything to fear from her again." I took a breath before I added, "You are not alone. We do this together, okay?"

She turned to me, something fragile and fierce in her eyes. "Then let's fight for this. You and me. Not for what we used to be, but for whatever comes next."

I reached across and took her hand. "Together," I whispered.

Chapter 35

It was after 10 p.m. as we laid in bed. The house was quiet. Sloane was asleep, her head resting lightly on my chest in the dim glow of the bedside lamp. I hadn't moved for nearly an hour, not wanting to disturb her.

My phone buzzed on the nightstand and I saw the familiar name that had haunted us: Angie.

Is she this fucking stupid?

A cold spike of dread shot through me. I carefully slid out from under Sloane, grabbed the phone and slipped into the hallway. My thumb hovered over the screen for only a second before I answered.

I didn't say anything. I stood in the silence of the hallway, listening to her breathing through the phone.

Then her voice: thin, saccharine, serpentine. "Leviiiiii, baby."

Anger flared in my chest, a warm, comforting ember of fury that steeled my resolve. "Leave me the fuck alone, cunt."

She giggled. "Oh, fuck, baby... I love when you talk dirty to me. I needed to hear your voice. I saw what happened at the clinic. How is our little Sloane?"

I seethed, "She is mine, not ours, and keep her name out of your filthy mouth."

"You know I didn't mean to hurt her, right? You know how I lose control when I feel cornered."

My grip tightened on my phone, nearly cracking the screen. "You came after a pregnant woman, Angie. You attacked her. You could have killed our baby. What. The fuck. Is wrong. With you?"

Her breathing was the only sound on the line for a moment, before she sighed. "Oh, baby... you used to understand me. Back then. When we were real."

"We were *never* real," I growled. "You were a distraction from my brokenness."

She laughed, quiet and brittle. "You keep telling yourself that, baby. But I know you don't mean it."

This bitch is crazy. She isn't going to listen to reason. We need to end this somehow.

"What do you want?" I asked, my voice low.

There was a pause before she whispered into the phone, "To remind you of who you really are, baby. Before you forget again." I heard rustling in the background as she raised her voice, "You know how much I hate being neglected, Levi."

Angie was a pampered mess, the product of her father's money and a lifetime of always having her way. She was also a living testament to my own damn stupidity.

I repeated with more force, "What do you want?"

"Mmm, baby," she pouted, "I want to suck your soul out of that thick cock of yours, to feel you ram it into me again, you trembling between my thighs, to drink your cu-"

"Enough! Fuck," I shouted, then whispered, practically begging, "please, stop this... and tell me what it is you really want from me right now."

"Right now? Well, I *do* want all of those things, baby. But for tonight?" Again, her breathing came through the phone like a living thing, writhing to wrap around me. "Tonight, I will settle on seeing you. Daddy says I have to leave town for a long time, and I want to say goodbye to you. In person."

"Where?" I growled, but I already knew the answer.

"Where it all started, baby."

Predictable psycho.

I mumbled, "The park. Near the lake."

She let loose a giggly squeal of excitement. "Oh, my baby! I knew you'd remember."

"I'll be there," I said, barely recognizing the sound of my own voice. "Midnight."

I ended the call and immediately dialed Detective Harlan.

"She just called," I said, keeping my voice steady despite the uneasiness I felt with the exchange. "She wants to meet. Midnight."

"I'll be damned. She's unhinged but desperate. She'll be vulnerable but also dangerous."

"She said her dad is trying to get her to skip town. Wants to say goodbye in person, but I think she might try something. You'll be there?"

"Already on it," he confirmed. "Where did she say to meet?"

Shame hits me then but I said, "The first place we met was at a park, near the restrooms. There's a lake nearby, too. A good place for her to dump my body."

"Let's not make assumptions. I will get moving on our side. Wear bright clothes so we can clearly see you. We'll move as soon as she makes a threat since she has already violated the no-contact." There was a pause. "Do you truly feel like she is a danger to your safety?"

"Honestly, I am not sure anymore what she is capable of, but I'm not afraid. I want this to be over."

"Then let's end it, Mr. Shaw. Text me the address of the park and what clothes you'll be wearing."

Things moved fast after we disconnected. So fast, in fact, that I accidentally texted Harlan the incorrect address. Which meant that I was unwittingly going to face this psychopath unarmed, in the middle of the woods, at midnight... alone.

Unfortunately, I wouldn't discover my mistake until far too late.

After the call with Harlan, I woke up Sloane and let her know what the plan was. I expected pushback, or resistance... but she said she trusted me to do the right thing. Even after everything I'd put her through and all she'd suffered because of me, she trusted me still.

If I'd had the time, I would have spent all night and most of the next day showing her just how much that meant to me. But I didn't.

I had a date with the devil, so I had to leave my goddess behind.

She hugged me before I left, tears in her eyes before whispering to me, "Be safe. I love you."

By midnight, the park was a frozen graveyard of rotten memories. The lake shimmered under the moonlight, still and cold. It was bitterly cold, each exhaled breath a steamy puff. I stood near the restrooms, the same place where I first gave in to every selfish impulse, where I first let Angie sink her claws into me.

She approached from the dark, hands stuffed in her thick black coat, blonde hair pulled into a tight braid. Her eyes gleamed in the low light like a wolf stalking its prey.

"You came," she whispered, her lips curving into that too-wide smile.

"I'm here," I said. "Say what you need to say." My phone was held in my hand, the recording app running.

She stepped closer, staying about five feet away, and reached her hands up towards me. "We could disappear, baby. Just us. Like we planned. Remember? Before everything got so... complicated."

I said nothing. Every muscle in my body was coiled tight. I shook my head at her.

Her smile faltered as she said, nearly begging me, "We could go back to Key West?"

We could go back to Key West?

Go back to Key West?

Back to?

The horror of realization must have been painted across my face, for I saw her manic grin return in full force.

"Baby," she said, "do you remember me now? How many times you fucked me all over the beaches of Key West?"

I shuddered as one hand tightened around my phone and the other covered my mouth. The sound of her voice, too knowing, too familiar, settled into the darkest most stained parts of me. Her voice was the sound of an irreparable wrong I could never right nor ever escape.

Angie wasn't haunted by our past and she wasn't delusional. This whole time, she had been taunting me with our future that hadn't happened yet. She was like me. She had lived beyond the present, beyond the boundaries of the *now*, and she carried the weight of an already lived future within her... just like I did.

She is like me.

Charlie is like us.

The unexpected randomness of that realization, to think of Charlie right then, was not something I had the luxury of examining in the moment. While I had been processing these revelations, she'd crept closer and was within arm's reach.

Her broken smile split her face in two and she cackled. "Yes! Oh, you remember now, baby? You remember how we used to be?"

How we used to be?

The constant fucking, then fighting, then fucking, then fighting. Our entire two years together had been nothing but empty orgasms and explosive outrage.

I struggled to speak, only managing a strangled, "How?"

"Because we're soulmates, Levi. Isn't that obvious?" She took one tentative step towards me and was so close I smelled her cloying perfume. "Our love transcended death and brought us back to when we first came together."

I violently shook my head. Her explanation forced bile to sear the back of my throat as my stomach roiled.

She reached up and touched my face. "We have one more chance to make it right this time."

I leapt back as if shocked.

Where the fuck are the cops?

"Levi, baby, it's okay." Her tone was coddling, as if she were soothing a frightened animal. She held her hands out, but didn't come closer. "I could pay for everything for us this time. Not with Daddy's money, either. I made my own."

The Angie I knew had no marketable skills and only syphoned from her family's wealth. Part of me was curious about what the hell she meant, but not enough to engage.

"No," is all I said.

She shook her head, the hints of a frown souring her face as she started spiraling, her words bursting out in a barely comprehensible blur. "You will be so proud of me, I know you will, so I have to tell you. When I woke up and realized what happened, realized the pandemic was coming, I thought of our first time in Key West, during the initial quarantine. I recalled the specific companies you said you'd have invested in if you'd had a crystal ball; do you remember saying that? I remember exactly which stocks you pointed out, because I believed in you, I've always believed in you, Levi! So I borrowed some of Daddy's money and bought shares of the companies you picked and, oh baby, you were so right!"

The fact she remembered the specifics of an idle conversation we'd had nearly twelve years ago unnerved me almost as much as her crazed eyes.

I tried to subtly scan the tree line, hoping to catch a glimpse of the police, while she kept rambling.

"Daddy never believed me. Never believed in me. Said I was chasing fantasies. But he lost three businesses. Three! Then when the stocks I'd bought finally took off, he lit up like Christmas morning!" Her voice broke up and it sounded as if she might cry, but I didn't care. "He told me he was proud of me. First time ever. You see, Daddy owes money to some really scary people. Despite how much he has, he's always saying it's for the Coven."

Where the fuck were the police? I wanted them to hurry up and grab her.

Then give them a reason to act. Poke the bear, big guy.

"Angie, I don't give a fuck about you, your dad, or your money." I looked down at her and with as much malice as I could muster I spat, "You wanted to see me to say goodbye. So? Say it."

"No," she said with confidence, "I told you. We're soulmates. Now? I know we are. Before we died? I was only pretty sure we were... that's why I got so furious when Raymond showed me those pictures of you and Sloane together."

"Who the fuck is Raymond?"

"The private investigator I hired to follow you after we broke up." She said it so matter-of-factly, as if I was expected to know that she'd paid somebody to keep tabs on me. "He showed me pictures of you and Sloane having coffee together to celebrate your birthday."

The little cafe at the corner of 7th and Spring... the one that doesn't exist yet.

"Coffee with Sloane?" I took two steps back as the enormity of everything she said hit me. "Angie, you and I... we had been separated for over a decade by then."

"Not a decade, baby," she said as she crept forward, keeping the same distance between us. "It had only been nine years, three hundred and forty-seven days. Don't pretend like you didn't know that."

Fuck, fuck, fuck, this crazy bitch.

She held her hands out again, imploring me to embrace her. "Baby, I never stopped watching you, I never stopped keeping other women away, I never stopped waiting for you to come back to me."

"For ten years?"

"True love doesn't have an expiration date, Levi. And once I woke back up here, once I knew we really were soulmates, I carved your name into my skin." She pulled down the collar of her coat, briefly showcasing her collarbone where red angry welts stared back at me, in a feeble attempt at my name. "I am yours in body and soul, baby."

"Good fucking god, Angie!" I stepped back, revolted. I felt dizzy and sick. This needed to end, I needed to get away. I didn't know where Harlan was or the rest of the police were, but it was obvious that I was on my own out there.

Just kill her. There's nobody around. There's nobody who will miss her. Fuck, you'd be doing the psycho bitch a favor, her mind is so far gone.

While I fought the urge to break my promise to Sloane and choke Angie to death, she continued to rant.

"After her husband killed himself and you started seeing Sloane again? I knew it would only be a matter of time. I saw you running into her open arms and I knew she'd forgive you eventually."

Angie's ranting became screaming. "It was as if you had forgotten about me! About us!" Her nails dragged across her cheeks, leaving angry red trails as if she were crying bloody tears. "I did the only thing I could to save you from her... I killed you."

Then her revolting smile returned, odious, ghastly, and now bloody, as the crack in her mind grew from a fracture to a canyon.

She killed me?

I asked, "The truck? That was you?"

She nodded.

"If you loved me," I struggled to say, "why kill me?"

She held her bloody hands over her heart and stepped closer. My mind screamed to run, to flee, but it was as if my feet had been frozen to the ground as she drew nearer.

"I wanted it to be a murder suicide," she pouted. "I wanted us to go out together; together in death forever, baby. It would have been a tragedy that made headlines... but I survived. I was trapped in the hospital, fading in and out of consciousness, delirious with the knowledge that I had killed you, but didn't get to die with you. After a few days of that personal Hell, I died from heartache."

You probably died from the massive internal bleeding and organ failure you incurred during your high speed vehicular murder.

"You crazy bitch." The words slipped out, reflexive.

"Levi, don't throw this second chance away. We can be together again. We can-"

"No." The word barely made it past the lump in my throat. I forced myself to stand tall, to stay composed as my voice came out jagged, but firm. "There's no 'we' Angie. There never was."

Her face contorted as her eyes went vacant; the rage, love, sorrow, heartache, hope all snuffed out. "I gave you everything, Levi."

"And you lost everything. This is over, Angie."

She slithered toward me, back to being within arm's reach, back to being far too close. "Sloane will never love you like I do, Levi," she hissed. "I know you. I know the real you. I know you in ways she never could. All the dark parts of you that you hide from the world, your rage, your hate, the rot underneath the mask you wear? You showed *me*. And I chose you."

Her presence was electric and unstable. The distance between us shrank as she slinked closer, her body a gliding shadow, and there it was... that kernel of midnight in my soul. A shriveled, abhorrent fragment of the Old Me that still craved her.

She reached a hand out to touch my face again, as if she sensed my weakness. Maybe she did. Her fingers, now caked with dried blood, grazed my cheek.

And all I thought of was Sloane's radiant beauty.

I slapped Angie's hand away, recoiled from her, and backpedaled away. "Stay the fuck away from me, my family, my life, and my Sloane. If I ever see you again, I will bury you."

And with that, any semblance she had of sanity snapped.

There was no hesitation in her body, no restraint, only the heat of a thousand Hells bursting from her throat as she screamed an ear shattering, incomprehensible, banshee wail. She crouched, as if she were about to pounce on me.

My thoughts scattered, panic crashing through me.

Would she kill me again? Will Sloane be safe if she does?

I heard a rustle in the trees. Movement caught my eye as Angie spun toward the sound, startled.

"Police! Hands in the air!"

Lights exploded around us, blinding in the darkness. Officers surged forward, weapons raised. Angie looked monstrous; bloodied face, wild-eyed, feral. She didn't run. Simply turned to glare at me, hurt and confusion etched deep across her face.

"You did this... to me?"

I held her gaze. "No. You did this to yourself the moment you hurt my wife."

The metallic click of cuffs snapped through the air as an officer lunged towards her. Angie kicked, thrashed, and screamed awful, inhuman sounds. I watched as one of the officers desperately tried to cuff her, but, in this moment of adrenaline, she was freakishly strong.

"Leviiiiii," she howled, "you'll regret this!"

Then chaos. A flash of metal in her hand. A gun, drawn from her coat during the struggle.

Everything slowed. Shouts from the officers of, *"Gun! Down! Get down!"* Their movements blurred as my world ticked by.

There was a hand that grabbed my shoulder, yanking me to the ground as Angie turned the weapon toward me.

Her eyes. Fuck, they weren't just wild. They were empty. Hollow. As if Angie had never even existed and it was some eldritch thing staring at me through her empty sockets.

I pitied her. Not only for what she'd become, but for all I had done to bring her there, to that moment. We were standing in the wreckage of choices I couldn't undo, burned-out husks of a ruined life I should have never touched. Hatred crackled between us, fueled by every mistake I let fester.

And in that moment of brutal clarity I realized… if the universe was cruel enough to give me one more chance, then it was cruel enough to take it away.

And how fitting would it be, if this were how my second chance ended?

Gunfire. Three sharp, echoing pops.

Her body jerked with each shot. Blood bloomed across her chest, and she stumbled back, her expression morphing into stunned confusion. She dropped to her knees. Her once-empty gaze, now filled to bursting from an unlived life of regrets, locked onto mine. Time snapped back into motion.

Radio static. Officers shouting.

Angie lay sprawled on the concrete, the gun kicked far from her outstretched fingers. One officer screamed for a medic, kneeling beside her as the others secured the scene.

I backed away, arms wrapped around myself. Detective Harlan was beside me, solid and steady, his presence the only thing keeping me grounded. I realized he'd been the one who pulled me to the ground.

"Come on, Levi. Let's get you away from here."

Later, I sat in the back of an ambulance, the coarse wool of a blanket scratching against my neck, the weight of it both comforting and suffocating. A styrofoam cup sat between my palms, its heat seeping into my frozen fingers, the faint scent of burnt coffee cutting through the metallic tang of blood.

I fixated on the steam rising from the cup, thin, wavering threads that disappeared into the cold night air. Sirens howled in the distance, sharp and rising, but underneath them, I could still hear it; the phantom snap of gunfire, reverberating through my bones.

Detective Harlan sat beside, both of us silent for a time.

With as much sarcasm as I could muster, which wasn't much at that moment, I said, "Thought you boys were waiting for Christmas with how long it took you to show up. You get lost on the way?"

Harlan laughed at that, deep and hearty. "As a matter of fact, we were exactly where you told us to be... which was not here, Levi."

And that was when I discovered I'd texted him the wrong address.

That particular park was massive, with multiple entrances, playgrounds, parking lots... restrooms. I'd texted Harlan the address for the main entrance, which was on the other side of the lake. The police had been set up and waiting over there the entire time.

When I asked him how he'd found me, my heart swelled and I nearly cried in front of him.

Harlan said, "I did the sensible thing any good detective would do when looking for a missing man; I called your wife. One hell of a woman you have, Levi. You're damned fortunate she keeps a GPS tracker on your phone."

"Yeah," I said as I nodded, "she's the best."

The best?

The only. Sloane had saved my life tonight without even trying or realizing it.

Then again, in a way, Sloane had saved my life every night.

Chapter 36

The days that followed were quiet in the way only devastation can be. The virus still choked the world like smoke, its presence a constant shadow. Despite the global panic, most businesses reopened, forcing employees to venture out from the safety of quarantine. There was a divide among the people; a threat of class warfare. Anger swelled within those who were considered essential workers as they decried how disposable they felt. Nurses, delivery drivers, janitors... all pushed to the brink while CEOs posted "we're in this together" from their lakeside homes. Frayed systems, shattered trust, and a fractured society struggling to remember what it meant to be human... if it ever had been.

And in the midst of all that chaos, life kept moving.

The new addition on the way was something we clung to at home; hope wrapped in something small and growing. Violet, ever the curious one, had a million questions: Did the baby sleep in your tummy? Could it hear us? Was it hungry? She tried talking to the bump like she already knew her little sister.

Liam, on the other hand, was coolly detached. He was older, more practical. He remembered what it had been like when Violet was born. The disrupted sleep, the crying, plus the way our attention shifted. His indifference wasn't cruelty; it was survival. I understood that.

Through it all, I did my best to stay grounded. To not let the fear or the guilt or the noise outside our walls pull me under. The shutdown meant most things were remote now, including the doctor appointments. That alone stirred quiet resentment in me.

Fuck, another thing the pandemic stole from us.

For the ultrasound, the doctor's office would only allow the mother to attend. I was devastated. When Sloane walked through that door afterward, holding the envelope with the sonogram inside, my heart ached in my chest like it had been carved hollow. She handed me the picture with a small smile and I held it like it was made of glass.

Our baby. Amber. A name we'd picked out together in one of those rare soft moments, curled up in bed. I stared at that blurry grayscale image like it was proof that maybe, just maybe, I was capable of changing this life's future.

I should've been there. I should've seen her face when she first saw Amber, when she heard our daughter's heartbeat thumping like a little drum of hope.

Sloane moved slower now due to the pain of her injuries, both seen and unseen, combined with her growing belly. I saw it in the tightness of her jaw when she had to pause to catch her breath, in the flicker of frustration when she dropped something and hesitated before asking for help.

She hated it.

She'd always been the strong one, the get-it-done-no-matter-what type. Being hampered by pain and pregnancy clawed at something deep within her.

But my woman had grit. Day after day, she logged in for her virtual therapy sessions, sat cross-legged on the couch with her laptop.

Me being home helped her, but it helped me, too. I'd promised to stay present, to carry the burden I'd once abandoned, to help our family find its way forward, one painful step at a time.

The monotony that the Old Me had once hated helped me stay grounded. I helped her up from the bed each morning, fetched her tea, cooked meals the kids could stomach, and listened to their input from the different gluten free recipes I tried.

We talked about many things. I confessed that I'd found her bottle of Alprazolam. She told me she had only started taking that after I left. We cried as we held each other.

There were times that I sat next to her during her virtual therapy sessions, sometimes outside the room, always available to hold her hand if she needed me. I didn't speak unless invited, but when she let me I listened. Goddamn, I listened to every word she shared with the screen, as if they were secrets not meant for mankind to know.

Sometimes, she cried. Sometimes, she didn't.

And slowly, like spring creeping past winter, there were better days. Evenings where Liam told me about a project he was proud of, or when Violet begged for ten more minutes of game time with me. I wasn't on the sidelines anymore. I was there. I was home.

Sloane let me in more; a touch on the shoulder; a look that lingered longer than before; her head resting on my chest after a long day. We didn't speak of forgiveness anymore. We spoke of rebuilding. It was happening in the quiet; in the way she no longer flinched when I held her; in the way she let me trace the curve of her stomach and whisper to the little life inside.

It had been an arduous, tense few weeks. The aftermath of Angie's death, the slow healing of Sloane, and the world still reeling from the chaos of the virus had all left a miasma in the air. It was as if we were all stuck, suspended between what had been and what might come, the knowledge of the future burning behind my eyes.

Early one morning I went to the clinic to pick up some things for Sloane in preparation for her maternity leave. I walked through the front door, an empty bag slung over my shoulder for Sloane's stuff, and there *he* was.

Charlie stood alone behind the front desk, flipping through paperwork, looking as composed as ever. He didn't notice me at first, which gave me a moment to just watch him. His handsome, composed frame felt like a contradiction to my own.

I couldn't explain why, but every time I saw the man a pit opened in my stomach. Maybe it was guilt, knowing he'd lost his chance at a future with Sloane because of the choices I'd made. Or maybe because I knew, ten or eleven years from now, he'd killed himself in my previous life.

Would he commit suicide even sooner without Sloane as his wife? Without her there to bring him joy, without her uplifting him as she uplifted everybody close to her?

Is it my fault if he does?

My own dark thoughts about his possible future aside, there was something else about him that unsettled me. Perhaps it was the effortless way he moved through the world, his overbearing confidence, as if he had already answered questions the rest of us hadn't yet asked.

When he finally saw me, his expression changed. The cool exterior cracked for a second, and there was a flicker of something behind his eyes... a hint of malice, or recognition, or regret.

I didn't know.

"Levi," he said, his voice even and words clipped. "I did not think I'd be seeing you around here."

"Had some things to pick up for Sloane." I shrugged as I walked over to the front desk. I tried to keep the tension out of my voice, but the lobby of the clinic felt much smaller as we stared at one another.

Do I ask him? Do I even want to know?

There had been a question circling my mind for weeks now, itching the dark edges of my brain. I set the bag down, avoiding his gaze for a moment, then I looked him dead in the eye. "Charlie, there's something I've been meaning to ask you."

He raised an eyebrow, leaned against the counter, and folded his arms as he casually asked, "Oh, yeah? Well, what's on your mind?"

God, he has a talent for getting under my skin. Was he this annoying in my previous life?

"Are we alone?" I asked.

"Between Sloane being on maternity leave, Sarah taking time off for mourning, and half the staff being sick at home from the virus?" he asked as he gestured to the empty lobby. "It's just us."

I took a deep, steady breath. "All of your well-timed and lucky investments you've made, the ones that Sloane has told me about... how did you do it?"

"Are you looking for investment advice, Levi?" he asked with a warm and friendly laugh.

It made me want to punch him.

"No, I'm not. I'm just curious how you pulled it off is all."

He stood there, smiling like he knew the punchline to a great joke he was about to share, before he said, "Well, I suppose I did the same thing you did. Sloane told me about your own 'well-timed and lucky investments' as you called them."

This fucking guy.

"Fair," I said before I moved on to my next point. "Sloane also told me about how you've managed to diagnose and identify cases that no other veterinarian could figure out. How you've always seemed to know what's wrong with your patients, even when there's no sensible way you could or should know. She said you were a Sherlock Holmes for pets."

That lit up his face, replacing the shit-eating-grin he'd had with a genuine, warm smile. "She said that? Sloane said that about me?"

"Not in those exact words," I lied, then asked, "But how do you do it?"

He shrugged as his mask of cordial calm slipped back over his face. "I'm a good doctor. There is no mystery to it."

We stood there in silence for awhile, watching one another, his unreadable smile twitching at the corner of his mouth.

Fuck beating around the bush, big guy.

I asked, "How do you know things before they happen? You're not normal, are you?"

I was so blunt that the briefest flicker of aghast panic flashed across his face. But he just deepened his smile and shook his head. "What is normal, Levi? Which of us are normal?" He picked up a clipboard off the desk and turned to leave. "As stimulating as this has been, you are here to collect Sloane's things and I need-"

"You remember what your life with her was like, don't you?"

The smothering silence in the clinic became a tangible thing, enveloping, entombing us like flies in amber.

Then he exhaled a ragged and stuttering breath as he sat his clipboard back on the desk, running a hand through his golden hair. I saw a brief flicker of guilt in his eyes.

"Yes, I remember," he said.

"Because you're from the future," I said.

To which, he laughed in my face.

"Oh, good god, Levi! What?" he asked as he gasped for breaths. "Did you just ask me if I'm from the future? Like a time traveler?"

My face burned and I knew I had to be fire engine red at that moment. I scrambled for what to say, how to turn this into a joke, or make a lame excuse about it being an idea for one of Sloane's paranormal romance books. I stood there, mouth agape, looking like a fish gasping for air.

Charlie managed to compose himself to say, "Levi, whatever happened to me obviously happened to both you and Angie... but it wasn't time travel."

I stared at him as if he'd lost his goddamn mind and said, "I know what happens over the next twelve years, because I've already lived through it and I know that you did, too. What the fuck would you that?"

"With the utmost respect, Levi, you don't know shit."

He must have seen my anger rising: brow furrowed, jaw clenched, hands balled into fists.

Charlie raised his hands in surrender as he said, "It's okay. I don't know shit, either. Too much has changed, and we have changed too much, for our futures to be the same."

How is it I refrained from killing Angie, but I'm about to murder this guy?

"Let's take this slow and walk through it step by step," I said.

"Sure. But if we're doing this, let's at least do it over coffee," he said as he walked down the hall and gestured for me to follow him.

"You remember living another life, one in which you married Sloane?"

He took a heavy breath and wistfully said, "Yes."

"And you remember how you died in that life?"

He winced as if I'd struck him. Then he nodded.

"And you woke up here, in the past, but you retained all of those memories?"

"Twelve years' worth of memories," he said as we entered the breakroom.

"And those memories actually come true, just like you've lived them once already?"

"Almost always."

"And you don't call that time travel?"

"No."

"And why the fuck not?"

"Because," he said matter-of-factly, "my body died and I imagine Sloane cremated me, as were my final wishes. It was only my consciousness that woke up in this reality. My body did not 'travel through time' as you put it."

Frustrated, I shouted, "Then what the fuck do you call it, Charlie?"

He was silent as he moved about the breakroom, putting a pod in a fancy new capsule coffee machine, before he selected something with multiple shots of espresso. I sat at the tiny table and waited. Eventually, coffee in hand, he sat down across from me.

"What do I call it? Limbo? Hell? A parallel world? An alternate dimension? A mass hallucination? A communal dream vision bestowed upon us by an unknown and unknowable higher power? A glitch in the simulation," he shrugged. "Who knows? I don't, which means you sure as hell don't."

"Why do you say that?"

"Because you are an idiot, and I am not."

He said we are alone, so there won't be any witnesses if I strangle him to death here in the breakroom.

I practiced my deep breathing before I said, "Well, I might be an idiot, but I figured you out."

Charlie nodded. "That is true. I was not planning on telling you, but it seems that miracles do happen and you managed to piece it together on your own."

I ignored the insult and asked, "How long have you known we were... the same?"

That wry smile returned to his face before he said, "As soon as I met you, that night you and Sloane brought Rufus here."

"Bullshit."

Charlie laughed and shrugged. "Well, think about it, Levi. My consciousness had been awake in this version of reality for over a year by that point. Nearly everything that I remembered from my first reality was the same, unless it was something that I directly impacted or changed. Ergo...?"

He spoke to me as if he were a teacher coaxing answers out of a student. To my annoyance, given our current circumstance, that wasn't too far off the mark.

I stood up to go make my own damned coffee and said, "When we showed up here with Rufus, that was a thing that you didn't recall from your previous life... because it never happened in your previous life."

"I don't think of it as my previous life, but other than that? Yes."

I tried to process the implications of what this could mean, the how and why of it all, but one thing leapt out at me. "You said you had twelve years' worth of memories and that you woke up in this life over a year ago?"

He nodded.

"It was twelve years for me as well," I said as I popped a coffee capsule in the machine. "I died almost a year after you did."

"Huh," he took a sip of his coffee. "Interesting. How'd you die?"

"Car crash, not important. Why twelve years? What does that mean?"

Charlie sat his mug down and turned to look at me. "Levi, how would I know that? How do you expect me to know what any of this means? Good god, man, we are in the same predicament and we have the same data to work with."

Neither of us spoke as my coffee brewed. When it finished, I sat across from him and we brooded together in silence. I was still contemplating what to ask next when he spoke.

"I wanted to make this reality a better one." He looked down into his coffee mug, his voice monotone, resigned, defeated. "I thought if I could start up my nonprofit and buy out this clinic, I could forge a path to a better future for us: me, Sloane, Liam, and Violet. I'd also be able to help the thousands of animals I had to put down in my first reality.

"I wanted to be there, ready and waiting, financially secure and emotionally available for Sloane when she needed me... for when you set her life on fire and walked away." Charlie looked at me then, his face ashen and haunted. "But she doesn't need me in this reality, because she has you."

Damn right she does.

I sipped my coffee then cleared my throat. "You were back for a whole year before me. You had to know what was coming, what I was going to do... you could have warned her. You could have-"

"You cannot be this fucking stupid," he said with venom in his voice. It may have been the first time, in either life, I'd heard Charlie angry. "I could have what? Warned her? Warned her that her husband, whom she loved very much, was going to obliterate her entire life and destroy her for the rest of her days? That you were going to knock her up, then leave her for a disposable, plastic, bimbo bitch while she gets sick, nearly dies, and has a miscarriage? Is that what I should have told her, Levi?"

"If you had come to me-"

"Oh! Brilliant," he nearly shouted. "I would have been approaching a man whom I had never met in this reality, but who I knew to be a heartless, selfish, egotistical, hot-blooded, short-tempered narcissist, and I would have told him... what, exactly?"

"You could have warned me about Angi-"

"Stop." He closed his eyes and put a hand over his face. "Please, stop talking."

We sat, breathed, sipped coffee, and hated each other for a bit.

Eventually, in a calm monotone, Charlie said, "I need you to understand that I thought of everything you are likely to suggest. I had time to contemplate every variable. I had a year and I was not idle. There was not a feasible way that I could warn anybody of anything without sounding like I was going completely mad."

I sat there across from him, my stomach churning, as I focused on just breathing. I couldn't decide if I should feel relieved that I wasn't alone in this fucked up rebirth, or terrified at the prospect that there could be even more of us out there.

"So," I asked with a shaky voice, "what happens now?"

He shook his head, a bitter smile pulling at the corner of his lips. "I do not know, Levi. We do our best to ensure this reality is better than the first one? We keep Liam out of trouble? We keep Violet safe? We are there for Sloane, each of us in our own way?" He asked this last part meekly before taking a sip of his coffee.

"That sounds like the most fucked up version of co-parenting in existence."

Charlie choked on his coffee and struggled to breathe as I laughed.

"Well," I said, "it is. You want to help me raise my kids and be a part of my wife's life, despite your decade of memories and emotions that you're saddled with? Memories that they don't share?"

He coughed a few more times, but managed to not drown on his coffee. "I will admit, the situation is unique."

"Sure as hell is," I agreed.

"Levi," he said, turning serious, "we cannot return to being prisoners in Plato's cave."

I opened my mouth to say... something. But nothing came.

Prisoners in a cave? The fuck is he talking about?

"I am sorry," he said, probably because he saw how confused I was. "Our situation is similar to Plato's cave. Each of us, in our former realities, believed that the shadows on the cave's wall were all there was to life; money, our jobs, our routines, all the things we'd been told were important. Those shadows were life, and that was all we believed there was to life.

"But now we, as in you and I, know better. We know more. We see the world differently now. Through violence, we were dragged from the safe, dark ignorance of the cave into the blinding light of the sun to see what none of the other prisoners could... that reality is vast and incomprehensible.

"And now, the hardest part? We cannot go back to share what we have seen. We cannot explain the sun to the prisoners still in the cave. They would think we went mad. They are still watching shadows and calling it reality. And I understand why... I really do. Afterall, I was them. But once you have seen the sun, you cannot pretend the shadows are enough anymore."

Fuck me, I wish I had taken a philosophy class at some point in my life.

"Listen Charlie," I said, "all I care about is keeping my family safe. And between everything I remember about you from my previous life and what we've just hashed out over coffee?" I offered him my hand. "I think I can trust you to help me do that."

He took my hand, firmly shook it, then said, "To the most fucked up version of co-parenting in existence."

Chapter 37

Night had swallowed the day, the sky bruised to ash when I logged into Violet's game. The screen's glow painted my face in cold light. The loading music crawled through my ears; oddly soothing, yet strangely haunting.

The kids were at Dawn's for some action-assassin movie marathon which Liam had talked of nothing else all week. Violet tagged along just to be one of the 'big kids' and Sloane worked the evening shift, covering for a tech who'd called out. Just me and the game that took Violet from me. Me and my thoughts.

My fingers froze above the mouse. A pixelated fox trotted circles beside a mushroom house. This had been Violet's refuge during the divorce in my previous life. *Robot Blocks* had served as her escape when the world crashed against her too hard, too loud.

Memory dragged me backward to that other life. That future where technology became poison in our veins. Where data proved, without mercy, the damage of social media, smartphones, reality TV, the constant and incessant noise of it all. Artificial connections breeding real isolation. Social media promising connection but delivering loneliness wrapped in perfect filters.

We'd invited it all in. Every algorithm, every infinite doom scroll. We thought we were evolving. Instead, we were distractedly dying.

How different would that world have been if we hadn't collectively surrendered our attention like lambs to slaughter? Would Violet even have needed this digital escape if the world outside hadn't fractured into jagged, screaming pieces?

Pain spread beneath my ribs as I pushed the thoughts away. The narrative in this life was already moving a different direction from the one I knew. Regardless, I knew I wasn't the hero of her story. But maybe keeping the monsters out was enough.

The pixel character sat on screen, blinking up expectantly. I didn't move.

I skimmed the chat log, my plan already spreading its roots. For weeks, I'd lurked, watching every interaction from the shadows. Violet had sworn not to reveal I was a parent in the channel. To her, it was a game. Our little secret joke.

She didn't know the truth: that her father haunted her game's chat channel, tracking every username that lingered too long, said too little, said too much.

Most chats were harmless. A few weird ones I shut down fast. Then I saw it. The one I'd been waiting for.

Prince_Harming has sent you a direct message.

My pulse quickened. *There's my monster.*

Prince_Harming: Hey! Love your screen name DogsRbetta. Wanna play together?

I stared at the message. My fingers hovered over the keyboard.

DogsRbetta: Prefer to hang out lrl insted.

The reply came fast.

Prince_Harming: Let's hang out!

There it was. The hook. Swallowed whole by a monster who took Violet away in my previous life.

Things unfolded quickly after that. Men like him always hunt, always hunger for the next easy target. I fed him a fake age, told him I was alone, and could find a ride. After a brief dance of messages, he dropped a GPS pin. It was bold, sloppy and disgusting.

I checked the forecast. Rain was coming. Perfect.

I grabbed my phone, my pulse steady now, sharpened to purpose. I dialed the number burned into my memory and waited. One ring. Two. Three.

"Levi, it's late for a call. Is everything okay?" Charlie's voice cut through, calm but edged.

"He took the bait." Silence stretched between us. I could practically hear him calculating, already working out his side of the alibi if shit turned sideways.

Finally, he breathed out. "Understood. When?"

"Tonight." I pulled the small duffel from its hiding place behind shoe boxes. Packed months ago when this seed first took root. Tactical boots and balaclava. Black thermal gear. Gloves. A burner phone.

Things I'd never imagined seeing outside of a suspense thriller. But thanks to Sloane's true crime obsession, I knew the setup.

Charlie said, "Forecast for tomorrow calls for heavy rain around that warehouse and the surrounding county. Should cover your tracks. If you run into trouble, call my burner. I'll keep it turned on."

"Sure. I don't think I'll need it." I zipped the bag closed with one clean pull, and caught my reflection in the mirror. A stranger stared back. I looked like a commando going to infiltrate a foreign country.

Good god, I look like one of Sloane's book boyfriends.

"Fuck me, I don't even recognize myself."

There was a pause before Charlie said, "I imagine you finally look useful. Sloane would be so proud."

I snorted. "She'd kill us both if she knew."

"That is why I said 'proud' and not 'happy.'" I heard the smirk in his voice.

"Yeah, yeah. Preach to the choir buddy."

"Levi?" Charlie's voice dropped back into seriousness. "You are only going to get one chance at this. Do not hesitate. Between the two of us, you are the only one who could... do this." He cleared his throat. "This is one of the reasons I conceded Sloane was safer with you."

"Yeah, well, we both know she gets better dickin' from me anyway."

That'll shut him up.

"Levi, are you still upset I am better hung than you?"

"No," I said, my lie evident to both of us. "Size isn't everything."

We had taken the kids camping, and when nature called we answered out in the bushes away from Sloane and the kids. I couldn't help but take a peek; morbid curiosity to a question I wished I'd never had answered.

Charlie let out a low sigh, equal parts exasperated and amused. "Levi." His voice shifted again as he tried to maintain a calm I knew he didn't feel. "You are Sloane's choice. And with what you are about to do... it is a testament to a parent's love."

I didn't answer. Not because I disagreed. But because I was already slipping on the gloves.

Damn right, I won't hesitate.

Not when it comes to Violet or anybody I love. Not when I remembered her stuffed fox lying untouched in her room for years while Sloane tried to process the moment we realized our daughter was gone.

I tucked the burner phone into my pocket and slid the knife into its sheath. No gun: too loud, too quick, too distant. A blade gave me time to look into his eyes if he fought back. I wanted that. No, I needed that.

This wasn't revenge. This was an offering to whatever gods had granted me this second chance to fix my mistakes.

I'd spent most of my life breaking things: hearts, promises, Sloane's trust.

But tonight? Tonight I am going to unmake something that has no right breathing the same air as my children.

Outside, the storm whispered overhead. Ozone curled in my lungs. The bruised sky hung low, dark with thunder; the kind of night nightmares vanish into.

Gravel crunched under my boots as I climbed into my truck, keeping it quiet with no music to distract except for the thunder of my pulse. I needed the silence.

I parked a quarter of a mile from the meeting spot and walked through the lightly forested woods. The warehouse stood exactly as it had in my previous life; steel bones rusting into the earth, a hollow shell against a moonless sky. I waited.

Ten minutes early, headlights sliced through darkness. A car pulled in as I crouched low, my heartbeat steady now. Time stretched thin as the car rolled closer, tires crunching over gravel. The engine died. A small man stepped out. He was balding and wiry. He popped his trunk, searched the darkness, his flashlight catching rope, tape, and a tarp.

This sick fuck came prepared for her. For Violet.

I moved in, my tactical boots silent over sand and loose dirt.

My pulse quickened as I came up behind him. "Boo."

He spun around in time to meet the crowbar.

To my disappointment, he dropped instantly, a dull thud echoing through the night. I checked his pulse, making sure he'd live for what came next. His heart beat steady under my fingertips.

Still alive. Good.

The laptop sat open in his trunk, angled like he'd stepped away mid-task, screen glowing faintly. It looked ordinary. Innocent.

I pulled on my black gloves and clicked through desktop folders. It didn't take long. A few clicks, and truth spilled across the screen in flickering images.

Just as Charlie and I suspected, he'd hidden behind a VPN, cloaking his IP address with false countries and shell locations. End-to-end encrypted messaging apps, some banned in half the world, synced directly to his laptop. Layers of protection that made him untouchable.

Until they didn't.

The screen filled with thumbnails. Flickering, grotesque, blurred by speed and pixelation but unmistakable. Kids. Rooms. Chains. Grainy footage captured through webcams or phones. Some couldn't have been more than five or six. Some smiled, like they'd been told this was a game.

Revulsion hit, sharp and choking, followed by an incandescent fury that shredded my brain to ribbons. My vision blurred but I kept breathing as I chanted to myself. *In through the nose. Out through the mouth.* Eventually, the rage quieted enough to think.

Good fucking god, how I would relish tearing him apart with my bare hands.

Not yet. Not here. I reined myself in. Justice would come on my terms.

With surgical precision, I closed the laptop, leaving behind whatever sickness he believed safely hidden, and turned away, every nerve burning with purpose.

I used his own tools against him; taped his mouth shut, bagged him like trash in the tarp, and left his wallet in the car. There would be neither screams nor words from him, only muffled whimpers whenever consciousness returned.

I had considered killing him there, but I wanted him to see his end; I wanted him to feel the same helpless dread those little boys and girls had felt because of him.

I dragged him back to my truck, dead weight through dirt and underbrush, then slung him in the back. The storm should cover my tracks, the wind and rain washing away any trace we'd been through here. All that would remain of this evening would be my memories of it.

And I planned to bury those, too.

I drove into darkness with my monster tied in the back, the engine humming beneath my hands. For the first time since my previous life, power replaced helplessness.

I am alive. I am saving my daughter this time.

Back at home, the concrete mixer churned slowly; a mechanical growl against a still winter night.

I stood over the barn foundation's skeleton, rebar stretching up like exposed ribs. A cigar burned between my fingers, flaring with each inhale. I'd checked every measurement twice. Ten feet deep. Reinforced. Secure.

At Charlie's request, I'd designed a shelter to go beneath the new barn. Hidden in plain sight, engineered to house two families, stocked with rations, backup power, clean water filtration, radiation shielding. Everything we'd need if the world cracked open again.

When I presented the idea to Sloane, I expected resistance. Questions. Suspicion. She surprised me, turning the concept over with that quiet, deliberate grace she carried then nodded.

"That's smart," she said. "Just in case."

No interrogation. No probing my motives. No asking why I'd drawn schematics months before Charlie even mentioned a shelter. Her trust was the most precious gift I'd ever earned.

I knew from the very first shovelful of dirt that this shelter would also serve as a tomb. A monument to my vengeance. The only missing piece was the monster I needed to bury in it. Cold concrete pressed into earth like judgment while above, we'd build something else: a home. A haven. A contradiction like my double lives.

But most importantly, a safe place for the one he tried to take from me.

The mixer groaned as I released the hatch, watching thick gray slurry pour into the wooden mold. I turned to my truck, staring at the already-lowered tailgate.

The bundle remained: black tarp, rope, shifting slightly with muffled sounds.

I grabbed it like drywall I'd carried a thousand times, muscles barely registering the weight. Give or take, he was a hundred pounds of dead weight.

Well, he isn't dead yet.

I carried him to the foundation's edge, his moans growing louder before I dropped him with a heavy thud. A muffled yelp sounded through the duct tape, and I fought the urge to kick him to death, to crush his balls beneath my boots and listen to him scream.

I crouched beside the bundle, yanked the tarp enough to reveal his face. Eyes wild, red-rimmed, drowning in panic. Jeremy Rogers, according to the license I'd left in his car. Middle-aged, soft, already sweating through his collar despite the night air.

This pathetic fuck took her from me.

"Jeremy," I said quietly, like greeting someone I'd passed in church.

His eyes screamed when his mouth couldn't. I grabbed his hair, forcing him to face the pit below. The concrete rose, slow and steady.

"You hurt someone I love," I told him, voice flat. "You sold children like objects. You built a market for monsters."

My heart beat against my throat like a steady reminder of what I must do. "And one day, you tried to take mine."

He shook his head violently, sobbing into the tape.

"But you found me instead of her," I continued, tightening my grip. "I saved her. And now I'm going to bury you."

Panic seized him as he twisted uselessly, but I was far stronger.

Ah fuck it.

I stood and stomped repeatedly where his balls should be, ensuring I used enough force to crush at least one. He convulsed, screaming into the tape. The smell of piss leaked from his tarp-wrapped body.

That's just the start of what you deserve, mother fucker.

I lifted and tossed him into the pit where he landed with a wet thud. He barely missed being impaled by a piece of rebar.

Pity.

I watched him writhe hopelessly, concrete already halfway up his chest. He screamed into the duct tape, the noise smothered by the mixer's drone.

Hmm, good thing we are far out from anyone. I looked back at the mixer. *The extra quicklime I added should mask any smell.*

No one would question me out here. Not my family, not the neighbors nearly a mile away behind trees I hadn't cut down, yet. I'd worked enough late nights to make this unremarkable. I flipped the mixer to high speed, watching as thick pour slowly engulfed the man below.

I didn't look away; not even as his eyes disappeared beneath gray. I watched until movement ceased, until breath stopped, until sound died. Only wet silence settling into finality. Into stone.

I should feel something. Remorse? Guilt? But all I feel is a satiated relief.

I stood for awhile afterward with my lit cigar, watching it dry, hardening like my resolve. The stars overhead seemed farther than usual, indifferent, as the air stilled after the mixer went silent.

No turning back from this now... not that I even want to.

Sloane had begged me to do things the right way with Angie; made me promise not to hurt her. But for this?

Fuck, I didn't flinch.

I thought of Violet from my previous life. Of my endless questions from years of not knowing. Of how desolate and empty I'd been after her disappearance.

Then I remembered the images on this monster's laptop and what he'd planned to do to her had I not intervened.

You're goddamn right you didn't flinch.

The cigar burned out in my hand, last embers dying as I tossed it aside. Night stretched into morning, and I heard the rumble of distant thunder before I walked the mile back toward the house.

That morning, rain fell heavy around the warehouse and nearby woods, as the forecast said it would. It would have been more than enough to wash out my tire tracks and render any of my footprints illegible. Thankfully, at the house we barely got a drizzle; not enough to prevent my new cement foundation from drying just fine.

Almost like Mother Nature herself is helping me bury that monster.

Weeks later, the town paper ran a short piece about an abandoned car near an old warehouse. Inside, a laptop left open, contents disturbing enough for police to request information.

I knew what they'd find. A catalogue of horror and digital confession of Jeremy Rogers. Thousands of videos. Each one was someone's son or daughter. Each one was someone's Violet.

I read it over coffee while Sloane hummed in the kitchen, her voice soft as she baked cookies. The kids tore through like wildfire, trailing laughter.

I will do it again in a heartbeat if I ever need to.

I knew what I'd done would stay buried: concrete and bone, silence and sin. Whatever came next, I'd carry the truth like a scar beneath my ribs, telling myself I did what needed doing. My regrets were few. My resolve, absolute.

Chapter 38

The ground was colder than I expected for early spring and my boots sank little into the thawing earth of our land behind the house. I unrolled the blueprints on my truck's tailgate, weighing one corner down with my tape measure. I stood there and admired what we'd designed: a twelve-stall barn with an attached four-bedroom, three-bathroom apartment.

All to be built over our emergency shelter, of course.

I took a step back to stare at the field again; the concrete foundation contrasted starkly against the earth. I knew it didn't look like much yet but it would be huge. Our success built this, and it would shelter anyone who needed it.

Behind me, I heard Sloane crunch through the dirt, steady and familiar. I turned to see her carrying two mugs, steam curling from the tops, her hair tied back in that quick, no-nonsense way that always made her look so damn sexy.

She handed me one without a word, and I took it, letting the heat soak into my hands.

"This'll be the north wall," I said, pointing toward the open stretch of land. "We can frame big windows here and add a bonus room. So if Violet or Liam ever want to move out here... they won't feel like they're living in a shed."

I glanced at her, half-waiting for a smile or a quip. She looked at the space like she could already see it, sunlight pouring through the stained windows, maybe an art study in the corner, bookshelves, and a desk covered in baby chicks.

"That sound okay to you?" I asked.

She smiled then. "Yeah. It does. A second home away from home."

That word still hit me sometimes: home. I used to take it for granted and now we built it with our hands and filled it with love, every single day.

We'd started this farm with the investment profits I made from the pandemic, the subsequent shutdowns, and the inevitable rebound. We'd discussed it quietly amongst ourselves and eventually with the children. Knew that we would grow it piece by piece. First vegetables, then chickens. We could sell eggs at the local market or in a farm box we could set outside. Over time, the rest of the farm would come together.

Including the bees.

That was Violet's idea. She mentioned it in passing, something about pollination and sustainability. She talked about the bees relying on pollen from our veggies and fruit trees when it was warm, the wax to make candles if we chose to. Her idea invigorated Sloane and me. Honestly, I didn't expect to fall in love with it. There's something humbling about bees as they work quietly, constantly helping each other, always moving together.

Maybe I can learn from them.

Liam had suggested we plant flowers, and as a family, we searched for ones that spoke to us. After much discussion, we settled on purple hyacinths, Texas bluebonnets, lilacs, marigolds, zinnias, and roses. Together, we dove into researching which would thrive best in the soil of our yard versus the protection of a greenhouse.

What began as a simple idea gradually blossomed into a full-fledged family project, filling our home with laughter, shared purpose, and conversations that carried on from morning to night.

Staring at the tilled earth before me, I glanced over to Sloane, noting the faded hoodie and work jeans, as she squinted at the field. She was beautiful, inside and out. She didn't know it, but every time she looked at something we'd built and nodded like that, like it was *good*. It felt like she chose us all over again; a life together.

"Dawn says all the kids are doing great by the way. Amber slept through the night." She pulled out a sketchbook and handed it to me, "Thoughts?"

"You still thinking navy for the barn doors?" I asked, thumbing through our drawings after placing my mug down.

"I was thinking daisy yellow."

I laughed, "Yellow? That's mighty bold."

She shrugged, sipping her coffee. "Yeah, well... maybe I want to be bold." Then she smiled, quick and unexpected, the sun catching her face just right as I felt the air get knocked out of my chest.

Without thinking, I reached down and laced my fingers through hers.

We weren't just building a barn. We were building something that could hold us, all of us. A place for Amber, Violet and Liam to return to, a place that could grow old with us, and a place where everyone could be safe.

"I hope this place does well enough for us to keep it for the grandkids," I said, half-joking, half-not.

She grinned, her eyes a little far away now. "You're assuming a lot."

"I like assuming," I said.

Her soft laugh curled around me. "Little feet again... running and playing through the mud. God, I'd love to see that."

I turned toward her, a teasing edge in my voice. "We could work on that, if you want." My fingers traced a slow, familiar pattern up her arm. "If you really want."

She tilted her face up to mine, eyes sparkling. "Why don't we go back inside... and you show me?"

I chuckled, already rolling up the plans and closing the sketchbook. "I am but a servant to your desires, my love."

We left the truck and walked the mile back home, our trip filled with jokes and banter. Slipping through the side of the house, I kissed her in the mudroom, the taste of coffee lingering on her lips as we fumbled like teenagers, then giggled our way toward the bedroom. Behind us, Rufus let out a whine, a soft protest lost beneath our laughter.

Sloane pulled away long enough to glance back. "He's judging us," she said, grinning as she took off her socks mid-step.

"He's jealous," I said, catching her around the waist and spinning her as we stumbled into the hallway. "He wishes he had someone to slow-dance with in the mornings."

"Slow-dance?" she snorted. "This feels more like a stampede."

We bumped into the wall with a thud that knocked a picture frame crooked, the photo a recent family shot of all of us with Amber, the newest addition, in the middle. Sloane burst into laughter, clutching her stomach as we toppled into another corner.

"Okay, okay," I said, pretending to steady us like we stood on a ship. "Next time, ballroom shoes."

"And a helmet," she added, grabbing my hand and pulling me into the bedroom. In a way, it felt like our first time all over again: no kids, no past, no regrets. Just us, together, breathless and giddy and alive in that moment as everything slowed.

The world spun for only us.

The laughter quieted to soft smiles, and our footsteps fell into a gentle rhythm; a dance only we knew. The morning light streamed through the curtains in pale gold, gilding the bedroom.

Her fingers found mine, and she spun into my arms, resting her head against my chest. I swayed us without music, letting the rhythm of our breathing lead. My hand brushed the small of her back, tracing the familiar curve.

"You still remember how to lead," she whispered, voice delicate.

"I never forgot," I murmured, dipping my head to kiss her temple.

We moved like that for a while, quiet, slow, present. No rush, no urgency. Simply the weight of her against me, warm and real.

Slowly, we undressed each other, each piece of clothing dropped to the floor like a layer of distance falling away. I slipped her hoodie off her as she helped me with my shirt. Her hands slid across my skin with the kind of tenderness that undid me, far more than any words could, before we fell into the bed.

"I want to try something," Sloane whispered against my neck.

My interest sparked. "I'm all ears."

She scrambled off the bed with a sudden burst of energy, heading straight for the closet. I heard shuffling, the creak of a box lid, then the unmistakable crinkle of plastic wrap.

"Jesus, Sloane... what did you get?" I asked, already half-laughing.

"You'll see!" she called over her shoulder, her voice sing-song and mischievous.

I propped myself up on my elbows, waiting, trying to imagine what on earth she would bring out. I thought of the two dozen different toys for her we'd discussed trying next, and I wondered which she'd purchased. When she finally turned around, she had something hidden behind her back and a sparkle in her eye.

"Ready?" she asked.

"As I'll ever be. Is it the new collar and leash we've talked about?"

"No, that's on back order."

She revealed it with a flourish; a soft, unmistakable toy. A flesh light. I blinked. "Is that...?"

"I ordered one of those custom kits," she said with a wicked grin. "I sent off the mold, and they returned it to match my uh... likeness."

I stared. "You're kidding."

For a flicker of a second, doubt flashed in her eyes, "Are you upse-"

I broke into full-blown laughter, clutching my stomach. "Sloane," I managed between laughs, "this is definitely... something we could've talked about first!"

She turned fire-engine red. "I wanted it to be a surprise!"

"Oh, it's a surprise alright."

She pouted. "Hopefully a good surprise?"

"You bet. So," I said, catching my breath and nodding toward the toy still in her hand, "you want to use it... together or solo?"

Her fingers tightened slightly on the base, and for the first time, I noticed a hint of nerves beneath her boldness. She shifted her weight from one foot to the other, suddenly shy.

"Together," she said softly, then looked up at me, uncertain. "If that's alright?"

I reached out, curled my fingers around her wrist and tugged her gently toward the bed. "Sloane," I said, voice low, "anything you want is alright. You think I'll turn down the opportunity to explore *you* in 4D?"

She let out a surprised laugh, shaking her head. "That's not how it works, but points for enthusiasm."

I kissed the inside of her wrist, holding her gaze. "You wanted it to be a surprise. Mission accomplished. But more than that... I love that you felt safe enough to share it with me."

She handed the flesh light to me. I looked at the toy in my hands; flesh-toned silicone, warm from her touch, molded in a way that made me pause. It felt surreal, holding something so intimate, made with me in mind.

I glanced up at her. "You really did this."

She shrugged, biting her bottom lip, suddenly shy despite the boldness it must've taken to order it. "I wanted you to have... me. In some way. I actually ordered it awhile ago. I didn't realize how long it would take for them to make the goddamn thing. It was supposed to be delivered before... well, before Amber was delivered."

I blinked, a knot catching in my chest as she continued.

"I know how much of a horndog you are, Levi. And six weeks without sex? I remember how tortuous it was for you after Liam and Violet were born."

A lump formed in my throat as I asked, "Even in the height of your pregnancy, with how difficult that was, you were thinking about me?"

"Of course I was," she whispered. "I've always thought of you, Levi. Even when I hated you."

That admission settled down, nestled between us. Despite everything I had put her through, she had chosen to love me all over again. Not blindly but bravely.

"Also," she said, "I've been thinking about more ways to explore. Ways to make things fun."

I fucking love this woman.

"Then let's have fun," I said.

She crawled into the bed next to me. With a half-laugh, half-growl, she said, "Alright, builder boy. Let's see how good you are with your hands *and* a user manual."

I grinned. "Challenge accepted."

I reached for her hand, guiding her gently onto my lap. "You want to show me how it works?"

Her eyes glinted. "You've already had tons of practice with the real thing." Then, she glanced down at me, cocking her head in amusement. "No. I want to see you use it on yourself."

My brows lifted. "Oh, authoritative. I like it. But only if you call me a good boy when I finish."

Her face didn't crack. Not even a smirk. Just a slow, deliberate tilt of her head as she leaned closer. "I will. But you have to be a good boy to be called one. You have to earn it, Levi."

She is hot when she gets like this.

I cleared my throat. "And how do I prove to you that... I'm a good boy?"

"You don't finish until I *allow* you to finish." Her voice was silk-wrapped steel, the commandment hanging between us like a dare.

My throat went dry. My cock twitched.

Fuck me, we're doing this.

I cleared my throat, hand still holding the toy like it might detonate. "Yes, ma'am."

She smirked now, ever so slightly, eyes raking down my chest to my lap like she inspected her property, already immersed in her role of goddess. "Good. Because you finish only when I say so. Not a fraction of a second before."

"Fuck." I exhaled a long breath. My pulse raced as she climbed off me, sat at the foot of the bed, and tucked her legs beneath her. Watching. Waiting.

"I want to see how you look when you're desperate," she said. "Not for release. For me."

I swallowed hard and nodded, lifting the toy slowly. My body already thrummed with anticipation, but her command made it something more. A challenge, a game, a twisted little trust fall wrapped in heat and love.

She didn't touch me. She didn't need to. Her presence was overwhelming, and she needed nothing more than her gaze to set every inch of me on fire. She reclaimed control over herself, me, us, everything.

The flesh light felt warm on me as I used it. Slick, tight, molded perfectly to replicate her likeness. It was surreal, obscene, and intimate all at once, and the fact that she watched me magnified every sensation.

Sloane didn't speak at first. She sat there, at the foot of the bed, her arms folded across her chest with a dangerous glint in her eye. She watched me like a warden, ensuring her helpless prisoner obeyed every unspoken command.

My breath caught as I slid deeper into it, the sensation so close to her it made my thighs tense. Despite the pleasure of the toy wrapped around me, it was her fiery gaze and how she studied me, burned me, that pushed me to a climax I was not allowed.

"Slower," she said, her voice calm but firm.

I obeyed.

She tilted her head. "I want you to remember what it feels like to want me. Earn it."

I groaned. My grip tightened involuntarily as my eyes rolled.

"Eyes on me," she snapped.

I looked up, throat tight. She filled the room, fuck, she filled my world. Confident, reclaiming control over her body as I lay there naked, humbled, and desperate to please.

"You do not come," she whispered. "You hold it. For me."

"For you," I repeated, breathless. "Always."

The flesh light was a tool. The real heat, the real connection, was her; the power she held over me, and the grace she gave by allowing me back in.

And I'd follow her rules until the end of my days.

Every.

Single.

One.

I neared my climax, the tension rising from deep in my loins, coiling tighter with each stroke. My thighs trembled. My abs clenched. The pace of my hand betrayed me, faster now, desperate, the edge so close it felt like falling.

"Sloane," I ground out, my voice rough and guttural. My chest heaved with the effort it took to hold back, to not spill my seed like an offering at her altar.

"Not... yet," she said, her voice thick with desire, but firm with restraint. Her gaze pinned me, unrelenting and hungry, as she slowly stood at the foot of the bed.

The room was silent but for the sound of my breath and the slick rhythm of my hand. She moved with maddening control, crossing the space between us one barefoot step at a time until she stood next to the bed, towering over me like a goddess from on high, heat radiating from her.

"You will obey me," she murmured, reaching down to cup my cheek, her touch gentle in contrast to the command in her tone. Her thumb stroked my jaw. "Stop."

I whimpered, actually fucking whimpered, and stopped. My hand froze mid-motion, the ache in me violent.

"Good boys get rewarded," she whispered in her deep sultry tone.

I nearly came undone then, just from the sound of her voice, the approval in her gaze, the sheer control she had over me. My body quaked, restrained on a hair trigger, obeying her because it was *her*. Because I would do anything she asked. Because I *needed* her to know she had that power over me. Fuck, that I *wanted* her to have it.

Her fingers trailed down my chest, nails scraping lightly. "You've been very good so far," she purred. "But let's see if you can keep being good... for a little longer."

"Sloane..." I begged again, breathless and raw.

Her smirk was devastating. "Oh, you'll thank me once I finally allow your release."

Then she straddled me and I forgot how to think.

If someone had told me years ago that my Sloane, the girl with the shy smile and the habit of folding laundry with military precision, would one day command me like a goddamn dominatrix in bed? I would've laughed in their face and asked what kind of psychic crystal ball bullshit they were peddling.

But after that moment?

I was a believer. Not because of some prophecy, but because of her sermons. Every whispered command, every deliberate touch, every rule she laid down and made me beg to follow.

This wasn't simply sex. It was a revelation.

And she? She had become a woman who knew exactly what she wanted, unflinching in her desires, and I worshipped the ground she walked on for it.

She straddled me with maddening slowness, knees bracketing my hips, her body hovering right above mine, close enough for heat to transfer, yet not enough for relief. Her skin brushed me like a whisper. My cock twitched against the air between us, painfully denied.

"You think you've been good?" she asked, tilting her head, fingers trailing down my sternum.

"I've done everything you asked," I choked out, my hand gripping the headboard like restraint was all I had left.

"But it's not only about obedience, Levi. It's about patience. Trust."

"I trust you," I said, eyes locked on hers, "But my patience is about to burst all over."

She leaned down, her lips grazing my ear as she loosed a silky laugh. "Prove it. Hands behind your back."

My heart slammed against my ribs. I did it without hesitation, locking my hands behind me, leaving myself completely exposed. Vulnerable. Hers.

"Good boy," she whispered, and the words struck me like lightning down my spine.

She reached down, took the flesh light from my lap, and set it aside carefully as if it was a tool she'd use later; for either punishment or reward.

Her hands wrapped around my cock instead, her grip purposeful, warm and knowing. I gasped, muscles twitching with the effort to stay still, to not thrust upward into her palm like a starving man.

She teased me with her fingers first. Light touches, soft glides from base to tip that made my toes curl and my eyes close.

"No looking away," she said firmly. "You watch me. You see who owns this moment."

I forced my eyes open. She was watching me, her eyes dark with power, but beneath it, something gentler. Something healing and trusting. I felt the rush of endorphins threaten to take me then.

"I hated you," she murmured as her hand tightened slightly, "for a long time. I hated how much I loved you. How much you broke me. But I never stopped wanting to be the only one who could bring you to your knees."

"You are," I said, voice breaking. "You always were."

She guided the head of my cock to her entrance, dragging herself across me, wet and ready, taunting me with the promise of everything craved.

"This is yours Levi, and your cock belongs *to me*."

And she sank down onto me: methodical, slow, deliberate. Her breath caught as she took me in inch by inch. My mouth fell open, a sound escaping that was part groan, part prayer.

I was home. Buried inside her. Owned. Forgiven.

She began to ride me, smooth and controlled. She dragged every ounce of desperation from me as her fingers laced into my hair.

"Do not touch me," she warned, her voice trembling now with her own need. "Not until I say."

I nodded, biting into my lip to force back the primal urge to grab her hips, to thrust savagely into her, to claim her.

She leaned forward and pressed her lips to mine with aching sweetness. "When I say, you'll let go. Not a second before."

"Yes, ma'am," I whispered, trembling underneath her. The weight of her love disguised as domination overwhelmed my senses.

And I waited, on the edge of madness, for her command.

She rode me slowly at first, her rhythm deliberate and devastating. Every movement squeezed the air from my lungs, her warmth gripping me like a velvet vise. Her hands were on my chest, grounding herself as she moved, her nails grazing over my skin. She was in charge, watching me with that fire in her eyes and I was barely holding it together.

"Sloane," I groaned, teeth gritted, every muscle in my body straining as if they would burst. "I-I'm so close."

"I know," she whispered, voice steady but her breathing ragged. "But you do not come until I do. You do not finish until I say."

She picked up the pace, hips moving in that perfect rhythm. Her body trembled, and I felt it. She was close too. We were right on the edge together, teetering over a precipice made of love and forgiveness.

"You're doing so well," she panted, her voice rough, her own heat spilling out into her words. "Such a good boy."

Good boy.

Those words undid something in me. My eyes clenched shut as I fought to hold back the impending orgasm.

Then her voice: "Come with me."

Permission. That was all it took.

I let go and shattered, exploding inside her as she cried out, her body tightening around me, her own climax crashing through her like a hurricane. We clung to each other, locked together, our bodies shaking, unraveling and binding all at once.

For a second, my vision blackened, stars prickling the edges of my sight. I caught her as she collapsed to the side, her breath coming in soft gasps against my neck. My body twitched against hers, nerves still alight, and I couldn't help but laugh.

"Sloane, that was... you were incredible," I gasped, pressing a kiss to her temple. "Fuck me."

She gave a dazed little hum, her voice muffled against my chest. "Hmm. I can't right now. My legs hurt."

I burst out laughing, the sound muffled into her hair. "Yeah, I guess three minutes of high intensity cardio is pretty tough for anyone."

She smacked my shoulder with the strength of a drunk kitten. "Oh, shut up. It was more like four. I added an extra minute with my commands, thank you very much."

"You should teach a class," I said, chuckling as I pulled the blanket over us. "Dominate your husband in ten minutes or less."

"Step one," she murmured, curling into me with a sleepy grin, "make him beg for it."

"Nailed it," I said, pulling her closer as we lay tangled together, the afterglow warm between us.

We didn't speak for a long time. There was only the sound of our breathing, the way our hearts pounded together like war drums turning into lullabies.

Afterwards, she looked at me, breathless and glowing, a soft smile curving her lips. "You are my everything."

"As you are mine, my love."

Chapter 39

L^{evi,}

Another therapy love letter. I've written a few at this point and I've tried reading them out loud with the therapist. You have no idea how awful it feels, listening to your own voice as you broadcast your feelings to someone who you've paid to listen to you. But hey, here goes.

I've been sitting with these thoughts for awhile now, unsure how to put them into words. I've realized through therapy that I don't need the perfect ones. I just need the honest ones.

When everything shattered between us, I thought I had shattered, too. There were days I could barely breathe, and nights I wanted to scream but didn't have the strength. Between work and the kids, I simply felt like an empty shell and I'll be honest, there were moments I didn't know if I could ever look at you again without feeling the pain of what you did. But the day you walked in and asked if we could start over, if we could try again, something stirred in me. It felt like hope, and it scared me.

While you were working tirelessly to show up for me, to prove yourself, I sought refuge with a community online. I found a group of women and men who had walked through the same storm and I listened to both sides. I spent sleepless nights reading through their D-Day stories, sitting with their pain and then I found a forum that talked about being whole after infidelity. I let you prove that you had changed. Working together in tandem to heal each other and understand that the needs of our relationship would change greatly.

For the first time, I didn't feel alone. I read stories of devastation, but also of strength, resilience, and hope. I started to realize that I didn't have to let what happened define me. I've learned I'm stronger than I ever gave myself credit for. I've learned I'm allowed to hurt and to heal. I'm not broken and I can rebuild myself on my own. Or, if I choose to, with you.

You've shown up, Levi. You didn't disappear into shame or excuses. You didn't just say the right things. God Levi, you did the hard things for my benefit and I am so grateful for that. You let me cry without rushing me. You let me rage without trying to fix it. You held space for my pain. Every time I've needed reassurance, even when I've asked a hundred times, you've offered it without hesitation or judgement because you know exactly what you did to me. I can see it in the shame that lights your eyes, and the way your tone breaks.

So, here's where I stand: I am proud of myself and I am proud of you. We are both choosing, every day, to lean in when it would be easier to run. You once broke my heart and now you're part of the reason it's healing. This isn't a letter of forgiveness, or of forgetting. It's not a bow tied around a broken story. It's a chapter, a real, honest, messy, brave chapter in something that still might be worth saving.

I'm strong on my own. I've proven that in my own ways but as I sit here, I realize too that I believe I can be strong with you too.

– Sloane

Chapter 40

10 years Later

It's been years since everything happened: Angie, the affair, my rebirth, the pandemic. The world has twisted into an unrecognizable thing, even when compared to my previous life. Some days I wondered if we, those of us who'd been reborn, had anything to do with that.

Charlie and I would discuss that at length, when it was just the two of us sipping whiskey on the back deck late into the night, certain we were the only ones awake. We hadn't met any others like us, but we both assumed they had to be out there... for good or for ill.

Over the past decade, society worldwide had slowly begun to segregate into two factions: the vaccinated versus the unvaccinated. We watched as businesses began to deny entry to the unvaxed, as countries made vaccines mandatory, and as more and more basic human rights were stripped from the unvaccinated.

In the USA, we'd been given the right to choose for ourselves. But even then, it felt like a hollow choice, as pressure was being applied to join the vaxed. As a family, we had chosen to vaccinate. The pros seemed to outweigh the cons, and the virus showed no signs of slowing down.

Going to get the vaccine was a surreal experience. The lines stretched for dozens of blocks outside of the stadium, where people huddled together against stark white tents that littered the football field.

Nurses with N95 masks called out names and led us to the Darken Pharmaceutical Representative, who read us the potential risks. We accepted with trepidation, reminding ourselves how swiftly the virus took Sloane's parents away from us, and told ourselves we were never looking back.

As the years progressed, things became more stable, but it was clear that there was a line between the two ideologies. The corporations in charge tried to appease both sides. I kept a watchful eye on Angie's father's businesses, all of which seemed to be profiting off of the misery from the changing times, and I ensured Master Builders Inc. stayed far away from his companies.

Despite all that depressing shitstorm raging in the background, today was a joyous day for me; I was helping Violet pack for her first day of college. Boxes littered our driveway as I shoved them into our company truck, reminding myself that she could visit home given the school was only an hour away.

She'll do fine. She's a big girl.

Violet had received several acceptance letters before she decided on this university: a school chosen for its vaccination requirement and its scholarship sponsorships for students who had impeccable academic backgrounds. Students like her. She had excelled in all of her classes growing up, often causing me to joke with Sloane whether I was really her father.

Thank fucking god she has her mother's brains.

At Sloane's suggestion, we helped Violet choose noncontemporary hobbies that not only interested her, but would help her stand out as an ideal candidate for a prestigious college: painting, sculpting, jiujitsu, fencing, equestrianism, archery. She managed to snag a full ride with dorms included.

That morning, Violet seemed subdued as she greeted me with dark circles under her red rimmed eyes. I assumed it was homesickness kicking in already, and imagined she didn't get much sleep last night; the last night before going off to college.

I didn't pry. I knew my baby girl would talk to me when and if she needed to.

She was quiet on the hour drive up, staring out the window, lost in thought. I tried a few conversation starters, light ones about campus life, her classes, the weather... but she responded absently, and eventually we drove in silence.

Once we arrived though, I caught a spark in her eyes as we found her dorm building and checked her in. The campus buzzed with parents and students, a swarm of goodbyes and last-minute hugs.

Somehow, I managed to haul an extra table up three flights of stairs for her, a "non-negotiable," she said for her art. My back protested with every step, years of construction and farm work catching up with me, but I didn't let her see that.

Sloane's joke about all delts kicked in as I laid the table down in the exact spot she wanted.

Inside her room, she walked around slowly, running her fingers across the mattress, greeting her roommate with a quiet, "Hey."

I introduced myself to the girl's mom and we laughed together about the chaos of college move-in day, the absurdity, the emotions, and the full car trunks.

That afternoon, Violet and I went to a small Italian restaurant near campus that prided itself on being Celiac safe, which was a shock given how hard it was to find safe foods for her. We squeezed into a secluded corner booth, and it felt as if we had the whole place to ourselves.

She sat across from me, and I could tell something was on her mind. There was a darkness behind her eyes that was more than nerves. She looked... haunted. After we received our drinks and food, I decided it was time to pry.

"Honey," I said gently, "do you want to tell me what's wrong?"

"Just thinking about how different the next few years are going to be." She paused, then asked, "The pandemic... that was a scary time, wasn't it?"

The question caught me off guard. "What? Oh, yeah. It was pretty horrific."

Especially all the shit I was trying to fix or stop from happening to us.

She took a sip of her tea. "You and Mom were going through a lot, even before the virus hit."

"That's a hell of an understatement," I said with a laugh, painfully aware of how much of a major fuck-up I must look like to her now.

"I remember how distant and distracted and... cold you used to be."

Oh Violet...

I thought of a hundred different ways to apologize for the Old Me that hadn't been there for her, that didn't cherish her. I opened my mouth, but before I could say anything she spoke.

"You changed so rapidly. Like... like somebody flipped a switch."

"I'm sorry, Vio-"

"No," she interrupted me, "Daddy, no. I'm not saying any of this to make you feel bad. I'm glad you changed."

"So am I." Decades of shame and regret still plagued me occasionally, and this was one of the moments as I stared at her.

She had her mothers face, sharp nose and gorgeous hazel eyes. Her auburn hair was braided just the way Sloane used to do it. Despite starting college, she was still my baby girl.

She was chewing on what she wanted to say next more than on her food. Eventually, she said, "You were a really cool dad back then, you know? Playing games with me online."

I took a sip of my water, trying to mask the tension rising in my chest. Back then, I wasn't only playing games with her. I was hunting a monster.

I cleared my throat. "Yeah, well... you were really into that game, *Robot Blocks*, and I wanted to spend time with you. I still remember those castles and bases we built," I said with a chuckle.

She didn't laugh. "Well, once we started doing all my other extra activities, it was hard to keep going." She gave me an analytical gaze and looked so much like her mother in that moment. "But it was more than that. You were watching out for me."

"Well... yeah. I mean, the internet was a scary place back then. You could never know who was out there. It used to be like the wild west."

Violet nodded, slowly. "Yeah. I mean, a child predator could totally convince someone to meet them at, like, an abandoned warehouse."

What?

A flashback of the warehouse struck me then, metal bones strutting from the ground. For a moment, I thought I was having a heart attack, the pain in my chest was so intense. "Baby girl? Is there something you want to tell me?"

"You used my account," she said, voice quiet but steady. "You pretended to be me. You met someone back then."

My mouth opened, but nothing came out. If I denied it, I was lying to her. If I admitted it, I was burdening her with a darkness she didn't deserve. How much did she already know and how did she know it?

She looked at me, calm, watchful, reserved. "Those investments you made... they weren't simply luck were they, Daddy?"

She can't be...

Horrified and stunned, I shook my head. "Violet-"

"Thank you." She said it with tears brimming in her eyes. "Thank you for finding me, Daddy."

Oh fuck, she's like Charlie and me. No please god, why?

I moved to her side and wrapped my arms around her as she broke down, heaving these deep, soul-wracking sobs that soaked through my shirt. I held her and kissed the top of her head as I cried with her, and whispered the only truth that mattered over and over into her hair.

"I love you. You're safe now."

Fuck, I couldn't save her.

The grim realization of just how little I could control hit me then. I had done everything I could to protect her in this life, and despite it all, she had somehow come back with those memories. A life of pain and sorrow that I knew I could never empathize with, much less understand.

Fuck you gods. Fuck your twisted god damn games.

I tried to wrap my mind around the horrors she would have seen, the unspeakable nightmare her life must have been after she'd been kidnapped... but I couldn't. I literally lacked the capacity to comprehend a life that would have been as dehumanizing and terrifying as what my baby girl would have experienced.

We sat like that, us crying and me soothing her, for hours. The staff checked in once, then gave us space and privacy as she shattered into a million jagged pieces.

"I love you," I whispered. "I'm here for whatever you need. In this life, you are safe."

At some point, I realized I wasn't only saying it to her; I was saying it for myself, to reinforce that she really was here and whole. I whispered that mantra until I'd become hoarse and her sobs quieted to whimpers.

Eventually, she sat up. We sipped water and blew our noses. I looked at her and saw that she'd cried so hard she'd burst blood vessels around her eyes.

"Oh god." I reached out and tenderly touched her temples. "Your eyes are fucked."

She chuckled at that. "I don't care. I've been holding that in since this morning."

I gave her a sad smile before dropping my hand. "When did you know?"

She quieted then, her posture going rigid as she tried to hide the tension in her body. "Since last night."

I closed my eyes as hot fresh pain tore my chest. "Violet, you know that if you ever want to talk-"

"No." She said with finality. "No. I don't ever want to remember. I'm not there anymore. I'm here."

With that, she rested her head on my chest as I wrapped an arm around her. She wasn't crying anymore, but her breathing still stuttered now and then.

"Violet. We both know that's not the healthy response. You were raised in this life with the tools to emotionally regulate and you have access to a therapist."

She reached up and grabbed the collar of my shirt between her thumb and index finger, rubbing the fabric repeatedly. It was a habit she'd learned from her mother, an anxiety tick she hadn't done in years.

"I know," she whispered. "But, I have all those years fighting for space in my head against what I know from this life. Everything feels... wrong. Fake. Like this is a dream and I am going to wake up again – owned by someone else."

My grip on her tightened as I kissed the top of her head. "Never again, Violet. I will bury whoever I need to again."

She chuckled at that. "Well, don't tell me where, yet. I'll ask when I'm ready."

We held each other for a while. When the server came by, quietly refilling our waters and dropping off extra napkins, neither of us made an effort to move. I gave the server a silent thank you, making the mental note to hook her up with a huge tip.

We stayed like that, a father and daughter bound not only by love but by a secret they shared. When she did look up at me her eyes were red-rimmed and swollen, but also filled with something I hadn't expected.

Joy.

She said, "Thank you for becoming a better person for us, Daddy."

My throat closed and I struggled to speak past the lump that had formed. "Of course. I love you, Violet. I love Liam. I couldn't make the same mistakes again."

She nodded, then asked, "Do you regret coming back?"

I laughed, the sound full of relief. "Good fucking god, no. Never. I've loved every single moment with you all."

Violet smiled. "You've been a great dad."

I cupped her cheek, tilting her face to look at me. "You deserved it, Violet. So did Liam. Just like your mother deserved a better partner. You all deserved the world."

When she looked at me, I saw in her eyes a woman who had lived a thousand lifetimes and witnessed atrocities that would make war criminals weep... but I also saw my brilliant and bright nineteen year old daughter, brimming with laughter and love.

"Thank you," she whispered. "I can't say it enough, Daddy." We pulled away, but stayed seated close to each other.

I wiped my eyes and said, "When I was reborn in this new life, I had a lot of mistakes to fix... but saving you was always my priority. I could not have survived losing you a second time."

Tell her about Charlie, big guy.

"Violet, I understand not wanting to recall your previous life... but if you ever feel the need to talk and you're not comfortable talking with me about it, you can also talk to Charlie."

Her eyes widened. "What?" Realization hit her then, "Uncle Charlie? He's... like us?"

"Yeah, reborn like us," I said with a laugh. "But he doesn't think of it that way. He has some very strong opinions about what it all means, or might mean, or doesn't mean, or theoretically could possibly mean. Ask him about Plato if you ever want to see him riled up."

Excitement spread across her face as she asked, "Have you met any others?"

I thought of Angie, then, for the first time in a very long time.

"No... no, we haven't."

She sipped her water and I already knew what her next question was going to be. She asked, "Did you ever tell Mom?"

I shook my head.

She nodded. "I think I can understand why. It's... heavy."

"Beyond heavy. I didn't want to tell her how my life was without her." Shame filled me, that drowning sensation I'd come to know as an old friend.

Understanding filtered between us and eventually we moved onto lighter topics. We did get around to finishing our lunch; we even split a gluten free chocolate torte for dessert. The rest of our day was filled with laughter, reviewing her class schedule, discussing which professors she was excited about, which weekends she'd like to come back home.

I stood at the door to her dorm getting ready to say our farewells. I knew we both looked like hell, with our puffy and bloodshot eyes, but I didn't care.

I wrapped her into a hug, but before I could say goodbye she fervently whispered, "You're my hero, Daddy."

This kid...

Her mother was the only other person in either of my lives who had ever been able to destroy me so utterly with nothing more than their honesty. The intensity and sincerity of her words filled me with a devastating euphoria, and I was humbled to know that this was my daughter.

"Always, Violet."

As I drove away from the university and pulled onto the main road, I thought back over the day's highs and lows and buffaloes.

Charlie is going to shit a brick when I tell him about Violet. He's already got his hands full with Rowan.

I'd been driving in a daze for awhile, so overwhelmed with everything the day had thrown at me, before I realized I should've called with an update the minute I left the campus.

I told my truck, "Call Home," and listened to the incessant ringing before the click of an answer.

Charlie's voice came over the speaker, "Hey, so how did our girl do?"

"She did great."

"You were gone for quite awhile. Did you run into any kind of trouble?"

I chuckled. "Not exactly, but trust me... you're going to fucking love what I found out today."

"Well, do not leave me in suspense," Charlie said. "Spill the tea, as Violet would say."

"Sorry, bud. You gotta wait. We'll discuss it tonight over whiskey."

"Oh... I see."

And I honestly believe the clever bastard somehow knew right then and there... and I hated him the tiniest bit for it.

I asked, "Hey, is Sloane around?"

"She was accepting a delivery at the door, but she is on her way now. Drive safe, Levi."

There was a moment of quiet, some rustling and jostling on the other line, and then Sloane's melodic voice filled the cab of my truck.

"Levi?"

I turned the volume up so I could feel her voice.

"Levi, you there?"

"I'm here, my love. I'm right here. What delivery did you get?"

She laughed. "You know damn well what it is, Levi. Thank you, they're as beautiful as always."

Blue hyacinths and white roses. Every week.

I said, "Violet did great. You would have been proud."

"Oh, I'm proud of her whether I can see her or not. But I'm glad the drop off went well. I hate that they wouldn't let both parents attend."

I shrugged, "Well, you know how these things go. They have their little rules and regulations they want everybody to march to."

She laughed. "I guess so. Amber stop that! Those are mine!" I heard rustling and then her breathless voice asked, "Will you be home soon?"

"Yeah. Thirty minutes. Should I grab anything?"

She made a noise like a ravenous animal. "A gluten-free pizza sounds fabulous right now."

"You got it. Veggie for you, Amber, and Charlie? Meat for me and Rowan?"

"Yessss!"

Her voice was warm, teasing. I felt a rush of love and a familiar pang of remorse.

"I love you, Sloane."

She heard the shift in my tone. "I love you, Levi. Are you okay?"

No. I don't think I can ever be truly okay... but that's okay.

"I miss her." A partial truth to the storm inside of me.

"Yeah," she said softly. "I miss her, too."

The phone was silent for a moment but connected us in the quiet. I heard Sloane moving something, maybe walking to the bedroom before she finally said, "We did it. We survived so much, haven't we?"

"Yeah. We really have. Thank you... for giving me another chance all those years ago. I don't think I'd know who I am if you didn't exist to keep me straight."

I heard her sniffle on the other end, "Thank you... for becoming a better person, Levi."

Tears slipped quietly down my cheeks. "Anything for you, my love." A moment of quiet before I said, "I'll be home soon with your disgusting fungus pizza."

She laughed, her exquisite, sonorous laugh that brightened the day of any who heard it, and I hung up, feeling whole.

Epilogue

The Atrium, the sacred heart of temporal existence, pulsed with silence. It was a place that existed in the stillness between moments, a place untouched by either gravity or light.

It was in that place where a pale, translucent piano sat, its ghostly keys untouched by fingers as it resonated with sound. Incorporeal birds and spectral butterflies drifted through dimensions, wavering in and out of existence to the rhythm of that ethereal music.

It was in that place where time measured itself in neither seconds nor centuries, but in ripples. In the waves of choices made and denied, in the tidal crush of lives lived and lost.

It was also in that place where three towering figures emerged from the folds of time itself, to speak of things beyond mortal ken.

Chronos stood at the center of The Atrium, his form vast and immutable, carved from the bedrock of reality older than matter either dark or light.

To his left drifted Aion, timeless and serene, his presence woven from the fabric that came before either starlight or shadow.

And to Chronos's right flickered Kairos, younger in form but older in chaos, brimming with the volatile spark of the perfect moment seized or missed or both.

A fractured soul hovered between them. Once human, now something else. It glowed faintly, barely holding a shape, torn between pasts, futures, and presents. What had been the coalescence of memory and experience, was now a shattered contradiction, screaming and reaching, as it struggled to stay together.

"It failed," Chronos said, his voice like the grinding of tectonic plates. He spoke without emotion, though the heaviness in his stance betrayed more than he would have admitted.

Aion, the god of cyclical time, responded softly, as if afraid to further disturb the frayed soul. "We tore the thread too soon. It snapped from the strain. You saw it. Memories at war, identities folding in on themselves. A mind displaced from causality, from all of that had happened before, and would or could happen again."

Kairos shook his head, fading in and out of the space between them. "No. Don't call it failure. The soul *reacted*. It screamed, yes, but it reached. That means something. It was an opportune moment, a time when action could potentially alter life or circumstances. Wasn't that the beginning of change?"

"Screaming is not success," Chronos replied coldly. "You pushed too early, before the moment had matured. The human mind was not ready for what you offered."

Kairos scoffed. "Moments don't wait. They burn. And in that burn, something new is born."

"Or something dies," Aion murmured.

Chronos's eyes darkened. "He aged in reverse, yet still decayed forward. His choices collapsed into noise. Meaning dissolved like mist."

"It was divine intervention was it not?" Kairos asked.

Aion watched them both with patience. "Possibility," he said gently, "was not stability. We gave him an abundance of simultaneity, past, present, and future all at once, with no separation. He could not hold it all. He could not remember whose death came first, his or his lover's. Which betrayal was his, and which he inherited."

Kairos turned away, as his form wavered in frustration. "You bind it in numbers and calendars and call it divine. But time *lived*. It *moved*. And he *saw* it. He said he could feel the now and the not."

"He also begged for death by the end," Aion reminded him. "He spoke in paradoxes, feared futures that never happened, and grieved children who had never been born. He wasn't evolving. He was drowning."

Chronos stepped forward. "And he took others with him. One choice in 2077 unraveled an act of kindness in 1961. A withheld kiss in 2002 silenced a revolution in 2098. We did not break only him. We tore the weave around him. Entropy bloomed and shattered the system."

Kairos spoke, voice ringing like bells, "Then the Grims knew. Shai and the Norns knew. Every god and goddess of fate and death knew what we had done. Some wept while others rejoiced." He paused and turned. "Ah, they come."

The fabric of The Atrium trembled as three new figures emerged from the nothing between time's creases. Hooded silhouettes woven in twilight threads, delicate feet never quite touching the ground.

The Moirai. The Fates. Daughters of Chronos.

Clotho stepped forward first, her fingers eternally weaving a new strand of thread. Life unborn, possibility yet unrealized.

Lachesis followed, a staff in hand, measuring strands no one mortal eye could see. She paused before the fractured soul, tilting her head, considering the weight of what had been and what could never be again.

Atropos, the smallest and quietest, came last. In her hand gleamed silver scissors, closed but twitching.

"The thread you tampered with," Clotho said softly, her voice the hush before birth, "was never meant for touching."

Lachesis looked at Chronos with a strange mix of awe and judgment. "You seeded chaos in the pattern," she said. "Do you think we don't feel it? That we don't *ache* every time you twist the loom for your grief?"

"I did not ask you to interfere," Chronos growled, space bending around him with the weight of unshed eons.

"No," Atropos whispered, stepping closer, her shears glinting under the eternal dusk of the chamber. "But you made us bleed anyway. You defied your own making by doing so."

Chronos stiffened but said no more as Clotho studied the broken soul before them, her circling feet light. "This one was never meant to stretch across so many timelines. He was singular. You made him plural."

"He held for a moment," Kairos said, with something like reverence.

"And then cracked," Lachesis snapped. "You call that transcendence?"

Kairos grinned. "I call it potential."

Chronos shook his head slowly. "You don't understand," he said, voice cracking at the edges. "This wasn't just an experiment. I felt her presence." He turned away, eyes searching the void beyond The Atrium as if hoping to glimpse something lost long ago.

Atropos turned to Chronos, her scissors trembling in her hand. "You speak of our Mother," she said. "The woman you lost after creation."

Kairos scoffed, though a flicker crossed his eyes. Something unspoken, perhaps even pity. "Forgotten gods and mortals are fleeting. Ephemeral. Why should one life matter so much?" He hesitated, just for a breath. "She might be dead, Chronos. In every reality."

Chronos flinched.

"She was never written into this age," Clotho murmured. "She drifted. When the timeline ruptured, we tried to catch her. But she slipped. She chose to fall rather than remain a ghost in your eternity."

"She remains lost," Aion continued. "If she lives among the mortals, you could not simply extract her. She became part of their fractured existence now."

"She's still out there," Chronos said, barely audible. "I felt her, her essence, in them."

Lachesis nodded slowly. "Yes. She haunted the mortals. She wove herself into their song. But that doesn't mean she is yours to reclaim."

Kairos stepped between them. "But what if he could find the moment? What if we tear a seam... enough to glimpse her thread?"

"Then you'll tear others," Atropos said flatly. "Every thread ties to a thousand more in one plane of existence. Imagine how many more you touch with the others?"

Aion placed a hand on Chronos's shoulder, his expression solemn. "You have always sought balance," he said gently. "But balance demands sacrifice. If you pursue her, if she still lives, you risk unraveling more than you intend. You cannot bend the universe for your grief without consequence."

Kairos's grin returned, electric and wild. "But isn't that the point?" he whispered. "The chaos. The rupture. That perfect moment when all certainty burns away and we begin again." His eyes glimmered with possibility. "Let me help you. I can create the moment. Enough of a tear to find her. We can speak with Thanatos. Surely he would -"

Chronos silenced him with a stare, his jaw clenched and heart torn. He knew the truth of Kairos's offer. He knew the danger.

"I know what you're suggesting," Chronos said at last. "You want to rip the threads apart. Create a breach. But we both know what happens when that line breaks. Entire realities collapse. Entire histories blink out."

Aion nodded solemnly. "You have always believed time was a river, flowing forward. Now you seek to dam it. To reroute its course for your own singular need. Even gods must learn to let go. Time is not ours to control."

Chronos's voice trembled now with pain worn raw. "Let The Library hold those forgotten stories. I *will* find her. Even if it breaks me."

"Break you, and you break us all," Lachesis said. "You are not only a god. You are the axis. If you unravel..."

"Then let it unravel," Kairos hissed, glowing brighter now. "Let us start again."

Chronos, offended, spoke to all who would hear. "Love cannot be contained and remains immortal to even time itself."

Clotho stopped spinning. "True," she murmured. "But it can unravel everything."

Lachesis' voice grew low, resonant, as if echoing through the centuries themselves. "It starts wars. It burns empires. It topples gods from their altars. What you call love, Timekeeper, is often grief disguised as devotion. A longing so fierce it breaks the structure of destiny."

"At Troy, love sailed a thousand ships into ruin," Atropos said. "At Carthage, love drove a queen to the blade. In Rome, love turned brothers against each other. Kingdoms fell, not because fate willed it but because love whispered rebellion into human hearts."

"And yet," Chronos said, "it is the only thing that defies time. The only force that remembers. That endures."

"You speak as if that redeems it," Lachesis countered, eyes narrowing. "But even immortality does not justify recklessness. You wove a tear in the fabric when you let your grief reshape the ages. And love, no matter how eternal, does not excuse the blood it spills."

Chronos turned from them, voice quieter now. "Perhaps not. But without it, history would be nothing more than a ledger of wars and kings, of empires rising then crumbling to dust. Love gives it all meaning. Love makes memory sacred. Love makes tragedy unforgettable."

Atropos watched him carefully. "Then maybe that is the true curse, that love was immortal. And now it stains every age with longing it cannot undo."

Aion, who had remained quiet, finally spoke, his voice laced with warning. "And when the storm ends, what's left? Do we truly want a world made of ash and memory? Ananke would never agree to this."

Chronos turned to his daughters. "If I asked you—"

"We would refuse," Clotho said, gently.

Lachesis's eyes met his. "Not because we do not love you. But because love is not permission."

Only Atropos hesitated. "There is one place," she said slowly. "A convergence point. A knot that has not yet tightened. You could see if she is there. But the cost-"

"-will be mine," Chronos said.

"No," Atropos replied. "It will be theirs. The mortal souls you touch and get sent back years, decades, even eons. The burden will be unfathomable. The Grims will know. Thanatos and Death will know. You will start a war, first with Nergal then all the others."

The room fell silent as all present absorbed the weight of her words. The ethereal piano's faint notes dimmed, swallowed by the stillness.

Still, Chronos stepped forward. "I won't let her fade. Ananke will understand the necessity of it all."

Aion nodded, his voice calm but dour. "Then the souls will be sacrificed. If they survive the transcendence, so be it."

Kairos grinned, and for once, so did Clotho.

"Then meet Khaos," Clotho whispered, eyes gleaming with a strange light. "She will guide you to that convergence point. Is that truly what you seek, Father?"

He nodded.

"Then so be it," Clotho said. "Let us hope Time can survive your grief, father."

TO MY READERS...

FATED REBIRTH PREVIEW NEXT! (VIOLET & ROWAN)

First of all—*thank you*. Seriously. Thank you for stepping into the beautiful chaos that is Sloane and Levi's story. It's complicated, messy, a little dramatic (okay, a *lot*), and very human. This story was never meant to be simple...it was meant to be *real* and somehow you stayed with them through the heartbreak, the awkward silences, the sharp words, and that stubborn little flicker of hope. That alone deserves a medal.

When I first started writing this, it was basically a glorified therapy session. (Spoiler: still is.) What began as emotional scribbles from prior traumas turned into a whole world I couldn't shake – a parallel universe that had been living rent-free in my head for way too long with stories pulled from my life and so many others.

Sloane and Levi's journey is a reminder that love can be a battlefield but also a place of growth, redemption, and occasional sarcasm. If their story resonated with you, challenged you, or even made you want to throw the book across the room (and then pick it back up), I'm honored. That means their voices reached you.

I also wanted to broadcast those living with celiac disease (cause man it's hard) and that therapy can be a wonderful resource if you find the right person.

To the beloved BookTok community and my gloriously unhinged, readers – I hope this scratched an itch you didn't even know you had (or maybe very much did). Whether you came for the angst, the spice, the fantastical elements, or the emotional damage, thank you for joining me on this wild, chaotic, potentially toxic, but ultimately heartfelt ride.

How can you help? Broadcast the story out there to others who might can live vicariously through the characters.

Here's to making questionable choices. Stay human. Stay messy. Stay hopeful.

With all my heart, thank you for reading.

Reno R. Mist

PS: if you're into fantasy worlds, epic story arcs, and the kind of slow-burn chaos that leaves emotional scars—the next set of books have got you covered (and then some).

While I know the next batch of stories might not connect with *everyone*, I hope they continue to speak to those of us who know love isn't always neat, or pretty, or Instagrammable (is that even still a thing?).

Fated Rebirth Preview

Rowan

The funny thing about dying is that you don't expect to be reborn.

You brace yourself for the end and hope for the void. If you're lucky? You get that sweet nothingness for eternity. If you're not? If some asshole god decides you've tipped one of their arbitrary scales too far? Well, it's fire and punishment till the end of time, thank you very much and go fuck yourself.

Those are your two options; either nothing or suffering. You don't get to come back. Not in a world like mine. Not unless the Grims, those busy-bodies who patrol the borders between life and death, have a reason to keep your soul tethered.

Tell me, do you think that by accepting your fate, you'd find some sort of solace in the quietude of slipping away? Would you go, if not happily, at least peacefully? Or would you die while cursing the gods and their fickle, prideful morals? Would you kick, scream, and spit into the eye of whoever tried to escort you on? I've found that most folks are on one end of those two extremes.

As for me? Well, at the time this story starts... I was somewhere in between.

I was no one special. I was one more scavenger scraping by in an entire world of vultures, all of us scrounging our meager way through a life barely worth living. I was one simple soul, with blood on my hands and ice in my veins.

The benefit of living this way was that I didn't fear death anymore. Being on the run for years strips you of that; strips you of everything, really. So you learn to make peace with death early. You have to, because once you hear the howling winds of the tundra and the shriek of a Nightbeast on your trail, you know there is no bargaining, no pleading.

In my world from before, dying in horrific fashion was an inevitability. Death with a capital D was a constant companion; silent, watchful, ever-present. He breathed down your neck with the kind of patience that only predators possess. And I had danced to His tune willingly, knowingly, the night I broke into The Library.

And I do mean *The* Library. The kind of place my people whispered about in the dark with heads bowed. A place none dared approach.

You see, The Library is more than a vault of forgotten knowledge. It's both a monument to power and a locus *of* powers, old and terrible. A place where the gods pay tribute to knowledge that doesn't simply live; it *hungers* as a ravenous beast.

The ink on the pages is known to bite, to shift, to slither across the parchment and vanish if it senses you're unworthy. And the shelves? The shelves rearrange themselves at will, curling away like offended beasts if they don't like your scent. All the doors are bound in spell-script that shimmers when you look too long.

And patrolling the aisles and halls of The Library are Constructs older than empires: sentinels carved of brass and bone. They don't sleep. They don't speak. They only protect and remember.

You could be forgiven for believing The Library's Constructs are its most terrifying servants; many uninformed folks do. But no, that honorific belongs to the one and only... Bounty Hunters. If the rumors are true, and everybody believes they are, neither mortal nor god has ever escaped one of The Library's Bounty Hunters.

Keep in mind... I knew all of this. I'd seen mangled bodies of fools flung from The Library, spit out as if they were the bones leftover after a beast's meal. I was not a fool. At least, not an ignorant one.

Maybe it was arrogance? Or maybe good old plain desperation. I'd been tempting the Fates for too long, pulling at the taut red strings they wove over our heads, as if I could cut them clean. Still I went. Because who doesn't love a challenge?

One book. That was the deal. One. In and out.

Steal the right tome and my debt – a lifetime of servitude, blood-oaths, and spell-bound contracts – would be forgiven.

No more running and no more looking over my shoulder from the kinds of people who forge pacts with blood and seal them with bone.

So I walked through the winding halls of ruined castles from crumbled kingdoms, forlorn temples to forgotten gods, and derelict palaces of fallen empires. I knew that each step could have been my last. I knew The Library was alive and aware. I *knew* it was a place that would recognize and remember thieves.

Yet still, I walked out of The Library with the tome hidden against my chest under my coat, laughing at how easy it had been. I mocked the cold corpses of those that tried and failed before me as I half-walked, half-skipped into the deep snows.

Of course, I didn't get very far before I realized I was soon to be one of those cold corpses.

Ice and frost crept up from the ground to wrap around my boots like skeletal fingers, biting through layers of leather and wool as I stumbled into the Forgotten Wastelands. A dead land, unmarked on maps and abandoned even by ghosts.

Each breath became a struggle, a cloud of steam that froze on my lips before it could escape fully. The wind screamed like it knew my name. My muscles burned with cold, but I clung to the stolen tome, its leather binding warm against my chest; unnaturally warm, as if it pulsed with its own heartbeat.

I didn't look back. I didn't have to. I knew *He* would come.

His presence wasn't just a shadow on the snow; it was a stain on my soul, an inkblot that spread slowly across my being, curling into my thoughts like smoke. I felt Him long before I saw Him. He was a constant pressure; an ache in my bones deeper than any cold could cause. The air around Him warped, bent, *listened* to His will as He hunted me with absolution.

I'd heard the rumors of those that hunted for The Library; nearly everybody had. Bounty Hunters possess eyes that pierce through the veil of all worlds and stare into what comes after. They don't see; they *know*.

Whatever The Library's Bounty Hunters seek, they find. Whatever they chase, they catch.

It will come as no shock to you, my friend, to learn that I was determined to make this chase as difficult as possible for them.

Each step through the Wastelands had only gotten heavier, dragged down by the weight of knowing He was behind me: patient, tireless, inevitable. The relentless snows swallowed my tracks in seconds, but I knew that would not matter. Not to a Bounty Hunter.

I trudged for far longer than I should have been able to, not stopping for food or sleep or even rest. I'd lost count of the number of sunrises and sunsets I marched through and a tiny part of me thought I'd already died; that this endless march through the Forgotten Wastelands was my own personal hellscape.

But all things end, my friend. That, more than anything else, I think is the point of this story.

By the time I could go no further, the wind had stripped the breath from my lungs. I took refuge in the husk of ancient ruins, so derelict I had no way of knowing what the structure used to even be, and I curled around the searing heat of the tome. I knew this book, eldritch and arcane, was the only thing that had kept me alive in the Forgotten Wastelands for who knew how long. I should have died a hundred times from starvation or cold.

Then, silent as the night, He came to me. His face was pale and angelic in the cruelest sense, an unearthly symmetry sculpted without softness: sharp lines, hollow cheeks, lips that had never known warmth. He held neither mercy nor malice, only undeniable, implacable purpose.

His dark, never-ending presence enveloped me, a second skin I couldn't shed, as He clutched me with invisible claws. By the time His blade slid through my torso, I neither screamed nor fought. Why would I? As I told you, I had made peace with Death long ago.

It was time to let go and hope – not *pray*, never pray – that I was lucky enough for the void.

The face of the Bounty Hunter faded to black, followed by the snows of the Forgotten Wastelands, then finally the world itself... gone. The searing heat of my own life's blood burning my hands and chest was the last sensation I remembered.

And that, my dearest friend, is where my story *should* have ended.

But, as you are very well aware, it did not.

You may have trouble imagining my surprise when I woke up to a reality so foreign, so sterile, so bright, that it struck me as a hallucination. I was in a bed in a who-spit-all: white, glaring, humming with mage-machines I had never seen. The whole place reeked of chemicals.

This was a place that should not have existed for someone like me.